The Silent Hour

Michael Koryta

HODDER

First published in Great Britain in 2013 by Hodder & Stoughton
An Hachette UK company

1

Copyright © Michael Koryta 2013

The right of Michael Koryta to be identified as the Author of the Work has been
asserted by him in accordance with the Copyright, Designs and Patents Act 1988.

A CIP catalogue record for this title is available from the British Library

ISBN 978 1 444 71396 1

Printed and bound by CPI Group (UK) Ltd, Croydon CR0 4YY

Hodder & Stoughton policy is to use papers that are natural, renewable
and recyclable products and made from wood grown in sustainable forests.
The logging and manufacturing processes are expected to conform to the
environmental regulations of the country of origin.

Hodder & Stoughton Ltd
338 Euston Road
London NW1 3BH

www.hodder.co.uk

To Don Johnson and Trace Investigations—
with deepest gratitude

PART ONE

Whisper Ridge

Chapter One

He'd sharpened his knife just an hour before the killing. The police, prosecutor, and media would all later make great use of this fact. Premeditation, they said. Proof of intent, they said. Cold-blooded murder, they said.

All Parker Harrison had to say was that he often sharpened his knife in the evening.

It wasn't much of a defense.

Harrison, an unemployed groundskeeper at the time of his arrest for murder, took a guilty plea that gave him a term of life in prison but allowed the possibility of parole, the sort of sentence that seems absurd to normal people but apparently makes sense to lawyers.

The guilty plea prevented a trial, and that meant Harrison's tenure as the media's villain of the moment was short-lived. Some editors and TV anchors around the state no doubt grumbled when they saw he was going to disappear quietly behind bars, taking a good bloody story with him. On the day of his arrest, he'd offered something special. Something none of them had seen before.

The victim was a man named John Maxwell, who was the new boyfriend of Harrison's former lover, Molly Nelson. The killing occurred in Nelson's rental house in the hills south of Xenia, Ohio, a town made infamous for a devastating tornado that occurred the same year Harrison went to high school, destroying homes, schools, and churches while killing thirty-four people and leaving nearly ten thousand—including the Harrison family—homeless. It wasn't the first storm of breathtaking malevolence to pass through the little town: The Shawnee had named the area "place of the devil winds" more than a century earlier. The winds certainly touched Harrison's life, and a few decades later the locals would claim the devil clearly had, too. A Xenia native who was half Shawnee, Harrison had been separated from Nelson for more than a year before he returned to town and they reunited for one night together. It was passionate and borderline violent, beginning in a shouting match and culminating in intercourse on the floor. Evidence technicians later agreed that the abrasions found on Harrison's knees were rug burns from that night and had no relevance to the killing that took place two days later.

After the night of sex and shouting, Nelson told Harrison she was done with him, that it was time to move on. Time to move *away*. Get out of town, she said; find something else to occupy your attention.

Apparently she didn't convince him. Harrison returned to her house two nights later, hoping, he would say, for more conversation. The police would insist he returned with murder on his mind and a recently sharpened knife in his truck. Harrison's story, of an argument that the new boyfriend turned into a physical contest, was never proved or disproved because there was no trial. What went undisputed was the result of the night: Harrison punched Nelson once in the jaw as she went for the phone, interrupting her as she hit the last of those three digits needed to summon help, and then turned on Maxwell and killed him with the knife. Harrison disconnected the phone, but a police car had already been dispatched, and a single sheriff's deputy entered the house through an open side door to find Nelson unconscious and Harrison sitting on the kitchen floor beside Maxwell's body, his cupped hands cradling a pool of blood. He was attempting, he said, to put the blood back into the corpse. To return it to Maxwell, to restore him to life. He was, he said, probably in shock.

That detail, of the attempt to return the blood, added a new twist on a classic small-town horror story, and the crime received significant media coverage. Front-page articles in the papers, precious minutes on the TV news. The murder was well documented, but I don't remember it. I was an infant when Harrison was arrested, and his name meant nothing to me until almost three decades later, when the letters started.

Chapter Two

He wrote me for the first time in the winter, about two weeks after my partner, Joe Pritchard, left for Florida. I remember that because my first instinct was to laugh out loud, and I was disappointed that there was nobody around to share my amusement. It was a crazy letter from a crazy killer who was already back on the streets. That life sentence only held him for fifteen years. He'd been out for thirteen when he made contact with me, sent a letter explaining that he had a matter of "grave importance" to discuss, but wanted to tell me his personal history before we met. It was an issue of honesty, he wrote. He had recently learned the importance of total honesty, of accountability, and therefore he would not hide from his history. He proceeded to describe, in a formal, matter-of-fact fashion, the crime he'd committed and the time he'd served, then left a phone number and asked that I call him when I was ready to meet.

The letter went into the trash without ceremony, and no call was made. More than a month passed before the second one arrived. This time, Harrison was more insistent and even stranger. He wrote that he'd followed my career in the newspapers and believed that I had been chosen for his task. He knew this must sound strange, but I needed to believe him, needed to meet with him just one time. There was talk of me being not a detective but a *storyteller*. Harrison had a story, and he needed to know the ending. No one could tell the ending but me. Was I intrigued?

I was not.

This time I considered burning the letter, or tearing it to shreds, but then decided that was too much of a gesture. Instead, I tucked it back into its envelope and tossed it into the garbage. Four companions soon found their way to a similar demise in the months that followed. Harrison was growing more persistent, writing so often that I at least took the time to look into his background to see what sort of psychopath I was dealing with. I considered contacting his parole officer but never did. His correspondence, while annoying, also seemed harmless.

He gave up on the letter campaign and decided to arrive in person on an unusually warm afternoon in the first week of May. I was in the office and engaged in critical business—browsing the ESPN Web site and pondering what lunch should be—when there was a single soft knock on the door. Walk-in business isn't just infrequent at our agency; it's nonexistent. There's no sign on the building, and that's by design. Joe had a theory about walk-in clients being the sort you wanted to avoid in this business, so we kept a low profile.

I pushed back from the desk, crossed the room, and opened the door to face a man who couldn't have stood an inch above five-six. He had a thick build, the natural sort rather than a weight-room product, and his hair was cut very close to his skull. There was one scar on his face, a dark imprint high on his cheekbone, offsetting a pair of coal-colored eyes that were fastened on my own.

"Mr. Perry." It wasn't a question; he knew who I was.

"Yes?"

"I'm Parker Harrison."

He saw the look that passed over my face in response.

"I'm sorry if the letters bothered you," he said. "I didn't want to be a bother. But I also thought . . . you were a police officer, and I thought maybe the name would mean something to you. So I said, well, better to be up-front about things, right?

Then, when you never called, I decided maybe that was a mistake. I was hoping you'd welcome me."

"Welcome you."

"Yes."

We stood there in silence for a moment, and then he made a nod at the interior of the room and said, "Are you going to let me in, or do we have to talk on our feet?"

"On our feet," I said. "It's not going to take long to finish the conversation, Harrison. I don't investigate thirty-year-old murders committed in front of a witness and then *confessed* to. Besides, you're already out. You did some time and now you're done. So what's the goal? I don't understand it, and I don't want any part of it."

For a moment he just stared at me, looking perplexed. Then his face split into a smile, one with some warmth to it.

"Of course you think that's what I want. Why wouldn't you? I'm sorry about that, Lincoln. May I call you Lincoln? I apologize for your confusion, but the last thing on my mind is my own case. I mean, there *isn't* a case. As you said, I confessed. That wasn't a joke, something I did for kicks because I wanted to spend my life in prison. I killed that man, Lincoln, killed him and never denied it."

He must have seen some reaction in my eyes, some hint of the chill that had gone through my stomach, because he stopped talking and frowned.

"I say that like it's nothing," he said, "but that's not how I feel about it. Not at all. I regret it terribly, would give anything to see him have his life back. So if you hear me talk of it like it's nothing, please understand that's just a product of familiarity. When you spend every day living with the price of destruction—of someone else's life and your own—it becomes awfully familiar."

He spoke very well, gracefully even. I said, "All right, it seems I misunderstood, but why tell me about your case in that first letter if it's not your current concern?"

"I told you," he said. "I wanted to be honest."

I raised my eyebrows. "You know, Harrison, there are some

things we all keep to ourselves. If I'd killed somebody with a knife, I'd probably put that one on the list."

"Are you going to let me in?" he said.

I hesitated for a moment, then sighed and swung the door open and walked back to my chair behind the desk. He sat across from me, on one of the stadium chairs. He gave it a curious look, as most people do.

"From the old stadium?"

I nodded.

"When I was a child I saw Jim Brown play there," he said.

"Lots of people did."

He frowned at that, bothered by my unfriendliness, and said, "I have six thousand dollars. A little more than that, but roughly six thousand. I meant to lead off with that, do this properly, with the retainer and all."

"I'm not really looking for work right now, Harrison. Pretty backed up, actually."

He looked at my desk then, perhaps noting the absence of paperwork, and I reached out and turned the computer monitor to hide the ESPN screen. Like I said, pretty backed up.

"I read about you in the papers," he said.

"Terrific. I wasn't real happy about being in them."

"I felt the same way when I made the front page."

I cocked my head and stared at him. "Is that supposed to be amusing?"

"No, it's supposed to be serious."

Neither of us said anything for a minute. I was studying him, that scar on his cheek and the steel in his eyes. He had a soft voice. Too soft for the eyes and the scar.

"When I read about you," he said, "I knew you were the right person for this. I *knew it*. You've shown compassion for people who have done wrong. You've done wrong yourself."

He seemed to want a response to that, but I didn't offer one. After a pause, he spoke again.

"I knew that you wouldn't treat me as worthless, as diseased, simply because one day I made a terrible mistake and somebody died."

A terrible mistake and somebody died. That was one way to phrase it. I pushed back from the desk and hooked one ankle over my knee, keeping my silence.

"You're looking at me with distaste," he said.

"I'm sorry."

"It bothers you very much. Being in this room with me, knowing that someone died at my hand."

"Being in the room doesn't bother me. Knowing that you killed someone does. Are you surprised by that?"

"You've never killed anyone, I take it?"

My hesitation provided his answer, and I disliked the look of satisfaction that passed over his face. Yes, I'd killed, but it was a hell of a lot different than what Harrison had done. Wasn't it? Of course it was. He'd murdered someone in a rage. I'd killed in self-defense—and never reported the death.

"Mr. Harrison, I'd like you to go on your way. I'm just not interested in continuing this conversation, or in doing any work for you. I'm sorry if that upsets you. There are plenty of PIs in this town, though. Go on and talk to another one of them, and do yourself a favor this time and keep the murder story quiet."

"You won't work for me."

"That's correct."

"Because I told you that I killed someone."

I was getting a dull headache behind my temples and wanted him out of my office. Instead of speaking, I just lifted my hand and pointed at the door. He looked at me for a long time and then got to his feet. He turned to the door, then looked back at me.

"Do you believe that prison can change someone?" he said.

"I'm sure that it does."

"I mean change them in the way that it is supposed to. Could it rehabilitate them?"

I didn't answer.

"You either don't believe that or you aren't sure," he said. "Yet you were a police officer. You sent people to prison. Shouldn't you have believed in that idea, then?"

"I believe that we don't have any better ideas in place at the current time. Does that satisfy you?"

"The question is, does it satisfy *you*, Lincoln."

"If all you wanted was a discussion about the system, you could have had it with your parole officer."

"I didn't want a discussion about the system. I wanted you to treat me like a functioning member of society. You've chosen not to do that."

I rubbed a hand over my eyes, thinking that I should have left for lunch ten minutes earlier.

"Prison didn't rehabilitate me," he said, "but another place did. Some other people did."

He was still standing there, hadn't moved for the door, and now I gave up. It apparently would be easier to hear him out than throw him out.

"The job," I said. "What is it? What do you want from me?"

He gestured down at the chair from which he'd just risen, and I sighed and nodded, and then he sat again.

"I got out thirteen years ago," he said. "Spent the first year working for the most amazing woman I ever met. She was someone who operated on a level above most of the world. Kind, compassionate, beautiful. She and her husband built a house in the woods that was as special a place as I've ever seen on this earth, just a gorgeous, haunting place. If you go to it, and I hope you will, you'll understand what I mean. There's an energy there, Lincoln, a spirit I know you'll be able to feel. They came up with the idea for the home themselves, and it was incredible. Built underground on one side, so that when you came up the drive all you saw was this single arched door in the earth."

He lifted his hands and made an arch with them, revealing tattoos on the insides of both wrists.

"The door was this massive piece of oak surrounded by hand-laid stone, and it was all you could see. Just this door to nowhere. Then you could walk up over the door, stand on a hill, and even though the house was directly beneath you, you couldn't tell. There were trees and plants growing all over the place, and no sign that a home was under your feet. At the top of the hill they built a well house out of stone, styled in a way that made you think it was two hundred years old. There was no well, of course, because the house was beneath. If you kept walking past that, you'd come to this sheer drop."

Again he lifted his hands, making a slashing motion this time. "That was the back wall. Two stories of glass, all these windows looking out on the creek and the pond and the woods. It was only from the back that you could see the house. From the front, it was just the door in the hillside. Alexandra wanted it to feel that way. She wanted it to be a place where you could escape from the world."

I had a strong sense that he was no longer seeing me, that I could stand up and do jumping jacks and he wouldn't blink. He was back at this place, this house in the earth, and from watching his face I knew that he recalled every detail perfectly, that it was the setting of a vivid movie he played regularly in his head.

"I helped them grow vegetables, and I kept the grass cut and the trees trimmed and the creek flowing and the pond clean," he said. "In the fall I cleared the leaves; in the winter I cleared the snow. No power tools, not even a mower. I did it all by hand, and at first I thought they were crazy for requiring that, but I needed the job. Then I came to understand how important it was. How the sound of an engine would have destroyed what was there."

"Who were they?" I asked, and the interruption seemed as harsh to him as a slap in the face. He blinked at me a few times, then nodded.

"The owners were Alexandra and Joshua Cantrell, and while I was not close to Joshua, I became closer to Alexandra in a year than I would have thought possible. She was a very spiritual person, deeply in touch with the earth, and when she learned I had Shawnee ancestry, she wanted to hear all of the stories I'd heard, was just fascinated with the culture. I learned from her, and she learned from me, and for that one single year everything in my life seemed to have some harmony."

He paused, lifted his head, tilted it slightly, and looked me in the eye.

"They left that place, that beautiful home they'd built, without any warning, just drove away and left it all behind. I never saw them or heard from them again. That was twelve years ago."

It was quiet, and I let it stay that way. One of the reasons I didn't speak, truth be told, was that I could feel a sort of electric tingle, and I wanted to hold on to it for a moment. It came not from his story, which was intriguing but could also be total bullshit, but from the way he told it. The light in his eyes, the energy that came from him when he spoke, had an almost rapturous quality. There was a depth of caring in what he said that I hadn't seen often before. The depth of caring you could probably develop if you spent more than a decade in a cell and then were released to the place he'd just described.

"I'm sure there's a simple explanation," I said. "One you could probably find with a little computer research. Maybe they overextended when they built that house, and the bank foreclosed. Maybe they moved to be closer to family. Maybe they decided to go overseas."

"You think I haven't done computer research?" he said. "You think that's a new idea to me? I've researched, Lincoln."

"You didn't find anything?"

"Nothing. I turned up some addresses for people with the same name, wrote some letters, never got a response unless the letter bounced back to me."

"Not all of them did? Then you probably got through to them and they didn't care to respond. No offense, Harrison, but correspondence with a murderer isn't high on most people's list of priorities. I can see why they'd ignore your letters. I tried to do the same."

He spoke with infinite patience. "Alexandra would never have ignored my letters. She was a better person than that."

"People change."

"I have six thousand dollars," he began again.

I waved him off. "I know, Harrison. You've told me."

He looked at me sadly, then spoke with his eyes on the floor.

"I need to know what happened. If it takes every dime I

have, I won't feel that it was wasted. What I told you in my letters came from the heart. I see you as a storyteller. You take something that's hidden from the world, and you bring it forward, give us answers to our questions, give us an ending. It's what you do, and you seem to be very good at it. I'm asking you, please, to do that for me. Give me those answers, give me the ending."

I didn't say anything. He shifted in his chair, looking uneasy for the first time, and I had an idea of how badly he wanted me to take this job.

"You just want to know where they went?" I said. "Is that it?"

He nodded. "I'd like to speak with her."

"I won't facilitate contact for you. I believe there is a very good chance that one of your letters got through, and they did not wish to hear from you. If that's the case, I'm not going to pass along any messages or give you their new address. I'll simply tell you what I can about why they left."

"The address is important to me, though, because I want to send a letter. I have some things I need to say."

I shook my head. "I'm not doing that. The most I will do is tell them where you are and say that you'd like to be in touch. If they want to hear from you, they can instigate it."

He paused with another objection on his lips, then let it die, and nodded instead.

"Fine. If you find her, she will be in touch. I'm sure of that."

"You said you weren't close with her husband," I said. "Perhaps you should consider the possibility that he didn't think highly of you, and that he's one of the reasons you haven't heard from her."

"He's not the reason."

"We'll see."

It went quiet again, both of us realizing that the back-and-forth was through, that I had actually agreed to do this. I'm not sure who was more surprised. Harrison shifted in his chair and began to speak of the six thousand again, to ask me what retainer fee I would require.

"None, Harrison. Not yet. I expect this won't be hard. What seems altogether mysterious probably won't be once I dig into it. Now, you gave me their names, but is there any chance you remember the address of that house?"

"It's 3730, Highway 606. Just outside of Hinckley."

Hinckley was less than an hour south of Cleveland. I took a notepad out of the desk drawer, then had him repeat the address.

"There's a stone post at the end of the drive that says Whisper Ridge," he said. "That's the name Alexandra gave to the place, and it was a good choice. Appropriate. It's the quietest place I've ever been. Alexandra said one of the contractors told her it was built in an acoustic shadow. Do you know what that is?"

I shook my head.

"I'd never heard the phrase, either, but apparently in the right terrain you can have a situation where the wind currents keep sounds from traveling the way they should. I have no idea if that's true of Whisper Ridge, but I can tell you that it's an unnaturally quiet place."

"The house will give me the start," I said, not interested in hearing another spiel about the property. "I'll be able to tell when they sold it and whether there was a foreclosure involved. Sudden departure like that, one could be likely."

He shook his head. "That's not going to be your start."

"No?"

"Well, the house will," he said. "The house absolutely should be. I'd like you to see the place before you do anything else, but there won't be any details in a sale that will help you."

"You say that with confidence."

"That's because they never sold it."

"You're sure."

"Yes."

"Then who lives there?"

"No one."

I cocked my head and studied him. "Positive about that?"

"I'm positive. I've had correspondence with the sheriff out

there. The house is still owned by the Cantrells, the taxes are current, and according to him, it's empty."

"It's been twelve years," I said.

"Yes."

"The house has just been sitting empty for that long?"

"That's my understanding."

"A house that is worth—"

"Several million, for the house and the property. I know you expect this to be easy, but I have a different sense than that. I think it will be anything but easy."

Chapter Three

I left the office a few minutes after Harrison did. I stood on the corner waiting to cross Rocky River and walk over to Gene's Place for some lunch, trying to enjoy the warm breeze and the sun and not dwell on the fact that I'd just agreed to work for a murderer. Not even an accused murderer, which was the sort of thing defense investigators did regularly, but an admitted murderer, a guy who'd sat across the desk from me and talked about the man he'd killed with a knife.

I'd had him on his feet, headed toward the door, and now I was working for him. So what had changed? Why, after ordering him to leave, had I agreed to his request? I could pretend part of it was the story, the intriguing question he'd presented, but I knew that wasn't enough.

You're looking at me with distaste, he'd said, and he'd been right. I was disgusted by him when he walked into the office, disgusted by him when he wrote the first letter back in the winter. He was a killer. He'd ended a life, shed innocent blood. I was entitled to my disgust, wasn't I? Then he'd looked at me and asked if I believed in his potential for rehabilitation, asked if I believed in the work I'd done with the police, and somehow in those questions he'd guaranteed himself my help. I didn't want to refuse him on the grounds that he was a lost cause. Didn't want to walk out of the office feeling like a smaller man than when I'd walked in.

The light changed, and I crossed the street and cut through

the parking lot to the restaurant, thinking that Harrison was a clever son of a bitch. It had been a nice play, that final question about rehabilitation, and in the end it got him what he wanted. Part of me felt honorable for my decision; another part felt manipulated. Played.

Maybe I'd made a mistake. This wasn't the sort of client I wanted on the books. Granted, we hadn't signed anything, and I could always back out . . .

"Joe will be furious," I said aloud, and then I managed a laugh. No, my partner was not going to be impressed with this story. I could hear him already, his voice rising in volume and exasperation as he explained to me the hundreds of obvious reasons why I shouldn't have taken this case. That alone could justify taking it. I had a hell of a time getting under Joe's skin now that he was in Florida. This one just might do it, though. This one just might have enough annoyance to bridge the miles.

It should be simple, too. I added that to the pro side of the list as I walked into Gene's Place and down the brick steps beside the old popcorn machine that had greeted people just inside the doors for years. Honestly, it should take me no more than a day or two to determine where this Cantrell couple had gone. I'd give them a call or drop them a note and explain where Harrison was and what he wanted. If they agreed to contact him, fine, and if they didn't, I would still have held up my end of the bargain—and, hopefully, would have satisfied Harrison into silence.

I ate a turkey club and drank black coffee and listened as people around me discussed what a beautiful day it was, how nice the sun felt. It had been a cold, angry April, with a late-season snowstorm that canceled the early baseball games and then settled into a few weeks of gray sky and chill rain. That looked to be behind us now, finally. Today's weather seemed to be an official announcement, winter waving a GOING OUT OF BUSINESS sign at the city. CLOSED FOR THE SEASON sign, rather. It'd be back soon enough, as everyone in Cleveland knew.

Still, today it was gone, and staying indoors seemed like a crime, unappreciative. I had no real need to make the drive to see the Cantrell house—this thing could probably be wrapped up without leaving the office—but the day called for an outing of some sort, and this was the only one that had offered itself. I finished my lunch and left, walked back to Lorain and past the office and a few blocks down until I got to my building. I own a small twenty-four-hour gym and live in the apartment above it. The original plan when I got kicked off the police force was to make a living on the gym. Then Joe retired and coaxed me into the PI business, which was fairly easy to do based upon the meager profits the gym had been turning. A few short years later, Joe was gone indefinitely, and I was running the agency by myself. Man plans, God laughs.

I stopped in the gym long enough to say hello to Grace, my gym manager, and then I got into my truck and headed south for Hinckley. The Cantrell house was supposed to be just off 606, which was a winding two-lane highway that cut through small towns and farm country. I came onto it too far south and had to backtrack. Ten minutes and one more turnaround later, I located 3730, a beat-up metal box on a weathered wood pole, the painted numerals chipped and peeling. The pole sat at an unnatural angle that suggested previous contact with a car. I wasn't surprised. Winter storms came in fast and hard out here, and the rural communities always had more roads than they had snowplows.

The mailbox was on the opposite side of the highway from the driveway, which was identified, as Harrison had promised, by a stone post calling it Whisper Ridge. I turned off the highway and drove past the sign onto the rutted gravel lane. Well, it *had* been a gravel lane, at least. Most of the stone had either washed away or been beaten into the dirt, and grass was beginning to reclaim the drive. I made it about fifty teeth-rattling feet before I saw the gate.

Parker Harrison hadn't mentioned the set of steel bars at least eight feet tall blocking the rest of the driveway, outfitted with an electronic lock. On either side of the gate was a metal fence with barbed wire at the top.

I turned the engine off, climbed out of my truck, and studied the obstacle ahead. There was no need to risk setting off

an alarm or angering a neighbor with an attempt at trespass-
ing, but now that I was all the way out here I wanted to actually see the damn house. There had to be a way down to it; it
just wasn't going to be as easy as I'd hoped.

My first choice was to walk the fence line to the left, and
that was a mistake. After battling through the undergrowth
for about thirty feet, I ran into water. The fence went all the
way to the edge of a creek that was maybe fifteen feet wide
and at least a few feet deep. Wetter than I wanted to be, that
was for sure. I backtracked and walked in the opposite direction only to find that on this side the fence ran into thickets of
thorns and tangled brush. On second thought, the creek might
not be that bad. It was closer to the drive, and Harrison had
talked about the house looking out onto a pond and fountain,
right? Well, the creek must feed the pond.

I clung to that belief as I set to work ruining a good pair of
shoes. Originally I'd had hopes of jumping from stone to stone,
but it turned out ol' Lincoln wasn't as nimble-footed as he remembered. I splashed my way around the fence, grumbling
and cursing, and then battled through more of the brambles
until I came back to the driveway, this time inside the gate.

From there it was an easy walk. It was a long driveway, at
least a half mile, and it curved through a border of pine trees
so that my truck was quickly hidden from sight. At one point
a dirt offshoot led to the right, but I figured that probably led
to some sort of outbuilding, so I stayed with the gravel, tramping along down the middle of the drive, stepping around the
occasional hole or downed branch until it came to an end in a
stone semicircle.

At first I couldn't see anything but trees and ivy. It was very
overgrown, and even though the sun was out, all the shade left
it dark and gloomy back here. Then I saw the hill rising steeply
in front of me, and the door in the middle of it.

Harrison's description was dead-on. The door was a massive piece of oak encased in an arch of rough stone, and everything was so weathered and unused that it just blended right
into the hillside.

There was one wide, flat stone inlaid beside the arched

door frame, with words carved into it. I walked closer, pushed ivy aside, and read the words.

WHISPER RIDGE
Home to Dreams
October 2, 1992–April 12, 1996

An epitaph for a house? I ran my fingertips over the carved stone, then across the heavy wood of the door, and let out a breath that I hadn't realized I was holding.

"Unreal," I said, and it was. I'd never seen anything else like it. There was nothing here but a hill covered in ivy and groundcover and this single, solitary door with the words carved beside it. On a second read, I decided I was wrong— the epitaph wasn't for the house, which, still standing, lived on. It was for the dreams.

I stepped away and looked around at the empty trees and the drive I'd just walked up. All right, the house was here, and he'd been honest about the door. Let's see about the rest of it.

I walked up the side of the hill, which flattened out on top. A stone path was barely visible in the tall weeds, and I followed that until I came to the well house. It, like the door casing, seemed to be built out of hand-laid creek stone, and Harrison was right—it looked like it was two hundred years old. As I walked past I felt a strange, powerful need *not* to peer down into the well, as if something might come snarling out. I forced a laugh and shook my head and then went up to the edge and looked over, ignoring the prickle that climbed my spine.

The bottom was covered with plywood that was rotted and broken, weeds and mud caking the jagged edges of the boards. I leaned back and surveyed the hilltop. It looked like hell now, all the thickets and tall weeds threatening to take over, but I could imagine how beautiful it had been when Parker Harrison tended the grounds and kept the woods at bay. It was a solitary place, that was for damn sure. I couldn't hear a sound except wind and birds. Even though the highway was less than a mile away, I couldn't hear any traffic.

That seemed impossible to me, so I listened harder and still couldn't hear a car. Finally I gave up and walked away from the well.

At the far end of the hill there was a little ridge of stone, and once I got up to it I realized it was the top edge of the back of the house. I walked along it until I came to the end, and there I found a little path that led back down the side of the hill and emptied out behind the house.

It was just as Harrison had said—two stories of almost sheer glass looking out on the water. There was no fountain now, and the pond was covered with a skim of algae and leaves and hidden behind a cluster of dried, broken reeds, but I hardly cared about the water. The house held all my attention. It should have been gorgeous, but instead it was buried under a heavy layer of grime and disrepair. The windows were broken in several places and covered with dirt, but even so you could see what it must have been, what it could *still* be if only someone had taken care of it.

I walked up to the lower-level window and used my shirt-sleeve to rub away some of the filth, then pressed my face to the glass, shielding my eyes with my hands like someone window-shopping at a store that had closed for the night.

A swimming pool was just inside, long and deep. A lap pool. Empty, of course, with stains and corrosion lining the cracked tank. Around the pool was a floor of Italian tile, many of the pieces broken, and behind that the thick plaster walls were bare. I could see two ornate columns rising behind the door that led into the next room, and a curving stone wall with a fireplace.

I stood there for a long time. Didn't move until my breath began to fog the glass and I could no longer see. Then I stepped away and looked from the house to the silent pond and back again, suddenly feeling very ill at ease.

This was not normal. The housing market in Medina County wasn't booming, but some people were willing to trade a long commute for a little country living, and the price tag on a place like this would have been mighty. So why not sell it? Why did you let a home like this sit empty and exposed to the elements for twelve years?

I walked away from the back of the house and up the other side of the hill. I found an angle that allowed me to look in at the second story, in at more beautiful but empty rooms. All the way around the hill was another entrance, a sunporch with almost all the glass broken out. I stepped over the jagged shards and walked to this door and repeated my face-to-the-window act. This time I saw a hallway bordered by a short partition that had recessed floodlights and doors opening to hidden rooms beyond. Back through the broken glass and into the woods, and now I was walking away from the house faster than I'd walked toward it, returning to my truck with a strange tightness in the middle of my back and sweat-dampened hair clinging to my forehead. I splashed back through the creek without a single muttered curse or a thought about my shoes and climbed up to the driveway.

People did not leave homes like this. I'd never seen anything like it, and maybe that was why it was affecting me in this way, why I felt almost relieved when I was back in the driver's seat and had the engine going. It was just something . . . different, that was all. Felt a little off because, well, it *was* a little off. Abnormal. Still, I could figure out what had happened, and I could tell Harrison, and I could be done with it. I owed him that much, because his request certainly seemed genuine, convicted murderer or not. This much of the truth he had told me: The door was there in the earth, and the house beyond it was empty.

Chapter Four

My shoes forced a return home. I was tempted to head straight for the Medina County Recorder's Office, find out who held the deed on the property and whether there was a mortgage, and then continue on to the auditor's office to see whether the taxes were truly paid up and who the hell was paying them. My shoes and the lower third of my pants were soaked and coated with a slimy creek mud, though, and I didn't want to go tramping into the county offices looking like I'd just emerged from a swamp.

I was back in the city, only a few blocks from my building, when Amy called.

"Guess who visited today?" I said in place of a hello.

"Who?"

"Parker Harrison."

Amy Ambrose, friend-turned-girlfriend—a process not without its bumps—was well aware of the letters I'd received from Harrison.

"The psycho?"

"The rehabilitated murderer, Amy."

"Fava beans," she said. "Tell me he talked about fava beans."

"Sadly, no."

"Well, what the hell did he want? How was it? Is he crazy? I bet he's charming. Those guys always are. Or did he get angry? I could see him getting—"

"Amy."

"Sorry. Got carried away."

"Indeed." I turned left across traffic and bounced into the alley beside my building.

"So?" she prompted.

"He is unique," I said. "More toward the charming side, definitely."

"Please don't tell me he *charmed* you into working on his case. From what I read, the guy couldn't be any guiltier."

"That isn't in dispute." I parked and shut off the engine. "He candidly admitted his guilt."

"What did he want with you, then?"

"Help with the most minor of investigations. I mean, it's odd that he went through all the dramatics of the letters, because this is something that shouldn't take much time—"

"Oh, no. You agreed to do it, didn't you?"

"Why do you say that?"

"Because you're trying to explain it in that rational, matter-of-fact tone you always use to justify something stupid."

I smiled and didn't answer.

"Speak," she said. "Tell me I'm wrong."

More silence.

"Lincoln!"

I explained it to her then, told her about Harrison's story as quickly as possible and went on to describe the house. I knew the house would pacify her. Amy's natural curiosity well exceeds my own.

"How much do you think the place is worth?" she asked when I was done, her voice softer.

"I'm not good with real estate, but I'd have to say a few million with all that property involved. The house is incredible, but it's also been ignored for a long time. It would take someone willing to invest in rehabilitation."

"I want to see it," she said.

"Bring some waders. That creek provides the best way in."

"Your psychopath didn't mention that? He didn't even know there was a gate?"

"My *client* did not, no."

"Hey, you work for a murderer, you better get used to the criticism and name-calling. Anyway, maybe that means the gate is new."

"Probably."

"I wonder who put it up."

"So do I. I'm going to change clothes and drive back down there and check with the auditor, see who has been paying the taxes."

"You're going back today?"

"Uh-huh."

"Lot of driving for one day."

It was, and with any other case I might have delayed the return trip. This was different, somehow. There was something about the place that had gotten under my skin after just one visit, and I wanted to know who was responsible for it, who'd kept it away from a sheriff's sale but still didn't bother to actually take care of the home.

"I'm not busy," I said. "Faster I get this worked out, the faster I can terminate my relationship with Harrison."

Two hours later, wearing fresh pants and shoes, I stood in the recorder's office and stared at a warranty deed confirming that, yes, Alexandra and Joshua Cantrell owned the home. There was no mortgage. They'd paid five hundred thousand for the property alone seventeen years earlier. It was a forty-eight-acre parcel.

So Harrison's information was accurate and up-to-date and the Cantrells still owned the home. Now came the second step, the auditor's office, where I'd find a new address for the couple.

Well, it was supposed to go that way. When I took the parcel number over to the auditor's office and requested the records, though, I learned that the taxes had been paid each year—in full and on time—by one Anthony Child, attorney at law, Hinckley, Ohio. Okay, maybe I was going to need a third step to finish this one off.

* * *

Child's office was on the second floor of a brick building on the square in Hinckley, which is a town known nationally for Buzzard Day, a bizarre ritual in which people gather each April to welcome a returning flock of turkey vultures. In some places, this return would be cause for alarm, or at least mild revulsion. In Ohio, it's a celebration. Hey, we have long, tedious winters, all right? You take your excitement where you can get it.

Attorney Child was in, and willing to see me. The entire firm seemed to consist of an angry-looking secretary in an outer room and Child alone in the office behind that. The door to the tiny attached bathroom stood open, showing a toilet with the seat up. First class. For a good thirty seconds after I'd been shown into his office he kept his back to me, staring at the TV. Weather report. Can't miss that.

"Hot," he said when he finally clicked the television off and turned to me. "Unusually hot for the first week of May."

"I know it."

"Going to be a rough summer. You can always tell."

Everyone else was rejoicing that winter had finally broken, and this guy was bitching about the summer to come. Cheerful. He sat and stared at me without much interest. Maybe fifty years old, small face with slack jowls and sleepy eyes. His tie was loosened, and his jacket was off.

"I was just explaining to your secretary that I found you through a tax record," I said. "I'm curious about some property, and when I pulled the records I found your office handled the payments."

That was all it took to wake the sleepy eyes up. They narrowed and focused, and he pushed away from the desk and ran both thumbs down the straps of his suspenders.

"What exactly is your line of work, Mr. Perry?"

I took out a business card and passed it across the desk to him. He looked at it long enough to read every word three times and then read them backward. Finally he set the card carefully on the desk and kept one hand on it while he looked back up at me.

"This is about the Cantrell house."

I nodded.

"Who are you working for?"

Here I hesitated, for the obvious reason. Parker Harrison's name hadn't meant anything to me until he'd taken to writing letters, but Child was a good deal older and more likely to remember a murderer from that era than I was.

"Someone who's interested in the property," I said after a beat of silence. "It's a damn expensive home to leave in that condition."

"I take it you've trespassed out there and seen the place? Don't worry, I'm not going to report you. Plenty of people have trespassed there before. It's a damn headache, that house is, and for as little money as I've made off the arrangements, I wish I'd never agreed to it."

He was warming up to me now, waving his hand around while he talked, looking more relaxed.

"You put up the gate," I said.

He nodded.

"At the Cantrells' request?"

A hesitation, as if I'd asked something odd, and then, "No, not exactly. I'd been out to the house a few times and saw that there'd been some vandalism. The sheriff called me to complain, because they'd had to go out there on several occasions and break up groups of drunk kids wandering the grounds. Word got out that the place was empty, and the kids immediately found their way to it. You know how that goes. Then there was a hitchhiker who found it and moved right in, had some insane idea about claiming squatter's rights. Sheriff was irritated, so I went ahead and put up the gate and the fence. It's helped."

"You paid for this?"

"I draw from an account she left. The money was there." He pulled himself back to the desk again, frowning, and said, "Mr. Perry, you clearly don't want to tell me who you're working for and why they want to find her, but I need to tell you this: Any number of people do want to find her, from the police to reporters to people like you, and I can't help. All I ask of you is to make that clear to your client. I don't know how to get in touch with her; I don't know where she is or what she's doing."

"Mr. Child, I don't understand exactly why she'd be so sought after. Who is the woman, anyhow?"

He looked at me as if I'd asked him how to spell my own name. Then his eyes turned reflective and he nodded. "Your client's interested in the property."

"That's right." It wasn't true, really, but I had the sense that was what he wanted to hear as some kind of reassurance.

"So you have no idea . . . shit, you guys really are clueless. Okay. That puts me at peace. It truly does."

"What don't I understand, Mr. Child?"

"Anything," he said. "You don't understand anything. What *do* you know about Alexandra and Joshua Cantrell?"

I shook my head. "Only that their names are on the deed."

"Okay," he said. "Then you absolutely don't understand a damn thing. Now I'm going to tell you two little details, and then I'm going to ask one more time who you're working for, and if you won't answer, I'll tell you to get the hell out of my office."

He braced his elbows on the desk and folded his hands together. "You've done amazingly poor research, Mr. Perry. Here are the two details you need to know: First, Joshua Cantrell is dead. Nobody had heard from him in twelve years, but last winter his bones were found near Pymatuning Reservoir. Buried in the woods. Case still under investigation."

He paused, and I was aware of how quiet it was in his office, so quiet that I could hear the dripping of a faucet in the little bathroom on the other side of the wall, a drop falling into the sink every few seconds. *Plip, plip, plip.*

"Detail number two," he said. "Do you know the lovely Mrs. Cantrell's maiden name?"

"I do not."

"Sanabria," he said. "Alexandra Sanabria."

"Shit," I said. "You're kidding."

He shook his head.

"Maiden name," I said. "Surely she's too old to be the daughter of—"

"Dominic? Yes, too old to be his daughter. Just the right age to be his sister. Sister of Dominic, daughter of Christopher, right there in the trunk of a very infamous family tree. Pride and joy of Crime Town, USA."

It was an old nickname, went back almost fifty years, but people still attached it to Youngstown, a gritty factory town an hour from Cleveland. While the Italian mob's heyday in Cleveland was during the sixties and seventies, Youngstown remained an epicenter for decades longer, featuring constant FBI attention as well as the occasional car bombing or sniper takedown of a major player. During one attempt to pay off the town's mayor, a *priest* was involved as a money handler. Ties run deep in Youngstown, and a lot of them run through the Sanabria family. Christopher was the patriarch, the focus of a major federal investigation when he was killed in the late seventies. Twenty years later, his son, Dominic, appeared in headlines for a few months during the Lenny Strollo and James Traficant trials. Something like seventy convictions were handed down in the fallout of those investigations—Traficant was a U.S. representative at the time, which only added to the circus—but Dominic Sanabria walked away with one of the lightest sentences, two years for minor crimes. It wasn't that he'd been a minor player, but he apparently left less evidence and trusted fewer people. At the time, one of the district attorneys suggested that Sanabria was the most dangerous of the lot, and the media made good use of that quote. People in the Cleveland area remembered the name.

"That house," I said, "is owned by Dominic Sanabria's sister? That's what you're telling me?"

Child's face turned unpleasant as he leaned across the desk, almost pulling out of his chair, and said, "Yes. Now, damn it, I need to know who you're working for."

"That information is confidential, Mr. Child. I'm sorry."

"Then get out. And tell your client to give up his inquiries on that house."

"Where is she?" I said as he got to his feet and walked to the door. "Where's Alexandra?"

I didn't ask because I believed he would provide an answer but simply because I wanted to gauge his reaction for myself, see if I smelled a lie.

He paused with his hand on the doorknob and turned back to me. "Nobody knows. Not me, not her family, and certainly not the police. If they did know, maybe they'd stop calling me all the time."

It felt like the truth.

He twisted the knob and swung the door open for me. "Goodbye, Mr. Perry."

Chapter Five

Outside, the air was thick with humidity, and a bank of angry dark clouds had gathered in the west. It was a heavy, cloaking warmth, and I opened the second button of my shirt and stood on the sidewalk and stared at the sleepy town square.

Joshua Cantrell is dead . . . bones found last winter . . . buried in the woods. Case still under investigation.

Without leaving the front steps of Child's office, I took out my cell phone and called Amy at the newspaper. For once, she was there. I asked her to do an archives search for Joshua Cantrell.

"The guy who owns the house?"

"Owned. He's dead."

"Lincoln—"

"Run the search, please. I'd like to know when they found the body."

I listened as she clicked keys and people in her office laughed over something. It took a few minutes, and neither of us spoke. Then she found the right article.

"Looks like a hunter found the body on the first weekend of December."

"That's just before Harrison wrote me the first letter. He knew. The son of a bitch knew."

"Lincoln, there's stuff in here . . . hang on. It says that Cantrell is related by marriage to organized crime. To the Sanabria family."

"Yeah," I said. "I was recently informed of that."

"What in the hell is Parker Harrison trying to do?"

"I have no idea, but I guarantee you he knew Cantrell was dead when he sent me out here. He knew, and he didn't tell me."

"You don't think he killed him? That he's playing some sick game now because the body was found?"

"I don't know if he killed him, but, yeah, he's playing some sick game—and I'm going to end it."

I called Harrison from my truck and told him to meet me at the office. I didn't say anything else. The clouds built overhead as I drove back to the city with both hands tight on the wheel and the stereo off, the cab of the truck silent. The rain started when I reached the stoplight across from the office and was falling steadily as I walked into the building, but the air was still warm, reassuring us that this was a spring, not winter, storm. Harrison was already inside, and he met me at the top of the stairs with a smile.

"When you said you'd be in touch, I was expecting a bit more of a wait."

I didn't say a word. Just unlocked the door and walked inside and sat behind the desk and stared at him while he took the chair across from me, waited while his smile faded and his eyes narrowed.

"What's the problem?" he said.

"Did you kill him?"

If I'd been expecting a visceral reaction to that, I was wrong. He lifted his hand and ran his fingertips over the scar on his cheekbone, let his eyes wander away from mine. "No, I didn't kill him. If you're referring to Joshua Cantrell."

"If I'm referring . . . listen, Harrison, you twisted prick, what the hell kind of game is this? Why do I need to play it?"

"Hang on, Lincoln."

"Shut up. I shouldn't have ever let you in the door, and when I made that mistake I *definitely* shouldn't have been stupid enough to buy your story. It was a good one, though, compelling, and you reeled me all the way in with those questions about whether I believed in rehabilitation, whether I believed in the system. A nice, subtle guilt trip. I'm sure there's a better word for it, some psychology term, and you probably know it because you had fifteen years to sit in a cell and read books and come up with games to play. But you shouldn't have involved me, Harrison."

I was leaning toward him, loud and aggressive, and if that made the slightest impact he didn't show it. He waited till I'd wound down, then said, "I told you the truth."

"Like hell you did."

"Lincoln, I worked for the Cantrells as a groundskeeper for one year, and ever since I've wondered what—"

"Oh, stop it already." I waved him off. "All that may be true, and I don't care if it is or if it isn't. What I care about is that you lied to me. You sat there and talked about Joshua Cantrell as if you didn't have the faintest idea that he was dead. Talked about wanting to find him."

"I said nothing about wanting to find him. I said I want to find *her*. In fact, I assured you he was not the reason she had stayed out of touch."

"You already knew he'd been murdered and didn't bother to tell me that. Like it's insignificant information, Harrison, that the guy is dead and the woman is the *sister* of a Youngstown mob figure? How did you get tied up with those guys in the first place? Last I knew, the requirement was to be Sicilian, not Shawnee."

"I was never tied up with them."

"Sure."

"I shared minimal facts," he said. "That I will admit."

My laugh was heavy with disgust. "Shared minimal facts? Shit, that's brilliant. You should've been an attorney, Harrison, instead of a murderer."

That seemed to sting him, and for a moment he looked entirely genuine again. Looked hurt.

"Would you have taken this case," he said, "if you knew all of that beforehand?"

"No."

"See, that was my reasoning. I didn't think you would, but

I knew if I could get you to go out to the house, to stand there in that spot under the trees and feel the energy of that place, that things might change. I knew that was possible, because I knew this one was meant for you, that you'd been—"

"*Shut up!*" I hammered my fist onto the desk between us. "I don't want to hear any more of it. I'm not going to take the case. We're done."

I stood up and walked to the door and opened it for him, just as Child had done for me an hour earlier.

"You saw the house?" he said without turning.

"Yeah."

"You didn't feel anything?"

"No, I did not," I said. Was there a tug somewhere along my spine at that? Some twinge that comes from telling a lie? No, couldn't be.

"All right," he said. "I'm sorry you're offended. Sorry you feel betrayed."

"I don't feel betrayed, I feel stupid. I'll give you this heads-up, though: I'm going to track down whatever police agency is investigating Cantrell's death and tell them about your request."

"You think I was involved?" He still had his head down, and now, standing above him, I could see another scar, long and ugly, across the back of his skull and neck.

"I don't know," I said, "but you've killed before, and you seem awfully fascinated with this couple, one of whom happens to be dead. I think the right cops ought to be told about that."

"It's my past that bothers you. That's why you refuse to give me any credibility."

"Yeah, Harrison, that does bother me. Just a touch. Sorry."

"Let me ask you one question," he said, keeping his back to me.

I was silent.

"Can a good man commit a horrible act?" he said.

I stood there at the door, looking at his bowed head, and then I said, "Harrison, get out."

He nodded and got to his feet. "Okay, Mr. Perry. Goodbye."

It was the first time he hadn't called me Lincoln.

I stood at the door while he went through it, and then I crossed to the window and looked down as he walked out of the building and into a hard, driving rain.

Chapter Six

Amy was in my apartment when I got home, and she was cooking, some sort of Italian dish that had filled the rooms with a thick scent of tomatoes and garlic and made the place feel more welcoming than at any time I could remember.

"Did anyone give you permission to touch my valuable implements?" I said, lifting a cheese grater off the counter. Amy had never cooked a meal in my apartment before.

"You want to be the only one to touch your implements, I can make that happen." She shifted a pan on the stove and adjusted the heat.

"Seriously, to what do I owe this?"

"You sounded a little rough on the phone. Like it hadn't been the best day."

I listened to that, and watched her move around the kitchen, and I was grateful to see her there. She was right; it hadn't been the best day—but those were the sort of days that could stack up on you easily, and it was a new and welcome thing for me to end them with Amy. It beat the hell out of ending it alone, with a bottle of beer and the mindless noise of some TV show.

"Thank you," I said. "Really."

"I wouldn't say that till you taste this."

"What is it?"

"I call it Mafia lasagna. In honor of the Sanabria family."

"Weak humor, Amy. Very weak."

She dried her hands on a towel and turned to face me. "If you're interested, I've got a bunch of printouts discussing Joshua Cantrell—or at least the discovery of his body—over on the table. As for Alexandra, there's not much out there. She's the quiet one of the Sanabria family, I suppose."

I walked over to the table and looked at the stack of papers there. Lots of articles. The discovery of Cantrell's body had made plenty of news.

"I can't believe the name didn't register with me," I said, flipping through the articles.

Amy turned to look at me over her shoulder, a few strands of hair glued to her cheek from the steam rising off the stove. After months of fighting to straighten her naturally curly blond hair, she'd finally given up again, and I was glad to see it. She'd looked too corporate with the straightened hair—an observation that had gotten a pen thrown at me once.

"You've been pretty removed from the news lately." She pulled the oven open and bent to look inside, leaving her voice muffled as she continued to speak. "Can't say the last time I've seen you with the paper."

It was a good point. Ordinarily I would've read about the discovery of Cantrell's body, and probably remembered the name when Harrison said it, but I'd stopped reading the papers and watching TV news shows back in the fall, when I was making all-too-frequent appearances in them. I hadn't gone back to them yet, but now I was thinking maybe I should. It's dangerous to be uninformed, as today had demonstrated.

"That's just good taste," I said. "You know the sort of crap they write in the newspaper these days. It's a wonder they still refer to those people as journalists."

She closed the oven and stood up. "I am close to knives, you know. Large, sharp knives."

"Good reminder." I moved the stack of articles out of the way. They could wait, or maybe I'd never read them at all. There was no need to. I'd taken a silly nibble today, but now I saw the lure and its hooks and knew better than to hang around.

The Cantrell case didn't need my attention, and I needed even less the attention of the Sanabria family.

"Food is almost done," Amy said, "and you better realize the only reason I'm feeding you is because I want to hear the story. Not some half-assed version of it, either. The real story, with all the details."

"You'll get it," I said, "but let me pour some wine first."

It was a nice evening that turned into a nice night, and she stayed with me and we slept comfortably and deeply in my bed while another round of storms blew in off the lake and hammered rain into the walls that sheltered us. Amy rose early and slipped out of the house sometime before seven to return to her own apartment before starting the day. We'd been together a while now, but still we both clung to own routines and our own space, and I wondered at times if maybe that wasn't the way it would and should always be, if maybe we were the sort of people who simply didn't cohabit well. At other times, I'd come home and sit alone in the apartment and wonder why in the hell I hadn't proposed.

She'd been gone for almost an hour, and I'd fallen back into a surface layer of sleep, not quite awake but never far from it, either, when the tapping began. A gentle series of taps, five or six at a time, then a pause followed by another sequence. I don't know how many sequences had passed before they finally carved into my brain and I sat up in bed and realized that someone was knocking on my door. Knocking, it seemed, with extraordinary consistency and patience. Never loud, never urgent, but never stopping, either. Tap, tap, tap, tap.

I got out of bed and tugged on a pair of jeans and a T-shirt, made it to the top of the stairs as another calm sequence of knocks began, reached the bottom just as it came to an end. Then I had the door open and was squinting out into the harsh daylight and the face of a small, dark-haired man with a raised fist. There was a ring on his finger that seemed brighter than the sunlight behind him, some hideous collection of gold and diamonds so heavy that I hoped he wore one on the other hand to keep from becoming lopsided. He was getting ready to bring it back down on the door, continue the knocking, but when he saw me he just held the pose for a second and then slowly lowered the hand to his side.

"Good morning, Mr. Perry."

I was barefoot and he was in shoes, but still I had a good four inches on him, and I'm not particularly tall. He was thin across the chest and shoulders, with small hands and weak wrists, and seemed like the kind of guy who would need his wife to open the pickle jar for him. Until you looked him in the eye. There, in that steady and unflinching gaze, was a quality I'd typically seen in much larger men, stronger men. Men who felt invincible.

"Did I wake you?" he said when I didn't respond to the greeting. "I apologize. I'm an early riser, though. Always have been."

He put out the hand with the ring and waited until I shook it, until my palm was firmly held in his, to say, "My name is Dominic Sanabria."

I pulled my hand free and stepped forward, out of my doorway and into the daylight.

"I'm sorry you made the trip," I said. "It was entirely unnecessary, Mr. Sanabria."

"You don't even know the purpose of my trip."

"I know the source of it, though."

"Do you?"

"A lawyer named Child probably gave you a call. Or somebody in the Medina County Recorder's Office, though that seems unlikely. Either way, somebody told you I was inquiring about your sister's home. That information is no longer correct."

"Is it not?"

I shook my head. "I've learned the house is not on the market and will not be on the market, and I've passed that information along to my client. We're done with it now."

He reached up and ran a hand over his mouth, as if drying his lips, and then he spoke without looking at me. "Let's go upstairs and talk—and I'd ask you not to continue lying to me. It's not something I appreciate."

He walked past me and headed up the stairs without another word, and I turned and hesitated and then followed, swinging the door shut and closing out the daylight behind us.

When I got to the top of the stairs he was already in my living room, standing in front of the bookshelf. He slid a Michael Connelly novel out with his index finger and studied the cover.

"I had a brother-in-law who was a big reader," he said. "Not these sort of books, though. Not fiction. He was an anthropologist. Studied people. Studied the, what's the word, indigenous types."

He pushed the book back into place and turned to face me.

"He didn't study me. Did not have the slightest desire to study me, or my people. Wanted very little to do with us. Oh, he was polite, you know, a hell of a nice guy, but he definitely wanted to know as little as possible about me and my associates and what it was that we did. I always liked that about him."

I didn't answer, didn't say a word as he crossed to an armchair and sat carefully on the edge of it. Dominic Sanabria was in my apartment. It was not yet nine in the morning, and Dominic Sanabria was sitting in my living room discussing dead men. I wasn't going to require coffee to get my nervous system energized today.

"My sister is a very special girl," he said, crossing his legs in a manner that would have looked effete from anyone but him. "A woman, of course, but I can't help but think of her as a girl. She's nine years younger than me, you know. By the time she was growing up, there was some awkwardness around my family. Some legal troubles that you might recall, or might not. You're pretty young. Anyhow, my father, who was not without his faults but always loved his children dearly, he thought it would be best to send Alexandra away to school."

I hadn't taken a seat, hadn't moved from the top of the stairs, because I thought it was better to simply stand there and listen. There are guys who bring out the smart-ass in me, the desire to throw some jabs back at them, show them the tough-guy bullshit isn't as intimidating as they'd like it to be. Dominic Sanabria was not one of those guys. All I wanted to do was listen and get him the hell out of my home. Even while that desire occupied my thoughts, though, I hadn't missed the tense shift. He'd referred to Joshua Cantrell in the past, and well he should—Joshua was past tense for this world, no doubt. Alexandra had received present tense. *My sister is a very special girl . . .*

"They found a school out east, somewhere in the Adirondacks, cost a friggin' fortune," he said, "but it was worth it, you know? It was worth it. Because Alexandra, she was always a special kid, but after being out there, being around those sort of teachers and those sort of . . . I dunno, *experiences*, I guess, it made a difference. She was a kind of, you know, a deeper spirit when she came home. A very compassionate person. She was not as close to the family as the rest of us were, but that was good. It was good for her to be around other people. Other influences. Every family has their darling, and she is ours."

He did that thing with his hand again, running it over his mouth, the way you might if your lips were chapped and bothering you.

"When she got married, the guy was, well, a different sort from the type we know. Probably from the type you know. Quiet guy, real studious, shit like that. Nose in a book, right? All the time with that. I liked him. He wasn't real comfortable around me, maybe, but he was good to my sister. They matched up where it counts." He touched his head with two fingers, then his heart. "Where it counts."

Out on the street a truck's gears hissed and someone blew a horn while Dominic Sanabria sat and stared at me.

"I liked Joshua," he said. "Used to call him Josh, and he never bitched about that, but then Alexandra said he didn't like it. Josh*ua*, she said. I liked him. Because I love my sister, and he made her happy."

He sighed and kneaded the back of his neck with his hand and looked at the floor.

"They found his bones a few months ago, and I cannot tell you how unhappy that makes me, because I know how unhappy that makes my sister. I feel that pain in my heart, you know? I feel it for her. There are people out there, somewhere in the world, who know some things that I will need to know."

"I'm not one of them." It was the first time I'd spoken since he entered my apartment.

"Probably not," he said, "but you may be working for one. I believe you probably are. I'd like to speak with that person."

Give him up! my brain screamed. *Give him up!* A quieter voice, the soft whisper of instinct, offered dissent.

"Mr. Sanabria," I said, "I run a business that would not exist without confidentiality. It would disappear if I did not maintain that, and I'd be out on the streets looking for work. I respect you, though, and I respect your interest in this, and here's what I will tell you: My relationship with this client is done. That's a promise, that's a guarantee. I ended it yesterday, and I will not resume it at any time, ever. I don't know anything—*anything*—that can help you. I assume Mr. Child communicated that idea to you. I was utterly clueless when I went into his office, and I remain that way now. Nor do I have any desire to learn more."

"Who hired you?"

I shook my head.

"You've been around," he said. "You understand that people can eventually be convinced to share information."

"I've also seen how stupid and wasteful all that convincing becomes when it doesn't produce any information of value. I've seen the problems that can arise as a result of the effort."

"You were a cop."

"I was."

"Cops tend to feel safe. Off-limits, protected. That sort of thing."

"I've been to a few police funerals. Enough to know better."

"Still you refuse me."

"The name can't help you, Mr. Sanabria. My client is a nobody. *Was* a nobody."

"Maybe you like me," he said. "Maybe you like having me around, want me to drop in again. That must be it, because here you have a chance to send me away for good, and you're refusing that."

"I like you fine. You're terrific, trust me. Even so, I sure as shit don't want you around."

"You sound a little uneasy there."

"I am."

"You sound, maybe, even afraid," he said, and there was a bite in his voice, a taunt.

"I'm afraid of my own stupidity," I answered. "There are people I'd rather not be involved with, at any level, at any time. You are one of those people."

"That could be viewed an insult."

"It should be viewed as a statement of fact. I don't want anything to do with you, and I don't know anything that can help you. Where we go from here, I guess you will decide and I'll deal with."

He nodded his head very slowly. "Yes. Yes, I guess I will decide."

Another pause, and then he got to his feet and walked toward me. Slowed just a touch when he reached me, then turned and went down the steps and opened the door and walked outside. He left the door open. I waited for a few seconds, and then I went down and closed it and turned the lock and sat on the steps. I sat there for a long time, and eventually a car engine started in the parking lot, and then it was gone, and I was alone.

Chapter Seven

For more than a week, it was quiet. At first I checked the locks with extra care, wore my gun when I left the apartment, and held my breath each time I turned the key in the ignition of my truck. Visits from a guy like Dominic Sanabria can make you conscious of such things.

Nothing happened. Sanabria didn't stop by, nor did anyone operating on his behalf. Parker Harrison made no contact. I was quiet, too—despite promising Harrison that I would pass his name along to the Joshua Cantrell death investigators, I didn't make any calls. After Sanabria visited, it somehow seemed better to do nothing. Amy and I discussed the situation frequently for the first few days, but then the topic faded, and soon I was leaving the gun at home and starting the truck without pause. I'd gotten out of the mess early enough, it seemed, and no damage had been done.

"Managed to escape yourself this time," Joe said when I called to say that seven days had passed without disaster following Sanabria's visit. "It's good that you're developing that skill, LP. Without me around, you've actually been forced to learn some common sense."

"Aren't you proud."

"Not particularly. If you'd had even an ordinary amount of that sense, you'd never have agreed to look at the house in the first place."

"Harrison assured me he'd been rehabilitated. What else could I do?"

"I've sat in on parole hearings and listened to true psychotics insist on the same thing."

"You wouldn't release a jaywalker until he'd done five years in solitary, Joe."

The conversation drifted away from Harrison then, on to more important things, like baseball, and eventually Joe asked after the weather.

"Warm," I said. "The sun's shining every day, and it's warm. So why are you still in Florida? I'm pretty sure the rest of your kind has migrated back north."

"My kind?"

"Snowbirds, Joseph. Men who sit around the pool all day talking about their experiences fighting in Korea and working for the Truman campaign. You know, your peers."

"My peers." Joe hated the idea of being one of those flee-for-Florida-in-winter retirees, so naturally I raised the subject during every phone call.

"Perhaps I'm wrong, though," I said. "Perhaps you're not part of that group. Like I said, most of them are already coming back north. So if you need to stay down there this late in the year, you must be even more old and frail."

"That must be it, yes," he said, determined not to rise to the bait this time around.

"When are you coming back?" I asked, serious now. I'd been expecting his return sometime in April, but that month had come and gone and he remained in Florida.

"I don't know yet. We'll see."

"We'll see? If it's pushing eighty degrees up here it has to be, what, a hundred and sixty down there? With ninety percent humidity?"

"Close to that, sure."

"And summer hasn't even hit yet. Only a damn fool would stay in Florida in the summer when he could retreat to a home near the beautiful shores of Lake Erie."

"I'll admit I'm not enjoying the weather as much lately."

"So why not come home? What did you do, meet a woman?"

He didn't answer.

I said, "Joe?"

"Could be the truth, LP. Could be the truth."

I'd made the initial remark as a joke, but his response seemed sincere, and that silenced me. Joe's wife of thirty years, Ruth, had been dead for five now, and in that time he'd not gone on a single date. The few people who'd attempted to make introductions for him had been shut down quickly and emphatically. If Joe was actually seeing someone, it was an awfully big step for him.

"Well, good for you," I said after the pause had gone on too long.

"Oh, shut up with the sincerity. Makes me sick. If I were anybody else, you'd be giving me hell right now, asking which strip club I met her at."

"A stripper? At your age? No way. I just assumed you'd done some volunteering at a home for the blind. Convinced her you were forty years younger and good-looking. Convinced her you were more like me, in other words."

"You're neither good-looking nor forty years younger than me."

"Close enough on both counts, grandpa. Close enough. Can I at least hear the young girl's name?"

"Gena," he said, "and she *is* a few years younger than me, smart-ass."

"You lecherous old dog. How many years? Is she even legal yet? Is this girl—"

"Goodbye, Lincoln."

"Oh, come on, you've got to give me more than—"

"Talk to you soon," he said, and he was laughing as he hung up.

I was laughing, too, and in a good mood as I went downstairs to check the mail, happy for him even if disappointed that this might delay his return. Had a smile on my face until I took the mail out of the box and saw my name written in unpleasantly familiar handwriting on the only envelope inside. *P. T. Harrison*, the return address said, but I didn't need that to identify the sender. I'd seen enough of his damn letters already.

I tore the envelope open as I walked back up the stairs, shook out the contents as I stepped inside the office, dreading whatever twisted manifesto he'd decided to write this time. There was no letter, though. Nothing but a check for five hundred dollars, with *thanks for your time* written in the memo portion.

I threw the envelope in the trash but kept the check in my hand for a minute. It was a simple design, blue on blue, standard font, the sort of check most banks issued cheaply. It told me nothing about Parker Harrison that I didn't already know, except that he had a checkbook. *I have six thousand dollars. I'll spend every dime . . .*

I smoothed the check against the top of the desk and wondered if it would bounce. If not, then Harrison had done all right for himself after serving fifteen years in prison. Managing to stay on the streets for twelve years and save at least a little bit of money might not seem like much, but it was more than most of his fellow offenders managed. Twelve years was a hell of a run for some of them. I had a friend who worked at the Cuyahoga County Jail and referred to the booking area as "the revolving door." Same faces went in and out, year after year, decade after decade. Harrison hadn't done that. From the small amount of research I'd done once he began his letter writing, I'd determined that he'd never been charged with any crime after his release, not even a traffic ticket. I didn't know where he worked or how he lived or what he did with himself, but he hadn't taken another bust. For years, he'd lived quietly and without incident. Then the remains of a former employer turned up in the woods and he'd decided to surface again, surface in my life.

"Go away, Harrison," I said quietly. "Go away." Then I took the check and held it over the trash can, opened my fingers, and watched as it fluttered down. I wouldn't take his money. Didn't want it, didn't need it.

For once, that was true. My former fiancée, Karen Jefferson, had mailed me a check for eighty thousand dollars after my investigation into her husband's death in the fall. She was worth millions now, could certainly afford it, but I'd thrown that check in the trash, too, and the two that followed it. Then she sent another, along with a letter insisting that I take the money. I had. Cashed the check but hadn't spent a dime of it. The money sat in a savings account, earning a pitiful interest rate, but that was enough for me. I didn't want to invest it or spend it, but I appreciated the sense of comfort it provided. The sense of freedom. If I didn't like a client, I didn't have to work for him. If I didn't like a case, I didn't have to take it. If for any reason I didn't feel like working, well, I didn't have to. For a while, anyway. That eighty grand kept me at least a few steps ahead of the thresher.

I spent the rest of the day at my desk writing a case report. A local insurance company had hired me to conduct background investigations on candidates vying for a management job, and by the time I'd summarized the findings on all seven of them it was midafternoon and I was sick of being in the office. I locked up and left, thinking that I'd have an early workout. My energy felt wrong, though, and by the time I got to my building I'd talked myself out of exercise. I got into my truck instead and drove toward Clark Avenue in search of a drink. If you give up on the healthy decision, why not go all out in the opposite direction?

I was headed for the Hideaway, which had reopened in April after being closed for nearly a year from fire damage. I'd found myself down there often in the past few weeks, maybe trying to recapture something that was already gone, maybe just enjoying the place. I didn't want to overthink it. The owner, Scott Draper, had been a good friend once, and maybe could be again. With Joe gone, I'd become more aware of just how many friendships had wandered off or watered down over the years. A lot of that was my fault—I'd retreated from the world for a while after losing Karen and my job. Hell, if Amy hadn't come around back then, when a kid who'd spent a lot of time at my gym was murdered and she was asked to write about it, I'd be pretty damn pathetic by now. Funny how having just one woman around is enough to make you look like a functioning member of society.

A week or even a few days earlier, I might have noticed the

car behind me while I was on the highway. When I was riding the peak of my paranoia, I'd done a good job of watching the mirrors. That was past, though, and I didn't pay attention to the cars behind me as I burned up I71 toward downtown, didn't register any of them until I pulled onto the Fulton Road exit ramp. Even then, it was a cursory thing, just an awareness that I'd been one of two cars leaving the highway.

When I turned off Fulton and onto Clark and the car stayed with me, I finally gave it a few seconds of study, memories of Dominic Sanabria's visit not completely purged yet. It was a Honda Pilot, newer model, red. Not the sort of thing you'd expect a mob enforcer to drive. I put my eyes back on the road and pulled into a parking space on the street a half block from the Hideaway. The Pilot kept going. Nothing to worry about.

By the time I was out of the car, though, I saw that the Pilot's driver had just pulled into a spot across the street, not far away. I stood on the sidewalk and watched as the door opened and a tall guy with blond hair stepped out and walked in my direction.

He came across the street and up the sidewalk without missing a step, even when he realized I was standing there watching him. Walked right up to me, lifted a hand as if he needed to catch my attention, and said, "Lincoln Perry?"

He didn't match the mob-enforcer mold any better than his car. Tall, maybe six three or four, with broad, knobby shoulders under his starched blue shirt. Something about him made me think of a baseball pitcher. He moved well but without any sense of speed or agility, seemed like the sort of guy who'd be good at most sports despite not being particularly athletic. There was a shadow of beard along his jaw, darker than his sandy hair. Light blue eyes.

"Why were you following me?" I said.

"You're Lincoln?"

"You know I am. You were following me."

He held up his hands, palms spread. "Sorry, man. Didn't mean to freak you out. I'd just stopped by the gym and was going down to your office when I saw you get into your truck. I was already in my car, so I just pulled out after you."

"I've never seen you before in my life," I said. "So how did you know that was me, and that it was my truck?"

He smiled. "The lady who was in the gym office looked out at your truck to see if it was still there before she sent me up to your office."

"And your natural inclination was to follow me?"

"Actually, yeah. I'm a PI. You should know how that goes."

"A PI?"

"Name's Ken Merriman. You the sort that likes to see ID?" He reached for his wallet, but I waved him off.

"Don't worry about it, Ken. I'm a little on edge lately. Not your fault."

"No problem—and, hey, give me *some* credit. If I'd been tailing you I could have done a better job than that." He laughed and nodded in the direction of the Hideaway. "You working or grabbing a beer?"

"The latter."

"Well, why don't you let me buy a round, and I'll try to talk you into doing the former."

"That kind of visit, huh?"

"That kind of visit," he said, starting toward the bar.

"Where are you from?" I asked, falling in step beside him. I knew most of the private investigators in the area, by name if not by face, but neither Ken Merriman's name or face was familiar.

"Pittsburgh," he said.

"Keep your voice down, man. People in this neighborhood hear Pittsburgh, they turn violent. It's the home of the Steelers, you know."

"The proud home," he agreed as we reached the front steps.

"I also haven't worked on anything that involved Pittsburgh in a long time," I said, reaching for the door handle. "So whatever brings you up here must have a local tie."

"It did once, at least."

"Did?"

"About twelve years ago."

I was holding the door open for him, but he stopped on the top step, looking at my face.

"Twelve years?" My voice was hollow.

He nodded.

"There's a name I don't want to hear you say," I said.

"Which one? Cantrell or Sanabria?" He winked at me and walked into the bar.

Chapter Eight

Draper wasn't behind the bar, but I didn't care anymore—
Ken Merriman had just obliterated my plan for a relaxed evening. I followed him as he walked to the back of the narrow
dining room and slid into a booth.

"What do you want to drink?" I said.

"No waitress?"

"Not till five. What do you want?"

"Guinness would be good."

He handed me a ten, and I walked back to the bar and got
his Guinness and a Moosehead for myself, then came back
and sat down across from him. There'd been a few guys at the
bar, but we were the only people in the dining room.

I lifted my beer and nodded at him. "Here's to unwanted
visitors from Pittsburgh."

"Come on, don't say that. Here's to fellow PIs, wouldn't
that be friendlier?" He grinned and lifted his glass. "To Sam
Spade."

"To Sam Spade," I agreed, then touched my bottle off his
glass and took a drink. He was a damned likable guy, easygoing and good-humored, but that didn't make the purpose of
his visit appealing.

"I wish you'd just made a phone call so I could've told you
not to waste your time," I said, "but as long as you made the
drive, I'll tell you what I can—*nothing*. Somebody asked me
to look into the property, see where the owners had gone. I

was dangerously uninformed and had no idea that what was left of one owner was in a coroner's lab somewhere and that the other owner was related to Lenny Strollo's best pal."

Merriman took a drink and shook his head. "Nah, Strollo wasn't that tight with Dominic. Acquainted with him, sure, colleagues you might say, but not that tight."

"What a wonderful reassurance."

He smiled again. "You sound damn edgy about this, Lincoln."

"You would be, too, had Dominic Sanabria paid a visit to your home."

"By all accounts, Sanabria has settled down these days. Living on the straight and narrow. Nary a complaint."

"Be that as it may, there were a few complaints in years past, and some of them involved car bombs."

He acknowledged that with a nod and drank some more of his beer. "Did he threaten you?"

"Not overtly, but he also went out of his way to make sure the notion was in my head. It wasn't a relaxing conversation."

"How do you think he got wind of you so fast?"

"The attorney."

"Anthony Child? That makes sense."

"Of course it does. He called you, too."

He wagged his finger at me. "Wrong. Nice try, but wrong."

"Okay, then who did call you, Ken? Who sent you up from Pittsburgh to ply me with booze and get me to talk?"

"Booze was your idea. I just fell in line."

"We're not going to accomplish much," I said, "if neither one of us is willing to say who we're working for. That's fine with me. There's nothing that I want to accomplish. That doesn't seem to be the case for you."

"If I tell you who tipped me, do I get reciprocity? Will you tell me your client's name?"

I shook my head.

"Damn," he said. "I was afraid of that. But the good news, Lincoln, is that ultimately I'm not too worried about your client. That's not why I'm here."

"No? Then what is it?"

"I want you to work with me. Or, rather, I'd like to work with you. I've done some background research. Seems like you're awfully good. I need help on this one."

"By this one, you mean . . ."

"Finding out who killed Joshua Cantrell."

I shook my head. "No thanks, Ken."

"Sanabria scared you that much, huh?"

"It's not just that, though I'll admit he did a damn good job. There's nothing in it for me. I have no interest in it."

"Really." His Guinness was almost gone. "I'm surprised to hear that. Because what this one has, man, is some intrigue, and most of the detectives I know, well, they go for that sort of thing. The challenge. At least the detectives who are worth a damn."

"Then I must not qualify for that list."

"So if I were to say I could fill you in on Cantrell's history, tell you about the happy couple, what they did up until the time they vanished, you'd say no thanks? Prefer not to hear about it?"

"All I care to hear about is how you learned that I'd inquired about their house."

"You want to know that, I'll tell you," he said, "but you'll have to sit through the rest of it, too. Because if I start, I'm starting at the beginning."

I didn't answer.

He slid out of the booth and got to his feet. "You want a pass on that, I'll walk out the door and drive back home. If you want to hear about it, though, then I think I better buy another round."

Somebody burst into loud laughter at the bar while Ken Merriman stood above me, waiting. Then the laughter faded and it was quiet.

Merriman shifted and spread his hands. "Well?"

"Bring me another Moosehead," I said, "and a bourbon. I think I'll need both."

He'd been hired by Joshua Cantrell's parents, James and Maria, about two months after their son and daughter-in-law left the house near Hinckley for places unknown. It wasn't an especially close-knit family—the Cantrells hadn't been on the best terms with their son in many years, too many social and ideological differences—but it was also unusual for weeks to pass without any word. When they finally called, they learned the phone was disconnected.

"Took them about another month to grow concerned enough to hire me," Ken said. "They drove out and saw the house was empty, then went to the local police, who nosed around enough to determine that Alexandra had made arrangements for the care of the place. That implied a willing departure, not a crime. Nothing illegal about ignoring your parents."

James and Maria Cantrell couldn't believe their son would have made such an abrupt, unannounced departure, and as the weeks went by and still no word came, they grew certain something was terribly wrong.

"When they came to see me that first time, they were petrified," Ken said. "It was difficult to get anything close to a fact out of them."

What he found, once he began looking into the situation, was that there weren't many facts. The only person who'd had any knowledge of the couple's plans to leave was Anthony Child, and he'd been contacted by phone. Child swore that he knew Alexandra's voice and believed without a doubt that she was the one who'd given him his instructions.

"For twelve years the police have refused to look into this because that woman's contact with Child suggested they'd just gotten a wild hair and taken off somewhere," Ken said when he returned from the bar with two more beers and two more bourbons. "Until the body was found, at least. That's shaken things up."

The problem, Ken admitted, was that the couple seemed like the type who *might* get a wild hair and take off. They were an eclectic pair, and most of their interests—holistic practices, faith healing, spiritual retreats—suggested a life outside of the ordinary. Those close to the Cantrells, while surprised by the disappearance, had to admit it seemed to suit them.

Ken worked the case for months and never developed a

lead on the missing couple's whereabouts or the reason for their departure. What he did learn was a great deal about their past, including one particularly interesting detail: For years, the couple had maintained a relationship with the state's department of corrections, helping to transition violent offenders through the early stages of parole.

"They met when they were both studying offender rehabilitation in graduate school," Ken told me. "Found some sort of mutual interest there. Academic for Joshua, personal for Alexandra. You can imagine why. Her father had been in and out of jail before being murdered, and her brothers were moving quickly down the same path. Anyhow, once they were married, she and Joshua teamed up to write a few papers, conducted some studies, and got hooked up with an alternative program that snagged a federal grant. At that time, the state was real concerned with engaging the offender's family to help with reentry. The problem that the Cantrells raised was, what about the offender who has no family, or whose family is a cancer to him?"

I sipped my beer and kept my eyes on the table while I listened, not wanting to react in a way that suggested this was anything but new to me. I still hadn't decided whether I'd disclose Harrison's identity, but this twist in the conversation had me wondering if Ken would bring him up of his own accord.

"A police detective called me a few months back, after Cantrell's body was found," he said. "They'd heard I'd investigated in the beginning, and he wanted to know if I'd come across anyone who could work as a homicide suspect. I told him, yeah, I've got twenty-eight names."

The twenty-eight names belonged to the violent offenders Alexandra and Joshua had helped transition back into the world. We had another round of drinks while Ken recited their crimes, which ranged from bank robbery to rape and murder. As of Ken's last count, nineteen of them were still free, and two were dead.

"That means only seven of the offenders who worked with the Cantrells returned to prison," he said. "You know anything about recidivism numbers?"

"Enough to know that's a hell of a lot better than average."

"Yes," he said. "It absolutely is. So whatever they were doing, it seemed to work."

"What were they doing, exactly?"

"At first, they were acting as, well, I guess you'd call it a sort of foster family. They kind of adopted these guys, stayed close to them, counseled them, things like that. By the end, after they bought that land in Hinckley, it changed. They would hire these guys to work for them, kept them on for six months to a year. They paid them well, but the catch was the guys also had to live there."

"In the house?"

"Yes. Imagine that, welcoming convicted killers into your home. Also, while everything out there was modern enough—running water, electricity, all that—they insisted that all the work be done by hand, and without power tools." He grinned at me. "Weird stuff, huh?"

At first I thought they were crazy for requiring that . . . Then I came to understand how important it was. How the sound of an engine would have destroyed what was there.

"Weird," I agreed and finished my beer.

"Alexandra contended that a great contributing factor to recidivism was a loss of touch with the natural world," Ken said. "That prolonged incarceration created this traumatic sense of isolation."

"Okay."

"I talked to a woman with the state parole office who worked with the Cantrells, and she said that Alexandra's vision was for a new sort of prison, one that didn't isolate the inmates from nature. As you can imagine, making *that* sort of change was going to be difficult. So she brought the same ideas over to the reentry side."

"She wanted the parolees to, what, bond with nature?"

"Evidently. She had all these studies. One demonstrated that just a view of nature from a hospital window reduced reliance on pain medication; another showed inmates who participated in a gardening program had improved recidivism rates. Since she couldn't get the support she wanted, she created the program of her desires on a very small scale."

"How were the parolees chosen?" I asked.

"The Cantrells would review their files, their case histories, and then extend the offer. The offenders were under no obligation to accept, but they always did. The pay was good. The Cantrells had one stipulation: They'd only take violent offenders. Preferably murderers."

"That's different from the requirements I've had for roommates over the years."

"Not a request you see in a lot of personal ads, either."

"So how many of these guys did they actually have out there, working for them?"

"Four," he said. "None of those have shown up back in prison—but one is dead."

"How'd he go?"

"Mysterious death," he said. "Not long after leaving the Cantrells' care."

It was quiet for a moment, and then I said, "Seems like it was a hit-or-miss program," and Ken's smile returned.

"Yes. Seems like it was. Apparently they were hoping to use the handful they'd worked with to get a larger program going. Those first four were test subjects, I guess."

"Okay. So you've got twenty-eight violent criminals who worked closely with the couple, and you've got the daughter of a bloody mob legacy. Not hurting for suspects."

"No."

"So where did you get with it?"

He looked down at his glass. Empty again. We'd gone through a few of them by now. I'd lost track. Bourbon with a beer back can do that.

"Absolutely nowhere, Lincoln. I got nothing. I wanted to pursue it, but the parents didn't have much money, and they couldn't pay to keep me running back and forth from Pittsburgh. Originally they hired me because they wanted someone they could meet with face-to-face, someone local, but I blew through their budget and didn't turn up a damn thing, and I couldn't justify taking more of their money. They didn't have much."

"This was twelve years ago?"

"Eleven years ago, by the time they pulled the plug."

"So what the hell are you doing up here now?"

His easygoing humor had faded, and he seemed uncomfortable. "You want another round?"

"I want you to answer the question."

He was quiet.

"Who told you about me?" I said.

"That's what you're worried about? It was your buddy Sanabria."

"*He* hired you?"

"Didn't hire me. I'd crossed paths with him briefly when I got started on this years back, and apparently he hadn't forgotten my name. Called me last week to ask if you were working with me or for Cantrell's parents. I told him no way to the former and no idea to the latter. He seemed dissatisfied with that."

"I've seen that reaction from him, yes."

"So that was how I got your name, and I was curious, right, because this case hadn't left my mind over the years, and it really came back to me when Joshua's body was found. I did a little research on you, saw that you've done some major work—some serious, serious stuff—and I thought, what the hell, why not drive up there and make a pitch."

"I don't understand the pitch."

"I want to work the case, man. With you, ideally. Without you, if you say no."

"You've got no client, Ken. What's the point?"

He braced both forearms on the table and leaned closer. "The point is I've been in this business for fourteen years and never investigated anything that mattered. You know what I've done, year in and year out? Insurance work and infidelity cases. That's it."

"That's how you pay the bills. Isn't that the goal?"

"No! Bullshit it's the goal." He slapped the table and leaned away again. "You're doing this just to pay the bills? Really? That's why you got into the business?"

"I got into the business because I got fired, Ken."

"I know that. You got canned as a police detective, and you set up shop as a private detective. Why?"

"It's all I was qualified for."

He blew out a disgusted breath and looked away from me.

"I get your point," I said. "This has more appeal than an insurance case. If there's one type of detective I've never trusted, though, it's a glory hound."

"That's not what I'm after, damn it. That's not what I mean at all." He sighed and ran both hands through his sandy hair. His face had taken on a flush, and his eyes were beginning to show the booze. "All I'm trying to say is, in fourteen years I've had just *one* case that really mattered, and I didn't accomplish anything on it. Didn't find their son. Now the son has been found, and he's dead, and I'd like to be able to tell them why."

I looked away from him, suddenly wishing I'd let him go for that next round.

"You've had cases like this," he said, voice soft. "I've read about you, Lincoln, I already told you that. You've had cases that mattered. Had cases that . . . that people cared about. People other than you, people other than your clients."

"Ken," I began, but he was still talking.

"My daughter—she's fourteen—she's a fan of the police shows. You know, the TV bullshit, none of it's close to reality, but she enjoys them. There are times . . . times when she asks me about my job, and I find myself . . . not lying maybe, but I'm spinning it, Lincoln. Trying to make it sound like more than it is. More than chasing cheating spouses and taking pictures of accident scenes." He pushed his empty glass away and forced a laugh. "I've had one too many if I'm telling you this."

I didn't say anything.

"You don't have kids," he said.

"No."

He nodded. "You don't have kids, you've never been divorced. You haven't watched some other guy step into your daughter's life. Some other guy who is a damn *doctor*, Lincoln. A surgeon. Saving lives, right? That's what he does. I'm out there taking photos next to a Dumpster, hoping to get a picture of some loser kissing some tramp, hoping to go back to my client and say, yeah, turns out your husband is an asshole—can I have my check now? Meanwhile, my daughter, she's going home to that big house, waiting for her stepfather to drive up in his Porsche with a story about a liver transplant or some shit."

His voice had been rising steadily, closing in on a shout, and he caught it at that point, paused. The bar had filled in as the night grew later, and there were other people in the dining room. I had my back to them, but I could feel the stares. We sat there in silence, though, and once the rest of the room realized Ken's rant had concluded, they lost interest and went back to their own conversations and drinks.

"I know it's petty to care," he said. "I know that, but you try not caring about something like that. You give that a shot."

He reached for his empty glass, wrapped his hand around it, and held it.

"Ken," I said. "This case . . . nothing good comes out of working it. You do understand that, don't you?"

He shook his head. "No. No, I do not understand that. What I understand is that the man and his wife went missing, Lincoln, vanished and did not appear again until his remains were found. So now he's dead, and she's still missing, and his parents still have no idea what the hell happened. They have no idea what went wrong in their son's life, how his bones ended up in the woods an hour's drive from the million-dollar home he left without a word."

He looked me in the eye. "I want to tell them what happened. I don't give a damn if it's the Sanabria family or the Manson family, or who that guy was married to, I want to be able to go back to those people and tell them, this is what happened to your son."

He lifted the glass, remembered it was empty, and lowered it again. "I'm not good enough to do that on my own."

I shook my head, but he was already shaking his own right back at me.

"Lincoln, I've tried to do it on my own. I didn't succeed."

"There's no reason to think I'd do any better."

"I disagree."

There was a long pause, and then he said, "How about this? How about I bring my case file by your office tomorrow. I run through it with you and talk about approach. Talk about where I'm going from here. You could offer some input, right? Is there a reason in the world why you couldn't at least do that?"

I was sure there was, but it didn't come to mind fast enough to save me.

"All right," I said. "I'll do that much."

He toasted me with the empty glass.

Chapter Nine

That night strips of coal-colored clouds skidded over a bright three-quarter moon, pushed by a spirited wind off the lake. I sat on the roof of my building and marveled at their speed, stared long enough that the lights and sounds of the street below faded and I was held by the rhythm of the clouds, by the vanishing and then resurfacing moon. If I looked long enough, it seemed I wasn't on the roof anymore, could instead be miles out at sea, nothing in sight but that moon and those clouds.

Yeah, I'd had a bit to drink.

I'd called Amy on the drive home, but she hadn't answered, and I'd soon realized that was for the best—I shouldn't have been driving, let alone driving and using a phone. I put the windows down and took Lorain all the way back, a simple and slow drive, stoplight to stoplight until I got home.

I missed her, though. That was different. That was something new. Any night I spent without her, I missed her. Sounds like a bad feeling, but it's not. Having somebody in your life to miss . . . always good. I missed Amy when she was gone, and I'd missed Joe for many months, and all of that meant I wasn't truly alone. There were people who belonged near me, and I felt their absence when it occurred. It was almost a healthy sort of existence. Didn't seem to suit me at all.

It was a warm night, overcast but without rain, and I didn't even turn the lights on in my apartment, just poured a glass of water in the dark kitchen and took it up on the roof. I settled into one of the lounge chairs and watched a sky that seemed determined to entertain.

For a while, bits of the conversation with Ken Merriman played through my head, the most frequent recurrence being the moment he'd confessed it was Dominic Sanabria who'd called him. He'd thrown that out casually enough. *It was your buddy Sanabria.* Too casually? Was it something to wonder about, or just alcohol adding a dose of paranoia to my brain? I meant to ponder that one, but then the wind blew harder and the clouds moved quicker, and eventually the water glass slid from my hand and I was asleep.

I dreamed that I woke. Sounds crazy, maybe, but it happens to me now and then, always when I fall asleep somewhere other than my bed, and often when the mind is encouraged toward odd behavior by alcohol or fatigue. This time I dreamed that when I came out of sleep I was facing the trapdoor that led to the stairs, still in the lounge chair. A figure stood beside the trapdoor, and my dream-mind registered that with surprise but not alarm. I didn't move from the chair, didn't speak, just watched the figure standing there in the dark, and eventually my vision adjusted and I saw that it was Parker Harrison.

He looked at me for a long time, and I knew that I should rise, say something, order him out of my home, but instead I watched silently. The longer I looked at him the more my surprise edged toward fear, a steady crawl, and I held my breath when he reached into the shadowed folds of his clothing with his right hand. The clouds blew past the moon and a shaft of white light fell onto him, and I saw that though his face was normal the flesh on his arm was gone, only thin bones protruding from his sleeve. When his hand came free again, it, too, was nothing but bones, a skeleton hand, and there was a silver coin between his fingers.

He looked across the roof at me, and then he flicked his thumb and spun the coin skyward. The moonlight gave it a bright, hard glint. He caught the coin and flipped it again, and again, and it seemed dangerous now, each flash as wicked as the edge of a sharp blade. My fear built with each toss and burst into pure terror when he caught the coin with an abrupt and theatrical slap of his hand, snatching it out of the air and folding it into his palm and hiding it from the light. When he clasped his hand shut, the bones shattered into a cloud of white powder that turned black as it drifted down to his feet. The coin landed on the roof and spun as the black dust settled around it, and suddenly I was awake and upright, my hands tight on the arms of the chair.

I held that position for a few seconds while the wind fanned over the roof. It was much colder now than when I'd fallen asleep, and below me the avenue was silent. I swung my feet off the chair and stood up, forgetting about the glass resting against my side. It rolled off me and fell away from the chair and shattered on the stone, and I nearly jumped off the roof at the sound.

The sparkle of the broken glass near my feet made me think of the coin from my dream, and like a child who can't trust that the dream world was a false one I turned and looked back at the trapdoor as if expecting to see Harrison there. The door was nothing but a dark square in the surface of the roof, and it was also behind me and not in front of me as it had been in the dream. I took a deep breath and walked toward the door, stepping over the broken glass. That could be dealt with in the morning. Down on the avenue a car finally passed by, rap music thumping out of its speakers, and I was grateful for the noise. I walked to the trapdoor and climbed carefully down the steps and then folded them back into the roof, the door snapping closed with a bang. It was dark inside the building, and my head pounded with a pressurized ache, as if someone had pumped it full of air, searching for leaks in the skull.

"No more bourbon," I said aloud. "No more bourbon."

I groped along the wall for the light switch, flicked it up, and flooded the hallway and stairs with light. Halfway to the apartment door, I paused and turned back, squinting against the brightness, and looked down the steps at the front door. Closed, and with the dead bolt turned. Of course it was. Of course.

I went into the apartment and drank another glass of water, this time with a few ibuprofen tablets, and then went into the bedroom and slept. There were no dreams.

Morning found me at the office with an extralarge cup of coffee and a continued headache, researching Ken Merriman. I spent most of an hour at it, and while everything he'd told me the previous night checked out—he was from Pittsburgh, had worked as a PI for fourteen years, was divorced, and had a fourteen-year-old daughter—there were a few details he'd chosen to omit. Namely, the unpleasant press he'd received from the Cantrell case.

James and Maria Cantrell had given an interview after their son disappeared, imploring the public to help in their quest. As a part of that interview, they let loose on Ken, claiming he'd taken thousands from them and done nothing on the case. James even suggested they would consider a lawsuit against Ken but couldn't afford the legal fees. The reporter had contacted Ken only to be given a "no comment" response. It wasn't necessarily a fair attack—every PI in the business knows the headaches that come from clients who believe they're paying for a specific result, not for work that may produce no result or one contrary to the client's wishes—but it was the sort of publicity that could damage a career, too. I was impressed that Ken had survived it, and I understood a little better why he seemed to be stuck with insurance and infidelity work now. Still, the Sanabria call lingered with me, and that odd personal revelation toward the end of the night. Had it been too much? A melodramatic sales technique?

I knew a PI in the Pittsburgh area through a group called NALI, the National Association of Legal Investigators, a generally high quality group of PIs. His name was Casey Hopper, and he was about Joe's age; he'd been around the business a long time and knew who was worth a shit and who wasn't. I decided it might be worth a call to see if he'd ever heard of Ken.

"Good guy," Casey said as soon as I mentioned the name. "I've worked with him several times."

"You trust him?"

"Much as I trust anyone I don't know particularly well, sure. He's always seemed genuine enough to me, but, you know, there've been some stories about him. Well, one story really."

He then proceeded to relate the Cantrell case to me, and I let him run with it. His take seemed to jibe with every other account—and that included Ken's.

"You thinking about giving him some work?" Casey asked.

"The other way around. He's wanting to partner up on something. I'm not sure about it."

"Well, I can tell you this: He's one hell of a surveillance expert. Good as anybody I've worked with, in that regard. Damn near invisible, and the most patient son of a bitch I've ever seen." He paused, then added, "You know I was a sniper in Vietnam, too."

"Yeah."

"So when I say somebody is patient . . ."

"Yeah."

"Thing with Ken, though, is that's really all the work he gets. He has a steady client base on the surveillance side, insurance and divorce work, shit like that, but as far as a field investigation goes, I don't know that he has much experience at all. I gave him an interview job once when I was out of town, subbed it out to him, and he screwed that up pretty royally. Just didn't know how to take a statement that would be worth a shit in court. So I've avoided giving him anything like that again, and that seems to be the general consensus about him around here. Give him any extra surveillance work you've got; otherwise, find somebody else. He wasn't a cop, wasn't mentored by a good PI, doesn't really have any background on a full-scale investigation, but the son of a bitch can hide in your rearview mirror."

That wasn't exactly encouraging, since the case he wanted a piece of now was going to require the polar opposite of his skill set.

"The Cantrell thing is what he's interested in coming back

to," I said. "I bumped into it inadvertently up here, and he looked me up and asked me to help."

"He's back at that? Who the hell is paying him?"

"Nobody. He claims he wants to finish now what he couldn't then. You buy it?"

Casey was quiet for a moment. "Yeah, I probably do. It did some real damage to his career basically *because* he didn't have any other experience to claim as proof that he knew what he was doing. Ordinary people might forget the story, but law firms and agencies who sub out work, the sort of people you need to rely on for quality business, they don't."

I thanked him for the insight and hung up. Then I went back to search for more information and found little else. Beyond that story, there was nothing that stood out, and certainly no indicators that Ken had been telling me anything but the truth. His loyalty to the family seemed odd, considering the charges they'd levied at him, but perhaps his real motivation was in proving them wrong all these years later.

It was ten thirty by the time Ken showed up, and he looked rough. Same clothes as he'd had on the previous day, only now his face had a darker shading of beard and the whites of his eyes wore pink cobwebs. He closed the door behind him with infinite care, as if a loud slam might shatter something in his brain, then looked over at me with a pained smile.

"Maybe I should have told you this last night," he said, "but I'm not a whiskey drinker."

"I like a good Scotch," I said, "but that swill wasn't it. It occurred to me sometime around three in the morning that what the Hideaway considers a well bourbon is probably closer to leaded gasoline."

He groaned and fell onto one of the stadium seats.

"Careful there," I said. "Those seats watched the Cleveland Browns beat the shit out of the Steelers many, many times."

"I'm too hungover to even rise to that argument."

"That bad, eh?"

"Yeah. You bounced back well. Sleep it off peacefully?"

I remembered the slap of Parker Harrison's skeleton hand,

the way the bones had burst into powder, how it had looked like fine black dust by the time it settled around the spinning coin.

"Peacefully," I echoed with a nod.

"Wish I could say the same," he said and then held up the scuffed briefcase he'd carried in with him. "Last night you agreed to look this over with me. In fairness, though, I thought I should give you a sober chance to back out of it. You don't owe me anything, and you're certainly not obligated to waste your time on this."

"I can give you a few hours."

He put the briefcase on his lap and folded his arms over it. "Look, Lincoln, I might have gotten a bit more, uh, personal than I should have last night. I mean, shit, you don't even know me, and I was dumping some information on you that probably made the whole thing awkward for you. All of that crap about my wife's new husband—"

"Don't worry about it, Ken."

"No, it wasn't anything you needed to hear, and to be honest, it embarrassed the hell out of me once I got back to the hotel and realized everything I'd said. So, you know, if you could just chalk that up to the booze and forget about it . . ."

"I just said not to worry about it. Okay? It's nothing, man."

He nodded, and an awkward pause settled into the room for a few seconds before he broke it by slapping a hand on the briefcase.

"Well, is this a good time, or you want me to come back in a bit, or—"

"Now's good. Let's see what you've got."

He set the case on the table beside him and opened it, and I raised my eyebrows when I saw all the papers that were inside, hundreds of pages.

"I've got a lot here," he said.

"No kidding."

"I don't want to drown you with shit you're not interested in, so if you've got any idea on where to start . . ."

"I'd be most interested in what you've got from the people who knew them best," I said. "Particularly the people who knew them best at the time they took off. Friends, co-workers, colleagues."

"They didn't work."

I lifted an eyebrow. "Neither of them?"

"Nope. Lived off her money."

"Well, how the hell did she get so much money?"

"The late Christopher Sanabria."

"Surely he wasn't worth that much."

"Was worth a lot, and when he got clipped, the family discovered he'd left the whole pile to Alexandra. It was several million at the time, and she had to wait about eight years until she turned twenty-one and the trust kicked in. By then it was worth a hell of a lot more. Christopher was well invested, it seemed."

"She got every dime?"

"Of his financial holdings, yes. House and possessions split among the sons."

"Nothing to the wife?"

"Wife was dead. Suicide a year before Christopher was murdered. That was the reason Alexandra was sent away. He thought she needed a female influence."

I shook my head. "How many sons did he have?"

"Two. Dominic and Thomas. Thomas was shot and killed by a cop in Youngstown about five years after the father died. Drug bust, but just one cop went in. Odd, right? Said he was checking out a tip he didn't have much faith in. Rumors went around that it was a setup, that the cop was paid for the hit, but nothing ever came of the investigation."

"Alexandra was away at her boarding school for this?"

He nodded. "She left when she was twelve, came back to Ohio after getting out of college."

"To work with the prison system."

"Yes."

I didn't say anything for a minute. I was remembering the way Dominic Sanabria had spoken of his sister. *Every family has their darling. She is ours.*

"Do you know anything about the family relationship after she got back?" I asked. "Was there any bitterness over the money? The mob connections don't even apply to that—father dies and leaves a few million to one kid but not the other, it would start personal problems in most families."

"No sign of that, but I always wondered," Ken said. "By the time she was old enough to take the trust, Dominic was a pretty big deal in Youngstown, had a lot of other things on his mind, and a decent pile of his own cash. He's more than ten years older than her."

I was quiet again, not entirely sold on the idea. Being jilted out of your family money in favor of another sibling was a difficult thing for a man to ignore, particularly a man like Dominic Sanabria. It wasn't easy to imagine the guy going after his own sister, though—that notion of honor among thieves applied more to family than anything else. I wasn't going to figure that out sitting at my desk, though, and I didn't want to have to leave my desk on this. Instead, I waved at Ken's briefcase.

"Well, if their parolees are the only people who saw the Cantrells regularly, what do you have on them?"

"Pretty detailed profiles. There were four of them who worked out there, and three are still alive."

"You ever talk to them?"

"Only two." His head was bowed while he rifled through the briefcase and pulled out a thick manila folder. "Had trouble tracking the other guy down, and then the budget ran out and I was off the case."

He opened the folder and pulled out a stapled sheaf of papers. "The one I never got in touch with, and he was working with them right up until they took off, was a guy named Parker Harrison. So maybe you want to start with—"

"No," I said. "Let's start with the first one, okay? Work forward."

He didn't react other than to nod and slide the Harrison papers back into the folder.

Chapter Ten

The four offenders who'd worked with the Cantrells at their strange home in the woods near Hinckley had all been sentenced for violent crimes. Three had been convicted of murder, another for armed robbery and assault.

The couple's first hire was a Serb named Mark Ruzity, who'd grown up in the Slavic Village on Cleveland's east side. It was a damn hard neighborhood. At one time Ruzity had a bright future. A blues guitarist of some renown, he'd been featured in a few newspaper and magazine articles after landing gigs with national acts. Ken had copies of those stories, glimpses of what could have been. Ruzity's success had always been short-lived, though; his drug problems limited his career. He bottomed out in New Orleans while touring with a band called Three Sheiks to the Wind, attacking an audience member who sat in the front of the club and talked loudly during the performance. Ruzity's luck was poor—not only did he break a good guitar on the gentleman's back, but it turned out his victim was an off-duty cop. That incident landed him in jail for six months, and when he got out he was broke and bandless.

After returning to Cleveland, Ruzity got a job in construction and began playing again, mostly in local bars and for little money. For more than a year he held it together, until he met a leggy redhead named Valerie after a gig one night. She was beautiful, he was stoned, and by morning he was in love. There was just one problem: Valerie was a prostitute.

He didn't remember paying her that night, though he apparently had, and when she informed him the relationship had been strictly professional, he viewed it not as a deal-breaker but as a challenge. The Montagues and the Capulets. After a day of brooding, with a few black beauties and some gin to clear his head, Ruzity determined there was only one way this mess could be sorted out: He murdered her pimp.

The beautiful romantic vision came to a fast and painful end when Valerie herself turned him in. The bad news was that he'd just been caught for murder; the good news was that he'd murdered a pimp with a record. The sentencing judge went easy, and Ruzity spent fifteen years in prison, writing songs and studying the blues. He had no living family and no close friends, and the state's department of rehabilitation placed him in a job with Joshua and Alexandra Cantrell, who had some ideas about offender reentry that seemed worth a try.

Ruzity lived and worked with them for six months before moving back into the city, where he made a living repairing instruments at a pawnshop and teaching guitar lessons.

The second parolee who found his way to Whisper Ridge was Nimir Farah, who'd used a machete in an attempt to murder his own cousin over a suspected affair with Farah's girlfriend. Farah had immigrated to the United States only two years earlier, fleeing a desperate situation in his home country, Sudan. He'd come to Columbus to live with a cousin who'd arrived years earlier on a student visa and was the last living member of Farah's family, or at least the last he'd been able to keep track of as war and famine swept Sudan.

It was thanks only to an exceptional emergency room surgeon that the cousin survived, a point made emphatically clear by the prosecuting attorney in the trial transcript Ken had photocopied. The charge was attempted murder, and the sentence was twenty years in prison. Farah served ten, then managed to avoid a criminal deportation hearing when Alexandra and Joshua Cantrell stepped in. Ken had tracked down a letter from the couple arguing quite eloquently against deporting Farah to a dangerous country where he no longer had ties. Instead, he was given parole and a job at Whisper Ridge.

He worked for the Cantrells for six months, then moved to Cleveland, where he finished the degree in environmental sciences he'd started while in prison. As of Ken's last check, he was employed by a nonprofit that specialized in water sanitation issues—particularly the challenges faced in arid areas much like Farah's homeland.

It seemed to be, once again, a striking success for the Cantrells.

I turned the last page of the Farah file over and found myself staring at a picture of Parker Harrison.

He'd been the third hire, and though I didn't need to refresh myself on his background, I read through Ken's notes anyhow. I wasn't ready to disclose my knowledge of Harrison yet, and skipping over him would be a clear tip of my hand. So I pored over the old information, found nothing new, and then moved to the fourth and final hire, a man named Salvatore Bertoli, who'd been raised in an orphanage after his mother died following their immigration from Italy.

"A lot of different ethnicities passed through," I said. "There a reason?"

"Yeah, that was the idea. Joshua was interested in culture and crime. It was a topic of a lot of the papers he wrote, and how he met Alexandra."

I thought about that and tried to fit Parker Harrison into the mix. His mother had been Shawnee, and he'd told me that Alexandra Cantrell was fascinated by the stories he'd heard and what he knew of the culture.

"I'll tell you something else about their boy Bertoli," Ken said. "He's Italian. As is, you might have heard, that Cosa Nostra thing to which brother Dominic is connected. Allegedly."

"Merriman, you profiling bastard."

He held his hands up. "Just making connections."

"So you think Salvatore was imported by Dominic Sanabria, orphaned, framed for a crime, then paroled and tucked away at the sister's house to steal back the dead father's money?" I considered it and nodded. "Yeah, that works. Let's call it a day."

"I can tell you this, wise-ass—Bertoli had been arrested

on two different occasions prior to the one he was finally convicted on. First was a car theft charge, second was assault. In both cases, the guys arrested with him were known associates of Dominic Sanabria."

The smirk dried off my face. "You're sure of that?"

"Positive. Arresting officers confirmed it for me. Said they were insignificant players—I believe he called them grunts— but that guy was an associate of Sanabria's crew. No doubt about it." Ken pointed at the file in my hands. "Interested now? Read on."

I read on. Bertoli's story was far and away the least interesting of the group. He'd beaten and then robbed the drug-pushing manager of a truck stop on I71, who claimed Bertoli took cash, though when police apprehended him he had no cash but did have some heroin. Truck stops are among the less wise locations for crime. Lonely places along the highway that stay open all night tend to be paranoid about their security. One of the parking lot security cameras caught Bertoli, who was smart enough to wear a mask and use a stolen plate, but not smart enough to use a stolen car. He put the fake plate on his own car—a custom Impala featuring chrome rims with silver diamond cutouts, hardly the sort of thing that stands out. It took police under two hours to locate it and arrest him. Bertoli had a sidekick in the car at the time of the robbery, but it was no high-level mob player. Rather, his passenger was a kid whose name was redacted from the report because he was a juvenile. The arresting officer believed Bertoli had promised to sell the boy the heroin. He was sixteen years old.

The boy wouldn't testify to Bertoli's intent to sell, claiming he was just along for the ride and oblivious to the crime, which weakened the case. Although Bertoli—who was only twenty-three himself—already had three arrests, he didn't have any convictions. He was offered a plea agreement sentence of five years, accepted, and served two and a half.

"Kind of a stiff sentence for somebody who beat up another guy just to take his drugs," I said, "and odd that he didn't want to take it to trial. Makes me wonder if—"

"They tried to get him to roll on somebody and he

wouldn't?" Ken said. "That he was scared of that sort of pressure, so he took the deal and did his time with his mouth shut to protect himself? Yeah, that was my idea, too—and where Sanabria figures in, maybe."

"This piece of criminal masterwork that got him busted hardly seems like a major mob play, though. He beats the shit out of some guy and steals a small amount of heroin so he can sell it to an underage kid? Doesn't feel like Dominic Sanabria's work."

"I agree, but Bertoli was associated with those guys, and it makes sense that the prosecutor and the police would have tried to lean on him, doesn't it?"

Yes, it did—but he'd taken his jail sentence instead of talking. Then, with just a few years of time behind him for a relatively mundane crime, he somehow became the next selection of the Cantrell rehabilitation effort. An effort that promptly went awry. Bertoli spent only three weeks on the property before leaving. When I saw Ken's note on the date he left, I looked up from the file.

"Hey," I said, and Ken turned his eyes away from the window as I held up the first sheet on Bertoli. "Is this accurate? The release date?"

"Yes."

I frowned and lowered the sheet. "Harrison was still there. Is that a mistake?"

"No. Harrison was the first one to stay longer than six months. I have no idea why. Maybe they thought he wasn't ready to move on. Maybe he was their favorite felon. I really have no idea. Anyway, he did his six months, stayed on, and then they brought Bertoli in, and the two of them lived there together briefly. Then Bertoli was killed, and the Cantrells took off."

"He was murdered?"

"Officially, no. It's listed as an accidental death. He somehow managed to tumble off the roof of a six-story building. Oops."

He looked at me with a grim smile, and I dropped my eyes and went back to the file and read the details. Bertoli left the

Cantrells abruptly, claiming to his parole officer that he was taking a job at a restaurant in Murray Hill, Cleveland's version of Little Italy. He never logged a day of work at the restaurant, though. A few days after he left Whisper Ridge, Salvatore Bertoli fell off the roof of an abandoned warehouse he had no reason to be in, and Joshua and Alexandra Cantrell fell off the face of the earth.

"If there's anything related to the Cantrells that feels wrong, it's Bertoli," Ken said.

He was right. Bertoli felt wrong.

"So let me ask you this," Ken said. "If you've got this case, who of that group interests you the most?"

"On the basis of his connection to her brother and his strange demise, Bertoli," I said. It was as complete a lie as I'd uttered in a while—Harrison interested me most, of course, but Ken's paperwork history pointed in a different direction.

He nodded. "So it would seem, but the detective I talked with, guy named Graham, was interested in only one person out of that group: Parker Harrison."

I was really hoping he'd say Ruzity.

"He tell you why?" I asked, thinking again of Harrison's letters, how they'd started just after Joshua Cantrell's bones were found.

"Nope. Was looking for information, not giving it out. He didn't ask any specific questions about what I'd found on the other guys, though. Just Harrison."

"The current detective? Guy who's working on the Pennsylvania side, where the body was found?"

"That's right. He was entirely focused on Harrison."

I didn't say anything. I'd been holding off on sharing my client's identity with Ken because it felt like the right thing to do, but how honest was it? If I didn't trust the guy enough to tell him that, then what in the hell was I doing offering my help to him? You had to pick a side, sooner or later.

I was quiet for a long time, and Ken was watching me with a touch of confusion, as if he didn't know what I was brooding over.

"Last night you wanted to know my client's name," I said.

Ken nodded.

"Parker Harrison."

He leaned forward, eyes wide. "You're shitting me."

I shook my head. "He'd written me letters for a few months, asking me to look into it, explaining his history to me. I threw them all out. Then he showed up in person and seemed reasonably sane and talked me into it. He didn't mention that Cantrell's body had been found. Once I learned that, I quit."

"Did he know it had been found?"

"Yes. That's what bothered me. It was like he was playing a game."

"You think he could have murdered Cantrell?"

"I have no idea, but now you've got a better idea of why I wanted to stay out of this."

"Did you talk to any cops about him?"

"No."

He said, "Maybe you should. This guy I talked with, Graham."

I didn't answer.

"You say he was writing you letters for a few *months*?" Ken asked.

"Yeah."

"Sounds pretty strange to me, Lincoln."

"He sent the first one the week Cantrell's body was discovered."

Ken leaned back and spread his hands, a what-more-do-you-need gesture.

I looked down at the file, stared at Harrison's photograph for a few seconds, then snapped the folder shut and tossed it on the desk.

"You got Graham's number?"

I called from the office, with Ken listening to my half of the conversation. He didn't hear much. I'd barely begun my explanation when Graham interrupted.

"He was writing you letters? Starting in December?"

"Yes."

"You still have them?"

"No."

"Damn it. That's okay, though. That's okay. You said you're in Cleveland?"

"That's right. Now I only—"

"About a two-hour drive," he said as if I hadn't spoken. "I have a few things to finish up, take maybe an hour, then I can head your way. You give me your address, I can be up there by two, two thirty at the latest."

"I can tell you everything over the phone."

"No, no. I'll come up."

So I gave him the address. When I hung up, Ken said, "Seem interested?"

"Enough to make a two-hour drive without even hearing the whole story," I said, and that made Ken smile. Odd. I didn't feel like smiling at all.

Chapter Eleven

Quinn Graham arrived just before two, and it didn't take him long to make me feel like a fool. He was probably in his late thirties, black, with a shaved head and a thin goatee. Not tall but powerful, with heavy arms and a substantial chest.

"So Harrison explained in the first letter that he was a convicted murderer, and you chose not to keep that letter or any that followed it?" he asked about thirty seconds after exchanging greetings.

"That's right."

He didn't shake his head or make a snort of disgust or a wiseass remark. He looked at me thoughtfully.

"Okay. Probably wanted to get it out of your sight. Is that it? Yeah, I don't blame you for that, but I wish you'd held on to them. It's a police thing, though. People with experience tend to be more concerned with potential evidence."

"I know," I said. "I used to be a police detective."

"Oh?" he said and gave me more of that stare, as if he were thinking it was no real surprise that I wasn't still a police detective.

"I remember the letters quite well, though," I said, "and while I do wish I'd kept them, I'm not sure how much evidentiary value they would have offered."

"We could have analyzed the language, given it to a profiler. Harrison might have even been crazy enough to incorporate some sort of code."

All right, I was an idiot. What else to say? I waited for him.

"Well, they're gone now," he said. "Nothing to do about that."

"Exactly."

"You say you remember them well, so let's hear what you remember."

I took him through the sequence as best as I remembered it, offering approximate dates for the letters, describing each message. Then I told him about Harrison's visit, the simplicity of his request, and the few brief hours I'd invested into working his case.

"Now when you told him off and said you were done," Graham said, scribbling notes onto a leather-bound legal pad on his lap, "was that in person or on the phone?"

"In person." I told him about that final meeting.

"Since then, no communication?"

"He mailed a check."

Graham lifted his head. "I assume you cashed it?"

I shook my head.

"Did you keep *that* at least?"

Another shake.

He frowned and scribbled a few more words onto the pad. "So you have no record of your relationship with Harrison? That's what I'm understanding? No record at all?"

"No, I do not. As I said, I wasn't expecting it would lead to a meeting like this. I just wanted to end it."

"So how *did* it lead to this meeting?" he asked, looking at Ken for the first time. "I've spoken to Kenny here, but how is it that the two of you found each other?"

Ken took it from there. I watched Graham, and when Ken explained that he'd been called by Dominic Sanabria, the pencil stopped moving across the pad, and he lifted his head much slower.

"Dominic Sanabria called you three days ago?"

"That's right. To ask if Lincoln was—"

"I've already heard the reason, Kenny. I'm wishing you might have found that information worthy of my attention. I believe I asked that you pass such things along."

"That was several months ago," Ken said.

"I don't recall putting an expiration date on the request." Graham stared at Ken for a few seconds, then sighed and looked back at his pad. He took his time with it, reading through all of the notes, and then he closed the notebook and set it on the edge of my desk.

"Was supposed to have the day off," he said. "I decided, well, go in this morning, get a few things done, be gone by eleven. Noon at the latest. Now I'm in Ohio. That's the way the damn days off always seem to go. You think you only got a few hours, then you're in Ohio."

"We could've waited," Ken said.

"Oh, no." Graham was shaking his big head. "No, this couldn't have waited. This, boys, this is important."

"Ken told me he had the sense that Harrison was the focus of your investigation," I said, trying to prompt a little information.

He was frowning at his notebook on the desk and spoke again without looking at me. "If you were with the police, then you understand what a nightmare this one is, Linc, my friend."

Apparently Graham liked to dispense nicknames. Too bad there was nobody in the world who called me Linc, and I could tell from Ken's face that he didn't go by Kenny, either.

"It's an awfully cold trail," I said.

"Not the only problem, Linc. Yes, the trail is cold, but it also starts in Pennsylvania, beautiful Crawford County, over which I have jurisdiction." He cocked his head and stared at me. "You know what's in Crawford County? Woods. You know where I'm from? Philadelphia. Now, the woods are nice, sure, but I miss sidewalks. Strange damn thing to miss, but it's true. I miss my sidewalks."

He looked from me to Ken and then back as if he were disappointed that we didn't chime in with our shared love of sidewalks.

"Now I work in Crawford County," he said, "and the wonderful thing about having a body dug up in the woods in Crawford County is that I get to go to work. Bad thing is that in this case, all of the work to be done seems to be in Ohio.

That limits me. I've been out here before, spent a few weeks driving back and forth after the body was ID'd, but it's a pain in the ass. An investigation that requires I spend time in Ohio when my superiors would like me to be spending it in the Commonwealth of Pennsylvania, which does in fact pay my salary."

He sighed again. "And, you're right, the trail is cold. Twelve years cold, and the people who left it, well, they're a different sort from you and me. A handful of people who knew them suggested that Joshua might have been suicidal, that he'd been depressed and secretive toward the end. You know what else those people had to say? That if Cantrell actually committed suicide it's possible his wife would have just buried his body, lit a few candles, and marched on. A different sort, yes, they were. Ah, but the family ties? Oh, the family ties, boys, they are *tremendous*. What I've got is a new-age, holistic healer of a sister to a Mafia hit man. How about that? You ever heard anything better?"

He turned his wide eyes to Ken. "Dominic Sanabria called you."

"Yes."

Graham's head swiveled toward me. "And he *visited* you."

"Yes."

"Keeps careful tabs, doesn't he?" Graham's eyes were on his notebook again, and he was frowning, as if he were reading right through the leather cover and didn't like what he read.

"Harrison sent you a check after you told him to get lost," he said. "That's really something. Why give up the money to a guy who said he didn't want it?"

"He was real worked up about giving me a retainer."

"Or maybe his motivations lay elsewhere. Like keeping open that door of communication that he'd been knocking at over several months." He leaned back. "What do you think, Linc? Could we open that door back up?"

"I was pretty happy to extract myself from this situation," I said. "Not as happy to plunge back into it. What's your idea? I'm supposed to play a game with this guy?"

"I love a good game, Linc. That is one hell of an idea. I'm really not sure yet. I'll need a few days to think on it. But I might ask you to play, yes."

I frowned. "Look, Graham, I understand the importance of what you're doing here, but if you expect me to contribute, then I'd like to know more about the situation. You still haven't said why you're so interested in Harrison."

"He lived with the victim at the time of the victim's disappearance."

"That's it?"

He didn't answer.

"Because I don't think that's enough. In fact, from what I've seen, there are plenty of other people worth your time and attention. Like the parolee who had a history of association with Sanabria, went to live with the Cantrells, and died soon after he left."

He nodded enthusiastically. "Oh, Bertoli's part of it, sure."

"Or her brother, shit, that guy—"

"Oh, yes, him, too." Still nodding.

"Seems to me there's more potential in those two areas than with Parker Harrison."

He stopped nodding, made a pained face, and then said, "No, I'm afraid I can't join you there. I was with you right up till the end, though."

"Why? What do you see in Harrison that makes him stand out from the pack?"

"I have my reasons."

"I'm going to need to have them, too, Graham, if you want my cooperation."

He was studying my face, and he kept his eyes hard on mine when he finally spoke again. "Only one of those parolees you mention ever had any direct contact with Dominic Sanabria," he said. "That was Parker Harrison. He made half a dozen phone calls to Sanabria in the same week the Cantrells left their home."

"Looking for information, maybe. Trying to track them down, just like he is now."

"Perhaps. Then there was a twelve-year gap between calls,

which ended not long ago, when Harrison made two more calls to Sanabria. That was in December, Linc. Same time Harrison contacted you."

"Following up with him, seeing if he'd heard the news," I said.

"Most interesting thing about the timing of those two calls? Harrison made them a day after the body was discovered."

"So?"

Graham smiled, his teeth brilliantly white against his dark skin. "Took a while to identify the corpse, Linc. Harrison didn't call after the ID. He called after the body was found. A body that, at the time, was an unidentified pile of bones in another state."

I didn't respond to that.

"Let me ask you something," Graham said. "When you talked to Harrison, he say anything about being part Shawnee? Talk about his, uh, culture?"

"Yes."

"Not surprised to hear that," he said. "The folks at Harrison's prison told me he did a lot of reading on the subject. A lot of study."

"That has some significance to you?"

He nodded but didn't speak.

"Well?"

Silence.

"Graham, I'm going to say this again: If you want me to cooperate in whatever game you cook up for Harrison, I'll need to know everything that you do."

"If it leaks," he said, "it jeopardizes an already weak investigation. That cold trail we keep talking about, it's not making this thing easy."

"It's not going to leak," I said. "Not from this room."

He looked at Ken, waited for the nod of agreement.

"We held one detail back from the report on the discovery of Cantrell's body," Graham said. "A detail of potential value."

"What is it?" I said.

"Joshua Cantrell was buried in a grave that was about four

feet deep, lined with bark, and laid carefully in an exact east-to-west fashion. Then poles were placed over his body, more bark laid over the poles, and dirt piled on top." He looked at Ken, then back at me. "Those are all elements of a traditional Shawnee burial."

Chapter Twelve

Something you learn early as a detective—your work is damn dependent on physical evidence and people who know things relevant to the crime. Have either of those, and you're going to get somewhere. Have neither? Not going far, at least not easily. Quinn Graham had spent six months determining he had none of the former and only suspicions of the latter.

Whatever physical evidence might have existed at Joshua Cantrell's grave at the time he went into it was gone by the time the body was discovered. The evidence techs worked it as thoroughly as they could and came back with nothing. The poles, bark, and arrangement of the grave were physical evidence, yes, but didn't link back to a killer.

"Except in circumstantial fashion," Graham told us, "and you both know that's not worth a shit in court. It's worth something to me, though. That grave and those phone calls to Sanabria, they're worth something to me."

Their worth, it seemed, had been a load of frustration. He'd attempted to talk to Dominic Sanabria and immediately been met by a team of attorneys. Then he'd shifted his focus to Harrison and found the same response.

"Harrison lawyered up?" I said, the surprise clear in my voice.

Graham swiveled his big head to me and nodded. "He's not confirming so much as his own name without his attorney present, Linc. That shouldn't surprise you."

It did. It surprised me because it didn't jibe with the Parker Harrison who'd given up on his letter campaign and come to see me in person, the Harrison who'd gazed at me with a mixture of sorrow and intensity as he implored me to find Alexandra Cantrell. Of course, Harrison hadn't mentioned he knew Joshua Cantrell was dead, either.

"The guy took a sentence for murder," Graham said. "If there's one thing he's not anxious to do these days, it's talk to a homicide detective. Does that imply guilt? Not necessarily, but it doesn't exactly clear his good name, either."

"How much did you push?"

"Interviewed him a few times, and it was an absolute bastard because he had this attorney with him, telling him exactly what to say and when to say it."

"You asked about the phone calls, though? And the burial?"

"Phone calls, yes, burial, no. Like I said, we decided to sit on that. We were hoping for a physical link between him and that grave. Didn't get it, but we're not done yet, either. Sent some of the stuff in for DNA testing months ago, still don't have results. You were on the job, you understand that."

"Cold case, out-of-state case, and a mile-long wait list at the lab."

"Check, check, and check."

"How about the phone calls?" Ken said. "What was his response?"

"Says he called Sanabria after the couple took off, hoping to get in touch with them. Then, after the body was found, says he was merely doing the same thing, checking in again for an update. I pointed out that was a hell of a twist of timing, waiting twelve years to check in and then doing it the same damn week the body was found, but of course he and his attorney refused to go down that road."

"Sanabria confirm that?" I asked.

Graham's face went sour. "Through his attorneys, yes, he did. It's too perfect, man, too rehearsed. They remember these phone calls like they're looking at a transcript."

"Still," I said, "seems to me you've got something to work with there."

"No shit, Linc? Seems that way? Well, hell, buddy, I'm glad to hear you think so. Now let me remind you what my superiors have to say—"

"I get that," I said. "At least I get it from the Pennsylvania side. I'm amazed you haven't stirred somebody with the FBI up about Sanabria."

"That's another part of the problem. I did, but they didn't stir in the way you are thinking and I was hoping. Didn't come into the game looking to help. Instead, they came in warning me that we'd have a nightmare on our hands if we hassled Sanabria. They took their run at him, hard as they could, back in the nineties and didn't get much to show for it. A couple years on a bullshit charge—and they were looking at the guy for, what, five, six murders? Who knows what else? Sense I got from the boys who worked on him back at the time, Linc, was that they didn't want any piece of it. They've kept tabs on him, shit, maybe kept *surveillance* on him, and he hasn't stepped wrong in fifteen years. If he killed his brother-in-law or had him killed, they don't seem to care. There's one guy who felt different, but he's retired now, and what he says doesn't carry water."

We fell silent. Graham got to his feet and walked to the window and stared down at the street.

"If I find Alexandra, it will be put to rest," he said. "That simple. I'm sure of it."

"You've looked for her? Pushed hard?" I said.

"Yes, I've pushed hard," Graham snapped, "and so did your buddy here and a lot of other people before us. Nobody found her. Not me, not anybody else. Right?"

He was looking at Ken, who didn't answer, just stared back at him as if waiting for more. Graham turned away and went back to staring at the street.

"Fact is, I was pretty well distracted from it until today. Got us a couple of dead girls a few months back. Raped, beaten, strangled, and dumped off the highway. Two in two weeks. One was hitchhiking, one a runaway. Two in two weeks, both on my highways . . . yeah, ain't nobody talked about Mr. Cantrell in quite a while."

He turned from the window. "Now you call, and I don't know what the hell to do with what you've got. Don't know yet. All I do know is I'm going to think on it, going to get back in touch, and when I do? I'm expecting cooperation."

He was looking at me, not at Ken. Had himself one hell of a stare. I braved it for a few seconds before I had to nod.

The day after I'd thrown Parker Harrison's check in the trash and promised myself that would be the end of it, I stood in the parking lot below my office and assured a Pennsylvania police detective I'd be willing to cooperate with his investigation if he asked it. I hoped he wouldn't. If he did, I knew my *cooperation* would amount to baiting a psychopath. It would be a game in which Graham would man one side of the board and Harrison the other. Me? The pawn shuffling around in the middle. Yeah, wouldn't break my heart if he decided not to pursue that avenue.

"I've got to head home tonight," Ken said as we watched Graham's Ford Explorer pull onto Rocky River. "How about we grab a bite to eat first?"

It was closing in on four, and we hadn't eaten any lunch.

"We can do that," I said, "and now that you've managed to involve me in the police investigation, I'd say it should be your treat."

We went to Sokolowski's University Inn in Tremont. It was one of my favorite places in the city, a third-generation family-owned restaurant with an exceptional vantage point of downtown. When I was still with the police, Joe and I would stop in and sit at the bar and admire the view. Today, Ken and I walked directly to the back dining room and found a quiet, dark corner.

"Four different varieties of sausage on the menu," he said, dropping his tray onto the table. "This is Cleveland's idea of gourmet?"

"Shut up and taste it."

He bit into the bratwurst and raised his eyebrows. "Okay. Point made."

I'd gotten perch, but the lingering hangover dulled my

appetite. Ken, on the other hand, seemed to make a full recovery at the first smell of food.

"Hell of an interesting talk with Graham," he said. "Got more out of him than I'd expected."

"Yeah, it was fantastic. Can't wait till he calls me and asks me to commence the game playing with Harrison."

"I don't know that he will." He cut into his potato pancake, forked about half of it into his mouth. "He gave us some starting points, that's for sure. I'd say it's safe to focus on Harrison."

I sipped some ice water and watched him eat, wondering if he'd stop when he got down to bare plate or just keep right on going until the tray was gone. I've known some people who could chase a hangover away with food, but I'm sure not one of them. Just watching him was making me queasy.

"Safe for *him* to focus on Harrison."

He finished the potato pancake, wiped his mouth with a napkin, and looked at me. "I've already told you. I want this one."

"Then talk to Graham about it."

"I intend to. You heard him bitching about how difficult this is for him when his other active cases are in Pennsylvania, how he's not getting the support he'd like. I think the man would appreciate the help."

"He also would have appreciated a phone call as soon as you heard from Sanabria. So if you're so eager to help him, why'd you wait on that?"

"I already told you, I wanted this one."

"So you've said. Yet you haven't done anything on it."

His face darkened. He looked at the table and slid a thumb along the edge of his knife. "I had some other things going on in my life at that time. Distractions."

"Like?"

"Like losing my daughter," he said and looked up. "My divorce was finalized in January. The ex had a new husband—and my daughter a new stepfather—by March. You do the math on that, Detective."

I nodded, drank some more water, waited.

"So here I am," he said. "Doing something about it, a few months too late—and I've got to thank you for wandering into this by mistake and pissing Sanabria off, because that led to the phone call that got me off my ass. I intend to push it as far as I can, Lincoln. With or without your help and with or without Graham's approval, I intend to do that. Know what I said about being distracted this spring? Well, summer's rolling on in now, buddy, and I'm *looking* for a distraction. This one fits fine."

His easy, amused manner had lost its grip and tumbled free, leaving behind a sheen of bitterness. I could sympathize with some of it—I'd lost a fiancée to another man—but what he was going through as a father was not an experience I knew. Or wanted to know.

"You know why I want that distraction?" he said, his hand returning to the knife. "Because when I have to sit around and think about what's happened in my life in the past year, nine times out of ten I conclude that my wife was right to go, and that my daughter's better off for it." He pressed his thumb into the blade. "That's the truth of it, but as you can imagine, it's not a truth I want to have to spend a hell of a lot of time considering."

"Why do you think it's the truth?"

"Sometimes you make decisions, Lincoln, that seem absolutely righteous at the time. Like there is no other possible option, you know? None. Then the years tick by and you see the way your decisions affected your family, and you wonder if it was a selfish choice."

He didn't offer any more details, and I didn't ask any more questions. There was a piano player in the corner of the room—seemed Sokolowski's always had a piano player—and for a while we just sat and listened to him play "Night Train" and didn't talk. When the song ended, Ken pushed the knife away. There was a hard white line down the middle of his thumb.

"All right," he said. "You've heard me out, and that's more than I had any right to ask, but I'll push it a bit more. I've been up-front with you, at the risk of bruising my ego, and admitted that I've never worked a homicide case. I know my way around an investigation, and I'm good at it, but I don't have the experience or the knowledge on a homicide, and you do. You also have some local credibility, which is going to be important. Those things are why I made the drive. I can move forward on this without you, and I will if I have to, but I'd rather have the help. So I'll ask you just once, with no pressure: Would you be willing to back me up on this?"

The piano player was into something upbeat and jazzy now, the sun was coming in warm through the windows behind him, and it had been many days since Dominic Sanabria stood in my living room. Easy to feel good about things. This one also felt like the sort of job that could get you into trouble, though, and generally you take those only when they're high-paying or personal. I didn't have that kind of excuse this time.

"Graham's assessment didn't exactly encourage me that this is something I want to be involved in, not even in a backup capacity," I said.

"You think he's going to leave you alone now?"

"I can make him. Police can solicit informant help, Ken, but they can't force it."

He shrugged.

It was quiet, and then he smiled, a cajoling, fraternal grin, and said, "Come on, Lincoln. This is what you are."

"Yeah," I said, but I couldn't match the smile. "It is."

"So?"

"Back you up. That was what you said, and it's what I'll hold you to. It's your baby, Ken, but I'll help you in whatever way I can, at least until it seems like that'll get me killed."

He smiled. "Can you ask any more of a man than that?"

Chapter Thirteen

Joe didn't like it. That was hardly a stunner. He grumbled and grunted and offered dire predictions and then told me I was an ass for not checking Ken's background out before agreeing to help him. When I explained that I had, he just grumbled and grunted some more.

"You had one of Ohio's last major mob figures standing in your apartment after one afternoon of work on the case, LP. That wasn't a clear enough warning sign to you?"

"Warning sign, sure. Stop sign, no."

"I knew there was a reason I always drive when I'm with you."

"Well, why don't you put that damn Taurus in gear and point it north, come back and run the show again."

"In time," he said. "In time."

Amy was a bit more receptive. That, too, wasn't exactly surprising—Amy's curiosity level can generally override her good judgment, a trait that Joe no longer shares. Or never shared. As a kid, he probably did background checks on the neighbors before trick-or-treating at their houses. Still, while Amy was at least lukewarm to the idea, her normal enthusiasm was tempered, and I understood that. It hadn't been so long ago that one of my cases invaded her life in a horrifying way. We rarely spoke of it now, and her typical bravado remained, but I'd also seen the pepper spray she'd added to her purse, and I'd heard the new steel security bar fasten behind me each time

I left her apartment. Those were good things, maybe, the sort of precautions that would have pleased me had I not known that I was the reason for them.

"It's a bizarre story, and I can see why you're intrigued, but I also understand what Joe's telling you about the risks," she said as we sat on my roof that night, after Ken Merriman left for Pittsburgh. We had the Indians game on the radio and a bottle of pinot noir within reaching distance. I'd swept up the broken glass from the previous night. Found plenty of dust on the roof, but nothing as black as what had come from Parker Harrison's shattered bones, and no silver coin. Reassuring.

"I understand that, too, Amy, but I only agreed to help the guy. Give him some advice."

"Lincoln Perry, technical adviser?" She rolled her eyes. "Yeah, that'll go well."

"What are you saying?"

"You know, I'm sorry. The more I think about it, the better it sounds. Instead of getting yourself arrested, like normal, you can get *him* arrested."

"It's not a long walk home to your apartment. I'd be happy to throw you down to the sidewalk so you can get a faster start."

"Ha, ha." She stretched out in the chair, put her feet up. "I'm not saying you should pass on this, Lincoln, but you can imagine what's going through my head, too. Sanabria already came to your home once."

The implication was heavy, an unspoken reminder of a day when a man I'd angered had come to her home instead of mine. It was a memory that chased me through my days, that could bring me up short with a grimace of agony seemingly out of nowhere, striking my heart like a sudden and unexpected muscle cramp. The possibilities of what *might* have happened loomed even larger than the pain of what had happened. I'd been in this business for far too long to keep such images at bay; I knew what the world could do, knew the savagery and senselessness of it all too well. It was this that had invaded my mind when Dominic Sanabria came to my apartment, and now she was remembering the same incident and worrying about me. I thought of him again, and of a body laid in a Shawnee grave in Pennsylvania. I thought of those things, and I looked at Amy, and I felt afraid.

"What?" she said. She was watching my face, and a frown had gathered on her own as she studied me.

"I can stay out of it," I said. "I should. It's the right thing for you."

"For *me*?"

I nodded.

"That can't be the issue, Lincoln. It needs to be the right thing for *you*."

"No," I said. "Not anymore. We're together, right? So we make decisions that are the best for both of us. That's the whole point."

She shook her head. "I don't want to let myself be shoved around by fear, Lincoln. It was hard for a while, after what happened. It still is, sometimes, but I'm trying not to let that dictate my life. If you start doing the opposite, you're going to scare me more. Can you understand that? I need support, not protection. There's a difference."

It was quiet for a while, and then I said, "I'm sorry."

"For?"

"For leading the sort of life that makes things like that go through your head."

"Hey, my fault, right? Nobody forced me to date a detective."

"You got a profession you'd prefer? Something safer? Sexier?"

She cocked her head to the side. "Now, that's a good question. What would the ideal profession for a romantic partner be? Hmm . . . do you have one?"

"Reporter, of course."

"Coward. Try again."

"Singer. Jazz or blues, or maybe a country-rock style. Someone with the right voice, you know, kind of smoky and sultry. Bit of an attitude when she's onstage, nice long legs—"

"Pig."

"What?"

"I ask about the ideal *profession* and you start describing the physical features of another woman."

"I was trying to play along."

"Try harder next time. Or smarter, at least." She laced her hands behind her head, smiled. "You know what I'd choose? A carpenter. Strong and capable, right? Handy."

"Hey, I replaced that shelf at your apartment."

She lifted her head and stared at me. "The shelf you broke?"

"Well, be that as it may, I also hung the new one—"

"How many trips to the hardware store did that take you?"

"Just because I didn't have all the materials at first—"

"You tried to put it up without using a level, Lincoln. It wasn't a shelf, it was a ramp."

"I corrected that."

"In a mere five hours. Yeah, stick to detecting, buddy. Even if it gets you into trouble."

I leaned forward and turned the volume on the radio down, a serious concession with two on and two out. "Think about another writer approaching you to guide them through a story, Amy, and then tell me what you'd say. Somebody in your business comes to you for help, you try to do it if you can. At least that's the way I've always operated. He put his ego on the shelf and came asking for help."

"Do you trust him?" she asked.

I hesitated, which is never a good sign when offered in response to a question of trust, but then nodded. "He checks out."

"I didn't ask if he checked out. I asked if you trust him."

"Yes." I nodded again. "So far, I haven't seen anything that warns me not to. The way he showed up after a call from Sanabria, I guess, but since then, in the conversations we've had . . . he seems genuine."

"Same thing you said about Parker Harrison at first."

That stopped me. I gave her a grudging nod.

"Maybe it is, but Ken doesn't share Harrison's history. Besides, I've been in his position, okay? In two regards. Once when Karen left"—Amy made the face one should expect when he mentions his ex—"and once with this sort of case, dealing with a client who came to me hoping I could explain what happened to his family. I remember the way that felt, the sort of burden John Weston handed over to me."

"As I recall, it didn't feel much better when you handed the answers back over to him."

I was quiet, and Amy reached out and laid her hand on my arm.

"I get what you're saying, Lincoln. I do. If you think you can help him and you want to try, then it's a simple choice."

"I really don't know how much of a choice it is. Ken's asked me to get involved. Graham probably will."

I was passing the blame off to every external party, but the truth was it came down to my decision, and I couldn't fully explain the motivation to her. Couldn't explain that when Ken had smiled at me and said, "This is what you are," it had felt less like he was trying to coerce me and more like he was defining me. While his definition was accurate, I didn't know how much I liked it.

This is what you are.

"All of it's irrelevant," I said.

"What do you mean?"

"The idea that I had some sort of choice to make about stepping into this. I was already in it, Amy. From the time Harrison sent that first letter. He picked me, and I've been in it ever since."

"Why?" she said. "Why did he pick you?"

The silence built and hung around us, and eventually I reached out and turned the radio back up. We listened until the final out, but I don't think either of us could have told you the details of the game.

PART TWO

Cold Trail Blues

Chapter Fourteen

By noon the next day my prediction to Amy was validated. I was involved now—thanks to Ken Merriman's urging and Quinn Graham's approval.

It was Graham who called, but he quickly blamed Ken.

"Your buddy doesn't have the best touch with police," he said. "Calls me up today, says he *wishes to inform me* that he'll be running his own investigation. Wishes to inform me. No bullshit, that's what he said. Not 'Yo, Detective Graham, I was wondering if I might be able to assist.' Not 'Excuse me, Detective Graham, I understand this is a cold case in another state and you might actually, for once in your career, be in favor of a PI's involvement.' No, Linc, instead he *wishes to inform me* that he's going out on his own. Whether I approve or not."

"Hmm," I said.

"Hmm? Hmm? Yeah, hmm is right, Linc. That's about what I had to say, too. Might have added a few more colorful terms, I don't recall. Your buddy, though—"

"Don't know that you can really call him my buddy, Graham. I met him two days ago. You two go back much longer than that. I figure, with that history, maybe he's really *your* buddy."

"Oh, you're not working with him on this? Because he said you were. He said, I believe this is a direct quote—'Perry and I are going to see what we can shake loose.' Shake loose, Linc. You not shaking? He shaking by himself?"

"I said I'd back him up. That's all. You know, give some advice—"

"Oh, some *ad*vice. Good, good. That's what I want to hear. You're giving advice to a guy who's never been any closer to a murder case than his TV screen."

"You don't want me to help him, then I'll just explain that and stay the hell out."

"Uh, no. Not at this point. Too late for that. Your buddy, he's in the game now. Already *informed* me, as I said. And if he's in the game, Linc? You better be, too. Because at least you been around. At least you know what you're doing. I did a little checking on you. Found out, my man Linc, he's a big shot."

"I wouldn't say that."

"Okay, we won't say that. Here's what we will say: I'm counting on you to keep Kenny from hurting this investigation. If he helps it, great, I'll be the first man down to shake his hand—but I am not going to let him *hurt* it, and I'm counting on you to help."

I rubbed my temples.

"Kenny does bring something to the table," Graham said. "I've got to admit that."

"Yeah?"

"He brings us an excuse to get you back in touch with Harrison. I was worrying on that one while I drove home yesterday. If you blew up on Harrison the way you said, then it'd feel wrong to have you go back, wanting to talk. Don't you think?"

"Sure."

"So we needed an excuse to open that door again. Needed one that felt right. I couldn't decide on it yesterday, but then this morning your buddy calls, and while I'm listening to him go on, I thought, yes, sir, this is the ticket. Kenny is the ticket. It'll be easy to sell as the truth, because it is the damn truth. Kenny looked you up, told you he wanted your client's name, and you agreed to give it to him. You might not want to work for Harrison, but he can. There's money in it, right?"

"Yeah." I could hear loud voices in the background, somebody swearing profusely, everybody else cracking up. Cops.

Something about it hit a chord of absence that had been quiet for a long time.

"So you two, you're going to go see Harrison," Graham said. "You're going to talk, and you're going to tape."

"A wire?"

"Yeah. I'll get you set up."

"I've got one. Got a couple."

"Good quality or cheap shit?"

"They're good."

"All right. I'm considering you an informant, not a cop, understand? This isn't your investigation, it's mine. What you hear, I hear."

"Tell it to Ken. I'm just an adviser, remember?" Even I wasn't buying that anymore.

"Yeah, my ass. Anyhow, go easy this first time. Feel Harrison out, check his attitude, see what you think."

"You want me to tape everything?"

"Every word, Linc. Every word. Now, you get a good talk going with him, there's a name I'd like you to drop. Bertoli. Salvatore Bertoli."

"He's of interest?"

"Man died at the same time the Cantrells decided to make their exit. Man also used to run with some boys in Youngstown and Cleveland who were close to Dominic. Man's *plenty* interesting, is what I'm saying."

"Is he tied to Dominic through ten degrees of separation or two?"

"Two would be high, I think. He was definitely in Dominic's circle, though. Definitely."

"Well, that's a hell of an important fact, don't you think? How did he end up with the sister if he's—"

"Just ask Harrison about him. See if he takes you somewhere different than he took me."

"Which was?"

"Nowhere. Now, I don't want you getting too heated with the questioning, Linc. You keep it toned down. We're just feeling our way in the dark here. So you introduce Harrison to Kenny, and if the chance is there, maybe you ask him what he thought of the Italian guy, Salvatore. Whatever, we're treading lightly at the start."

Does it matter how lightly you tread on a land mine? I wondered.

Ken Merriman returned the next afternoon, to a hotel just off I71 where he'd reserved a room for a full week. It was called a business suite and consisted of a bedroom, living room, and kitchen jammed into the same space as an ordinary hotel room, and when I made a joke about the place he told me I'd be more impressed by it if I'd seen the apartment he'd been living in since the divorce. I didn't make any more jokes after that.

I'd already located Parker Harrison's address and decided the way to approach him was in person and without warning. His sort of style. Besides, I wanted to see where he lived. There aren't many things that give you a sense of people faster than seeing them at home, in their own environment. Maybe he wouldn't let us in, but it was worth the try.

By the time I picked Ken up I was wearing the wire, just a simple seed mike that clipped to the inside of my collar and connected to a digital recorder fastened on my belt. I had a button-down shirt on, untucked over jeans, and it hung low enough that it covered the recorder even when I lifted my arms over my head.

In addition to the recorder, I had my Glock in its holster at my spine, and the feel of those things, the hard press of the gun and the cool, light touch of the wire running along my back, reminded me what I loved about my job. At some point during that preparation, testing the equipment and putting it on, I began to relish my role. After a few weeks of insisting I wanted no part of it, I was ready to go. A man had been killed and buried in the woods, and for twelve years nobody had answered for it. Whether Parker Harrison had killed him or not, he'd wanted to play games with me, writing his letters and telling his half-truths. Well, all right. If he wanted a game, I was ready to give him one.

The adrenaline was still riding with me when I got to

Ken's hotel, and as I stood in his cramped room and explained things to him, he began to grin.

"What?" I said.

"You're fired up, aren't you?"

"Just ready to go. That's all."

"I was expecting more of the whining," he said. "You know, gloom and doom, all the reasons we should be playing chess or knitting or whatever instead of working this case."

I thought about what he'd just said and shook my head. Holy shit, I was turning into my partner. I was turning into Joe.

"You want me to take the gun out, fire a few rounds into the ceiling?" I asked. "Maybe bring along a pump shotgun?"

"It doesn't need to be that exciting."

"All right. Then let's get to work."

Harrison lived in an apartment in Old Brooklyn, not far from what had been Deaconess Hospital when I was a kid. My father was an EMT who'd worked out of Deaconess for a while. It was an area that had gone through plenty of cycles in a fairly short time, hit hard by poverty and crime only to come back a few decades later with skyrocketing house values. Harrison's apartment building wasn't attractive—a two-story brick rectangle with all the aesthetic appeal of a shoe box—but it was clean and bordered on either side by nice homes. There were only ten units in the building, and Harrison's was located at the front, on the ground floor. I had no idea what he did for a living or what he drove, so it was anybody's guess whether he'd be home. One way to find out, and that was a knock at the door.

He didn't answer. Nobody did. It was pushing on toward five, but early enough that most people would still be at work. We got back in my truck and went up to Pearl Road, found a restaurant with a bar, and killed an hour and a few Coronas. At six we returned to the apartment building. There were more cars in the lot, including an older Toyota pickup parked directly in front of Harrison's unit.

I pulled in next to it, cut the engine, and resisted the urge to double-check my recorder on the off chance that Harrison was watching. That's one of the challenges of wearing a wire: You're constantly aware of it, but your goal is to make sure nobody else is. I've found the best approach is to try to let it float at the back of your brain. Don't forget you have the thing on—do that and you're bound to screw up—but don't worry about it, either.

When we reached the door, I could hear music inside the apartment, some soft blues that was turned off as soon as I knocked. A brief pause, Harrison probably taking a look through the peephole, and then the door opened inward and he said, "Don't tell me the check bounced."

It sounded like a joke, but his face held all the humor of a brick wall.

"Didn't even cash it," I said. "Mind if we come in?"

He was wearing jeans and no shirt, and his body was more muscular than I would've guessed. Not cut from working out, but strong and free of fat in the way you can be if you eat right. Something told me Harrison probably ate right. He regarded Ken with a curious but not unfriendly gaze, and then he nodded and stepped back, and we followed him into the apartment.

It wasn't spacious—the rooms were narrow, and the ceilings felt low—but it was clean and laid out with a nice touch, furniture carefully situated to keep the small space from seeming cramped. There was a large piece of art on one wall, an elaborate wood carving in a symbol that meant nothing to me.

Harrison watched me look around and said, "It's not my first choice. I don't like living in apartments. I'd rather have some space, but I can't afford that yet, and the neighborhood here is quiet. Besides, I spend all day outside."

"Do you?" I looked away from the wood carving, back at him. "What is it that you do for a living, Harrison?"

"I'm a groundskeeper. For a cemetery."

"Really?"

He nodded. "It suits me."

Ken said, "How unsettling," in a flat voice that was pure Bogart and would have made me smile anywhere and anytime else. Harrison gave him one quick, hard stare, then returned his attention to me.

"Can I ask—" he began, but I interrupted and pointed at Ken.

"He's the one who wants to talk with you. It wasn't my choice."

His eyes went to Ken and lingered there, studying, but when he spoke again it was still to me.

"If he wants to talk to me, why did he go through you?"

"I'll let him explain that." I walked past Harrison and sat on his couch. He watched me but didn't say anything, and after a short pause Ken sat down, too. Harrison stayed on his feet.

"Well?" he said, speaking directly to Ken this time.

Ken launched into his story, explaining the twelve-year-old case, the way it had eaten at him, how he'd promised Joshua Cantrell's parents he'd deliver an answer. I listened and tried to look bored, a little put out, as I was claiming to be. The seed microphone was cool and firm against my collarbone, but so far it hadn't taken in anything worth hearing, just Ken talking and Harrison staying silent.

"So when I found out Lincoln had looked into the house, I asked him about it," Ken was saying. "Wanted to know who his client was, who had an interest in the family."

Harrison looked over at me, no trace of emotion showing yet. "You provided that information."

I nodded.

"That's not confidential?"

"Usually."

He waited for more, but I didn't say anything. Finally he said, "Why wasn't it in my case?"

"You'd already broken my trust, Harrison. I told you that. You sent me out there asking questions like a fool, no idea the man was dead and his sister was related to Dominic Sanabria. You know who showed up at my home the other day? Sanabria. That's your doing, Harrison. You think I owed you confidentiality after that bullshit?"

I'd put some heat into the words, but he didn't change

expression or break eye contact. Just listened, gave it a few seconds to make sure I was done, and then turned back to Ken.

"So what do you want from me?"

"A job," Ken said.

"A job?"

"Why not? You wanted Lincoln to work for you, right? Well, he backed out. I won't. I want to see this through, and I need someone to bankroll it, Mr. Harrison. I'm not going to take any more money from the family, and they don't have any to give me. They're not well off. They still want to know what happened to their son, though, and supposedly so do you."

"What will you do?" Harrison asked. "No offense meant, but if you've had twelve years at this . . ."

I was surprised by the flush that rose into Ken's cheeks. Either he was a hell of an actor or that sort of remark got to him even when it came from the lead suspect.

"It wasn't like I worked at it full-time for twelve years," he said, his voice measured and tight. "When I got started there was no body, no evidence of a crime. They just went away, that's all. Went away and didn't leave a trace. Now there's a trace."

"The buried body," Harrison said. "That's your trace?"

His tone had changed when he said *the buried body*, dropped and chilled. Ken hesitated, as if he'd heard it, too.

"Sure," he said. "That's one hell of a trace, don't you think?"

"The body was found months ago. Has the trace helped you since then?"

It felt cold in the room now, and there was something in Harrison's eyes and the set of his jaw that I didn't like. Ken was sitting forward on the couch, his arms braced on his knees, and I was leaning back, out of his view. Ken shifted his head slightly, as if he wanted to look at me, but then stopped, realizing Harrison would see any exchange between us.

"Well?" Harrison said. "Has the trace helped you?"

"Sure," Ken said.

"In what way?"

Again a pause, Ken unsure of himself now, and Harrison repeated his question.

"In what way?"

"It's given me some suspects."

"Really? Who?"

"Salvatore Bertoli," Ken said.

This was no longer going according to script—Graham had asked that we mention Bertoli, not identify him as a suspect—but Harrison's reaction was worth the gamble. He'd been unusually still, one of those rare people who can stand in front of others without fidgeting or shifting, but now he stepped closer to Ken and took the back of a chair in his hand and gripped it tight.

"Why do you say that?" he asked.

This time Ken did look at me, just one quick glance, and then he said, "You're not my client yet, Mr. Harrison. I'm not going to disclose any of the work I've done. You want to hire me, that would change."

"I'll write you a check tonight," Harrison said, "if you tell me why you said Salvatore's name."

"I've got my reasons."

"I want to hear them."

Ken was in a corner now—he had no reasons for suspecting Bertoli, and no way to avoid answering the question that wouldn't seem false. He was silent for a minute, weighing his options, and I decided to speak for the first time since he'd gotten started, just to divert the conversation if possible.

"You worked with him, Harrison," I said. "So you tell us—what did you think of Salvatore?"

He frowned and shook his head, then pointed at Ken. "I'd like to know why you think he's a suspect."

"He took a tumble off a warehouse roof the same time they disappeared," Ken said. "I've got a feeling those events weren't coincidental."

It was a cop-out, and not enough to satisfy Harrison. He said, "That's all? That's the only reason you called him a suspect?"

"It's the only one I'm prepared to share tonight. Now, if you want to write that check . . ."

"Is he the only suspect?"

"Everyone's a—"

"That's a silly cliché. Is he *your only suspect*?" Harrison was leaning forward now, his weight against the back of the chair, cords of muscle tight in his dark arms.

"He's a favorite," Ken said, still dancing, still evading. It wasn't working well, though. The one thing I was becoming more and more certain about with Harrison was that he could read people, and if Ken kept playing him there was a damn good chance we'd expose too much and learn too little. Every time Harrison looked at me I felt like he was following the wire with his eyes, tracing its path as if my shirt were transparent.

"He's a favorite," Harrison echoed. "Well, who are the others?"

"Mr. Harrison, do you want me to work for you or not?" Ken said, and I was glad he hadn't answered the question, that he seemed to want to bring this to an end, probably sensing the same dangers I had.

"There are some people who would tell you that I was a suspect," Harrison said.

Ken didn't answer.

"You said you're from Pennsylvania?"

"That's right."

"Have you talked with Detective Graham?"

Again Ken was quiet.

"Of course you have," Harrison said. "That would be a formality. A requirement. Who is his *favorite suspect*?"

"I'm not working with him, or for him."

"Are you not?" Harrison said, and then he turned and looked at me, as if the question applied to us both.

"You told me you didn't kill Cantrell," I said.

"That's right."

"So why are you worried, Harrison?"

His eyes seemed darker now than when we'd walked in. He said, "The evidence can always be twisted, can't it, Lincoln?"

"There something specific on your mind when you say that?"

Harrison looked at me for a long time, and then he let go of the chair and stepped back and turned to Ken. "I'll think about this."

"Well, I'd ask you to think fast," Ken said. "I'll leave a card, and if you could decide by—"

"When I decide, I'll let Lincoln know. You keep your card."

I shook my head. "I'm out, Harrison. If you—"

"No. When I decide, I'll let you know. You brought him to me, Lincoln."

His eyes were hard on me, still searching, distrustful. I felt a tingle at my collarbone, where the microphone rested, and I wanted to cover it with my hands.

Ken got to his feet and offered a hand to Harrison, who shook it after a moment's pause. I stood then, and we moved for the door together. Ken opened it, and I followed him outside, then turned back to face Harrison before closing the door.

"Hey, Harrison. One last question."

He waited.

"Everybody else came and went from the Cantrells' in six months. Everybody else worked alone. Why were you there for a year, and why'd you stick when they hired Bertoli?"

He stood in the doorway, framed by the lighted room behind him.

"Because she asked me to," he said eventually.

"Alexandra?"

A nod.

"Why?"

He stepped out of the apartment, reaching for the door, his hand passing close to my face as he grasped the edge.

"Because she trusted me, and she was afraid."

"Of who? Bertoli? Her brother?"

He pulled away, and my hand fell from the knob as the door swung shut. A second later the lock turned.

Chapter Fifteen

It was quiet in the truck as I drove away from Parker Harrison's apartment. A disconcerted feeling hung in the air between us, and not just from Harrison's final statement but from the way Ken had handled the interview. He was older than me by several years, but it didn't feel that way, because he was so damn green. Anytime I'd done an interview with Joe, I could afford to worry about my own end of it, assured that Joe, with thirty years of experience and one hell of an intellect, wasn't going to say anything that jeopardized us. Ken was a bright guy, certainly, but he didn't have those thirty years of experience. Didn't have one, even, not in the way that counted. Working divorce cases and insurance fraud and accident reconstructions didn't prepare you for a homicide investigation, didn't prepare you for a back-and-forth with someone like Parker Harrison.

It wasn't just Ken's end of that exchange that left me ill at ease, though. Harrison had taken a different tone than in either of my previous meetings with him, somehow both more guarded and aggressive. He'd seemed . . . cunning. Like he knew not to trust us from the moment we walked through his door, but he also didn't want to throw us out. Wanted us there, instead, so he could find some things out for himself. I remembered the way he'd looked at me when he asked if we were working for Graham, and once again, even in the truck, miles from him, I felt exposed.

"You think anything good was accomplished back there?" Ken said at length.

"We did what Graham asked of us."

"I don't think this was what he had in mind." Ken's voice was low, his face turned away from me, to the window. "I screwed it up, didn't I?"

"Tough to say."

He shook his head. "No, it's not. You were sitting there, you know how it went. He didn't believe a word I was saying."

"Didn't seem to believe much of it," I conceded, "but maybe we were reading too much into it, too. That's how it goes on undercover stuff, you're more sensitive than the target ninety percent of the time."

"Maybe," Ken said, "but that's sure not how I wanted it to play. Doubt it's how Graham wanted it to play, either."

"No."

He was quiet for a while again, then said, "Maybe we could run a few days of surveillance on him. Think that would help?"

"We're not going to do that without Graham signing off on it," I said, "and my guess is he's not going to."

"I might suggest it anyhow."

He was playing back to his strengths, to what he knew— surveillance. The conversation with Harrison had rattled him more than it had me, even, and that was a bad sign. If he wanted to keep moving on an investigation of this magnitude, he was going to need to come up with some confidence fast.

"Lincoln?" Ken said, and I realized I'd tuned him out, fallen away into my own thoughts.

"Sorry," I said. "What was that last bit?"

"Asking if we have to sit around and wait for Harrison to contact us again, or if we can move forward on this in some way. I was thinking if we pursued the Bertoli angle, it'd match up with what we told Harrison."

"Maybe."

"Well, what do you want to do? That's what I'm asking. What's next?"

"I've got to talk to Graham."

He fell silent for the first time as I turned off the interstate at the exit for his hotel. We were waiting at a red light just across from the parking lot when he turned to me and said, "Thank you, Lincoln."

"For?"

"For getting me up here, man. For agreeing to take it on. I needed this. I mean, I *needed* this."

He spoke with intensity, but his eyes were sad. I thought his mind was probably on his daughter again, his daughter and his ex-wife and the new stepfather. What was it he'd said that day at Sokolowski's? *Nine times out of ten I conclude that my wife was right to go, and that my daughter's better off for it.* I wondered which one of the ten he was on right now.

"Maybe tonight wasn't an impressive audition," he said, "but I'm not going to worry about it. I'm here to see it through, and I'll do that."

The light changed, and I pulled across the street and into the parking lot, bringing the truck to a stop outside the door closest to his room.

"I'll talk to Graham, and give you a call in the morning," I said.

"All right." He opened the door, then paused with one foot on the pavement and one still in the cab. "We're going to see this thing to the end, Lincoln. Twelve years I've been waiting for that."

"Maybe we will, or maybe we'll still be talking about it, pissed off and annoyed, ten years from now. That happens sometimes, Ken."

He shook his head. "Not this time. No, I've got a feeling about it."

My apartment was dark and empty when I came inside, and I felt a surge of disappointment that Amy wasn't there. No surprise—we hadn't made plans for the night, and she rarely came by unannounced—but some nights you can't help wishing that someone were waiting for you, had a light on. Of course, the first time that happened I'd probably wince at the sight of the light in the window and think longingly of a quiet, empty, and dark home. What can I say? We private eyes are dualistic creatures. It's one of our human traits.

I wanted to call Amy but figured Graham should come first. Sitting on the couch, I unbuttoned my shirt, removed the wire, and checked the recorder to see if all looked right. It did, but I wouldn't be sure until I hooked it up to the computer, ripped the audio file, and played it back. That would wait until morning. I found Graham's number and called.

"I'm about to get in bed with my wife, Linc. In other words, you best have something worthwhile to say."

I looked at the clock. "It's not even nine, Graham."

"Said I was getting into bed with her. Didn't say anything about sleeping."

"Ah."

"Yeah, ah. Now, what do you have?"

I took him through it as accurately as I could, albeit with a touch of varnish on my description of Ken's contributions. It wasn't a heavy enough coat.

"He told Harrison that Bertoli was a *suspect*?"

"You wanted us to drop the name."

"Drop the name, not call him a suspect! You think that's one and the same?"

"The implication would've been there anyhow."

He grumbled at that but let it go. "So Salvatore's name gave Harrison a little stir, did it?"

"Felt that way."

"Interesting. What do you think of that bit he said to you at the door?"

"That Alexandra asked him to stay because she was afraid? I'm not sure what to think of it."

"I'll ask you this, then—suppose you a woman, and you afraid. A convicted murderer is who you turn to for help?"

"Could be she trusted him."

"Uh-huh, even if I buy that, I still go back to the convicted murderer element. She wants a guy with those credentials around for help, then what do you think she was afraid of?"

"Husband, maybe."

"Guy's a scholar, Linc. Weighed maybe a hundred and forty pounds, spent his day stuck in a book."

"You've been around long enough to know that doesn't mean a thing."

"No, but if she's afraid of him, why not call her brother?"

"So maybe it was the brother she was afraid of."

"That's what I like about your mind, Linc. It works just like mine, only slower."

"That's a big jump, man, suggesting Dominic would go after his own sister."

"Who said anything about going after her? We've got one person confirmed dead, Linc, and it ain't Alexandra."

"You think she was afraid for her husband."

"Makes sense, since he turned up dead," Graham said, but then rushed out, "Look, let's don't get too sidetracked with this. Only reason we're even talking about it is because of what Harrison said, and I don't know how high he'd score in truthfulness. What do you think?"

"About Harrison?"

"Yeah. You were the one sat there and talked with him tonight. Give me your instinct. You feel he's being straight? That he doesn't know a hell of a lot more about this than he's saying?"

I thought about it, remembering his words, his body language, his eyes.

"No," I said. "I don't trust him."

"Exactly. Now, you expect to hear from him? Think he'll take the bait?"

"Here's what I expect—if he takes it, he'll do so knowing damn well that it's bait. He's smart, Graham. He's awfully smart."

"I'm not so sure about that," Graham said.

I was—And that's why, when I got to the office at eight thirty the next morning to discover Harrison had left a message three hours earlier, I didn't view it as any sort of victory.

He'd called at five twenty in the morning and prefaced the message with an apology for the early hour, explaining that he needed to be at work by six.

I know this is your office number, though, so I assume it's not a problem. I gave your offer some consideration, Lincoln, and I've decided to accept. I'll put a new retainer check in the mail today. For one thousand dollars. If that's not enough, let me know. The check will be made out to you. If you'd like to pay Ken Merriman the full sum, that's your decision, but the only way I'll approach this is with you as a go-between. I think that's fair, seeing how you're the one who brought him to me. It wouldn't be right for you to be completely removed from this. I'm not comfortable with that.

He paused there, and I could hear his breathing, fast and shallow, in direct contrast with his patient, careful manner of speaking.

I imagine you might be speaking with Detective Graham at some point. Feel free to give him my regards.

Another pause.

All right, so, I'll mail the check. Now, I don't mean to tell you how to do your business, but I suppose since you're working for me, it's fine if I make a request. Leave Mark Ruzity alone. He shouldn't be of interest to you, and he shouldn't be bothered. I'd like you to keep your distance from Mark.

That was the end of the message. I listened to it a few times before Ken showed up, and as soon as he sat down I played it again and watched his face darken as Harrison talked.

"You get the sense he may know exactly what we're doing?" he said when the message was done.

"I suggested that to Graham last night."

"And?"

"Graham doesn't agree, or doesn't care. I'm not sure which."

"What Harrison said about him . . . that felt like a message, didn't it? Like he was telling us—"

"That he knows we're doing this at Graham's direction? Yeah."

"You talk to Graham since this call?"

"Tried and didn't get him. Left a message."

"Harrison still seems quite taken with you, Lincoln. Supposedly he just hired me, right? But he did that through a call to you and a check made out to you. What do you think of that?"

I shook my head. "No idea. Why'd he come to me in the first place? Why keep writing letters after it was clear I wouldn't respond? Why show up at my office after months of being ignored?"

"You don't like it."

"Would you?"

His grin slipped back into place. "Shit, he's sending you checks. How bad can it be?"

"Yeah, right."

"So what now, we wait on Graham?"

"Uh-huh, that's the drill."

"That last bit of the message is pretty damn strange," Ken said. "Telling us to stay away from Ruzity."

"I was waiting for you to comment on that."

"As far as I knew, the two of them had no relationship. They were with the Cantrells at different times, and I had no idea their paths would have crossed."

"Seems like they did."

"Yeah. With Harrison being our client and all, I suppose we have to respect his wishes and leave Ruzity alone."

"That would be the ethical decision, certainly. We are in his employ."

"So as long as you got that message, we'd be required to keep our distance from Ruzity."

"Exactly."

"Imagine what might have happened if you didn't come into the office right away, though."

I nodded. "Why, there's a chance we might have blundered our way to Mr. Ruzity, oblivious to the wishes of our client. In fact, until that message came through, he *wasn't* our client. He was still considering things."

"An excellent point." He flicked his eyes to the phone, and a smile drifted across his face. "So, let me ask you, Lincoln: When did you play that message?"

"It's tough to recall, Ken. My memory isn't what it used to be. But I can't imagine it was *before* we looked Ruzity up."

"Oh, no," he said. "I can't imagine it was."

Chapter Sixteen

Finding Mark Ruzity was like looking for a lost dog in a neighborhood overrun by strays—nobody wanted to help, and nobody understood why in the hell you'd want to find him in the first place.

We started at the pawnshop on Storer Avenue where, according to Ken's notes, Ruzity worked repairing guitars. The notes were more than a decade old, though, and the pawnshop was now a vacant building with boarded windows. From there we went to his house on Denison, found nobody home, and started knocking on doors to see if anyone could tell us where to find him. Most of the people on the street seemed to know who he was, but nobody wanted to direct us to him.

"He's one of those guys," said a Puerto Rican woman who kept the chain on the door while she talked to us, "you just keep your distance from him, you know? He's lived here as long as we have, never caused a problem, but he looks like he *could*, right? He don't bother nobody, but I sure as shit wouldn't bother him, either. I don't think you should bother him."

It was the same sentiment Harrison had expressed. For a guy who hadn't taken a fall in fifteen years, Ruzity had one hell of a rep.

Ken finally had the inspiration that got us to him.

"He's a musician, right? Is there anyplace in this neighborhood where a musician would want to go?"

We found one: a used instrument store ten blocks from his house. They knew him, all right.

"Dude can shred a guitar," the kid behind the counter informed us from behind his protective layer of piercings. "I mean just melt the amp, really. But he won't play with anybody else now. Only solo. Calls himself El Caballo Loco."

He paused, waiting for a reaction, and then said, "It means the crazy horse. Badass, right?"

Badass, we agreed. Now where can we find him?

"He's a stone carver, man. Works with a guy named Ben down on Forty-eighth. Does all sorts of cool shit. You should see some of the gravestones."

"Gravestones?"

"Yeah, awesome, right? Like I said, he's pretty badass."

He didn't have an address for the carving shop, but he gave us a close enough description. Ken and I didn't speak until we were back in my truck.

"So he carves the gravestones," Ken said, "and Harrison keeps them clean? That's the idea? A pair of murderers making a living in the cemetery business?"

"Steady work," I said. "They're never going to run out of clients. Hell, they've helped produce some."

The carving shop—Strawn Stoneworks—occupied the bottom floor of a three-story brick building near the old stockyard district. Nobody answered our knock, but there were lights on in the back, and the door was unlocked. We went in.

The front of the room was scattered with samples of carvings laid out on old wooden tables—a fireplace mantel, a small gargoyle, and a handful of headstones. There was a narrow corridor separating this room from the next, and at the opposite end fluorescent lights glowed and a steady tapping sound could be heard. Metal on stone.

I led the way down the hall, and we came out in a workshop that smelled of sweat and dust. There were pieces of stone on the floor and on heavy-duty steel shelves, and tools littered the rest of the space—grinders and hammers and racks of chisels, an air compressor with hoses draped around it. A man was working with his back to us, chipping away at a piece of marble with a hammer and chisel. I was just opening my mouth to speak when he turned and said, "The hell you think you're doing?"

He was of average height, wiry in a hard way, with gray hair and a goatee. He wore an earring, and there were thin lines of sweat snaking down his forehead.

"Hey, sorry, there wasn't anybody out front," I said.

"Strawn left for a while. Said he was getting lunch, but he's probably buying comic books. That's what he does at lunch." He wiped sweat away with the back of his hand. "Anyhow, he's the owner; he's the one you talk to. Not me. And nobody comes back into the workshop."

"We're not looking for Strawn," I said. "We're looking for Mark Ruzity."

He didn't answer.

"Are you—" I began, but then he cut me off.

"Maybe I wasn't clear. Nobody comes into the workshop." He cocked his head and stared us down, first me, then Ken. "Lot of tools back here. People wander in, they could get hurt."

It didn't feel like a public safety announcement.

"Mark," I said, "wouldn't it be easier to answer five minutes of questions?"

"Would be *easiest* to throw your asses out. Nobody—"

"Comes into the workshop. We get it. But if you throw us out now, we'll just have to go back to your place on Denison and wait around. What's the point?"

His eyes flickered and went dark when I said that. Didn't like it that we knew where he lived.

"Okay," he said. "I can tell you what I've told every other cop: I'm clean. Haven't killed anyone in a while. If you're asking about something that went down in the neighborhood, you're asking the wrong man. I'm not involved, and I don't drop dimes."

"It's not about the neighborhood," Ken said. "It's about Alexandra and Joshua Cantrell."

Ruzity seemed to draw in air without taking a breath. Just absorbed it, sucked it right out of the dust-filled room until the walls felt tight around us. He didn't speak, but he looked at

Ken in a way that made me wish I were wearing a gun. There were pneumatic hammers on a table beside him, but he was using hand tools, a hammer in his right and a carbide chisel in his left. He turned the chisel in his fingers now. It looked natural in his hand. Familiar.

"I suspect the time has come," he said, "for us to share some names. You already know mine. What are yours?"

We told him. Names and occupation. He kept rotating the chisel. It had a flared point, ridged with small, sharp teeth. Sweat had slipped behind his glasses and found his eyes, and he blinked it away without dropping his stare.

"Private investigators," he said. "Then police didn't send you. So who did? Dunbar?"

I could feel Ken's *who's Dunbar?* question on the way, could also feel the price of it if he let it escape his lips, and rushed out my own response first. "What's your problem with Dunbar?"

Mark Ruzity switched his eyes to me. "My problem? The son of a bitch has spent *twelve years* harassing me and sending cops my way. You ask what my *problem* is?"

I shrugged, and he narrowed his gaze. "Dunbar does his own hassling, though. FBI guys don't hire anybody else to do it for them. So who the hell you working for?"

"If you don't mind," Ken said, "maybe you could answer a question or two and then we will. You know, fair trade."

"Fair trade?" He took a step closer and drew himself up to his full height, and the muscles in his forearms stood out tight around the chisel and the hammer. Then he paused, as if something had interrupted his forthcoming words, and frowned at Ken.

"Merriman," he said. "That's your name?"

"Yes."

"You came around a long time ago," he said. "Back at the start."

"You wouldn't agree to see me," Ken said.

"No. And I won't now. You were working for his parents." His frown deepened. "What in the hell brings you back all these years later?"

"The case remains unsolved, Mark."

"No shit. You been working it for the whole time?"

"No. I'm back because they found his body. It . . . stimulated my interest."

Ruzity pulled his head back, stared down at Ken with his eyes thoughtful and his mouth open, as if Ken had just told him a riddle and Ruzity wanted to be damn sure he got the right answer.

"His body," Ruzity said at length, "doesn't mean shit to me. Okay? Unless you want me to carve his headstone, it doesn't mean shit to me. It shouldn't to you, either."

"No? Like I said, the crime remains—"

"Unsolved," he said. "Yeah, I got it. Maybe it's better that way, too."

"Think you can explain that remark?" I said, and he ignored me, still focused on Ken.

"His parents hired you again when the body turned up? That's what you're telling me?"

"No. I'm not working for them anymore."

"Bullshit. Or, wait—give a shit. As in: I don't. Who sent you here is irrelevant. What's relevant is that you haul your asses out the door and go back to your clients and tell them to stay the hell away from Mark Ruzity."

"Odd response," I said, "coming from someone the Cantrells helped. I'd think you would care about seeing Joshua's death and his wife's disappearance resolved."

His head swiveled to me, and I felt a cold tightness along my spine.

"You think you know something about what the Cantrells did for me?" he said. "You think you know a *damn* thing about that? Let me tell you what they did—showed me that I'm the sort of man who needs his space. Why? To keep from losing a temper that I don't have real good control over. I've controlled it for a while now. Some years, in fact. But it's a daily chore, and it only works when I keep my space, and other people keep theirs."

He lifted the chisel, put the tip to my forehead, and then gave it a gentle tap with the hammer. The tiny teeth bit into my skin. Enough that I felt it, but not enough to draw blood. Ken shifted toward us, but Ruzity appeared unconcerned with him.

"Right now?" he said. "You're in my space, brother."

He'd lowered the hammer but was still holding the chisel against my forehead. Now he leaned close, so close that his goatee brushed my jaw, and spoke into my ear.

"You want to know what Alexandra Cantrell did for me?" he said. "She taught me how to keep myself from putting that chisel through your brain."

He popped the chisel free, and I could feel the imprint of the teeth lingering in my skin.

"The door is where you left it," he said. "Turn your asses around and find it again."

Chapter Seventeen

"Rehabilitated?" Ken said as we walked to my truck. "Really?"

"Clean since the day he stepped out of prison, is what you said."

"It's the truth. But the man seems to have an edge, doesn't he?"

"An edge," I said. "Yeah. That's the word."

"He's the only guy Harrison singled out, the only person he told us not to talk to. I wonder what he—"

"I'll tell you what we need to be wondering about right now: Dunbar. That's the name. You didn't mention him to me before. Have you heard the name?"

"No."

"Ruzity said he was FBI."

"As far as I know, the FBI had nothing to do with the case."

"They shouldn't have," I said, "but evidently they did."

"Think we should track him down?"

"Until I hear otherwise from Graham, yeah. And guess what? Graham still hasn't called."

John Dunbar had retired from the Bureau four years earlier, but fortunately for us he hadn't left the Cleveland area. He was living in Sheffield Lake, a small town west of the city and directly on the shore of Lake Erie. I didn't know the place well, but I'd been there several times, always to a bar called

Risko's Tavern. My father had been close with the guy who'd owned the place when I was a kid, and he used to make the drive out there on the weekend to sip a few beers, talk, and watch the water. Every now and then they'd have a clambake or a cookout outside, and he'd take me along. All I remembered of the place from those early visits was that they'd had a piranha tank inside and that my father always seemed to be in a hell of a good mood when he was there. The bar had changed hands since then, but I still stopped in occasionally to sit with a few drinks and some memories.

The waterfront property in the town had gone through a dramatic transformation in recent years, rich people buying up the old cottages that had lined the shore and tearing them down, building ostentatious temples of wealth in their place. When we got out there and I realized from the addresses that Dunbar's property would be on the north side of Lake Road, right on the water, my first thought was one of suspicion— these places were going for several million, so how in the hell did a retired FBI agent afford one? Cop on the take?

Then we found his house and that suspicion faded. It was wedged between two brick behemoths but didn't fit the mold. A simple home, white siding with blue trim, it had just enough room across the front for a door and two square windows on either side. To say the place was tiny didn't do it justice— beside those sprawling homes, it looked like something made by Lionel.

What the house lacked in size, it made up for in location, though. The perfectly trimmed lawn ran all the way down to a stone retaining wall at the lakeshore's edge, and beyond it the tossing, petulant gray water spread as far as you could see. There were some beautiful trees in the front yard, with flowers planted around their bases, but the backyard had been wisely kept free of visual obstructions, letting the lake stand out in all its power. The house was as well cared for as the lawn. When we pulled to a stop behind the carport—there was a Honda Civic parked inside—I could see that all the blue trim was fresh, and the roof looked new.

"Not much house, but I'd take the view," I said.

"No kidding." Ken popped open his door, nodding at the Civic. "We're in luck, too. Looks like somebody's home."

We got out of the car and walked up a concrete path to the front door. There were iron railings beside the two steps up to the door, and those, too, were shiny with a fresh coat of black paint. I pulled open the storm door to knock, but the someone was already at the door, swinging it open.

"Can I help you?"

"Mr. Dunbar?"

"That's right." He was probably late sixties and seemed more like an engineer or a math teacher than a retired cop. Neatly parted gray hair, slight build, three mechanical pencils and one red pen tucked into the pocket of a starched white shirt that he wore with black suit pants but no jacket or tie, so that it looked like a waiter's uniform.

"My name's Lincoln Perry. I'm a PI from Cleveland. Used to be with the department out there."

"Am I the target of your investigation or a potential source for it?" he said dryly, a hint of humor showing in the eyes.

"With any luck, a source."

"Come on in."

We walked inside, and I crossed through the cramped living room to stand at the back window and look out at the lake while Ken introduced himself. Everything in the house spoke of an exceeding level of care, but you could see the age in it, too—old-fashioned doorknobs and hinges, a Formica countertop in the little kitchen beside us.

"Hell of a location," I said when Dunbar finished addressing Ken and they joined me in the living room.

His smile seemed bitter. "You have no idea how often I've heard *that* in the past few years."

"Sorry."

"No, no. It is a great spot, but you've seen what's going up around it. Last fall someone offered me three-quarters of a million for the property. You know what my parents paid for it?"

"Fifty?"

He smiled. "Thirty-eight. We lived in Cleveland, and my

father wanted a place on the lake for summer, and back then there was nothing out here."

"You ever consider selling it?" Ken asked. "Money talks, is the rumor."

"Money screams in your ear. No, I haven't and I won't. I'm retired, I live simply, and I cannot imagine being any happier than I am right here."

Retired, and he was wearing a starched shirt and dress pants in his own home. Yes, the more I saw of him, the more he reminded me of Joe.

"Besides, I enjoy my legend in the neighborhood," he said. "Would you believe that the garage next door is more than a thousand square feet bigger than my entire house? The *garage*."

He laughed and turned away from the window, then went and sat on an overstuffed blue armchair and waved at the matching couch across from it.

"All right, if you're not here to buy the house, then what is it? One of you from Cleveland and the other from Pennsylvania, this has to be interesting."

"I'm basically riding shotgun on this one," I said. "It's Ken's case, but I'm helping out with the Ohio end of it. We're trying to find out what happened to a man named Joshua Cantrell. I don't know if that name means anything to you."

Even before I got that last part out, it was clear that the name meant plenty to him. The easygoing look went tense and, maybe, a bit sad.

"Oh, my," John Dunbar said. "That one."

"Yes," I said. "That one."

He was quiet for a moment, looking at the coffee table. "When you say you want to know what happened to him, you mean why was he killed. You mean, of course, what transpired that led to the man's body being buried in the woods."

"Yep," Ken said. "That's the gist."

"Well, you came to the right place," Dunbar said, and when he looked up at us there was no mistaking it this time— his face held sorrow. "I can tell you who I believe murdered him, but I can't prove it. What I can prove, though, is who *got* him killed. There is a difference. Would you like to know who *got* him killed?"

Ken shot me a quick glance, eyebrows raised, and nodded. "We sure would."

John Dunbar lifted his hand and gave us a child's wave, all from the wrist. "Right here," he said. "I got him killed, gentlemen. If you don't mind, I might pour myself a drink before I tell you the story."

Chapter Eighteen

He went into the kitchen and opened a cupboard and withdrew a bottle of Scotch that was nearly full. We waited while he opened another cupboard and spent a few seconds scanning the inside before selecting a juice glass. When he twisted the cap off the bottle it made a cracking sound, breaking a seal that had evidently enjoyed plenty of hardening time.

"Ken Merriman," Dunbar said in a flat voice. "You're the one the Cantrells hired."

Ken raised his eyebrows. "How do you know that?"

"I was trying to assist with the investigation. The police side. I knew everyone who was involved, at every level. I never spoke with you because, frankly, I wasn't interested in seeing a PI step into the case. Are you still working for them?"

"No."

Dunbar waited, but Ken didn't volunteer a client, so eventually he just nodded and sat down. He took one sip of the whiskey.

"We found you through a man named Mark Ruzity," I said. "He told us you'd been sending police his way for years."

"That's right."

"Why?"

"Because he knows something that could help," Dunbar said, and then he set the whiskey aside and got up and walked into another room, closing the door behind him. He was gone for maybe five minutes before he came back out and dropped a photograph in my lap.

Ken moved so he could look over my shoulder, and we studied the picture. It showed Dominic Sanabria and Mark Ruzity standing together on a sidewalk bordered by a wrought-iron fence. They both looked much younger. Ruzity was saying something to Sanabria, speaking directly into his ear. Whispering, perhaps. He had one hand clasped on the back of Sanabria's neck, and Sanabria was leaning forward and listening with intense eyes.

"They knew one another?" Ken said. "How?"

"I'm not certain," Dunbar said, "but you'll be interested in the date that photograph was taken. It came a matter of days after the Cantrells disappeared."

"Why do you have it?" I asked. "What's your connection to their case?"

"You don't know my personal history with Dominic?" he said, sounding genuinely surprised.

"John, we really don't know much at all," I said. "We're not as far around the curve as you think. More lucky than good, maybe."

"Oh, I doubt that. Still, in the interest of having us all caught up, let me explain. I assumed you read some articles about Dominic, the charges he always managed to slide out from under. I had the bastard once. *Had him.*"

"How so?" Ken said.

Another drink of Scotch, little more than a sip. He hadn't offered us any, which wasn't a problem but confirmed that he wasn't much of a drinker. This glass was for him while he told his story, and it didn't even cross his mind that anybody else would want a drink in the middle of the day.

"There was a motel out on the east side—a big old place with lots of separate units—that Dominic and his team were using. The owner of the place was a sleaze, and he knew they were dirty, but they paid well and tipped better, and so he kept his eyes wide shut to everything they did. Well, I put some energy into turning him, put some pressure on, and he agreed to cooperate with us. The idea was that he'd be a pretty general snitch. I wasn't asking him to do anything out of line, just tip us to comings and goings. I wanted to do some wiretaps out there—the whole reason they were using the place for meetings was to avoid wiretaps—but they were smart enough to get different units every time, and the judge wouldn't sign off on a warrant for the whole damn place. Even if he had, we couldn't have gotten that much equipment. It just wasn't practical.

"So instead I'm using the guy as a source of information on movement, nothing more. About a month after I turned him, I get a call from him. A page, actually—back then we were still using pagers. I call him back, and the guy's frantic. Says Sanabria and another guy had just checked into the motel, and that there were blood splatters on Sanabria's shirt and that he looked all disheveled and out of breath, like he'd just come out of a fight or something. They asked for a unit all the way in the back of the place and then pulled the car up right outside the door, and when they go in Sanabria carries a handgun in with him. This is good news, because he's a convicted felon and not allowed to have a handgun."

This time, Dunbar took more than a sip of the Scotch.

"I haul ass out to the motel. When I get there, the owner tells me somebody else showed up at the room and then drove away, but the car Sanabria and the other guy came in originally is still parked out front. So I go down there, with the owner, and bang on the door, and this guy named Johnny DiPietro answers. Remember that name. He's the guy that checked into the motel with Sanabria. I badge him and tell him I've got the owner there. I stand there in the door, and I say to the owner—this is your property, and I have consent to search. Right? He says yes. All this, DiPietro hears. So then I turn back to him, and I say, okay, you heard that, now are you going to make trouble? He shakes his head and steps aside, and then I say to him, *I repeat it carefully,* I say—do I have your permission to search the room, then? He tells me that I do, he tells me this in front of the hotel owner, who has also given consent, and, you know, it's *his* property anyhow."

Dunbar paused again. There was a flush building in his face.

"I search the room and find a gun and a shirt that's soaking in the shower, has blood on it. DiPietro is panicking now, but Sanabria is gone. He left with the other guy. We arrested him eventually, first for the handgun charge, and then later we got his fingerprints off the gun and a ballistic match to the homicide of a kid named Lamarca, who had just been shot that day. After that, we even got a blood match—Lamarca's blood was on Sanabria's shirt. We had that confirmed by the lab. Ballistic and blood evidence tying Sanabria to a homicide, and if nothing else we've got him on the gun charge."

He paused then, and it was quiet for a moment before Ken said, "So how the hell did he walk?"

I answered for Dunbar.

"DiPietro didn't rent the motel room."

Dunbar raised his eyebrows, then gave a short nod and lifted his glass to me. "Well done, Detective."

"You had ballistic and blood matches that you got through a good-faith search, though," Ken said, incredulous.

"He wasn't a cop," I told Dunbar. "Doesn't know the lovely law of the exclusionary rule."

"Fruit of the poisonous tree," Dunbar said, nodding. "Sanabria, piece of shit that he is, is legally entitled to privacy in a motel room that he rented. If he wants to leave a homicide weapon and a bloody shirt in that room, he's allowed to do that in private. It's his reasonable expectation. Fourth Amendment right."

Ken looked shocked. "You had consent from an occupant and the *property owner.*"

"I know," Dunbar said. "I thought that would be enough. I really did. I knew there was a chance the owner might not be able to grant consent to a rented room without a warrant—honestly, I wasn't sure about that, which I probably shouldn't admit, but then I'm not a lawyer. That's why I used him to bait DiPietro into opening up, though, because I figured DiPietro had to believe it was the owner's right. What I didn't count on was DiPietro being a visitor and not the registered guest. It was Sanabria's room, legally. That means nobody else could give consent."

"So he walked?"

"Yes."

Dunbar put the glass down on the coffee table. "Well, I suppose you don't care about that. I suppose that's not relevant. What you're interested in, I imagine, is how I happened to get Joshua Cantrell killed."

He said this through his teeth, eyes still on the glass. Ken and I were silent.

"So I had Sanabria once and couldn't deliver," Dunbar said. "There's your background. That's all that really need be said. The details, well, the details are mine to worry about, not yours. The point is, we went back after him again. I went back after him. I also went to Joshua Cantrell."

"As an informant?" I said.

"That was the original idea. It didn't go well. Not only did he refuse to talk with us about Sanabria, he insisted he didn't know anything about the man. Said he only knew what his wife told him, and that was old news. His impression was that we knew more of the family he'd married into than he did."

"Did you believe him?"

"Actually, I did. In any event, it was clear he wasn't going to cooperate, so we didn't waste any time on him. I kept tabs on him, though. Made the occasional call. We did that sort of thing with the idea of keeping the pressure up, both on Cantrell and Sanabria. We wanted Sanabria to know that we were always around, always talking to the people who surrounded him, looking for a chink in the armor."

"Was Alexandra a part of this?" Ken asked.

He shook his head. "She wouldn't have anything to do with us. Joshua, though, was almost as scared of us as he was of Sanabria. So while he didn't help, he also didn't refuse to communicate. He was afraid to do that. Now, as I said, we'd check in with him every so often. I caught him alone one day when I came out to their house to show him some photographs. No reason at all that he or Alexandra would be able to ID anyone in the photos, but we wanted to rattle Sanabria's cage a little. He *hated* it when we talked to his family, but we could pretend it was necessary investigation, not harassment. Truth was, we just wanted him sweating.

"So this time, Joshua seemed a little different. He looked at the photographs, told me he didn't recognize any of the people in them, which was of course true, but he was cooperative, too, and as I was leaving he made a remark about wishing he *could* help, and it sounded genuine, and almost angry. We talked for a while, and he told me about the new houseguest they had, a guy who'd done a long stretch for murder. Mark Ruzity."

"Are you saying he wasn't in favor of the hands-on approach his wife brought to the mission?" I said.

"I'm saying he was absolutely opposed to it. The phrase he used was 'she's bringing them into our home.' Apparently against his strongest objections."

"So you made a suggestion," I said. "A pitch. If he was willing to help with Sanabria, why not take advantage of the situation."

His nod seemed embarrassed. "It was almost a joke. On that day, in that conversation, it really was almost a joke. I mean, it was that ludicrous—place an informant in Sanabria's sister's home and use her husband to work him? Crazy, right?"

"But he agreed," Ken said.

"No. He rejected the idea, emphatically, and as time passed, I stopped dropping in on them, refocused in other areas. Then he came back to me. Contacted me by phone and asked if we could meet in person. He seemed very nervous, very agitated. So I drove out to a restaurant in Shaker Heights and met him, and he told me that he'd reconsidered."

"Why the change of heart?" Ken asked.

Dunbar frowned. "The motivation, I'm afraid, was anything but noble. What led him to pick up the phone and call was a complete collapse of his marriage, I believe. His wife wasn't aware of it yet, but that's what it was." He cocked his head at us. "What do you know about Joshua?"

"Quiet, academic sort," Ken said. "Interested in the prison system."

"*Interested*," Dunbar said and nodded. "He was interested in it as a student, not as a participant. Here's what I can tell you about Joshua—he was a nervous man, a scared man. Insecure. I believe that played a role when he met Alexandra. He saw her fascination with those issues of rehabilitation and reentry, and he ran with it. She was a beautiful woman, and a rich one, the sort who had never before given him the time of day. What more motivation did he need?

"Joshua's vision of their married life was that his wife's obsession would pass, or that a few papers, maybe some small donations, would satisfy it. He was wrong. I'm not surprised the final straw came when she began to hire inmates to work for them. As I've said, he was an insecure man. I think those insecurities took his imagination to some wild, dark places."

He looked directly at me with a sudden, sharp gaze. "Understand this—while I sit here and discuss the man's paranoia, I didn't do anything at that time except feed it. I'm not proud of that, but I won't lie about it, either. He felt betrayed by his wife, pushed aside in favor of murderers and thieves, and he wanted to hurt her. That was the sum of it. He wanted to *hurt* her, but he didn't know how. What could he do? Leave her? Then he'd lose everything. Have an affair? He was an awkward, introverted man, hardly capable of becoming a crusading Casanova. Withhold his money? He didn't have any. Alexandra was so much stronger than he was in virtually every way a person can have strength. He saw no way to strike back, no way to retaliate for what he viewed as disregard and betrayal. Until he found my card."

It had started to rain, and the wind was blowing even stronger now. Dunbar turned his head and looked out at the tossing lake.

"He was going to feed you information about his brother-in-law?" Ken said.

"I'm sure he would have been happy to do that," Dunbar said, looking back at us, "provided he knew anything, but he didn't. No, he remembered my earlier proposal, the one I'd made as a throwaway line, about seeing that one of the inmates placed in their care was someone who could snitch."

"Enter Salvatore Bertoli," I said.

"What did he know?" Ken asked. "What was he supposed to know, at least?"

"I told you to remember Johnny DiPietro's name from that story about the hotel. Well, Sanabria and he were both partners and rivals. We heard rumors that Sanabria wanted to clip him even before the motel arrest. After the way DiPietro stood pat and didn't talk he eased up on it temporarily, but before long they were at odds again."

"Over what?"

"Key issues were drugs and associates. Sanabria was very reluctant to be involved with the drug trade at any level. Had heard too many stories about how it brought down his mob buddies all over the country. DiPietro was all about it. DiPietro was also not only willing to network outside the Italians but enthusiastic about it. Sanabria, being old school, didn't support that or trust it. One of the reasons Sanabria was so furious with DiPietro was his tendency to trust people like Bertoli who committed ignorant, poorly thought-out crimes. He also was at odds with him over his desire to move into the east side drug market, which was generally black territory. Eventually the feud boiled over and Sanabria had him whacked. Bertoli was a witness."

"How did you know that?"

"Wiretaps. We got lucky. Almost got lucky, I should say. Caught a conversation between Bertoli and another guy—who's actually in prison now—and Bertoli started in on DiPietro, saying he knew what happened, but his buddy was smart enough to shut him up and get off the phone. Still, it was clear he'd seen it."

"You didn't question him?"

"Of course, but he didn't talk. He was facing prison time on another charge, and we thought we might be able to leverage him then, but . . ." He shrugged. "Sanabria's not the sort of person you want to snitch on. There was a side element, too. When DiPietro was killed, a significant quantity of heroin and coke disappeared. We had credible information that he'd bought into the supply end of things, that he intended to push his influence into the east side drug trade. This was in direct conflict with what Sanabria wanted, and when the hit was made, the drugs seemed to vanish."

"Bertoli's other charge was for beating the shit out of the truck stop guy and stealing his drugs," I said. "You think he went after DiPietro's product?"

"All we're sure of is that the product seemed to disappear from Italian hands. My guess is Sanabria claimed it and got rid of it. Sold it to someone else, outside of his circle, probably. Maybe just destroyed it. He didn't trust drugs."

"Let me be clear on the time line," Ken said. "DiPietro was killed *after* Bertoli was arrested and went to jail, but you somehow think he was a witness? That makes no sense."

"He wasn't in jail yet. He'd been charged, bonded out, and was awaiting trial. Then DiPietro was murdered, Bertoli witnessed it, and we came back at him hard, pushing for him to talk. He panicked and took the plea bargain and did his time. You want to know why? Because he was afraid of Sanabria. He thought going to jail would prove his trustworthiness, prove that he'd kept his mouth shut. He thought, gentlemen, that jail was the safer place to be. As I just said, Sanabria is not the sort of person you want to snitch on."

"You understood that, but you still decided to try again with Cantrell?" I said. "If Bertoli didn't give Sanabria up to avoid prison, why would he do it after he got out?"

"I should have turned him away?" Dunbar snapped. "A potential source of Cantrell's level comes to me and offers to help and I should have turned him away? That's what you think?"

I waited a few seconds, wanting to diffuse the tension, and then spoke as gently as I could. "I'm not second-guessing you. I'm just trying to conceive of the situation—all of them living in that house, working against one another. You turned it into a damned gothic mansion, Dunbar. How surprised could you have been when it imploded?"

"Sanabria had been a target of our investigation for years. *Years.* We'd had him once, and he slipped out, and we were determined to have him again and make it stick."

How'd that work for you? I wanted to ask, but neither Ken nor I spoke, and for a long time all you could hear was the wind.

"I don't feel like that was the end of your story," Ken said eventually. "You told us you got him killed. Who killed him, and why?"

"Sanabria, of course. For the obvious reason. Can I prove that? No. If I could have, that bastard would be in prison where he belongs. So, yes, what you're thinking is right—I screwed up again, and he laughed his way through it again."

"That's not what I was thinking," Ken said.

"Well, it should be. It damn well should be."

"How did it happen?" I said. "Did you have no idea things were going wrong until they disappeared, or . . ."

"I had an idea, but it all went to hell pretty fast. Joshua Cantrell was clumsy in his attempts with Bertoli, displayed his true intentions too early and awkwardly, and Bertoli took off. Moved out of the house. Joshua called to notify me of that, and I thought, well, there's another missed opportunity. That's all that I thought. That we'd taken another swing, hadn't made contact, but no big deal. Then a week later Bertoli was dead. As soon as I found out about that, I went looking for Joshua. He and his wife were gone."

"How are you so sure it was Sanabria, then?" Ken said.

Dunbar frowned. "Did you miss the summary your partner gave? That bit about the gothic mansion? To use his word, it imploded. It surely did. Think about it—we were attempting to get information about Sanabria, we panicked Bertoli, and then he was killed and the Cantrells vanished. Where do you think the blame rests?"

Ken didn't answer. Dunbar stared at him for a moment, and then he said softly, "That's a poor question. The blame, as I've already told you, rests here. Rests with me. But the bloodshed, Mr. Merriman? That's not my doing. That's Dominic Sanabria."

"You must have questioned him," I said. "Tried to connect him to Bertoli's death."

"Of course we did. True to form, he had an alibi seven

layers deep. Actually, calling it an alibi wouldn't be fair. He didn't kill Bertoli personally—I'm fairly certain of that—but he had it done. I am even *more* certain of that."

"Then who got the call?" I said, thinking Harrison or Ruzity. "Who carried out the orders?"

"That one, I cannot answer. Only one person alive can. Sanabria himself—and good luck getting him to tell you."

"Two people," I said.

"Pardon?"

"Sanabria could answer it, and so could the person he used. That's who we're looking for."

"I'm not going to be much more help with that," Dunbar said. "You should talk to the detective who got the Cantrell case in Pennsylvania. Graham."

I raised my eyebrows. "You know Graham?"

"Not well. I've had this same conversation with him, that's all." Then, seeing the rise of anger in my face, he said, "Surely you didn't think you were the first people to make these connections?"

"Not anymore," I said. Part of me was embarrassed for being naive enough to believe just that, but more of me was pissed off at Graham. I'd told him I'd help provided I was given the real score, understood the situation as well as he did. The lying prick had promised me that was the case.

"You're sure Sanabria killed Joshua Cantrell, or had him killed," Ken said to Dunbar.

"That's right."

"Well, what about Alexandra?" I said. "Do you really think he murdered his own sister, or do you think she's still alive somewhere?"

"That," John Dunbar said, "is the one question I've been wondering about for the past twelve years."

Chapter Nineteen

I never knew my mother, but I know plenty of her expressions. She died when I was three, hit by a drunk driver at noon on a Sunday. She'd just left church; he'd just left a tip for the waitress who delivered his fifth Bloody Mary. Ordinarily, we'd have all been in the car together, but my sister and I were sick, sharing some sort of virus, and my father stayed home to watch us. Mom decided to go by herself. Every now and then, generally when my mind's immersed in something, I'll have a sudden sense that I can remember her voice, that I can *hear* the way she spoke. Then my conscious brain shifts over to try to trap it and it's gone. Just that quick. I'll hear her cadence perfectly in some secret lobe of memory, try to focus on it, and scare it off. She's in there somewhere, though. I know that she is.

While the voice eludes me, the expressions do not. My father recalled them often when I was growing up, and in a way that's how she came to exist for me: *Your mother always said . . .*

One favorite phrase, evidently, was head-spinner. As in, *How was your day? Well, it was a head-spinner.* It was how she referred to those days when things came too fast, too unexpected, too complicated.

My day? One hell of a head-spinner.

We'd gone out that morning thinking that Mark Ruzity might be able to give us some insight into the Cantrells.

Instead, he'd given us John Dunbar, which at the time had felt like a significant breakthrough. Felt even more like that when Dunbar poured himself a Scotch and settled in to explain how he'd gotten Joshua Cantrell killed. Then he'd delivered the capstone: *Talk to Detective Graham; of course he already knows this.*

A head-spinner.

Had we gained anything? As I sat on the roof watching the sun fade and streetlamps come on and waiting for Amy to arrive, I tried to determine that, and couldn't. A hell of a lot of information had come our way, and that felt like progress. The realization that Graham already had the information, though . . . yeah, that pretty well killed the sense of progress.

A head-spinner. You bet your ass.

I'd dropped Ken at his hotel and left him on his own for the night. Inhospitable, maybe, but I felt a strong need to be away from him and Graham and Dunbar and anyone else who'd ever heard of the Cantrells. We'd meet again in the morning, and then we'd see where it stood. Graham was the one who could tell us that. He hadn't answered when I called him, so I left a message informing him we'd made a major break and he needed to drive up the next morning to discuss it. Since then, he'd called five times and I hadn't answered or called him back. He probably wanted to avoid the trip, and I wanted him to make it. The son of a bitch could explain his lies in person.

Couldn't be mad at him for lying, though. That's what Joe would tell me. I was a civilian, Graham was a cop. Why would he tell me everything he knew? When had I ever done that for a civilian? It was a game, all of it was, and Graham was playing one version with me while I played another with Harrison. I wondered who in the hell kept track of the big board, though.

It was full night when Amy finally arrived, and we sat together as the temperature dropped. No radio tonight, no baseball game. Just talk, lots of it, the two of us tossing questions but no answers.

"You know who I feel sorry for?" Amy said after one long lull. She was curled up tight in her chair, sleeves pulled down over her hands, clearly freezing but not willing to speak of going inside until I did.

"Lincoln Perry, for getting sucked into this nightmare?"

"No, you're doing a good enough job of feeling sorry for Lincoln Perry tonight."

"This is why I gave up being single. Support like that."

"Stop. You know it's true. I've never seen anyone get as melodramatic over anything as you do when you've been lied to."

I smiled. "It's my subtle way of ensuring you always tell me the truth."

"Subtle, sure. Now, can I say who *I* feel sorry for? Alexandra. I mean, step back and think about it. This woman comes from a family that should have its own HBO series, she somehow emerges sane and motivated to help people, and when she tries to do that her husband turns against her, tries to betray her brother, and gets himself killed. All of this just to hurt her."

"Her brother talked about her as if she's alive," I said. "If that's true, how does he know it? And if that's true, how much does she understand?"

Amy tried to nod but lost it in midshiver as the wind picked up. I got to my feet, pulled her up and toward me, and wrapped my arms around her and rubbed her back. She was shaking against me.

"You look like you're ready to go in," I said.

"Only if you are."

I laughed. "Okay, *that's* support."

I turned, ready to move for the stairs, but she stopped me.

"Imagine what that would feel like," she said, her voice muffled against my chest.

"Imagine what?"

"If she is alive, and she does understand. If she knows that her brother killed her husband, and if she knows why it happened."

I didn't answer, just took her hand and guided her toward the steps. The wind was blowing harder now, and I was feeling the cold, too.

* * *

Graham rose to the bait. When I finally played his messages the next morning, he cursed me for not returning his calls, then said he'd be up, though not until afternoon. He sounded curious, and I was glad. We didn't have a damn thing that was new to him, but if he wanted to jerk me around, I was happy to return the favor.

Ken came into the office ten minutes after I did, with a cup of coffee in each hand and a stack of papers held between his chin and his chest. He swung the door shut with his foot, set one cup down in front of me, and then lifted his chin, spilling the papers across my desk.

"Thanks."

"No problem."

I took a drink of the coffee and waved at the papers he'd dumped on the desk. "So what's all this?"

"When do you think that first bust with Dunbar and Sanabria went down?" he said. "The one that got screwed up by the informant and the motel room?"

"A while ago. He was talking about using a pager."

"Try twenty years."

"*Twenty?*"

"I was surprised, too. Dunbar talked about it like it had been a few years, right? Not twenty of them."

"I don't suppose it changes anything," I said, gathering the pages into a stack and pulling them toward me. "How'd you find that out?"

"Library. They've got good newspaper archives."

"You went last night?" Now I felt guilty about blowing him off, spending the night with Amy while he was working.

"What else am I going to do? Can only watch so much ESPN."

He'd apparently printed out every article mentioning Sanabria or Dunbar or Bertoli, and it amounted to quite a collection. I flipped through them, skimming most, reading a few completely. Dunbar's account seemed accurate enough.

"Dunbar's been around for a long time," I said, looking at

the dates on the articles that referenced him. They started in the late seventies.

"Yeah, he has. Tell you something else that stood out to me from those articles—Bertoli's death was ruled an accident. We already knew that, but reading it again made me think about how firm Dunbar was on the idea that the guy was murdered. He was white on rice with that, you know? Which makes me wonder—if there was an FBI agent involved who knew all the background, and believed Bertoli was murdered, then why rule it an accident and close the door to an investigation? Why weren't the cops out looking for the Cantrells years ago as witnesses for the Bertoli case? Joshua Cantrell's parents told me that the police brushed off the idea of a crime. How could they do that, if what Dunbar told us is true?"

"All good questions," I said. "Bertoli died in Cleveland, didn't he?"

"Yes. Warehouse district, down by the river."

"So it was Cleveland police jurisdiction. Who had the case?"

"His name is in there."

I found the article and read through it, and nodded as soon as I got to the lead investigator's name—Mike London. I knew he'd take my call.

"How about we get you some answers to those questions while we wait on Graham's arrival, Kenny boy?"

"Sounds good, Linc. Sounds good."

Mike London always reminded me of a circus bear—enormous and threatening, but a crowd-pleaser at heart. He was one of the better-known wise-asses in a department full of them, but he was a good detective, too. Didn't have the sort of mind that Joe or some of the others had, that gift for problem solving, but he compensated with a good eye for detail and a dogged work ethic. Give Mike thirty leads at the start of the day, and he wasn't going home until he'd tried all of them, and a few others generated along the way. That effort was what kept him in favor with the brass despite his sense of humor, which superiors never found quite as hilarious as the rest of the department did.

He was out on the east side when I called, interviewing witnesses to a drive-by shooting that had missed the intended target and wounded a sixteen-year-old kid on Euclid Avenue the previous week, and said he'd give us some time provided I bought him lunch. Mike's appetite had been the stuff of department lore for years, so that was no small concession.

"Bertoli," he said when I agreed. "That's an old one, Lincoln. Old and cold."

"I know it. Just want to see what you remember about it."

"What I remember is that I did a bunch of interviews out Murray Hill way, because that's where his family was. Say, you know what Murray Hill makes me think of?"

"Food?"

"Hell, boy, you always were a good detective. Now, you want to ask me some questions, you can feed me out there at Murray Hill. That little Italian place."

"Murray Hill's nothing *but* little Italian places, Mike."

"The one with all the red, white, and green," he said. Real help narrowing it down. When I finally determined he meant Mama Santa's, we agreed to meet at noon.

Ken and I left early, largely by virtue of having nothing else to do. There'd been no more word from Graham, so I assumed he was still planning to show up that afternoon. If he came by while we were with London, he could wait. I wasn't feeling particularly gracious toward Quinn Graham.

We got to Murray Hill around eleven thirty, which meant we were in for a long wait, because London was never early and rarely on time.

"Here we are," I said as we drove up Mayfield Road and passed by Holy Rosary's brick facade and stained glass windows, the building more than a hundred years old now but still looking solid and clean. "Cleveland's fierce Little Italy. Do you want to go to an art gallery first or a bakery?"

"Yeah, yeah, I get it, not a threatening place anymore—but remember, we're here to talk about a murder. Speaking of murder—"

"I love that segue."

"Thought you would. I forgot to tell you, I checked my office voice mail last night. There was a message from an attorney representing Cantrell's parents."

"Did somebody call them to ask about what you're doing up here?"

"Nope. Wanted to inform me that I may be called for a deposition. They're trying to claim the property."

"That house?"

He nodded. "You've been out there, you know how much it must be worth. The thing's held free and clear in Alexandra and Joshua's names, but they're gone. So his parents want a piece of the estate."

"I don't see how they could get it if there's no proof that Alexandra is dead. The taxes are paid and current, there's no mortgage, no excuse to take it away from her."

"That's what I thought, but their attorney intends to file suit to have her declared dead. They're going to subpoena her attorney to see if he's had any contact with her in the last seven years. Apparently that's some sort of legal standard. They're sure nobody else has been in touch with her for that long."

It sounded crazy, seeking a courtroom ruling over whether or not a life still existed, but I supposed it was reasonable for them to try. Just the night before, Amy and I had wondered if Alexandra was still alive.

"Supposing Child says he hasn't heard from her in the last seven years, then . . ."

"They'll have to publish a notice of her presumed death. Run that for sixty days or something, I'm not sure of the specifics. If she doesn't respond in that time frame, and nobody else comes forward with proof of life, they can get a judge to rule that she's legally deceased. Once that's done, they can put a claim on the property."

I sat with my car keys in my hand and thought about the house, that arched doorway into the earth, the quiet that surrounded it. "They're going to sell it, aren't they?"

"I'm sure that's the idea. They aren't well-off."

It was tough to imagine anyone moving into the place. I

tried to picture it—a moving truck parked outside under the trees, a family inside sorting through boxes, kids running around the grounds, ready to transform the empty home into someplace full of life. It didn't seem right.

"That's interesting," I said finally, when I realized Ken was still looking at me and I hadn't said anything for a long time. "I'll be curious to see what happens."

"She'll come back to it," he said.

"What?"

"I think Alexandra will come back to it if she's still alive."

"I don't know why she would."

"Because the place is a grave to her, Lincoln. It's a memorial. You have to see that. She left a home that's worth millions sitting empty and alone for twelve years. She had a damn epitaph carved beside the door. That place means something to her. So let me tell you—if she's alive, I bet she'll come back to see it again."

Chapter Twenty

There are plenty of good restaurants on Murray Hill, but Mama Santa's pizzeria is one of the oldest and best known. Ken and I were ahead of the lunch crowd and got a table in the back of the dark, wood-paneled dining room.

"I hope Mike sits next to you," I said as we took our seats.

"He's that big?"

"Three hundred at least."

"That's not tiny."

"I knew a guy who worked a surveillance with him once, said Mike brought this feed bag of beef jerky along, like five pounds of the stuff. Went through that in the first hour, then spent the rest of the night bitching about how hungry he was. Guy said the longer the surveillance went on, the less he liked the way Mike looked at him, started to feel like he was out with the Donner Party."

Ken smiled as he leaned back from the table, stretched out his long legs, and crossed his feet at the ankles. "What's your best surveillance story? Or worst experience, rather. Those usually make the best stories."

"That's easy. I was in an unmarked car by myself not long after I switched to narcotics and started working with Joe. This is early on, and Joe was something of a legend, so I'm trying to impress, right? Well, it's February, bad snowstorm had just blown through, left it cold as a bastard, and my lovely and charming fiancée—yes, I was engaged, and no, it didn't stick—she's feeling bad for me and decides to give me a present. One of these heated pads for the car seat, you plug it into the cigarette lighter. I was embarrassed by the damn thing since it didn't exactly feed the tough-guy image I was trying to cultivate. I threw it in the car, though, because I didn't want to hurt her feelings.

"So, the night of this surveillance, we sit on the guy's house for hours, and nothing happens. Started in late afternoon, and now it's two in the morning and our guy hasn't moved, which means neither have we. It's getting colder and colder, just crawling into my bones, you know, and I figure, hell, might as well her gift for a little while, just long enough to warm up. I plugged it in for maybe twenty minutes. Half hour at best."

Ken's smile widened as he saw where I was headed.

"Thing warms me up, and now I understand why—it must have been burning watts like a set of stadium lights. I unplug it about an hour before our guy moves. He comes out of the house and gets into his car, and I think, *finally*, and turn the key."

"Click," Ken said, and laughed.

I nodded. "Click. Absolutely no juice, battery's dead. So I have to get on the radio with Joe and say, uh, our boy's in motion, but I can't tail him until I get a jump."

"You tell him what killed the battery?"

"Hell no. You kidding me? I spent the next three weeks bitching about the shitty unmarked cars they gave us. Joe *still* doesn't know the truth about that one."

"Nice."

"All right, your turn," I said.

"You'll like this—worst surveillance I ever went on was a fake surveillance."

"A fake surveillance?"

"I have—*had*, rather—a brother-in-law who I simply could not stand. He was older than my wife, had the protective big brother thing going on, but he was also just a dick, you know? Owned a car lot, made piles of money, told bad jokes and laughed at them way too loud. Only his own jokes, though. Never cracked a smile at anything anybody else had to say, but when *he'd* make a joke he always cut up, roared at his own dazzling wit. When we first got married, my patience with him could last about an hour. That's how long I could stand to be in the same room. That time frame diminished over the years."

"I can imagine."

"One Friday night my wife informs me that he's coming by for dinner, and I thought, oh, shit, not on a weekend. Because on the weekends he liked to hit the bottle, and when he did that, he lingered longer and laughed louder. So I thought, just tell one little white lie and give yourself a night off. Tell them you have to work, a rush surveillance job came up, and then go sit in a bar and watch a basketball game."

"Good plan."

"That's what I thought. When I came home that night, I planned to sell the story to my wife by picking up a tripod and acting real annoyed at this last-minute development. Well, the son of a bitch was already there. He'd shown up early. So he started asking a thousand questions about the surveillance, what it is that I do, all of that. I was edging for the door, he was following me with beer in hand, and just as I was about to escape, he turned to my wife and said, 'Hey, you wouldn't mind if I skipped dinner and tagged along with Ken, would you?'"

I started to laugh.

"Yeah," Ken said, nodding. "Of course she agreed to it. So now instead of dealing with this asshole over dinner in my own home, with my wife to distract him, I've got him alone, and in my car."

"Without any surveillance to do."

"Exactly. So I thought, well, what the hell can you do at this point but play it out? I drove us to some apartment complex, just picked one at random, and gave him a story about what we were watching for. We sat there for five hours, him drinking and talking and pointing at every car that came and went—'is that them, is that them?'"

"That's fantastic," I said. "A cautionary tale."

We traded a few more war stories while we waited. Ken asked if I had a surveillance theme song, and I had to laugh.

"A theme song? Are you kidding me? You play the *Mission Impossible* sound track when you're working?"

"Everybody should have a theme song," he said, unbothered, "and, no, mine's not the *Mission Impossible* sound track. Song's called 'Cold Trail Blues.' By a guy named Peter Case. Ever heard it?"

I shook my head.

"Thing speaks to me," he said with a faint grin. "Speaks about the Cantrells, too. All about some guy searching through the gloom, wondering if he'll ever find what he's looking for. Thinking it's too late, and he's too far behind."

"If that's your theme song," I said, "it's no damn wonder that you haven't found Alexandra yet. Encouraging shit."

His smile was hollow. "I'll burn you a copy."

When Mike finally entered, it was twenty past twelve. He wedged in through the door, lumbered across the room, extended his hand, and set to work crushing my fingers. A Mike London handshake was both a greeting and a warning, I always thought.

"How are you, Mike?"

"Hungry. I am hungry, Lincoln, my boy." He turned and cast an interrogator's stare down at Ken. "You're Pennsylvania?"

"Ken Merriman."

"From Pennsylvania," Mike said, as if that dismissed any need for Ken to have a name. A location would suffice. He dropped into the chair beside Ken and heaved his bulk up to the table's edge. I saw Ken trying to slide closer to the wall to make room for him, and I had to hide a grin.

"The way we got to Bertoli," I began, but Mike lifted a hand to silence me.

"I need a menu and a waitress. Then you can tell me all that shit."

We got him a menu and a waitress, and once the food was ordered he drained his glass of water as if it were a shot and said, "All right, get to it."

"Ken was hired by the parents of Joshua Cantrell a while back," I said. "Do you remember that story?"

"Guy went missing with his wife and was found last winter."

"That's him, yeah. We're trying to figure out how he ended up dead and in Pennsylvania, and where the wife went."

"We? How'd you get involved?"

It froze me for a moment, and even Ken gave me an odd look, because it shouldn't have been that difficult a question to answer. Eventually I forced a grin and said, "Just doing what I do, Mike. Just doing what I do."

His eyebrows knit together, as if he thought it was a bullshit answer or at least a strange one, and then he said, "Whatever. None of my business. Let's hear the questions."

"Seems the Cantrells were involved in an offender reentry program, had a bunch of parolees working out at their place, and Bertoli was one of them," I said. It was a cursory version, certainly, but that's all I wanted to give him right now. He didn't need to know about Harrison or Graham or Dunbar. Not yet.

"He was," Mike said, nodding his enormous head. He'd grown a beard since I'd last seen him, which added even more size. "You probably know that their vanishing act was almost simultaneous with Bertoli getting whacked."

"You say getting whacked," Ken said. "That's the perspective we've heard from some others, too, but the cause of death was given as an accident."

"That's right."

"Well, why wasn't there an investigation, if the evidence pointed to homicide?"

"There was an investigation, friend. I ran it. As for the death ruling, you got to look at physical evidence. That's the key. And the *physical* evidence didn't point to a homicide, necessarily. Guy took a fall off a warehouse, clipped his head on a Dumpster, then bounced off the pavement, and turned his face inside out. Nasty way to go, but the cause of death was the fall. That's something I won't dispute. Whether he took that fall willingly . . . I have strong feelings about that, but my strong feelings weren't going to get the cause of death changed. Fall killed him. What triggered the fall, we couldn't say for sure. No physical evidence to suggest that anybody pitched him off the roof. Someone could have, and probably did, but we couldn't prove that."

"There's an FBI agent named John Dunbar," I said, "who knew a hell of a lot about what was going on with Bertoli. Did he approach you?"

Mike smiled. "Oh, you know Dunbar, eh?"

"Uh-huh. You have some problems with him?"

"Not exactly. He was cooperative as hell once Bertoli was dead, but more hindrance than help. He might not have realized it, but other people did."

"What do you mean?"

"Dunbar told you what, exactly? About Bertoli?"

"That he was a potential witness against Dominic Sanabria, and Dunbar was working with Joshua Cantrell to get information out of him."

"He mention that he was retired at the time?"

"What?"

"Yeah, Lincoln. Dunbar was retired from the Bureau when all this shit went down. Everything he told you about his plan with Bertoli and Cantrell is accurate, but it was also unofficial. The Feds had no idea what was going on, because he wasn't working for them anymore. There was no law enforcement involvement, period. Dunbar's idea was that he'd go to them when he had something to show. Didn't pan out, did it?"

My disbelief turned quickly to understanding. The previous day I'd had trouble believing that the FBI could have implemented such a ludicrous plan, placing Bertoli in the home of Sanabria's sister and using Cantrell as an informant. Now I understood—the FBI *hadn't* implemented the plan. It had been Dunbar and Cantrell, working alone.

"That makes sense," I said. "Hell, that's the only way it makes sense. The whole idea was insane. If they never approved it, that means—"

"He was running his own show with Cantrell," Mike said. "Which tells you two things. One, the only official version is the one Dunbar provided, because everybody else who was involved is dead or missing, and, two, the man had a king-sized hard-on for Dominic Sanabria. I mean, he turned

Sanabria into a retirement project? Pro bono prosecution? Crazy shit."

Ken said, "So everything Dunbar did with Cantrell was completely—"

"Unsupervised," Mike said. "Yes. When Bertoli took his header off the roof—with or without assistance—and Dunbar came forward with his story, you can imagine how elated his Feeb buddies were. Then the Cantrells bailed, and the whole thing started to smell even worse."

"So they squashed the investigation?" I said. "Are you kidding me? To protect Dunbar?"

"I wouldn't say that they squashed it, really. I mean, I did work the case for a while, and worked it hard. We couldn't get anything convincing to go on. Everybody understood that Sanabria probably had the guy killed, but we couldn't get a lead to work with. Bertoli was a piece of shit anyhow, nobody was crying over his loss, and the last thing the FBI wanted was Dunbar's story going public. Wouldn't have been anything criminal, but it also wouldn't have made them look good. A rogue retiree placing informants without anybody's knowledge, and then the informant gets killed? No, that wouldn't have made them look good."

"Nobody thought it was worth looking for the Cantrells?"

"We looked."

"Not very forcefully," Ken said. "The police told his family that they wouldn't investigate. Told them—"

"Cantrells left of their own volition. That's the way it looked at the time, at least. Packed a bunch of shit into storage and made arrangements for the house. There was no sign that one of them had been killed. Not until the body showed up."

"You said you worked the Bertoli case hard," I said.

"I did. Even if the death ruling wasn't a homicide, we treated it like one as soon as Dunbar came forward. You have to give the guy that much credit, too—at least he showed up and told the truth when Bertoli got killed. A lot of people wouldn't have the balls to do that. He had to know it wasn't going to go over well with his buddies at the Bureau. Took some swallowed pride to come forward, I'm sure."

"You never got anything that showed a connection between his death and Sanabria, though?"

"I got something, but it was weak. It wasn't enough to build a case on." He stopped talking as the waitress passed nearby and eyed her tray hopefully, then sighed with disappointment when she delivered the food to the table beside us.

"What did you get?" I said.

"Lasagna and—"

"Not the food, Mike. I mean on the case. What was the connection?"

"Oh, right. Well, there was a place across from the warehouse where Bertoli died that had parking lot surveillance cameras. It didn't show the scene, but it caught cars coming and going. Problem was, the street was fairly busy. In just one hour around Bertoli's time of death, there were sixty-two cars on the tape. I got all the plate numbers I could, ran registrations."

This was the sort of work ethic that Mike was famous for, a determined pursuit of any angle, no matter how long the odds.

"I got one car, and one car only, that had some possibility," he said. "A tricked-out Oldsmobile Cutlass, all sorts of custom shit on it, spinners and crap like that. The plate ran back to a Darius Neloms. Big D, as he is generally known."

I shook my head. "Doesn't mean anything to me."

"There's a bunch of Neloms in East Cleveland, and the whole family is nothing but pushers and hustlers. Darius runs a body shop over on Eddy and St. Clair."

"Tough neighborhood."

"You ain't kidding. These days, Big D's doing well for himself. Making money putting in hydraulics and fancy rims and stereos, all the toys that the young thugs like, makes 'em feel like they're in a rap video. There was a time, though, when he took a bust for running a chop shop. Taking in stolen cars, repainting them, adding some window tint, maybe changing the headlights or the grille, and sending 'em back out. He didn't take a hard fall because they had trouble proving he knew the cars were stolen. I'm sure that was crap, but the guys bringing him the cars worked for Dominic Sanabria and a guy named Johnny DiPietro."

"Later murdered," I said, "and Dunbar thinks it was by Sanabria, and Bertoli was a witness."

"You got it."

"You think Sanabria hired this Darius guy to kill Bertoli?" Ken asked.

"No way," Mike said. "He would've handled that in-house."

"It was his car at the scene."

"It was registered to him. One of about nine vehicles he had registered to him or his shop. When Bertoli died, Darius was at a party at a nightclub, which I verified by their security tapes."

"So maybe it's a meaningless connection," Ken said.

"Could be, but Darius Neloms was connected to Dominic Sanabria and Johnny DiPietro, had gone to jail for working with them on stolen cars in the past. If somebody in their crew wanted to borrow a car, Darius was a likely source."

"Why in the hell would they borrow a car," I said, "instead of stealing one?"

Mike smiled. "Look at the result. I spent time chasing leads on Darius—and don't kid yourself into thinking the Italians viewed him as some sort of compatriot. A bunch of racist fucks, those guys. They're not above working with a black guy to bring in some dollars, but they damn sure aren't going to worry about redirecting police his way, either."

"You talk to Darius?"

"Uh-huh, and got nothing. 'I own lots of cars, lots of people have access to them cars, no way I could possibly remember who might've been driving that car on that night.'"

"What was your sense of him?"

"That he was lying, of course—but was he lying with a real purpose? Guy like Darius Neloms, he doesn't necessarily need the extra motivation to lie to me. See a badge, lie to the badge."

"So that's where the case died?"

"That's where it died. I ran that up the ladder, you know,

showing there was at least a weak link between one of the cars and Sanabria, but of course it wasn't enough. No evidence for a homicide, nobody talking to us, the FBI boys embarrassed by the whole thing because of Dunbar, it's almost surprising I got that far with it."

I saw the waitress headed our way again and figured this time the food would be ours, and that meant Mike wasn't going to be answering any more questions for a while. Best to slide in one more while I had his attention.

"A few minutes ago you made a good point, saying that Dunbar's version is the only official one, since the whole damn circus he put together was so *un*official."

Mike nodded, waiting.

"So I'm wondering—did you believe that version? That one unsupported but also unconfirmed version?"

Mike said, "Look, Dunbar was one of a group of FBI guys that did some righteous work on the mob around here. Put a lot of those boys in prison."

"But?"

"But Dunbar also wore a suit every day, and one of the rules I've developed after twenty years at this game, Lincoln, is never trust a man in a suit."

Chapter Twenty-one

Amazing, the way one fact can change your entire perception of something.

John Dunbar was *retired* at the time he launched his plan with Bertoli and Cantrell? Nobody else approved it, or even knew about it? Yeah, that changed things.

His plan had been terrible, too, a perversion of an old cop game that had never worked well in my experience—planting a snitch in a jail cell. There were plenty of narcs in the prison system, and it was a tactic that had been used for decades, generally off the books, and rarely well. The problem was that the snitches lied, that they had no credibility in court, and that the targets were rarely anywhere near as stupid as required for the tactic to work. Joshua Cantrell had effectively played the role of a jail cell snitch in his own home, welcoming Bertoli in and trying to talk to him about a mob hit. Made it a great deal more difficult to be sneaky about that sort of thing when your wife was the sister of the suspect. They could have concealed that from Bertoli initially—and surely did, otherwise I couldn't imagine he'd have actually agreed to the parole assignment—but eventually it would have had to surface, wouldn't it?

Yes, it was stupid, and Dunbar had known that all along; otherwise he wouldn't have operated without FBI approval, and that made me wonder about both his motivations and his story. I hadn't doubted him at first, not in our initial talk, but at the time I had felt like everything he said was a breakthrough, had been almost overwhelmed by the story he told. Now I looked back on it, playing through the conversation again in my mind, looking for holes, signs of lies.

There were dozens of them. Maybe. Or the whole story could have been entirely truthful. No way to know because every other person who could confirm it was dead or missing, and had been for years.

Except for Parker Harrison.

He was on my mind during our drive back from Murray Hill, and because of that it didn't feel like much of a surprise when I checked the office voice mail and found a message from him.

The request was simple this time, no tips or names or suggestions. Harrison wanted to see me that evening, if possible, and he wanted me to be alone. He didn't leave any other details, just said he'd be home after five and repeated that he wanted it to be only me.

I played the message on speakerphone, so Ken heard it, too.

"Guy doesn't seem to like me, does he?" he said.

"Your client relationship does seem a bit strained."

"Because he knows damn well he's not really a client. The way we tried to play it didn't fool him. Not enough, at least."

"Not at all, would be my guess," I said.

There were no messages from Graham, even though we'd been late getting back from Murray Hill, almost two thirty, and Graham had predicted an arrival time of one. I assumed he would've called if he'd come in early, though; it was too long a drive to give up on us just because nobody was at the office.

I kept staring at the phone, even though the blinking message light was now gone, nobody but Harrison leaving words behind for me. I wished Joe would call, so I could throw all of this at him, let him offer some perspective. It had been a few days since we'd last talked.

"I'll tell you what," Ken said, "the more I think about it, the more I wonder what Harrison did out there. Or what he saw. We're making sense of everything else, slowly but surely.

We understand Bertoli's role now, know that they were trying to use him as a witness and it went bad—but Harrison? I can't make sense of him. Not even close."

Nor could I. Or Graham, or Dunbar, or Mike London. A lot of people had considered Harrison, and nobody had made sense of him yet.

While I was staring at the phone and pondering Harrison, there were footsteps on the stairs, and then the door opened without any knock and Quinn Graham entered. He was dressed sharp—black pants with a gold shirt and black-and-gold tie, and when I looked at him I thought of Mike London's warning never to trust a man in a suit and smiled. Most detectives wore suits every day. Only a guy like Mike could distrust the daily wardrobe of his own peers.

"Happy to see me?" Graham said, noting my amused face.

"Sure, Graham. We're elated."

He shook hands with Ken and then took a chair, looked at me, and spread his hands. "Brother, this better be good. I'll tell you something about the drive between my home and here—it ain't pretty. Not gonna be on anyone's scenic route list real soon. I keep making it, though, because of you boys, because of Linc and Kenny. Hope you appreciate that."

"Graham, you'll be thanking us by the time you leave," I said. "We've made some breakthroughs for you, buddy. Big stuff."

"Yeah?" His interest was genuine.

"Yesterday we learned"—I threw in a pause, enjoying the impatience in his eye—"that Salvatore Bertoli was, in fact, placed in the Cantrell home by an FBI agent named John Dunbar."

I said this with heavy drama, straight-faced, as if I really believed he'd be impressed.

"He was believed to be a witness to a killing committed by Dominic Sanabria," I continued after another pause. "Joshua Cantrell was working with Dunbar to extract information from Bertoli. Evidently it did not work well."

Graham stayed silent.

"Pretty big stuff, eh?" I said.

"Right," he said, but the disgust was clear in his voice.

"What's the matter, Graham? You thinking about those hours you wasted on the road?"

"You know all of this is old to me," he said, "yet you made me drive up here."

"I know it's old to *you*, yes. It wasn't old to us, and it's something we wasted a day on, when you could have told us the same things in about fifteen minutes. So you want to worry about the time you spent driving up here, tough shit, man. You let us walk around like a couple of—"

"I didn't want you walking anywhere, Perry. Don't you get that? I don't know how you found Dunbar, but I wish you hadn't. If you'd have called—"

"I did call. Yesterday morning, after we got Dunbar's name and were standing downtown feeling like hot shit. It's embarrassing to admit now, but that's the truth of it. You got a problem with us talking to Dunbar? Well, you could've prevented that easy enough."

He sighed and leaned forward, then ran a hand along the side of his head and gripped the back of his own neck and squeezed as if he were trying to calm himself down.

"I know you were police, Linc," he said, "but you gotta realize, you are *not* police anymore. So when you get all fired up over shit you weren't told, slow down and think about the situation from my point of view, which is: I'm not telling anybody a *damn thing* that I don't have to. Ever. I'm trying to maintain control of my investigation."

It was exactly what I'd expected he'd say, but that didn't mean it pleased me.

"Graham, you asked for our help. Sat right there in that chair and asked for—"

"No, no, no." He looked up, shaking his head. "Didn't ask for anybody's *help*, Linc. What I asked for, and what I expected to receive, was your *cooperation*. Big difference, boy. You had access to Harrison, and that's where I wanted your cooperation. What I did *not* want, at any time, was for you two to go running around the city interviewing people and knocking on doors and potentially damaging my case. I as good as told you that, too."

"When?"

"I said that I was counting on you to keep him from stepping to trouble." Graham jerked his head at Ken, and I saw a flush of anger—or embarrassment—cross Ken's face. "Now I find out I should've been just as worried about you as him."

He sighed again, shook his head again, and then leaned back and loosened his tie. "Here's what I want out of you two, okay? Communication with Harrison. That's it, and that's all. I don't want you to *force* the communication, either. I just want to be aware of it. Tape the talks when he initiates them, and that's great. As far as street work goes, I don't want you on this."

"That's not really your call," Ken said.

Graham looked at him with wide, challenging eyes, his index finger still hooked in the knot of his tie. "It's not? You get in the way of a police investigation, and don't think I can shut you down? Boy, you don't even have a client."

"I do now," Ken said.

"Who?"

"Parker Harrison. He retained me through Lincoln. I believe that scenario was your idea, too."

Graham scowled and released his tie after one last angry jerk.

"Hang on a minute," I said as he was getting ready to start in on Ken again. "We can all fight this one out later. Fact is, Ken's got a client, and you gave it to him, Graham. Regardless, I don't think Ken has any desire to hinder what you've done, or what you're trying to do. If we don't know what that is, though, we're bound to cause you some headaches."

"I told you my reasoning."

"Yes, and I understand it, but what I'd like to hear you say is what you actually think of John Dunbar. I'm assuming you know he was retired at the time all this went down?"

Graham gave one last stare to Ken, not ready to let that battle fade so quickly, but then he returned his attention to me.

"Dunbar's straight," he said. "I know it doesn't feel right, but he's straight."

"How can you say that with any confidence when there's nobody around to support his story?"

"Nobody around to contradict it, either, but the fact is the man could not be more cooperative," he said. "The day after we ID'd the body as Joshua Cantrell, I got a call from Dunbar, wanting to fill me in. He initiated the contact. I had no idea who he was at that point, or what his connection was, and I would've wasted a lot of hours developing that. Instead, he drove out to see me, brought boxes of shit out with him, photos and notes that he'd taken. Left it all with me, for my review. If the man's got anything to hide, he's got a strange manner of hiding it. He was calling me a couple times a week for a while, throwing theories and suggestions until I stopped calling him back because he was underfoot so damn much. Hell, it was him that pointed me to Sanabria's phone records, showed he'd been in touch with Harrison."

"Did you make any attempt to verify his version of events?"

"Of course I did, and the man checks out, Linc. You want to do the same, go ahead. He served thirty years in the FBI, thirty *strong* years, and if you can get anyone to say a bad word about him, it'll be in the way things went with Bertoli."

"Well, I'd imagine. You've got someone murdering an FBI informant that nobody in the FBI knew was an informant, yeah, that's a problem."

"Sure it is. Everyone involved acknowledged that, both at the time and when I got in touch this year. That doesn't make Dunbar corrupt, though."

"What about Mark Ruzity?" I said. "The guy seems to have some anger issues. Put a chisel to my forehead while telling us the case was better off unsolved. Then Dunbar showed us a photo of him with Sanabria just days after the Cantrells vanished. How do you explain that?"

"I can't. You know who took that picture? Dunbar himself. He'd started following Sanabria after he realized Joshua was MIA. Yes, while he was retired. Yes, acting unofficially. I get your problem with that, Linc, I do, but I'm telling you the man is truly trying to help. Without him, we'd never know Ruzity and Sanabria had any association."

"So now you know that they do, but you don't know *why*."

"Not yet."

"Bertoli was openly connected to Sanabria's circle before he went into prison," I said. "Now we know that both Ruzity and Harrison had contact with him after they came out. What in the hell was going on in that house, Graham?"

"I'm not sure."

"Yet you want our help, and you expect to get it without telling us a damn thing."

Graham lifted his hands, palms out, and made a patting gesture. Soothing. *Step back, relax, everybody be happy.*

"Look, I understand your irritation, but what we need to make clear is that I can't afford to have you guys in my way. What've you done here, it's no big deal. Talking to Dunbar is nothing, but I can't have you keep after it. Eventually you may talk to the wrong person, maybe before I do, and then we've got a real problem."

"So you're telling us to stop the investigation?" Ken said.

"No, I'm telling you not to harm the *real* investigation. The one that'll get somebody arrested and convicted if it's done right, and will let 'em walk if it's done wrong. I'm here to see that it's done right."

"Which means—"

"Which means you probably ought to go on back home." He said it gently but met Ken's eyes. "That's no disrespect, Kenny. Okay? The truth of it is, man, there ain't nothing for you to do that the police can't do better."

Ken looked at me, eyes hot, as if he were waiting for me to jump into the fray and argue. When I stayed silent, he turned back to Graham.

"What *are* the police doing? A few days ago you were in here telling us how overstretched you are. Sounded to me like you needed the help."

"All right," Graham said, still with the temperate touch in his voice, "then why don't you tell me what you're going to do to help?"

Again Ken looked at me. "Detective work, Graham. That's what we're going to do."

"And that means?"

"Getting out on the street, talking to witnesses, running down leads," Ken said, anger in his voice now. He seemed to think Graham was talking down to him, patronizing, but I didn't read it that way. Graham was trying not to bruise egos, but the reality was he wanted us out of the way because he didn't think we could do anything but harm.

"All of which I've done, and will continue to do," Graham said. "You'll end up right where I am now, Kenny—staring down Sanabria and Harrison."

"So you're saying this one's unsolvable?" Ken said. "Time to put it under wraps, nothing left to do?"

Graham shook his head. "I intend to solve it. I think we will. We should have lab results from the body and the grave in a few months, maybe in a few weeks if we're lucky, and hopefully those will open up some doors. I expect that they will."

"So you want to shut us down," Ken said, "but at the same time you want us to communicate with Harrison. Well, the communication he wants is about our progress on the investigation. Going to be pretty difficult to sit around and chat with him if we're not doing anything."

Graham's jaw worked as he looked at Ken.

"He makes a fair point," I said. "You can't have it both ways, Graham. Either we're involved or we're not. You make the call."

"Okay—you're out."

Ken bristled, but I just nodded. "All right. I guess I better call Harrison, then, tell him tonight's meeting is off."

"You plan a meeting with him?"

"No. He called today and requested one. Seems he's got some things on his mind. Wanted to have a talk."

Graham was looking at me as if considering how satisfying it would be to pop my head right off my neck, but finally he sighed and nodded.

"Go talk to him, then. See what he says, get it on tape, and then call me. Do *not*, under any circumstance, talk to anyone else until you've cleared it with me. Got it?"

"Got it."

"While I'm here, I want a copy of the tape from your last talk, too."

"I burned it onto a CD for you."

"Good. At least I'll get something out of this drive." He stood up and reached for the CD. "You have any idea what Harrison wants?"

"None," I said.

Graham slid the CD into his pocket, then looked at both of us silently.

"Don't worry, Graham," I said. "You'll learn to love us."

"That's what my wife told me when she got a dog—and you know what?"

"What?"

"Time to time, dog still shits on my rug."

Chapter Twenty-two

Ken wanted to ride out to Harrison's house with me, but I didn't like that idea. Harrison had requested a one-on-one meeting, for whatever reason, and I didn't want to irritate him by leaving Ken sitting in my car in the parking lot. So instead I left him sitting at a bar, with Amy for a conversation partner.

"You're not real good with the art of relationships," she observed as I drove her to the Rocky River Brewing Company, a microbrewery that was one of Amy's favorite drinking venues. "It's not exactly standard for a guy to take his girlfriend to a bar and drop her off with orders to entertain another man."

"I'm not telling you to sleep with him. Just buy him some drinks, maybe give him a shoulder rub."

"Yeah, it's a stunner that your fiancée ended up with another guy. A true puzzle."

By the time we got there, Ken was already at the bar, halfway through a beer called the Lakeshore Electric. He stood up when we approached, and I made introductions, wishing like hell that I could just stay with the two of them instead of driving off for yet another strange conversation with Parker Harrison.

"I'll head back this way when I'm done with our boy," I said to Ken. "Until then, watch your ass around Amy. She's a mean drinker."

By the time I got to the door, I could already hear her apologizing for me. It's not an uncommon occurrence.

Then it was back to Old Brooklyn, as the twilight settled in warm and still and with the wet touch of humidity that promised real summer. I kept the windows down and turned James McMurtry up loud on the stereo and thought that it would be a perfect night to sit in the outfield, watching one of those spring games that can't help but be fun because it's too early to feel much concern or disappointment over your team. Maybe if Harrison didn't want too much of my time, we could do that. I knew Amy would be up for it, and what else did Ken have to do?

By the time I reached Harrison's apartment, there was nothing left of the sun but a thin orange line on the horizon, the streetlights were on, and James McMurtry had just finished explaining why he was tired of walking and wanted to ride. I'd put the recorder and wire on before I left my apartment, and now I adjusted my collar and gave one quick look in the mirror to be sure the microphone wasn't visible. It wasn't. I got out and walked up to Harrison's apartment, found the window dark. The door opened at my first knock, though, and Harrison stood in front of me with a dish towel in his hands, his forearms streaked with moisture. Behind him I could see a light on in the kitchen, the living room gloomy with nothing but the fading daylight.

"Lincoln. Come in."

I stepped through the door, and he closed it behind me. Now I wanted a lamp on.

"You mind turning on a—"

"You both need to stop."

"What?"

"You and Ken Merriman. Tell him to keep the money. Or you keep the money. Either way, I think you both need to stop. Send him home."

"Why?"

He didn't answer but also didn't look away.

"Harrison? What the hell is going on?"

He wet his lips. "Lincoln, do you remember what I told you at first? The reason I wanted to find Alexandra?"

"You wanted to be in touch with her."

"No. Well, yes, that was part of it, but what I told you I wanted most was—"

"To know what happened. To know the story."

He nodded. "It's not worth it."

"Not worth *what*?"

He shifted his weight and dropped his eyes for the first time, saw the towel in his hands, and used it to dry his arms.

"Harrison, damn it, tell me what the hell is going on."

"It's not worth the potential for harm," he said.

"Harm to . . ."

"You, Ken Merriman, anyone else. Everyone else. At the end of the day, Lincoln, I think I made a mistake. She left because she wanted to leave, and if she hasn't been back . . . well, I suppose she wants to stay where she is. Right? Unfound and unbothered. If that's what Alexandra wants, then I won't fight for something contrary to it."

"I'm still not following this sudden worry about harm."

"It doesn't matter if you're following it. The last time we talked, you told me you didn't want to work for me, so now I'm giving you good news—I don't want you to work for me, either. Not you, or Merriman, or anybody else."

What had changed his mind? Something we'd done that he knew about? Had he seen us with Graham or Mike London, somehow developed the idea that we were working with police? Or was it entirely different and unrelated to us?

"Harrison—"

"This isn't a discussion. I appreciate your reconsideration, the way you brought an investigator to me, but I'm done."

Now I was more aware of the recorder and the possibilities that were about to be terminated when Harrison threw me out. We'd gotten nothing from him. Not a word that would help the investigation.

"What do you know about the Cantrells?" I said, taking a step toward him even though there wasn't much space between us. "About what happened to them?"

"What I know isn't enough to matter."

"Bullshit. I saw your eyes when we mentioned Bertoli's name, Harrison. Why?"

"Lincoln, there's nothing I can say."

"According to the police, that's always been your response. Nothing to say—but it's a lie, Harrison, and you know it."

"You've talked to the police about me? To Graham?"

I hesitated only briefly. "Of course I did. You're a convicted killer, like it or not, and you wanted me to look into a murder case. Don't you think that raised some questions in my head?"

He stood where he was and looked into my eyes as if he were taking inventory, and then he reached out with a quick and sure motion and grasped the edge of my shirt collar, and tugged it back, tearing the first button loose. As he did that, he ran his other hand down my spine, checking for a wire. I tried to counter, shoving his hand away and stepping back, but it was too late. His eyes had found the thin black wire, standing out stark against my white skin.

"Whose idea?" he said. "Yours or Graham's?"

"Mine." I took a few steps back, feeling exposed now, vulnerable. He hadn't moved again, but as I stood there in the dark living room facing him I found myself wishing I had my gun. I hadn't brought it in because Harrison hadn't seemed the least bit threatening in our previous meetings. Now his stance and his face made the Glock noticeably absent.

"Leave, Lincoln," he said. "Leave, and let it go. Don't let anybody else keep you involved. Not Graham, not Merriman, not anybody."

I waited for a moment, staring back at a face that looked to be caught between fear and anger, and then I went for the door. Harrison didn't move as I opened it and stepped out.

I stood on the welcome mat in front of his apartment and blew out a trapped breath and looked down at my shirt, the microphone dangling bare and obvious. I took it off and untucked my shirt and slid the whole contraption out and kept it in my hand as I walked to my truck. When I started the engine, the headlights came on automatically, shining directly into Harrison's windows. The glass reflected an image of my truck back at me, but beyond that I could see the shadows of Harrison's apartment, and his silhouette standing directly in the middle of the room, watching me. He was holding a phone to his ear.

Chapter Twenty-three

I called Graham as I drove away from Harrison's building, got the phone out and dialed without pause because I knew if I stopped to think about it I'd delay calling him. He wasn't going to be pleased with this.

It took about twenty seconds of conversation before he confirmed that idea, breaking into a burst of sustained profanity that might have impressed me had I not been its target. No, he wasn't pleased.

"Graham, there's nothing I would have done differently," I said when he finally paused for a breath.

"Nothing you would have done—"

"No. There's not. It was nothing I said that convinced him I was wearing a wire; he was already pretty sure of it. The way he went for my shirt, Graham—he knew I was wearing one. He was sure he'd find it."

"Beautiful, Perry."

"I don't know what to say, Graham. Sorry it went like that, but it was your idea."

"My bad idea," he said. "I'll readily admit that. I let you and your buddy get into this, and I shouldn't have."

I kept the phone pressed to my ear as I hammered the accelerator and pulled onto the interstate, took it up to eighty-five before letting off. It was silent for a while, Graham's breathing heavy with irritation.

"Okay," he said finally. "Okay, it's done. It was a bad idea, and it didn't work, and maybe it did some harm. We can't really tell yet."

"I'm more interested in what changed his mind."

"What changed his mind was the fact that he knew you were trying to con him. What changed his mind was knowing you were taping every conversation."

There was biting accusation in every word, as if he thought I'd gone into Harrison's home with a microphone labeled POLICE PROPERTY in my hand and started asking him questions about Cantrell's death. I gave it a few beats of silence again, not wanting to let this turn into a clash of egos.

"I warned you after our first attempt that I thought he saw through it," I said. "Back then, you didn't want to believe me. That's fine. What I'm telling you tonight is, I don't think that's all there was to it. Something else rattled him."

"That's terrific, Linc. I'll find out what it was. In the meantime, you—"

"He called somebody as soon as I left. You might want to check that."

"How do you know?"

"He was standing with the phone to his ear when I drove away. Kind of curious who he felt deserved such an immediate call."

"Could be somebody called him."

"I didn't hear the phone ring."

"All right, look, I'll see about that, but as I was saying, *in the meantime*, you go find Kenny and you send him home. I want you both off of this, immediately. Like I said before, I take some of the blame. Maybe it was a bad idea from the start, but now it's done. I want you and him as far away from this as possible."

"I'm not sure how easy it'll be to convince Ken."

"It'll be damn easy when I arrest him for interference. You tell him that, and if he has a problem with it, you tell him to call me. He doesn't have a client anymore, and he's not licensed in Ohio. In other words, he's mine, Linc. If I want to shut him down, I can."

Not much was said after that. I disconnected, threw the

phone onto the floor of the passenger seat, and drove back to the brewery. It was more crowded than when I'd left; I had to shoulder past people bottlenecked just inside the doors. Amy and Ken were where I'd left them, though, fresh pints on the bar in front of them. They were facing each other, and Ken was grinning at Amy's animated words.

"Hey," she said, turning when she saw Ken's eyes go over her shoulder to me. "I was just explaining my favorite psychological phenomenon to Ken."

"Which one is that?"

"The way the world's most pathologically narcissistic people seem drawn to careers in newspaper management."

Ken started to laugh, but then he stopped, eyes still on me, a frown replacing his smile. "Didn't go well with Harrison?"

I shook my head and leaned on the bar in between them, gesturing at the bartender for a beer. "Didn't go well, no."

"What happened?"

I told them about it while I drank the beer. When I got to the part about Harrison finding the wire, Amy sighed and turned away from me, fear disguised as anger.

"Not your fault," Ken said, shaking his head. "He didn't have to find the wire. He already knew."

"That's exactly what I told Graham."

"Oh, you already talked to him? What'd he have to say?"

I took a long drink of my beer, staring up at the TV. Indians had been up one when I walked in, and now they were down two.

"Well?" Ken said.

"He wasn't happy. Spent a while swearing at me and calling me incompetent before he decided to man up and accept part of the blame, realized it was probably a silly ploy to try in the first place."

"He say what comes next?"

"I assume it'll be back to waiting on the lab work. He seems pretty convinced that's where any break will come from."

"What about us?"

I finished my beer, slid the glass across the bar. "We're done."

"What?"

"He told me in no uncertain terms that we are to stay away from this."

"That's not his decision."

I didn't say anything.

"Is it?" he said. "Lincoln? You want to let that guy back us off?"

"It's not that simple, Ken. He can if he wants to. We don't have a client anymore. If he wants to jump up and down and scream about interference and tampering, he can do that. I don't think he wants to, but I also don't think he's going to let us keep digging on this without a fight."

Amy was quiet, watching us, and I could imagine Ken's expression from the concern in her eyes. This case mattered to him. I knew that by now; he'd made it damn clear. Still, I didn't know what else to tell him.

"So you want to stop?" he said. "This is the end? Go home and forget about it?"

"I'm not saying that."

"Yeah, you're not saying *anything*. What do you think, Lincoln?"

I drummed my fingers on the bar, not looking at either of them for a minute. The bartender pointed at my empty glass and gave me a questioning eye, and I nodded at him. I didn't speak again until the fresh beer was in my hand.

"I think that you care about this one too much to go home and forget about it—but I also want to point out that it's been twelve years since they took off, and six months since his body was found. Plenty of time's already passed, right? So I don't see the harm, really, in letting it breathe for a few more weeks. Let Graham get his lab results. On a case this old, the breaks usually do come from the lab."

"What if they don't?"

"If they don't, we figure out how to move forward, yet after talking to Graham tonight, I think it's a good idea to let it breathe, Ken. At least for a few weeks. We want to assist the police investigation, not slow it down by fighting with them."

He was quiet, clearly unsatisfied. He looked up at Amy as

if searching for support, then flicked his eyes down when he didn't find any there.

"So I head home," he said.

"I'm not telling you that. Graham is. Although I think there's probably more smoke than fire to that. Besides, he's angry."

"You just said you wanted to let it breathe."

I shrugged.

"Basically, Graham wants me out of it. Right?"

"It wasn't a one-person decree."

He shook his head. "Maybe not, but I'm the one he doesn't trust in it. What was it he said today? Something about how he'd essentially asked you to babysit me, make sure I didn't cause any trouble. That makes sense, too. I can't fault him for that. You've got the experience on a real investigation. I don't. Hell, I'm the one who already had a shot at this and couldn't come up with a damn thing to show for it, right?"

"Nobody else has, either."

"I guess I can take comfort in being part of a group failure." He sighed and rubbed a hand over his eyes. "So what's your take, then? Should I listen to him and pull off?"

"Let's figure it out tomorrow. Come to the office in the morning and we'll talk."

He nodded, but the energy had gone out of the night, all of us quiet now, flat.

"Hey." I slapped the bar, got both of them to look up. "I think we should tie one on tonight. Go downtown, hit some bars. Got six innings left to play, we could even buy some cheap tickets and watch the end of the game. Drink to crazy graveyard groundskeepers and asshole cops."

"And pompous, untalented editors," Amy said, lifting her glass, trying to fall in line with my forced enthusiasm. "I'm game."

Ken gave an empty smile and shook his head, standing and reaching for his wallet. "I'm out," he said. "Sorry. Not tonight."

"Oh, come on," I said. "What else do you have to do?"

"Call my daughter, for one thing."

"So call her, and then we'll go out. Show you what this beautiful city of Cleveland is all about."

"Not tonight, Lincoln. I think I'll head back to the hotel and go over my case file, make some notes."

"How many times have you been over that file? What's going to be gained from one more look?"

"You never know. Maybe I'll shake something loose yet. Convince Graham he's making a mistake." He tossed some money on the bar, then put out his hand. "We'll talk tomorrow, right?"

"Absolutely," I said, shaking his hand, then watching as Amy stood up to do the same. "Come on down to the office, and we'll get things figured out."

It didn't feel like enough, though.

Last words never do.

Chapter Twenty-four

It took a while for me to determine anything was wrong. I lingered at the bar with Amy long after Ken left, and when we finally departed it was for her apartment and a night that began in the shower and ended in the bedroom. I was aware of her moving around the next morning but managed to tune it out and return to sleep, didn't come fully awake until almost nine.

By the time I returned to my own apartment, showered, shaved, and dressed, it was nearly ten, and when I finally got to the office I expected Ken might be waiting. He wasn't, but a voice mail from him was. His voice was hurried, almost breathless.

Lincoln, I think we've got something. You got us there, we just needed to see it. Last night, I finally saw it. I'm telling you, man, I think you got us there. I'm going to check something out first, though. I don't want to throw this at you and then have you explain what I'm missing, how crazy it is—but stay tuned. Stay tuned.

I called him immediately. Five rings, then voice mail.

"What in the hell are you talking about?" I said. "Get your ass down here and tell me what you've got cooking."

I hung up and sat and stared at the phone, both impatient and irritated. My excitement was up, certainly—or at least curiosity—but I also didn't like being shut out so suddenly. He'd come all the way up here to ask for my help, practically beg for it, and against all better judgment I'd cooperated. Now he felt like he had a break and he'd gone off to field it solo? It was a greedy move, and I'd known some other investigators who pulled it when they had a chance for glory. This case was Ken's baby—he'd been working it for twelve years, not me—but I still wasn't impressed.

Thirty minutes passed. I called him again, got voice mail, didn't leave a message. Waited an hour, called again, left another message, hearing the annoyance in my own voice and not caring. It wasn't just a greedy move, I'd decided, it was a damned foolish one. With his total lack of experience on homicide cases, he could screw this up. Whatever *this* was.

Noon came and went, and I thought about lunch but didn't go for it, not wanting to leave the office phone. I was seething over the fact that he'd called the office line instead of my cell anyhow. He'd wanted to be sure he got a head start on this thing by himself, which was bullshit. I didn't give a damn who got the credit, supposing he *had* made a break—though that seemed like one hell of a long shot to me—but it was my ass that was on the line with Graham.

At two o'clock, Graham called. I recognized his number and hesitated before answering, part of me afraid he was already aware of whatever Ken was attempting and pissed off about it, another part thinking it was my job to warn him. Either way, it wasn't a conversation I wanted to have, but I answered.

"I don't know whether I should give you blame or credit," he said, "but whatever you did to stir Harrison up, he's in action again. That could be good or bad."

"What do you mean, he's in action?"

"I checked the phone call from last night. The one you mentioned."

"Yeah?"

"He called Sanabria."

Neither of us spoke for a minute, just sat there across the miles holding our respective phones and considering the possibilities.

"Okay," I said. "That's one call. Right after I left. Right after he'd told me to hang it up. Were there any others?"

"Uh-huh. One more, made day before yesterday, in the evening."

Just before Harrison had called me to ask for a meeting.

"Sanabria told him to get rid of me," I said.

"Possibly."

"How did he know I was working with Harrison to begin with? You said there hadn't been any other calls between them. Not since the body was discovered."

"They don't always have to use the phone, Linc. In fact, I'm surprised they do it this often."

"I guess."

"Another possibility is your buddy."

"Ken? Are you crazy?"

"Linc, you remember how he found his way to you?"

I was quiet.

"Sanabria," he said. "Right? Dominic Sanabria called him. That's what he told you, that's what he told me. So they've been in communication. Who says it stopped with that call?"

"Do you have any records saying it didn't?"

"No."

"Then I'm not—"

"Remember, there are plenty of other ways they could have had contact. Face-to-face, through an associate, emails, other phones. All I'm saying is let's not rule Kenny out of the mix entirely. He around?"

"No."

"Gone home?"

"No. He's in the field."

"In the *field*, you say? Doing what?"

"I have no clue."

"Excuse me?"

I told him about the message and said it was the only thing I'd heard from him all day. He responded, as expected, by reaming me for letting Ken head off into unknown avenues of investigation. My patience wasn't strong enough to take it today.

"I'm not his caretaker, Graham. I don't know the guy any better than you do, and if you want somebody monitoring him, you better get an officer on it. Last night, I told him I was done. That it was time to back off. If he doesn't do that, it's your problem, not mine."

The words sounded childish, petulant, and that only contributed to my growing anger. It had been directed at Ken originally, for cutting me out, now at Graham for blaming me for that, and only built after I hung up the phone. Another hour passed before I finally forced myself to admit that another emotion was bubbling beneath the surface: fear. I was beginning to hear the first drumbeats of dread. Where was Ken?

In the next hour, I called his cell six times and got voice mail every time. I left two messages, then called his hotel and asked to be put through to the room. Again, just rings and a voice mail option.

At twenty till five, I got in my truck and drove to his hotel, went up to room 712 and pounded on the door. No answer. I took the elevator back down to the lobby, stood in the corner, and looked the reception desk over. Two clerks working, one male and one female. I'd talked to a guy on the phone, which meant he'd be more sensitive to Ken's name. Ken had been there a few days, and there was a chance both of the clerks knew him by now, but it was a big hotel, busy, and I thought I'd take a chance. I waited until the guy took a phone call, then approached the woman with a rapid step, feigning great annoyance, and told her I'd locked my keycard in the room.

"Okay, sir, if you could tell me—"

"Room 712, the name is Merriman."

"All right, 712 . . . I've got it. Now, can I see some ID?"

I gave her my best look of condescending patience, as if I were dealing with a child, and said, "Um, I'm locked out, remember?"

She stared at me.

"Wallet's in the room," I said. "I was just running down the hall to get some ice."

No ice bucket in hand, but she didn't seem likely to notice that or care.

"Well, I would have no way of knowing that, would I?" Snippy now, offended. She looked down at the computer screen, then over at her co-worker, who was still talking on the phone.

"I'll just scan you another one. Hang on." She grabbed a blank keycard, ran it through the scanner, hit a few keys, and passed it over. I thanked her and went back to the elevator, rose up to the seventh floor, and walked back to stand in front of the closed door to 712.

I knocked again, just in case. Nothing. Then I slid the key in, waited for the green light to flick on, and pushed the door open.

The so-called living room was in front of me, the bedroom beyond it, with the little kitchen jammed in between. Nothing seemed out of place—no corpse on the bed, no blood splatters on the walls.

Ken's suitcase remained, a pair of pants and a sport coat draped over it. Tossed there casually, the way you would if you knew you were coming back soon. The air-conditioning was humming away even though it wasn't much past seventy outside, turning the room into an icebox. I let the door swing shut, stepped into the cold room, and made a quick circuit through it, looking for anything noteworthy and finding nothing. Housekeeping had already made a pass through—the bed was made and the bathroom cleaned, with fresh towels and soap out. If anything had gone wrong in this room, word would have been out long before I conned my way into a keycard.

I saw a charging cord trailing from the bedside table to a wall outlet, and that made me wonder if he could have left his cell phone behind in the room, explaining why he hadn't answered. I took my phone out and called his number, waiting hopefully as it began to ring, thinking I might hear it in the room. There was nothing, though.

As I stood there amid his things, I began to feel intrusive. I had no right to be there, not just from the hotel's point of view but also from Ken's. He'd been gone a few hours, that was all. Hadn't returned my calls yet. That hardly gave me justification to break into his room and go through his things. Now that I was in here, away from Graham's suspicions and Harrison's questions and the collision those things had with my faith in Ken, the sense of urgency faded a bit. He'd turn up soon, and then I'd have to admit that I'd done this and hope he'd be more amused than angry. It would be an embarrassing moment for me. Right then, though, I was looking forward to that embarrassment. By the time I could feel shame over my actions, he'd be back.

I walked out of the bedroom and back toward the door, then stopped in the living room and looked down at the coffee table. His laptop sat there, closed but with a blinking green light indicating it was still on. There was a blank CD in a clear plastic case on top of the computer. I leaned over and picked it up, read the scrawled *Peter Case, CTB* written with a black marker across the disc. "Cold Trail Blues." The song he'd promised to burn me, his surveillance song.

I put the CD into my pocket. Even the guilt I was feeling about breaking into his room didn't give me pause. I don't know why that was. Maybe it was just that I knew the CD was for me. Maybe it was something darker and more instinctive. Either way, I took it.

I'm glad that I did.

The day faded to evening, and I went back to my apartment and called Amy, asked her to come by. She picked up some Chinese takeout on the way, and while we ate that together I told her about Graham's call and Ken being MIA. She put her fork down and looked at the clock, and her forehead creased with worry lines.

"He's not obligated to call, Amy. He's not our kid, staying out past curfew."

It was forced nonchalance, though, and she knew it.

"You could call someone else, ask if they've heard from him," Amy said.

"Who? His ex-wife?"

That silenced the conversation, but it shouldn't have, because the idea wasn't bad. His ex-wife did hear something before me, when she was called as next of kin and notified that Ken Merriman's body had been found in one of the Metroparks with two small-caliber bullet wounds, one through his heart and one through his forehead.

The ex-wife heard first, and she gave the police my name. Apparently Ken had spoken of me to his daughter. It was eleven thirty when the phone rang. I was sitting on the couch with my arm around Amy, trying without success to focus on the TV, and for a few seconds before I got to the phone I was sure it would be Ken. They were a pleasant few seconds.

I wish I could have them back.

Chapter Twenty-five

Where his life ended, the police weren't sure. They knew only where the body had been found, and at four o'clock in the morning, long after I'd widened their eyes with my list of possible suspects, I stood there alone in the dark.

Ken Merriman's corpse had been discovered on a short but steep hill near the edge of the tree line in Mill Stream Run Reservation, snagged in a thicket of undergrowth that was full and green with late-spring enthusiasm. There was honeysuckle nearby, the sweet cloying scent pushed at me by a breeze that rose and fell like long rollers breaking on an empty beach. The breeze was warmer than the still air, and damp, a messenger sent ahead with promises of rain.

At the top of the hill and beyond the tree line, a small field ran across a parking lot. A walking and bike path snaked away from the lot, a silver thread in the darkness. No cars were in the lot but mine, and no traces of police activity remained. The body had been found at eight that evening, and the Metroparks Rangers who interviewed me said they thought it was found soon after it was dumped. Twenty, thirty minutes earlier and they might've had an eyewitness.

Instead, there'd been only the discovery, made by two brothers from Berea who'd ridden their bikes down past the YMCA camp with a glow-in-the-dark football. The police had the football now, because one end of its neon green body carried a crimson smear. The kids had tossed it into the woods, where it took one good bounce into the thicket and landed directly on Ken's body. Throw got away from him, the older brother, who was fourteen, told the police. Then he started to cry.

Maybe I'd come down here to cry myself. Or maybe to rage and swear. Maybe I thought Ken Merriman would speak to me somehow, that alone in the dark in the place where his blood had drained into the earth and then gone dry under the wind I'd be able to feel his presence, understand something about his end and find direction for the justice this required.

None of that happened. I didn't scream, I didn't weep, I didn't hear any voices of dead men. Instead I smelled the honeysuckle and felt that warm, ebbing breeze and wished that I'd turned Ken away the night he arrived from Pennsylvania.

Where had he gone, what had he done, who had he provoked? Why was his body out here in the brambles instead of mine? We'd worked side by side on this since he'd arrived in Cleveland, right up until those last twenty-four hours when I sat at the office waiting on him to show up and he'd gone out and gotten killed.

What did you do, Ken? What button did you push, what thread did you pull?

There would be no answers here, nothing but wind sounds and sorrow, but I stayed anyhow. When my legs got tired I sat on the top of the hill and stared into the shadows and did not turn when the occasional car passed, disrupting the silence and throwing harsh white light into the trees.

We're going to see this thing to the end, Lincoln. Twelve years I've been waiting for that.

That's what he'd told me at the start, sitting in my truck with one hand on the door handle, ready to go up to the hotel room where he would spend his last night alive, sleeping alone with a too-loud air conditioner blasting away beside him. I'd responded by telling him . . . what had I said? That we might not get there. Something to that effect, some warning that all the effort might yield no result. He'd shaken his head.

Not this time. No, I've got a feeling about it.

* * *

My anger rose with the dawn. As the shadows around me changed from shades of dark to patterns of gray and then golden light, I noticed my jaw had begun to ache from the force of my clenched, grinding teeth. I'd had thoughts of Ken earlier in the night, but now he was gone, and Dominic Sanabria and Parker Harrison filled my mind in his stead.

They had done this. I didn't know who had put the bullets through Ken's heart and forehead, didn't know whose hands had carried him from the trunk of a car and released him at the top of this hill, but I knew who'd put it all in motion. I'd seen them personally, looked into their faces and heard their words, and now the intimacy of that filled me with anger that spread like steam. They had left me alive. They had killed Ken Merriman and yet they had left me alive, and in that action their regard for me was clear—they viewed me as impotent. Of course I would accuse them, of course I would come at them with all the resources I could muster. They knew this, and they did not care.

Harrison had told me to step aside before harm was done. That had not been a wild notion, clearly. He'd warned me, and then he'd reached for the phone and called Dominic Sanabria, and a day later Ken—who had not gone home, who had not heeded the warning—was dead.

Harrison had answers.

It was time to get them.

I was close to Old Brooklyn, and that was important, because Harrison left early for work. I didn't know what cemetery employed him, and I didn't want to take the time to find out. The MetroParks Rangers who'd drawn Ken's homicide would surely be looking for Harrison this morning, and I didn't want to follow in on their heels. By then it would probably be too late. The good fortune I had was that they'd been alarmed by all of the information I'd shared. The stories about Sanabria and Harrison and Bertoli had overwhelmed them, and I knew when they finally released me that they'd take a few hours to talk to Graham and others, working to confirm my claims, before they moved in on people with mob ties and murder convictions. I had a window this morning. It was going to be small and closing fast, but I had a window.

By the time I got to Harrison's apartment it was nearly six, and the soft predawn light was giving way to a deep red sunrise, the sort of that age-old sailor's caution. I'd cut it close—almost too close. I was pulling into the parking lot when the door to Harrison's apartment opened and he stepped out. He was wearing jeans and one of those tan work coats favored by farmers, with a thin knit cap pulled over his head. He wouldn't need the jacket and the cap—the day was dawning hot and humid—but he was probably used to chill early morning hours, and he wouldn't yet know of the weather change. He hadn't spent the night sitting in the woods above a body-dump scene.

Harrison didn't look up at my truck as he shut the door and turned to lock it. I pulled in at an angle a few doors down from him, leaving the truck across three parking spaces as I threw it in park and stepped out without bothering to cut the engine. Only then, as he put his key back in his pocket and turned from the door, did he look toward the headlights of my truck. When he saw me his face registered first surprise, then concern, and he said, "What happened?" just as I reached him, grabbed fistfuls of his coat, and pushed him against his own door.

When I left the truck I'd intended to say something immediately, shout in his face, but when I caught him and slammed him against the door I didn't speak at all, wanting instead to just stare into his eyes and see what I saw there. It was only a few seconds of silence as I held him pinned by his shoulders, but what I saw added coal to those fires of anger. His face held secrets. I could no longer tolerate the secrets.

"He's dead, you piece of shit."

"Ken?" he said, and the sound of the name leaving his lips, the way he wanted confirmation of it, was too much for me. I lifted him off the door and then slammed him back into it, maybe three times, maybe four, and when he finally made a move to resist I stepped sideways and sent him spinning off the sidewalk and into the hood of the closest car.

He hit it hard, his ribs catching the bulk of the fall, and when he righted himself and turned back to me I saw a new Parker Harrison. He stood with a wide stance, balanced and ready to move in any direction, and took two steps toward me with his hands raised and no hint of fear or uncertainty in his eyes. He was coming to do harm, coming with violence and confidence, and as I stepped off the sidewalk to meet him I wasn't at all sure that I could win this encounter, knew in a flash of recognition that he had been places and seen things that I had not, and that it was the sort of experience that might well make my advantage in size irrelevant.

That new Harrison lasted only those two steps, though. He brought himself up short as I approached, and there was a moment of hesitation before he moved backward. To a spectator it might have appeared he was giving way to me, but I knew it wasn't that. He didn't fear me at all. Not physically. For a few seconds he'd been sure he could take me and ready to do it. The latter aspect had passed. The former had not.

"What happened?" he said, circling away from me as I continued to pursue him, back on the sidewalk now.

"Somebody killed him, and you know who, you son of a bitch."

"I don't."

"Harrison—"

"I didn't want this," he said. "Lincoln, I did not want this. When I told you to leave it alone, this is what I wanted to avoid."

"What do you know?" I shouted it and was dimly aware of a light going on in the apartment beside Harrison's.

He didn't answer, moving backward in short, shuffling steps.

"This is what you wanted to avoid? How did you know it would happen? *Stop lying and say what you know!*"

We were beside his apartment now, and I punctuated the last shout by pounding my first into his door.

"You called Sanabria," I said. "You told me to quit, and then you called him. Didn't even wait until I was out of the parking lot. Why?"

"How do you know that?"

"Answer the question!"

"You'll have to ask him."

I almost went for him again. Almost gave up the questions and came at him swinging. It was close for a second, but I held back. My hands were trembling at my sides.

"Did Sanabria have you kill him, or did somebody else do it this time?"

"I haven't killed anyone."

"Did fifteen years in prison for shoplifting?"

"That's got nothing to do—"

"It doesn't? You're a *murderer.*"

The muscles in his jaw flexed, his eyes going flat.

"You killed Joshua Cantrell," I said. "Didn't you?"

"No."

"Bullshit. Somebody else gave him a Shawnee burial?"

"I didn't kill—"

"Bullshit!" As I moved toward him, the door to the apartment next door opened and a young woman in a pink robe stepped out and pointed a gun at me.

"Stop it," she said. The voice was weak, but the gun was strong. A compact Kahr 9 mm, and though her voice shook, the gun didn't do much bouncing, just stayed trained on my chest.

"I called the police," she said. "You can wait for them, or you can leave."

Parker Harrison said, "Kelly, go inside. I'm sorry."

She didn't move. Behind her, the door was open, and somewhere in the apartment a child was crying. This woman, who looked maybe twenty-five, was wearing a pink robe and standing barefoot on the sidewalk and was pointing a gun at me while her child cried in their home.

I said, "There's going to be a lot of police here in the next few days, ma'am. They're coming for him, not me."

Neither she nor Harrison responded.

"Do you know he's a murderer?" I said. "Do you know that he killed a man with a knife?"

She said, "Please leave," and now the gun had started to tremble.

I nodded. "I'm going to. I'm sorry. I'm sorry . . . but he . . ." The words left me then, and my strength seemed to go with them, and suddenly standing seemed difficult.

"I'll burn your lies down," I said to Harrison. "All of them. Every lie you've told and every secret you have. Understand that. Tell Sanabria."

I could hear the sirens when I drove out of the parking lot.

Chapter Twenty-six

I went to the office, walked upstairs, and logged on to the computer. For a moment I stared at the phone, thinking of calling Amy. The last time I'd talked to her had been after the police released me and before I'd gone to Mill Stream Run to see the place where Ken's body had been found. She'd been awake then, and I had a feeling she'd be awake now.

I also knew what she'd tell me. She'd tell me to go home, tell me to wait on the police, tell me to do anything but drive out to see Dominic Sanabria. I left the phone untouched while I ran a database search for his address.

A few minutes later, back in my truck with a printed-out map of Sanabria's neighborhood in Shaker Heights beside me, I reached over to the glove compartment, opened it, and took out my gun. It felt in my hand. Too good. I sat there for a while, caressing the stock with my thumb, and pleasure spread through me and filled my brain and circled around my heart. When I put the gun back, I made sure I locked the glove compartment. Wouldn't want the wrong person getting in there. The sort of person who would use a weapon without need, who'd pull the trigger for reasons of rage and vengeance rather than self-defense. No, I didn't want anybody like that getting ahold of my gun.

It was a slow drive out to Shaker Heights, fighting the build of rush-hour traffic. The house turned out to be in a gated community, which gave me a few seconds of pause, sitting just outside the main drive with my truck idling while I wondered how to get through. I decided it was always a better bet to try the straightforward approach first, so I pulled up to the gate and put my window down and told the kid in the security uniform that I was here to see Dominic Sanabria. I doubted Sanabria had many house calls at eight in the morning, but you never know.

The kid nodded at my request, asked for my name, and then waved me ahead, but he was looking at me strangely as he put the gate up. I kept my eyes in the mirror as I pulled forward and saw that he reached for the phone even before the gate was down. Standard procedure, or was this something he'd worked out with Sanabria, always to call if somebody showed up? Most of the gated communities I'd been through wouldn't let you pass until it had been cleared by the resident. I'd expected him to call before he let me through, not after.

That curiosity stayed with me as I followed the curving road to the right, past dozens of ostentatious homes that all looked generally alike. A few people were out on the sidewalks, walking small dogs that yipped hysterically at my truck. Sprinklers hissed here and there in the perfect lawns, and every car I saw was high-end, lots of Lexus and Mercedes SUVs, one Jaguar sedan. It was a place where most people went off to work each day in law firms or brokerage houses, maybe showing commercial real estate. Sanabria was probably their favorite neighbor. Nothing made better conversation at a cocktail party than saying you had a mob player living in your gated community.

According to my map, Sanabria's house was four right turns—or right curves, really—from the gatehouse, and I made it through all of them before I finally understood why the kid had waved me in and then picked up the phone. The police were waiting.

There was a single cruiser parked on the street across from Sanabria's house, and even before I slowed my truck they hit the lights without turning the siren on. Yeah, they had a description of my vehicle.

I brought my truck to a stop facing the cruiser, and both

doors opened and two police in uniform got out. The one behind the wheel was a woman, tall, close to six feet, and her partner was a young guy with a ruddy, freckled face. He hung back while she approached, and when I started to put the window down she shook her head and motioned with her hand.

"Step out, please."

I took a deep breath, put the truck in park, and got out, giving the cruiser another look as I did. Shaker Heights Police Department. All right, they hadn't come here from Harrison's. They'd been sent to wait for me.

"There's no problem," I said as I got out. "I just came here to talk to him."

The cop smiled. She was young, couldn't be thirty yet, but she had cool, no-bullshit eyes.

"I'm sure that's the case," she said, "but we got a call from Cleveland city, said they didn't want you talking to him, Mr. Perry. Said they want to talk to you, and then they'll talk to him."

"I've got every right to knock on the man's door."

She shook her head. "I'm going to have to bring you in to talk to city, Mr. Perry. They have a complaint. Woman says you assaulted her neighbor."

"I didn't assault anyone."

"I'm sure you didn't. Still, like I said, they have the complaint."

"They sent you out here?"

"That's right. They said you threatened Mr. Sanabria."

I started to object again, started to say I'd never threatened anyone, but the energy went out of me then, and I sighed and nodded.

"Call them," I said. "Tell them I'll come in to talk. You don't need to take me."

She frowned. "I was asked—"

"To arrest me, or to keep me from bothering Sanabria? Doesn't look like you're arresting me."

"No."

"Then tell them I'll come in. Tell them I'm cooperative and I'll come in."

She studied me for a moment, then shot her partner a glance and nodded. "Okay. Do me a favor and go wait in your truck. Let me see what they say."

I turned back to my truck, and my eyes passed over it and went up to the house, and I saw for the first time that Dominic Sanabria was standing in front of the door. He hadn't been there when I pulled up, must have come outside when he saw the police lights go on, but now he was standing on his front step wearing workout pants and a fleece jacket, holding a cup of coffee in his hand. I stopped short when I saw him, and when he realized he had my attention he lifted the cup of coffee at me and nodded his head. A neighborly greeting. I was too far away to see if he was smiling, but I imagined he was.

"Mr. Perry?" There was a warning in the female cop's voice, and when I looked at her I saw that she was watching Sanabria, too. "Get in the vehicle, please."

For a moment I didn't move, and then she spoke in a gentler tone. "I know who he is, Mr. Perry. I don't know the details of your situation, but I know who he is. All the same, though, I need you to get in the vehicle."

I nodded without speaking, and I got into the truck, and while I waited on her to come back I did not let myself look at Sanabria. Or at my glove compartment.

Chapter Twenty-seven

Things didn't get ugly until Graham got to town. The first few hours I spent with the Cleveland cops who'd responded to Harrison's house and the Metroparks Rangers, getting everyone updated. Nobody arrested me, and it seemed Harrison's version of events had been largely sympathetic. When Graham arrived around noon, I let him have a short briefing and then asked if I could speak to him alone. I wanted it to be just the two of us when I told him about the mistake I'd made, the one I hadn't even considered until I was driving back through the gatehouse of Sanabria's neighborhood.

"You had anything to eat?" he said when the other cops left the room. "Any breakfast, lunch, cup of coffee?"

I shook my head.

"Let's get out of here, then. Go somewhere, grab a sandwich."

He was calm, contained, but he'd never had trouble meeting my eyes before, and today he did. Anger, maybe, but probably some guilt in there, too. Ken was dead, and Graham had been in charge.

We left the station and drove back to my office, Graham following behind me, then walked across the street to Gene's Place. It was close and it was comfortable, and only after we walked through the doors did I remember that it was also where I'd gone for lunch on the day Harrison came to see me and I agreed to take his case. That weird, warm day, when all

I'd wanted to do was stand outside and drink in the air, feel the sun and the wind and the knowledge that we'd finally shaken winter.

Graham got a cheeseburger, and I had a cup of soup and picked at a club sandwich while I went through cup after cup of coffee, the fatigue slamming me now. I told him everything I could tell him. He listened and ate his burger and didn't look at me often.

When I was done talking, he leaned back from the table, wiped his mouth with a napkin, and said, "I'm sorry."

"Yeah. Both of us. We're sorry, and he's dead."

His chest filled with air, and he shook his head. "Maybe we didn't do everything perfect, but . . . well, let me correct that, Linc. I *know* we didn't do everything perfect, know that I didn't, but we also didn't kill the guy. We didn't get him killed, either."

The waitress came back and refilled my coffee yet again. "You'll be bouncing off the walls today," she said and laughed. Yeah. Bouncing off the walls.

"No," I said when she was gone, "we didn't get him killed. Sanabria did, I think, and Harrison's involved."

"The phone calls suggest that, at least."

"Speaking of which, why don't you have a damn wiretap on these guys?"

"Don't have the probable cause, and you know that. Maybe I can get it now, but not before."

"Great," I said. "Ken's made a break in the case. That's all the poor bastard wanted to do. Don't think he wanted to die to get it, though."

Graham sighed again. "Linc, how's your head?"

"What, the coffee?"

"No, not the coffee. The way you went at it today, brother . . . I can't have you doing that. You're lucky Harrison's not pressing charges. He may change his mind. Either way, I can't afford to have you—"

"I screwed up with him."

"No shit you screwed up with him, and I'm just saying—"

"No." I shook my head. "You don't understand, Graham. I

don't mean in general terms. I mean specifically. In the heat of the moment, when I had him out there in the parking lot, I said something I shouldn't have."

He looked at me like a man who was waiting for a diagnosis and wasn't optimistic.

"I told him you know about the burial," I said. "The Shawnee elements."

Diagnosis delivered, and the result was what I'd expected—a flash of shock, replaced quickly by anger. Deep anger. He stared at me and then turned and looked down at the table and blew his breath out between his teeth.

"You told him we know about the burial. The one thing we've got hope on, waiting on those damn lab results—"

"If you get the lab results, it doesn't matter that he knows. Maybe it doesn't anyhow. How can he prepare to deal with that, Graham? How can that knowledge really help him?"

I was arguing out of a natural sense of self-defense, but I still knew it had been a mistake, and a potentially damaging one. The detail of the grave was the one card Graham had to play on this one, the only thing he'd held back from the media and the only firm link he had to Harrison. It wasn't all that firm—the definition of circumstantial, actually—but it was what he had.

"That's beautiful," he said, shaking his head. "That is just beautiful, Linc."

"Graham, I'm sorry. Like I said, heat of the moment."

"Yeah, heat of a moment you shouldn't have been in. You were *police*, you know better than that." Another head shake. "No, it's on me. It's on me, damn it, I know that, I see that, I got him dead and you knocking suspects around and divulging information and driving out to Sanabria's with intentions I don't even want to guess at . . . yeah, Linc, I made the wrong play when you boys called me. I did. No question."

I didn't say anything to that, didn't want to argue anymore, wanted to try to retain some dignity. Graham and I were feeling a lot of the same things, really. We'd both made some mistakes we'd be thinking about for a long time to come.

"So he knows," Graham said eventually. "He knows what I know now. Level field now, right? Level field."

"It's not level. He knows a hell of a lot more than you do."

He looked up at me then, held my eye for a moment, then nodded. The waitress came back and dropped a check off and Graham reached out and took it and folded it.

"Linc, there's something I need to ask of you."

"You want me out."

"Oh, yeah. Wanted you out yesterday, you know that, but after this morning, the way you went driving around, stirring shit up—that cannot continue."

"Let me head you off here," I said. "I *am* out."

He leaned back and gave me a bemused look, not buying it.

"That's a promise, Graham. The minute you and I finish this talk, I'm done. When I say that, I mean it."

"Why?" he said.

"Why do I want out? Because it's got nothing to do with me."

"Never did, though."

"I know it, and I should have paid more attention to that. Ken showed up and asked, and I went along with him because it is what I do, Graham. This is what I know how to do. He gave me a case and said here is what we know and here is what we need to know, and I couldn't stop myself from joining up. I've done it for too long to stop, evidently. Until today. Because I'll tell you something—I went down to see the spot where his body was found. I stood down there and I thought about my girlfriend's body ending up there instead, or my partner's. They've both come close over the last two years. I stood there and I realized what you just said: that it never did have anything to do with me, and that I can't make a decision to put people in danger for things that aren't personal. Call it a revelation, an epiphany, whatever you'd like. Here's what I'm promising you: I will not put other people at risk for a case anymore. I'm done with it. If I'd sent that poor bastard back to Pennsylvania the day he arrived, he'd be alive, too."

"Can't put all that on yourself, Linc."

"Oh, I'm not. Some of it's on you, and plenty is on him. Then there are the guys who actually, you know, *killed* him. They probably require a bit of blame, too. What I'm saying, though, is that I'm not going to be involved in any attempt to settle up with them. I burned that desire out this morning, and screwed things up for you while doing it. Now I'm just going to apologize and step aside. So save whatever speech you have prepared."

He was watching me with a deep frown, and now he braced his forearms on the table and leaned close, eyes on mine.

"I'll close this case," he said. "Word as bond, Linc, I'll close it."

"I hope so, Graham. You have to try, at least. It's your job—but you know what? It doesn't have to be mine. I'm finally understanding that." I stood up and tossed some money on the table. "I wish you luck, and if you have more questions, you know how to reach me. Otherwise, though, save yourself any worry on my part. I'm gone."

John Dunbar came by my apartment that afternoon. I'd been waiting for Amy, but when I heard a knock instead of a key turning I grimaced, knowing it wouldn't be good. I let him up, and he sat in my living room, loosened his tie, and told me that we had to get to work.

"Look, Perry, I understand how you feel right now. The anger, the sense of futility. You feel that way because you *know* who's responsible and yet he's walking around free. Sanabria's done that too long. We can't let it continue. We can't."

"Did you ever consider," I said, "that you might be responsible for this?"

"What?"

"Everything that happened with the Cantrells. Think about it. Do they ever leave that house if you don't conceive of the brilliant idea of planting Bertoli there? Does anyone ever get killed? Or are they still living in that place and helping people, Dunbar?"

He shook his head. "I'm not going to let you put that at my feet. I didn't invent the trouble they had as a couple, didn't even come to Joshua with the idea. He came to me. I don't regret what we tried to do."

I stayed silent and made a point of looking at my watch. *Anytime you want to leave, Dunbar . . .*

"Your idea," he said, "would be that if we just gave up on justice, fewer people would get hurt? If we just let Sanabria run wild, without persecution or prosecution, the rest of us are fine? That's a pretty selfish idea, Perry. He killed other people before your friend, and he'll kill other people again."

"How long have you been chasing him?"

He couldn't hold my eyes. "A long time."

"How many years?"

"Twenty. About twenty."

"And you've done nothing but add to his body count."

"I don't have to listen to—"

"If you want him that bad, why didn't you just kill the son of a bitch, Dunbar? You'd have had an easier time doing that and getting away with it than you would have getting anything useful with Bertoli and that half-assed sting attempt."

He got to his feet slowly, his jaw tight. "That's not how it's done. I do it right."

"You haven't yet."

"I will," he snapped. "I will. I'm retired, Perry, and still I'm here, asking for your help. That doesn't mean anything to you? Doesn't tell you anything about me?"

"It means something to me," I said, "but not what you want it to."

He stood there for a moment and stared at me, and I saw contempt in his eyes.

"You could do something about this," he said. "A real detective would."

He left my apartment then. I thought about what he'd said, and thought that a year ago the words would have been coming out of my lips. A year ago, I wouldn't be back in my apartment right now or for many hours yet to come, I'd be chasing every lead, believing that I could do something to set things right. Why didn't I now?

It stacked up on you, after a while. The violence. If you

kept your distance, maybe you could avoid that; if every corpse and every crime scene photograph you looked at represented somebody else's friend, somebody's else's brother, somebody else's daughter, maybe you could hold that distance. It wasn't working that way for me anymore, though. I sat in my living room after Dunbar left and I began to see the ghosts, Ken Merriman and Ed Gradduk and Joe before the bullets found him that day by the bridge over Rocky River. There was Keith Appleton, a sweet kid who'd been one of the first members my gym had and was murdered before his high school graduation, and Alex Jefferson, my onetime nemesis, and Julie and Betsy Weston, mother and child, long gone from this city and still present in my mind every single day.

It stacked up on you.

That afternoon I got out the CD Ken had burned for me and played it for the first time: *Something I need that I just can't find. Is it too late now? Am I too far behind?*

I heard those lyrics, and I thought of Ken, chasing Alexandra twelve years after she'd left, and of Dunbar, pursuing Sanabria two decades after he'd missed a chance to stick him in prison, and I wondered why they no longer felt like colleagues to me, like comrades.

Now there's a whole new crowd out here, and they just don't seem to care. Still I keep searching through this gloom . . .

I wouldn't keep searching through the gloom. Because you couldn't catch them all. Look at Dunbar. A full career behind him, and years after retirement he was still consumed by Sanabria, still hungered for him every day—and if he got him, finally? It wouldn't mean much. There'd be another to take his place. Every detective had his white whale. I wondered how many of them ever lifted their heads long enough to see that the seas were teeming with white whales.

I took the CD out and put it back in its case and put it away, and when Amy came by that night I asked her if she could take a few days off. I wanted to go to Florida, I said. I wanted to see Joe.

"What about the funeral?"

"I don't know anybody he knew, Amy. It'll be a roomful of

strangers, maybe strangers who won't want to see me there. He was working with me when he got killed."

"Still, it's a gesture."

"One he's gonna see?"

She didn't answer that, and I said, "Amy, I need to talk things out with Joe. I need you with me."

She nodded. "I'll call my boss."

I went to the Hideaway alone that night. I drank a beer and a bourbon and I toasted to a dead man. Scott Draper, used to dealing with the emotions of the drunk or the emotion-drunk, left me alone until I waved him over and launched into a debate about the prospects of the Cleveland Browns. He saw the forced nature of it, but he asked no questions, and I was glad. I had one last bourbon before calling it a night, muttered a toast to Sam Spade, and then spun the whiskey glass back across the bar. It was done for me now. It was absolutely done for me.

Chapter Twenty-eight

We left two days later, took a direct flight from Cleveland to Tampa and then rented a car. Even in the airport parking garage, among the shadows of cold concrete, you could feel the intensity of the Florida summer heat, opening your pores and baking into your bones. I put our bags in the trunk of the convertible Amy had insisted we rent—*if I'm going to sweat, I might as well get tan*—and then tossed the keys to her. I didn't want to drive. Felt more like riding.

We took I-275 south out of Tampa and drove over the Howard Frankland bridge toward St. Petersburg. A few miles past the bridge, I pointed at a sign indicating "gulf beaches," and Amy turned off the interstate. Joe was staying in a place called Indian Rocks, one of the hotel-and-condo communities that lined the beach from Clearwater to St. Pete. The last time I'd been on the gulf side of Florida, I was nineteen and on a spring break trip. We'd been much farther south then, too, so none of this was familiar to me. I could understand why Joe had enjoyed it during the winter, but now, with the unrelenting sun and humidity that you felt deep in your chest, enveloping your lungs, his motivation for staying seemed a little less clear. This Gena must be one hell of a woman.

We hit a stoplight just outside of Indian Rocks and watched an obese man with no shirt and blistered red skin walk in front of the car, shouting obscenities into a cell phone and carrying a bright blue drink in a plastic cup. Amy turned to me, her amusement clear despite the sunglasses that shielded her eyes, and said, "Think Joe's turned into one of those?"

"I'm sure of it."

Joe had told me to call when we got to the little town, so now I took out my cell phone and called, and he provided directions to the condo that had been his home for the past six months. We drove slowly, searching for the place, a different collection of oceanfront granite and glass everywhere you looked. When I finally saw the sign for Joe's building, I laughed. Trust him to find this one.

Squatting beneath two of the more extravagant hotels on the beach was a two-story L-shaped building that looked as if it had been built in the late 1950s and tuned up maybe once since then—perhaps after a hurricane. The old-fashioned sign out front boasted of shuffleboard and a weekly potluck.

"Oh, no," Amy said. "It's worse than I thought."

We pulled into the parking lot and got out and stretched, and then Joe appeared, walking toward us with an easier stride than I'd seen from him in a long time, some of his old athlete's grace coming back.

"Trust LP to wait until it hits ninety-five before he brings you down," he said, going first to Amy, who hugged him hard. He looked good. Some of his weight was back, and the pallor he'd had when he left Cleveland in December was gone, replaced by a tan that made his gray hair seem almost white. He stepped away from Amy and put out his hand, and I liked the strength I felt in his grip, the steady look in his eyes. It was a far cry from the way he'd looked when he left. These months had been good to him.

He let go of my hand but continued to search my eyes. We'd had a few talks since Ken had been killed, but nothing at length. I'm not a big fan of phone conversations.

"Please tell me you don't play shuffleboard," Amy said.

"No. The place is better than it looks, really."

"What's the median age of the occupants?"

"There are some kids. One guy just retired from Visa, can't be more than sixty."

He led us out of the parking lot and around the building,

past a sparkling pool with nobody in the water and up the steps to a corner room with a view of the ocean. Now that we were out of the car, the heat was staggering. Even down here on the water the humidity settled on you like lead. There were maybe fifteen steps going up to the second floor, and I felt each one of them the way I'd feel an entire flight of stairs back home. I've never been so happy to hear the grinding of an air conditioner as I was when Joe unlocked the door and let us in.

His room was larger than I would've expected, and bright, with all that sun bouncing in off the water, palm trees rustling just outside. Not a bad place to spend a winter. Also, tucked inside here next to the AC unit, probably not a terrible place to spend the summer. Just don't open that door.

We spent the afternoon in or around his hotel, talking and laughing and generally doing a fine job of pretending this visit was a carefree vacation. He wasn't fooled, though, but he waited, and so did I. We'd get our chance to talk soon enough, but we needed to be alone for it.

In midafternoon I left them in the room and wandered outside and down to the beach and the blistering heat and called the office to check my messages. Nothing new from Graham or Harrison or anyone else. I had an old saved message, though. I couldn't stop myself from playing it again.

Lincoln, I think we've got something. You got us there, we just needed to see it. Last night, I finally saw it. I'm telling you, man, I think you got us there. I'm going to check something out first, though. I don't want to throw this at you and then have you explain what I'm missing, how crazy it is—but stay tuned. Stay tuned.

I played it three times, as if listening to it over and over would reveal something I had missed.

You got us there, we just needed to see it.

I'd gotten us nowhere. In the entire course of our investigation, we had interviewed a grand total of three people beyond Harrison: John Dunbar, Mark Ruzity, Mike London. What had he seen? What could he possibly have seen?

It didn't matter. I told myself that with a silent vigor—it did *not* matter. I was out of it, and needed to stay out.

Chapter Twenty-nine

That night we got to meet the much-heralded Gena. Of course, she hadn't been heralded at all—that wasn't Joe's style—which had only made the anticipation greater. If I'd expected someone like Ruth, I was surprised. Gena was about a foot taller, for starters, brunette when Ruth had been blond, blue eyes instead of green, from Idaho instead of Cleveland. She was younger than Joe, too, probably by ten years, and Ruth had been significantly older than him. She was, in almost all ways, the polar opposite of his longtime wife, but that didn't make her any less likable. She was attractive and witty and intelligent, and Joe's eyes lingered on her in a way that made me continuously want to hide a smile.

We left the beach and drove all the way into St. Pete to go to a restaurant Joe liked called Pacific Wave. The food was outstanding, and Amy and Gena ran away with the conversation. Joe hadn't found himself a journalist, but something close. She was an attorney who'd become an advocate for public records and government access, and with those credentials it didn't take long for her to endear herself to Amy. I also began to understand why Joe was still here in the summer but hadn't made any remarks about a permanent relocation. Gena was in Florida only temporarily, as a visiting faculty member at the Poynter Institute, a renowned journalism center in St. Petersburg. She'd come down on a grant, and that grant would be up in September.

"Then it's back to Idaho?" Amy asked.

She nodded, and I saw Joe take his eyes off her for the first time while she was speaking.

"How'd you meet, anyhow?" Amy asked. It was a classic female question, I thought, and one that guys never seemed to ask. They'd met, that was all. Wasn't that enough knowledge? It's no surprise that some of the best detectives I know are women.

"One of my colleagues at Poynter has a time-share up here," Gena said. "I came to a party there, got bored, and went for a walk. Joe was sitting on the beach in his lawn chair. Not so noteworthy, you might think, but this was at ten o'clock at night. It stood out."

Amy looked at Joe, and he shrugged. "There were always a bunch of people out during the day. They got annoying."

"We got to talking a little, and he was explaining why palm trees are so resistant to wind, even in hurricanes," Gena continued, and now it was my turn to look at Joe.

"You learn a lot about palm trees growing up in Cleveland?"

"I did some reading."

"Evidently."

Gena smiled. "After a while I realized I'd been gone too long, and I had to get back, but I also wanted to see him again. He didn't seem to be picking up on that—"

"You can imagine what a great detective he is," I said.

"Well, that's what I finally had to use. By then I knew what he'd done, and he knew why I was here, so I told him I needed to have someone with police experience come speak at one of my seminars. Talk about public access and the back-and-forth with the media, things like that. It ended up being a fine idea, but I'll confess it hadn't been part of the original plan."

"You spoke to students?" I said to Joe. "To *journalism* students?"

He nodded.

"Tell them about the good old days, when there were no

recorders in interrogation rooms and every cop's favorite tools were the rubber hose and the prewritten confession?"

"I might have held a few things back."

After dinner, we drove back to Joe's building. He mixed drinks for the three of us and grabbed a bottle of water for himself, and we went out to the patio as the heat faded to tolerable levels and the moon rose over the gulf. It was quiet here, and I thought of Gena's story, of Joe on his lawn chair alone on the dark beach, and I realized that it had probably been a hell of a good choice for him to come here, to be away from the things that he knew and the people that knew him, for at least a little while. We all burn out, time to time. Some people never find that dark beach and that solitary lawn chair, though. I was glad that he had.

At one point, as the conversation between Amy and Gena became more animated and I thought my absence would be less noticed, I got up and walked down to the water and finished my drink standing in the sand. After a while a light, sprinkling rain began, and I realized the voices from the patio had faded. When I went back up, Amy and Gena were gone. Joe was sitting alone, watching me.

"They go inside?" I asked.

He nodded. I took the chair next to him again. It wasn't really raining yet, just putting forth a few suggestions.

"Amy was telling us about your friend," Joe said. "Ken."

"Friend? I'd known him about a week, Joseph."

"That make it easier, telling yourself that?"

I didn't answer.

"I'm surprised you're here," he said. "Right now, I mean. Something like that happens . . . the guy working with you gets killed, I just assumed you'd dig in."

"When your partner gets killed, you're supposed to do something about it, that what you mean? The classic PI line? Well, I don't have it in me anymore. So try not to get killed."

"Understandable. Sometimes it's good to take a few days—"

"No, Joe." I shook my head. "I don't need a few days, and

when I say I don't have it in me anymore, I don't mean to go find out what happened to Ken. I should do that, I know. I should be back in Cleveland right now, working on that."

"I didn't say that. I'm just surprised you're not, because it seems to be your way."

"Sometimes your ways change. Or get changed."

He was quiet. The sprinkling rain had stopped, but the wind was blowing harder, and there was no longer any trace of the moon through the clouds.

"Are you coming back?" I said. "It's why I'm here, and you know that. I need to know if you're coming back."

"To Cleveland?"

"No. Well, yes, I care about that, too, but I mean to work. Are you coming back to work with me?"

He said, "I got a call from Tony Mitchell two weeks ago. You remember Tony?"

"Sure. Good cop, good guy. Funny as hell. What this has to do with anything . . ."

"Tony's retired from the department, too. I expected he'd become a Jimmy Buffett roadie, but evidently that didn't work out, because he got himself a job doing corporate security for some big manufacturing firm. Place is constantly hiring new employees, taking in hundreds of applications a month. They've had some problems with bad hires in the past and want to put a preemployment screening program in place. Tony called me, asked if we'd be interested in running it. Would be real steady work."

"Screenings," I said.

"I'd be willing to do something like that," he said. "Make some money, keep busy. The street work . . . I've done it for too long, Lincoln."

"So you're coming back, but you don't intend to do any street work."

"That's about it, yeah."

"Where does Gena figure in?"

"I don't know yet."

I nodded.

"What do you think?" he asked.

"That maybe it's time to fold it," I said and hated the sound of my voice. I'd gone for detached and gotten choked instead.

He didn't answer.

"I don't want to be in this business alone, Joe. I'm not sure I even want to be in it at all anymore, but I don't want to go at it alone. Hell, you're the one who dragged me into it. I was running the gym and—"

"And losing your mind. You were so miserable—"

"That was a different time. I'd gotten fired, I'd lost Karen . . . things were different."

"This job gave you something back. Did it not?"

"Sure," I said. "It gives, and maybe it takes away a little, too. You're proof."

"I'm sorry?"

"Look at yourself. You're happy down here. Are you not?"

"Generally, yeah. It's been good. I'm not sure how—"

"You had to go fifteen hundred miles to separate yourself from it," I said. "From the work. The work was you, and you were the work. I saw it every damn day."

"I could take that comment the wrong way if I wanted to."

"You didn't have anything else, Joe. Nothing."

"I *know* I could take that one the wrong way."

"It was all you were," I said. "Being a detective didn't define you, it devoured you, and you know it. Why else did you have to leave, to go so far and for so long? You did it because if you stayed any closer you knew you'd go right back to the job, and you were scared of that. Scared, or tired."

"You seeing a therapist or just reading their books?"

"Tell me I'm wrong," I said.

He shifted in his chair, shook his head. "I won't argue it. I could, but I won't. Certainly not tonight."

I didn't say anything, and after a while he spoke again, voice low. "I thought the biggest headache would be getting you to let me step aside. Didn't figure you'd be racing me for the door."

"I'm tired of the collateral damage."

"Meaning what?"

It came out in a rush. For a long time, I spoke, and he

listened. Never said a word, didn't look at me, just listened. I talked about watching Joe in the hospital when he'd been shot, about John Dunbar's frightening fixation on a case he'd lost, about the way I felt every time I heard that new security bar click into place at Amy's apartment, and the uncomfortable pull my gun had on me while I drove to Dominic Sanabria's house.

"I've seen a lot of people around me get hurt," I said. "You, and Amy, and now Ken Merriman. I'm always untouched, but—"

"You're untouched?"

I nodded.

"Really?" he said. "Because you don't look that way right now, Lincoln. Don't sound it, either."

We let silence ride for a while then. The rain held off, and once I heard a door open and then close again after a brief pause, and I was certain without turning to look that it was Amy, that she'd walked out onto the balcony and seen me down here with Joe and gone back inside.

"So what will you do?" Joe asked.

"I don't know yet. I've still got the gym. Maybe put some of Karen's money into that. Get new equipment, do a remodel, try to expand. Help you out with the employment screening thing, if you need it."

"And stay away from case work."

"Yes. Stay away from case work."

He was quiet again, then said, "I'm sorry it didn't work out better for you, Lincoln. Like you said, I'm the one who brought you into it. At the time, I thought I was doing the right thing. You were a detective. That was as natural and deeply ingrained in you as in anybody else I'd ever seen. I thought it would be good for you, but more than that, I thought you needed it."

That night, when we were alone in our hotel room, I told Amy about my conversation with Joe. I was sitting in a chair by the sliding glass door, she was on the bed and outside the rain fell in sheets. I thought she might make some arguments, raise some of the same points that Joe had, remind me that when we'd met I was trying to make a living off the gym alone and I was a generally unhappy person. She didn't say any of those things, though. When I was done talking she got to her feet and walked across the room to me and sat on my lap, straddling me, her hands on either side of my face.

"If you can't do it anymore, then there's no decision to be made," she said. "You just need to step back. Don't feel bad about it, just do it."

I nodded.

"One rule," she said.

"Yeah?"

"You can leave the job. You can leave the city if you want to. You can leave damn near anything, but you better not leave me."

I shook my head. "Not going to happen."

"I've invested way too much into this ill-advised Lincoln Perry rehabilitation plan to give up now."

"If anybody ends this, it'll be you."

"Remember that," she said, and then she leaned forward and kissed me before moving to rest her head on my chest. We sat like that for a long time, and then she stood and took my hand and brought me to the bed.

When she was asleep and the rain was gone, sometime around four in the morning, I sat on the balcony with a pad of the hotel stationery and tried to write a letter to Ken's daughter, the one who'd loved TV cop shows. I wanted to apologize for missing the funeral, tell her how much I'd thought of her father, and explain that he'd been a damn fine detective and that his work had mattered, that what he'd been doing on the day he was murdered had an impact on her world. I sat there for more than an hour, wrote a few poor sentences, and then crumpled the pages in my hand and went back inside.

Chapter Thirty

Amy and I stayed for a week. We hung out with Joe and sometimes Gena, ate seafood, had drinks of fruit juice and rum, bitched about the heat. All the things you're supposed to do in Florida.

I checked the office voice mail daily. There was no word about Ken. Many days, I played his last message again. I listened to words I already knew by heart, and I tried to imagine what had provoked them. I had no luck. You rarely do with that approach to detective work. The way it gets done is out on the street. I stayed on the beach.

On the day before we left, I ended up sitting on a chair outside Joe's hotel, alone, while he and Amy made a run to the store. Gena was coming by for an afternoon cocktail before dinner, and she showed up before they got back and came down to join me. We made small talk for a bit. I found out that while she had lived in other states and, for one year, in Europe, she always came back to Idaho in the end. Both parents were still alive, and she had two sisters; all of them lived within a fifteen-minute drive.

"So are you going to move to Cleveland or make him move to Idaho?" It was supposed to be a joke, but her pause told me it was a discussion they'd actually had.

"Maybe either, maybe neither, maybe something completely different," she said.

"Egypt?" I was still trying to keep it light, because I was caught off guard by the idea that they were this serious.

"One person moving to join the other is the obvious option," she said, stretching out on the chair beside me and kicking off her sandals, "but there's an element of it that could feel selfish either way, you know? We both have our own lives at home, so to have one person make the sacrifice seems unfair. So we've talked about a compromise. Moving somewhere new to both of us."

"Oh," I said. Can always count on me for insight.

She looked over at me, sunglasses shading her eyes. The wind was fanning her brown hair out. "Would I like Cleveland?"

"Probably not."

"Really?"

"You live in a college town in the mountains, right? Well, the city's a change. Most people head the other way. Leave the city for mountains." I waved out at the water. "Or a beach."

"I lived in New York for seven years. Never minded being in a city. Of course, I was twenty-five then, too."

I didn't say anything.

"Either way, it won't be happening overnight," she said. "Joe's not the sort of person who rushes into things."

That made me laugh. "No, he's not."

She smiled but looked away from me. "He's worried about you."

"Doesn't need to be."

"I couldn't speak to that. I don't know you well enough to say. I do know that he's worried. He's afraid that the way he left was unfair to you. That you're carrying guilt about it when you shouldn't be."

"I got him shot, Gena. Seems to warrant a small dose of guilt. But that's really not the issue, not anymore. He's happy again, and I'm glad of that. Thrilled."

"You're not. Happy, I mean."

"Happy," I said, "seems like a hell of a subjective thing. I'm working on it. So is Joe. So is everybody. And I can tell you this—you're good for him. I can see that so clearly, and you have no idea how nice it is. He's been alone for a long time."

"Had you, though."

"Yeah, but he never liked my hairstyle as much as yours." She smiled. "There's one thing I'd like you to know."

"Yeah?"

"When we've talked about moving," she said, "and the things that we'd miss the most, just hate the idea of being away from, I talk about my family. Joe talks about you."

A call from Graham came later that night, and the message he left offered no sense of progress but some news—Joshua Cantrell's family had won a preliminary legal motion to claim the house on Whisper Ridge.

Chapter Thirty-one

Life, or the lack thereof, always seemed to me like something that had to be established medically, not legally, through beating hearts and functioning brains rather than notarized paperwork. That's not always the case. The judge had ruled that the Cantrells were entitled to post legal notice of Alexandra's presumed death, which would run in a variety of newspapers, and there would be a ninety-day period to contest the claim. Either Alexandra herself could appear, proving it wrong while welcoming the approaches of police, or someone else could bring forward proof of life. If those ninety days passed without either occurrence, the Cantrells could begin maneuvering to claim their share of the estate. Graham's understanding was that they'd have to split the estate with Dominic Sanabria.

"He probably killed their son," I said when I called him back the next morning, "and now they're going to have to share the money with him?"

"That's what the law seems to say."

When we got back to Cleveland, I bought a paper in the airport and flipped through it to the public notice section while we stood beside the luggage carousel. There was the first notice of Alexandra Cantrell, buried amid pages of fine-print legalese. It seemed too quiet a way to announce the end of a life.

"You should do an article," I told Amy. "If anything's going to produce Alexandra or proof she's alive, it won't be this notice. It'll take more publicity than that."

She agreed with me, and a day later so did her editor. The story appeared on the following Sunday, front page and above the fold. The TV news picked it up by that evening, and several Associated Press papers around the country ran shortened versions of the "missing, presumed dead" story in the days to come. The story never gathered the national steam I'd hoped for—CNN, talk show features, that sort of thing—but for several weeks, Graham, the newspaper, and the Cantrell legal team were flooded with tips. I called Graham to see if anything was coming of it. Just the tips, he said, most crazy, none credible. If Alexandra was still alive, there was no sign.

I wrapped up what case work I had left when I got back to the city, then put out a memo to our core clients explaining that Joe and I were stepping aside from field investigations. I referred them to other people in town, brushed aside inquiries, and waited for the outcry of disappointment and anger. It never came. Perry and Pritchard Investigations wasn't the community institution I'd believed it to be, evidently.

I listened to Ken's message daily for a while. Then, a month after he'd been killed, the voice mail informed me the message would be deleted from the system. It had been there too long, evidently. You couldn't keep it forever. Eventually the computer decided that the time elapsed required the message to go away even if I didn't want it to. By the next morning, it was gone.

I invested thirty thousand dollars into new equipment for the gym. I paid for a larger phone-book ad and hired a friend of Amy's to create a Web site. I did most of the work on the gym by myself, largely because it kept me busy. When I wasn't working on it, I was working out in it. That summer I took thirty seconds off my time in the mile and added forty pounds to my bench press, got it back up to a max of three hundred and ten pounds, my all-time high and a mark I'd set when I was a rookie. My attention to diet changed, and I started taking amino acids and fish oils and any number of other things that were rumored to have some sort of health benefit. By August, if I wasn't in the best shape of my life, I was damn close to it. My workouts had become feverish, almost obsessive. Do one more rep, Lincoln, run one more mile, take one more pill. You'll be stronger, leaner, faster. You'll have no vulnerability. None.

I'd been spending more and more nights at Amy's apartment, and one evening I felt her eyes on me and turned to see her watching me with a frown from across the room.

"What have I done?"

"Quit your job," she said.

"This is an unemployment lecture?"

"That gym won't be enough for you."

"You don't know that. I could make plenty of money—"

"Not money, Lincoln. It won't be *enough* for you. Don't you get that?"

"You're enough for me," I said.

"Romantically speaking? I sure as shit better be. If I'm not, then you're a cheating bastard. If you mean I'm *enough*, period, all you need . . . that's not true."

"Actually, it is."

"Well, it shouldn't be. You're not enough for me."

I raised my eyebrows. "Gee, thanks. You're a sweetheart tonight."

"I'm serious. I love you, but you don't define my entire existence, either. You wouldn't want to be around me if you did. So to sit there and tell me that I'm *enough* for you, that's a lot of pressure, and when you finally realize it's not the truth, I don't want to be the one who gets hurt."

"I'm not sure I follow your logic there, but I don't intend to hurt you, Amy."

She came over and kissed me, then leaned back and stood with her hands on my shoulders and looked into my eyes.

"You just removed a large piece of yourself, and now you're pretending that it was never there. It's been a hell of a thing to watch, trust me. Impressive at times. You're a master of denial, Lincoln, an absolute master—but I'm scared of where it's going to take you."

She kissed me again then and walked out of the room. I sat

and watched her go and thought that I should follow and say more. I didn't know what I would say, though. I really didn't.

At the end of August, Graham called again, this time to tell me that he finally had his lab results on Joshua Cantrell's grave. The backlog had loosened up, and he'd used Ken's murder as a means to bump his request higher in priority.

"We got nothing," he said. "No DNA results. Nothing that connects to Harrison, or anybody else. The only DNA they could find was Cantrell's."

I felt defeat sweep through me, realized just how much hope I'd been holding out.

"What next?" I said.

Graham was quiet.

"You're done?"

"I'm not done, Linc, but it's a cold case, and without new—"

"Ken Merriman was murdered in May, Graham. That's not a cold case."

"That's also not my case. Talk to your boys in Cleveland on that one. I'm sitting here in Pennsylvania with a full case-load and a bunch of supervisors who don't want me spending time in Cleveland. Look, nobody's more disappointed about this than me. I come to a case with one goal—to close it. I haven't done that on this one. I won't deny that, but I also won't bullshit you. My focus has to be out here, where I'm paid to work. I'd love to take Sanabria down, love to take Harrison down, but I can't."

"Somebody will," I said. "In time."

"Right," he said, and then neither of us was comfortable with the other's silence, so we said a hurried goodbye and hung up.

Chapter Thirty-two

The same day Graham gave me the news about the lack of lab results from the grave, he gave it to John Dunbar, who, evidently, had continued his regular calls asking for updates and offering his help. I hadn't heard from Dunbar since I'd asked him to leave my apartment, but at noon on the day after Graham's call he showed up again.

I was on a ladder in the gym, applying paint to a band around the ceiling I'd decided to make a different color than the rest of the wall. It was an aesthetic effect, completely unnecessary, but I'd decided to do it anyhow, because it was good to stay busy. I was finding all sorts of ways to stay busy.

Grace told him where to find me, and he came and stood quietly beneath the ladder and watched me paint until I felt his presence and turned and looked down.

"What are you doing here?" I said.

"Wanted to buy you a beer."

"I don't drink in the middle of the day."

"A cup of coffee, then."

"I'm off caffeine."

"A bottle of water."

He never blinked, just stood with his hands in his pockets and an even stare on his face, watching me. I gave it a moment, and then I sighed and came down off the ladder.

"Let me rinse out the brush."

* * *

We walked up the street to an Irish pub that had gone in on the corner. Neither of us spoke. Once inside, I went to a table across from the bar and ordered a beer.

"Thought you didn't drink in the middle of the day," Dunbar said.

I didn't answer.

"So you're not happy to see me," he said. "I get it."

"I just don't know why you came. Why you're not willing to make phone calls instead of personal visits, at least."

"Tougher to blow me off in person," he said. It was a line straight out of Joe's mouth, one of his guiding principles for detective work—you wore out shoe leather before you burned up the phone lines.

"I'll give you that much," I said.

They brought my beer, and he asked for a Jameson and water, and we waited while they poured that and brought it over.

"I talked to Graham," he said after taking an experimental sip.

"As did I."

"Pretty disappointing news."

"It was."

"It'll go back to where it was twelve years ago now," he said. "Go back to nobody looking or even thinking about looking. It'll be unsolved, and forgotten."

I drank some beer.

"Ken Merriman's case is open," he said. "You talked to anybody on that?"

"Not lately."

"I have. I was calling a couple times a week. Guy I've talked to down there got tired of it, though. Asked me to stop. Said he'd let me know if they got an update. So in my professional opinion, that one's moving along about as well as the Cantrell investigation. Which is to say, it's not."

"That could be an unfair assessment."

"You think?"

"The rangers aren't bad at what they do, Dunbar. Give them time."

"Time." He nodded and turned the glass with his fingers. "Twelve years of time, that's what we've had on Cantrell. I don't want to see Ken Merriman's case go another twelve."

"I know it."

"But you're not doing anything to help," he said, "and I don't understand that. Somebody else, sure, they'd feel hopeless and useless and I'd get that. I've read about you though. I've talked to people. Your reputation as a detective is extraordinary, Perry. Good instincts, they tell me, good experience, a real natural—but what people talk about most? It's how damned dogged you've been. How determined. How relentless."

I blew out a breath, looked away.

"I see you've closed your office," he said, "and now it's the middle of the week and you're in the gym, painting. Is that the new you?"

"What if it is?"

"I'd say that's a shame. I'd say that's as much of a shame as anything I've heard in a long time, because the world is full of evil, and there aren't enough people who can do something about it."

He paused. "Dominic Sanabria is a killer. He has gone unpunished for that. He sits around in his fancy house drinking afternoon cocktails and smiling about it. I cannot let that last."

When I didn't answer, a glow of anger came into his face, and he took a deep breath and looked away, as if he couldn't stand the sight of me.

"You remember the kid Sanabria killed, Lamarca?" he said after a while. "I told you about him. It's the case we had him for at the motel if the son of a bitch had only rented his own room."

"I remember."

"The reason he was killed? Sanabria thought the kid was talking to an informant. *Thought* he was. In truth, he wasn't, but that didn't matter to Sanabria. When Joseph Lamarca's body was found, seven of his fingers were broken. Smashed. Bone showing."

It was quiet. He said, "That's what he did to someone he *thought* betrayed him, Perry. Then Joshua Cantrell. Then Ken Merriman. It all goes back to the same place, every single one of those bodies goes back to the damned motel room that he didn't rent. It's about atonement. You bet your ass I'm looking for it, buddy. You better believe it."

I finished my beer, and we sat in silence for a while and watched the TV without really seeing it. Then I ordered another beer and asked if he wanted a second whiskey, and he shook his head. Most of his first was still in the glass.

"I got upset the last time I talked with you," he said eventually, voice soft. "I thought you were being a bastard, to be honest. You said some very cutting things."

"I was having a bad day."

"That doesn't matter. The things you said were cutting, but I know that's because they were true. I screwed that situation up, Perry, I screwed it up *bad*, and a man died. A man was murdered, and I have that blood on my hands. Do you understand that? His blood is on *my* hands."

His eyes were red, and his voice sounded thin.

"I've got to live with that," he said, "and all I can do, the only way I know to cope with it, is by looking for atonement. Because while his blood might be on my hands, I didn't kill him—and if I can see that whoever did kill him is punished? Perry, that's the closest thing I've got to redemption."

I'd lost my taste for the beer now.

"I know Joshua Cantrell doesn't mean anything to you," he said, "but Ken Merriman should. So think of him, and help me. Let's see it through."

"What Ken Merriman means to me," I said, "is that it's time for me to walk away. What you're asking for, I just cannot do. I'm tired of being in the game. Tired of having to spend my days immersed in some filthy, foolish crime, trying to determine what son of a bitch killed a good man and dumped his body in a park where children play. It's not for me anymore. I'm sorry."

"I understand that you're tired," he said, "but I'm trying to tell you that you can't afford to be. Because there are too many people saying they're tired. The whole world is tired now, the whole damn world doesn't have the energy to set anything right. We want to wait on somebody else to do it, and yeah, maybe we believe that it should be done, but we just don't have it in us to *try* anymore. We're a sideline species these days, Perry. We turn the news on and see some tragedy or crisis and shake our heads and say, 'Boy, hope somebody gets to that. It is just outrageous that nobody's addressed that one yet.' Then we put on *American Idol* and go to bed."

"You watch *American Idol*?" I said.

"Don't be an asshole."

It was quiet then, and he waited a while, and eventually I said, "Dunbar, good luck. Really and truly—good luck—but I'm out."

His face fell and he looked away from me. Then he reached into his pocket and pulled out a bill and dropped it on the table. He got to his feet and shook my hand silently, and then he went to the door and stepped out into the wind, shoulders hunched and head down and alone.

Chapter Thirty-three

I couldn't sleep the night after Dunbar's visit. I'd worked out for two hours that afternoon, then gone to the Hideaway and caught up with Scott Draper for a few beers while we watched the Indians game. They were on a losing streak. I knew the feeling.

It was midnight when I got back to my apartment, and I went right to bed, hoping that the lingering effects of the alcohol would take care of the rest, put me to sleep quickly. They didn't. Two hours passed, then three, then four. I stared at the ceiling, wandered out to the couch, went back to bed, turned the TV on, turned it off, tried to read, tried to control my breathing, tried damn near everything I could think of and still couldn't find sleep.

I gave up around five, dressed in workout clothes, and went downstairs, thinking I'd punish my body for refusing sleep by going for yet another run. Break its will before it broke mine. By the time I got outside, though, I knew I didn't have it in me. I stretched out in the parking lot in the dark, breathing in the last cool air of night, another hot and humid day ready to replace it. If not a run, maybe a drive. That seemed better. I could drive to Edgewater Park before the traffic started, watch the sun rise over the lake and the city. I hadn't done that in years. Or maybe go down to the West Side Market, hang around and watch as the vendors arrived and set up their wares before the doors opened. I used to do that when I was a patrol officer, come off a night shift and head down to the market, a place that always felt like a step back in time.

There were plenty of possibilities, and they all sounded good. How I found myself in Old Brooklyn, then, parked across the street from Parker Harrison's apartment building, I really couldn't say.

He left the house just before six, exactly as he had the last time I'd seen him. He walked out of the apartment, turned and locked the door carefully with his key, then tested it once to be sure before he headed to his truck. It was a Chevy S10, at least fifteen years old, and for a second as he drove out of the lot he was facing directly toward me. Then he made the turn and pulled away and I started the Silverado and followed. I wanted to watch him. That was all. Didn't want another confrontation, didn't want to say a word to him, just wanted to watch him.

He drove to Riverside Cemetery, and I passed the entrance when he turned in, knowing it was too early in the morning not to attract attention by following him in. I gave it fifteen minutes, then circled back around and entered the cemetery, which was one of the city's oldest and largest. It was a beautiful place, really. More than a hundred acres of rolling green valley and flowering trees and marble monuments and the dead. There were plenty of them at Riverside.

I drove through the cemetery until I found Harrison's truck, parked in front of the maintenance building, empty. I'd missed him. I drove back up to the chapel, where I assumed my truck would be less noticeable, parked, and set out on foot. It was a huge place, and it would take a while to find him. I had the time.

I left the road and walked through the grounds, my shoes soon soaked by the dew. After a pass along the south side without any luck, I looped around and headed toward the north, away from the maintenance building. I was not alone in the cemetery. During the walk I saw two people beside graves, paying early-morning respects. I thought that it had been a long time since I'd been to see my mother and father's stones.

I was approaching the northeast bend of the road, ready to

head west and walk back toward the entrance, when I heard the buzz of a weed trimmer. A few minutes later I found Harrison trimming the base of a monument, head bowed.

For a moment I just stood there, unsure of what to do. He was at work, and that's all he'd be doing for the rest of the day. No need to watch him tend the grass and weeds in a graveyard. If I really wanted to begin surveillance on him, I could come back in the afternoon, wait for him to get off work, and see where he went. That was what mattered, surely. This did not.

I couldn't leave, though. Now that I'd found him, I wanted to watch just a little bit longer. Just a few minutes. I retreated across the grounds, looking for someplace where I could sit unnoticed and keep an eye on him. Sitting was key. I was suddenly feeling the groggy, mind-numbing weariness of an entirely sleepless night.

About a hundred yards from where Harrison was working, I found an enormous monument with a granite lion resting on top. The lion was lying down with its front paws stretched forward, its head up. The carving job was exquisite. I couldn't imagine how long something like that took. The name on the stone read simply DAYKIN. No first name, no dates. It was probably a family monument, I decided as I looked around the other stones and saw the Daykin name repeatedly. The patriarch making his claim.

I sat in the grass beneath the lion and leaned back until my head rested against the stone. Out across the way, Harrison's weeder buzzed and his shoulders swung back and forth methodically. What a place for a murderer to work.

That thought took me back to Harrison's apartment, to the night Ken and I had made our initial visit and Harrison first told us he worked in a cemetery, told us that it suited him. Ken's response—*how unsettling.*

"How unsettling." I said it aloud and laughed. Man, what a line. How unsettling. I laughed again, softer this time, an under-the-breath chuckle, and then I laid my head back against the stone again and closed my eyes and tried to find a moment of peace. It was there, sitting upright in a graveyard with my head on a piece of granite, that I finally fell asleep.

* * *

I woke only minutes later, but it felt longer than that, and I came around slowly, like that moment of awakening was at the end of a long, difficult climb. When my eyes opened it took me a second to place myself, and then I realized that Harrison was out of view and I could no longer hear the sound of his machine. I pushed off the stone and looked around and saw him not ten feet away, standing with his arms folded across his chest, watching me.

"Hello, Lincoln," he said. "I'm going to assume this is not a coincidence."

I thought about getting to my feet, but what was the point? Instead, I just leaned forward, rested my arms on my knees, and looked up at him. "Great place to work."

"I like it."

I nodded up at the lion above me. "Hell of a cat, too."

"Do you know who he was?"

"Daykin?" I shook my head.

"A railroad man," Harrison said. "Specifically, a conductor. He was one of the conductors on Lincoln's funeral train. John Daykin. This is one of my favorite monuments in the cemetery."

"You know them all?"

"More than you'd think," he said.

"You keep the graves clean," I said, "and Mark Ruzity carves them. Can you explain that?"

"Alexandra taught us the importance of honoring the dead. Mark took up the carving as his way of doing that. By the time I left Whisper Ridge, he'd met people out here, and got me the job. Not so sinister, really. I hate to disappoint you."

"You know that he's talked to Sanabria?" I said. "There's a photo of it, Harrison. Ruzity and Sanabria together around the time your beloved Alexandra and Joshua disappeared. You were on the phone with Sanabria then, yourself."

He didn't respond. I looked away from him and out across the sea of weathered stones left to mark lives long finished.

"They haven't made an arrest in Ken's murder yet, Harrison."

"If I could tell them who to arrest, I would."

"Yeah?"

"Why are you here? Why would you sit here and watch me work?"

"I need an answer," I said, "to just one question, Harrison. There are so many questions I think you can answer, but I need just this one: Why me? Why did you have to come to me? I ignored your first letter, so you wrote me more. I ignored those, so you came to see me. Why?"

"You've already asked me that."

"I know it. This time I'd like you to tell me the truth."

He sighed and lowered his weed trimmer to the ground, straightened again, and took a rag off his belt and ran it over his face and neck, soaking up the sweat from the morning's rapidly rising heat.

"It was the truth then, and it will be the truth this time, too," he said. "I came to you because of what I'd read. Because of what I hoped you would be."

"What was that?" I said. "Supposing I believed you, which I do not, what was it that you thought I would be, Harrison?"

"Someone who knew how to see the guilty."

"What?"

"Not how to find the guilty, Lincoln. How to see them. How to . . . consider them. The people behind the crime. I'm a murderer. I get that. Well, Joshua Cantrell was murdered, and not by me. I wanted to know who did it—and why."

"That's not what you asked me to do."

"No, and that was my mistake. I held on to the truth when I shouldn't have, but I wanted to get you to the house."

"Why was that so damn special? Why did I have to see the house?"

He spread his hand, waved it around us. "You see all these stones? What are they?"

I sat and stared up at him, searching his face and trying, yet again, to come to a judgment about him. I wanted to believe him.

"What would you call them?" he said. "These stones."

"Graves."

"That's beneath the stone. What are the—"

"Markers, monuments."

He nodded. "Joshua Cantrell has one. You've seen it. That house is his monument. She left it for him, Lincoln. Something to sit in his memory."

It was the same comparison Ken Merriman had made. The sort of comparison that came easily when a house had been outfitted with an epitaph.

"Home to dreams," I said.

"Yes. Dreams she'd shared with her husband. It's important to remember the dead. Alexandra understood that, and so do I. It's why I work here, Lincoln—and before you ask the question, yes, I think of the man I killed. I remember him. Every single day, I think of him, and of what I took from him and those who loved him. It's important to remember."

"You know that she left the house so Joshua would be remembered. You're sure of that."

He nodded.

"Do you know who killed him?"

He shook his head. I watched for the lie and couldn't find it.

"I wanted to know," he said. "That's why I came to you. You wish I never had, and I'm sorry about that. I picked you because I hoped you'd see past my prison sentence, see past my crime. The police can't do that. Neither could you, and that's all right. I took a chance with you. It didn't work out. Sometimes they don't."

"It didn't work out for *you*? Ken's dead, Harrison."

"That wasn't me. I'm sorry about it, more sorry than I can probably make you believe, but it was not me who killed him."

A car passed on the road, circling slowly through the cemetery, and neither Harrison nor I spoke until it was gone.

"Why were you talking to Dominic Sanabria?" I said.

"When?"

"Any of the times. You called him when Cantrell was killed, you called him when the body was found, you called him just before Ken was killed."

He hesitated before saying, "At first I was trying to get information out of him. Trying to get in touch with Alexandra."

"What did you tell him the day before Ken was killed?"

"I told him that you were done with the case. He'd called me earlier to say that his sister and her memory needed to be left alone. That was when I asked you to quit. I was worried for you, and I didn't want to be the one who put you in harm's way. I didn't trust Dominic."

"All of that might be believable, Harrison, but there's one call missing in that explanation. Why did you call him when the body was found? When it was found and *before* it was identified."

He looked uncomfortable, failed to meet my eyes for the first time. "I really can't speak of that."

"You piece of shit." I shook my head in disgust. "You know things that could help, and you won't say them. You don't really want to see anything resolved, don't give a damn about Ken or Cantrell or anybody else. It's all some sort of sick game to you."

"It's not that at—"

"*Then tell the rest of it!*" I got to my feet, shouted it at him.

He stood in silence and watched me. I waited for him to speak, and he did not. After a few minutes of staring at him, I shook my head again.

"I made a promise," he said, his voice very soft, "to someone who mattered more to me than anyone I've ever known. Can you understand that? I gave my *word*."

"To Alexandra? She's gone, Harrison. Gone, and maybe dead. She's been gone for twelve years. You want to let your promise to her prevent justice?"

No confirmation, no denial, no response.

"Why do you have such loyalty to that woman?" I said, weariness in my voice.

He didn't answer right away. I stood beside the Daykin monument, resting one hand on the lion's side, and I waited. Finally he spoke.

"It's never really quiet in prison," he said. "People think of it as a quiet place, solitary, but it's not. Doors bang, and guards walk around, and the other prisoners talk and shout and laugh and cough. It's loud all the time. Even at night, you hear sounds of other people. You're never really alone."

He paused, and I didn't say anything. Another car drove past.

"You're never alone," he said again, "and it's not an easy place to be. It shouldn't be, right? It's a place where you're sent to be punished, a place that's supposed to painful. You walk around with other murderers, with rapists, drug dealers. Some violent people, some crazy people. You're one of them, and you've got a role to play. You've got to seem more violent and more crazy than them. You got to be the *craziest* man in the place, understand? Because otherwise you will not survive."

He wet his lips, shifted in the grass.

"I'd been in for four years before I decided I couldn't finish. I just gave up, knew there was no way I could make it to the other side. There was a cleaning detail, and I got assigned to that, and I started stealing Drano. They had a big bottle, I knew I'd never get that out, so I emptied toothpaste tubes and filled them with the stuff, brought them back to my cell. You have any idea how hard it is to fill a toothpaste tube with Drano? Takes dedication, I assure you. I waited until I had three of them filled. I did *not* want to have too little to do the job. I thought there would probably be enough in those three tubes to kill me."

"You're still here," I said. "So it wasn't enough?"

"I think it would have been. I didn't take it."

"Why not?"

"It got quiet," he said. "The night I was going to take it, the place got quiet. For one hour. I can tell you that almost exactly. I was waiting, and I was scared, and then it got quiet. I had one silent hour. I couldn't believe it. Nobody was talking, or moving, or screaming, and in that hour I remembered, for the first time in a long time, that this was not all that I was. I'd killed somebody, and it was a terrible thing, and I was in this terrible place and I would be for years to come, but that was not all I was. If I committed suicide in there, though, if I died in that place, then it would be different. That would be my identity, all the world would ever know or remember about me, that I was another murderer who died in the place where murderers belong."

He took the rag off his belt again, ran it over his face, soaked up the fresh sweat on his forehead.

"I told that story to Alexandra Sanabria a few weeks before I was released," he said. "She put out her hand and took mine, and she promised me that we would take that one hour and make it my life. That everything I had been and pretended to be aside from it would no longer matter."

He squeezed the rag in his hand, and drops of sweat fell into the grass.

"She kept her promise, Lincoln. So I'll keep mine. I'm sorry, but I'll keep mine."

PART THREE

Honors and Epitaphs

Chapter Thirty-four

The summer went down quietly. The heat broke and the humidity dropped and the kids went back to school. The Indians put together one of their classic late-season runs to ensure you'd spend the winter with that bitter oh-so-close taste in your mouth. The gym attracted a few new members. The PI office stayed closed and locked.

Joe came back to town in the middle of September. He'd been gone for more than nine months without a single trip back, and when he opened up his house and stepped inside and looked around, I couldn't read his feelings.

"So much dust," he said. He'd left Florida at the end of August but headed west instead of north, making the drive to Idaho with Gena. Just keeping her company on a long drive, he'd said. He spent two weeks there, though, and I wondered if it had been a scouting trip of sorts. He'd told me the two of them had not made any future plans but had also not closed any doors. I left it at that.

We reopened the office on the last day of September and devoted a morning to cleaning and reorganizing. We'd share the background check duties and the profits. It wouldn't be enough to support both of us, but that was okay—we each had a supplemental income, mine through the gym and Joe's through his police pension. The screenings provided extra cash as well as something to do.

By mid-October we'd developed a comfortable rhythm,

spending a few mornings a week in the office together, processing reports and requesting local court record checks where we needed them. It felt good to have Joe back, good to exchange some of our old jabs and barbs. What we were doing was not detective work, not in any sense that I'd come to know, but it was important, too. We routinely discovered applicants with criminal charges in their histories, from misdemeanors to felonies. These were the kind of people you didn't want in your employ, the sort who could bring real problems inside the walls of your company. In some circumstances, the charges were very old—ten, fifteen, twenty years—but we recorded them just the same. Old charges or not, there was a risk factor associated with the hiring of those people, and our new employer didn't want to take that risk. Couldn't afford to, they told us. Not in this day and age.

It was late October when I heard from Quinn Graham. He called the office and seemed surprised when I answered.

"I thought you'd quit."

"Just case work. We've got some other things on the table."

"I see."

"What's up, Graham? You got something?"

"No," he said, and I could hear embarrassment in his voice. "Not the sort of thing you're looking for, at least."

"Then what is it?"

"Thought you might like to know that Joshua Cantrell's parents won their case yesterday."

"Alexandra's legally declared dead?"

"Yeah, that happened a few weeks back, actually. Yesterday they came to a settlement. The house is going to be claimed by the estate and sold."

"Money split between them and Sanabria?"

"No. Sanabria's attorneys showed up and said he wanted no part of it. Went through whatever legal process they had to for him to waive his interest. It all goes to the Cantrells now."

At least that bastard wasn't taking the money. It wasn't much, but it helped.

"They going to put the house on the market soon?" I asked.

"Immediately, is my understanding."

We talked a little while longer, and he told me that a few weeks earlier he had made an arrest in the case of the murdered girls that he'd been working that summer. The perp was a thirty-year-old graduate student at Penn State who was working on a thesis about pornography. I was glad Graham got him. I was glad he'd told me about it, too. It was good to know these things.

Two days later a short article ran in the newspaper. It wasn't much, but it explained the legal situation and announced the pending sale of the house. Asking price hadn't been set yet but was rumored to be around four million. The Cantrell family was considering subdividing the land, though, so there would be a delay in the sale while they studied their options.

The morning the article ran, I stopped in the office and asked Joe if he could handle a few days without me.

"Where you going to be?"

"Sitting in the woods with binoculars and a camera."

He looked at me for a long time without speaking.

"I know you'll think it's crazy," I said, "but I want to watch that house."

"The Cantrell house? You want to watch it?"

I nodded. "I want to see who shows."

"What makes you think anyone will except a Realtor?"

"Because that place is sacred to people, Joe. Was, at least. I'd like to know if anyone comes to say goodbye."

"Alexandra?"

"I don't know. There might be a chance. Or maybe Dominic. Or Harrison. Or somebody else entirely."

He frowned. "Even if someone does—and I have trouble believing that anyone will—what the hell will that tell you?"

I didn't answer that. Couldn't. Still, I wanted to see it. I was remembering Ken Merriman's remark that day on Murray Hill. *She had a damn epitaph carved beside the door. That place means something to her. So let me tell you—if she's alive, I bet she'll come back to see it again.*

"If you feel it's worth a shot, then knock yourself out," Joe said. He paused, then said, "Hell, maybe I could take a day or two at it with you. Been a while since I did any surveillance. Old time's sake, why not, right?"

We logged a full week at it. I spent more time there than Joe, rising early each morning and sitting until dusk each night, but he put in plenty of hours. I didn't think it was wise to sit inside the gate, so instead we parked up the road and watched.

In the first two days, there was a decent amount of activity, but it was casual interest, people who drove up to the gate and then pulled back out and went on their way. The newspaper story had sparked some curiosity, that was all.

On the third day, someone drove a black BMW up to the gate, unlocked it, and drove through. I was intrigued by that one until the driver stepped out of the car, and then I recognized him as Anthony Child. Checking on the property one last time, maybe, before it was taken out of his care. He would probably be glad to see the hassle go.

The next afternoon there were more visitors. An old van arrived just after one and parked at the end of the drive. I watched through my long-range camera lens as the doors opened and two men stepped out—Parker Harrison from the passenger side and a rangy, gray-haired guy I'd never seen from the driver's seat. The gray-haired guy was carrying a bouquet of flowers. He kept them in his hand as he and Harrison walked around the gate and began to fight their way up through the woods, just as I had in the spring. I snapped a few pictures before they disappeared into the trees, including one clear shot of the van and the license plate.

Joe had been out with me for the morning but left around noon. I called him at the office now. "Guess who's here. Parker Harrison."

"Really?"

"Uh-huh. Just showed up with another guy I didn't recognize, and they aren't in Harrison's truck. You want to run the plate for me?"

I gave him the license number, and a few minutes later he

called back and told me the truck was registered to a Mark Ruzity.

"Mean anything to you?"

"Yeah. He was another of Alexandra's murderers. The first one."

"What do you think they're doing?"

"Paying respects," I said. "He brought flowers, Joe. I'm telling you, the place is a damn memorial at this point."

Ruzity and Harrison came back out twenty minutes later, sans flowers, and got back into the truck and drove away.

So now I had an answer. I'd seen what I told him I wanted to see, and yet I knew nothing more than I had before. Ken's bizarre prediction—*she'll come back to see it*—was as foolish as I should have known it was.

I stayed, though. For the rest of that day, and the three that followed. By the end of the week I was starting to lose my mind from sitting in one spot so long, and Joe was quiet on the topic, which meant he thought it was time to give up. Even Amy asked how much longer I intended to keep watch, and her tone made her feelings clear—it was time to call the surveillance off.

I told them I wanted one more day. Spent twelve hours watching that lonely drive and the gate and didn't see a soul.

"You knew it was a long shot anyhow," Amy said. "Time to let it pass."

I agreed with her, told her the whole thing had gone on too long. Then the next morning I got up and took my camera and my binoculars and drove back and watched nothing. I did it the day after that, too, then came home and told Amy I'd spent the day at the gym. The next morning I rose before dawn and returned.

That was the coldest day of the fall so far, and by seven my coffee was gone and the sun wasn't even up yet and the chill had already filled the cab of the truck and gone to work on my knotted back and shoulder muscles. It was time to quit, I realized. This was lunacy, or close to it.

I was parked just off the road beside a cluster of saplings

and brush, squeezed in the back of the extended cab with blackout curtains hung in the windows. I'd now spent about a hundred hours in this position, the most surveillance time I'd logged on a case in years, and I wasn't making a dime from it.

When the headlights crested the hill and slowed near the drive, I didn't even lift my camera. I'd seen too many cars pass to get excited about this one. Then it came to a complete stop, and I sat up and pushed the blackout curtain farther aside and watched as the car—a small red sedan—turned into the gravel track and drove right up to the gate. I finally got my shit together then, reached for the camera and got it up and turned on as the driver's door swung open. My zoom was good, but it wasn't built for low-light conditions, and all I could see in the predawn gloom was that the driver looked like a woman, and she was walking around the gate and through the trees. She was walking toward the house.

Chapter Thirty-five

For a moment, I wasn't sure what to do. I just sat there holding my camera and looking at the dark trees she'd vanished into, wondering if I should wait for her to reemerge and then follow her, or set off now with hopes of catching her at the house. After a brief hesitation, I decided to take action over patience.

I got out of the truck, leaving my camera but wearing my gun, and walked down the road toward the drive. I took my time, knowing that any attempt to follow her quietly through the woods around the creek would be hopeless. It was important to give her a little lead time. When I reached the red sedan, I knelt by the back bumper and took a photograph of the license plate with my cell phone's built-in camera, a device I'd come to appreciate in moments like this. It was an Ohio plate. Surely, then, this couldn't be Alexandra. She couldn't be living so close to home. It would be an aggressive Realtor checking on the house before going to the office, and nothing more. When I walked around to the front of the car I spotted an Avis sticker, though. A rental.

I walked toward the woods bordering the gate. The trees didn't seem nearly so dark when I was in them as they'd looked through the camera, and I found I was able to walk without much difficulty. It was easier now, in late fall, than it had been in spring, when everything was green and growing and the water in the creek rode high on the banks. Once I was around the gate and away from the creek I slowed again, focusing on a quiet approach now. I made my way back to the rutted drive and followed it along, seeing and hearing nothing of the woman ahead.

When the drive curled around its final bend and came out at the base of the hill that hid the house, I stopped and scanned the trees, searching for her. I gave it a careful study, made absolutely certain she wasn't in sight, and then continued forward. I'd taken at least five steps toward the hill when I finally realized she was at the door.

I hadn't seen her at first because the door was beneath that stone arch, covered in shadows, and she was no longer standing. She was kneeling before the door, and as I walked closer, in slow, silent strides, I saw that her head was bowed and her arm extended, her palm resting on the oaken door.

It was her. Other women might make a trip out to this home before the sun rose, but none would drop to their knees and touch its door as if at an altar.

Alexandra had come home.

I stopped walking when I was about thirty feet from her, stood and waited. She held her position for a while, maybe a minute, maybe two. Didn't move at all, didn't make a sound, just knelt there with her head bowed and her hand on the door. When she finally moved it was to rub her hand gently across the wood, and then she got to her feet and turned and saw me.

"It's a beautiful house," I said. "One of a kind. Do you miss it?"

Her eyes left me and flicked to either side, searching for others.

"I'm alone," I said, "and I don't intend to bring you any trouble. I would just like to hear you talk for a while. I'd like you to tell me some things. I need that very much."

She stepped away from the door, out of the stone arch and into the light, toward me. She was not tall, no more than five foot two or three, with a slender build and graceful movements. When she came closer I saw that much remained from the face that had stared at me in photographs—the fine bones and small nose and mouth, the impossibly dark eyes. Her hair was different, chopped short and close to her skull, but for the most part she looked the same.

"I wear a wig most of the time," she said, watching me study her. "I have glasses even though I don't need them. They're clear, no prescription. I wear makeup now when I never used to, lots of eyeliner and foundation and other junk that I just hate to put on my face."

She came to within a few feet of me, then tilted her head, frowned at me, and said, "You're Lincoln."

I hadn't been mentioned in any newspaper article; there was no public record of my involvement with any of the cases surrounding this woman.

"How do you know that?"

She ignored me, turned and looked over her shoulder at the door.

"You were right," she said. "It is a beautiful home, and I do miss it. I miss it terribly, the house and all of the other things I left behind. The life I left behind."

"Alexandra," I said, "how do you know my name?"

"From Ken Merriman."

I stood still and silent and stared at the calm set of her face. Then I said, slowly and carefully, "You don't mean that you spoke to Ken Merriman."

"Of course I do," she said. "I hired him."

Chapter Thirty-six

The sentence left her lips almost carelessly and struck me like lead.

"You hired Ken Merriman?" I said. "You *hired* him?"

She nodded.

"No," I said. "Joshua's parents hired him. That was in the papers. He'd been looking for you for twelve years."

"He looked for me for about nine months," she said, "and then he found me."

"Explain it," I said. It felt hard to get the words out.

"You understand how it began. Joshua's parents hired him. If there is one thing I felt worst about in all of this, it's the uncertainty they had to deal with. That was terrible, I'm sure. They were not kind people, and Joshua's relationship with them had been a painful and difficult one, but that was not enough to justify what I did."

She fell silent for a few seconds before saying, "There's probably no way for people to understand the decisions I made. All I can say is that once I was gone, once it was already under way, I wasn't brave enough to return. There was nothing that could be done to bring Joshua back, not for me or for them."

"Tell me about Ken," I said. The sun was beginning to show pink through the trees. I could hear the birds and the wind but nothing of the road. "How did he find you?"

"The same way you did."

"He watched the house?"

"He asked everyone he talked with about the words by the door, the inscription that's carved there. Everyone told him they'd not seen the carving until we were gone, and he believed that it had been left as an epitaph. He was right, of course."

She lifted her hand and waved at the eastern sky, now beginning to glow red with the rising sun. "Let's walk up top, okay? I loved to sit up there and watch the sunrise. It's just gorgeous."

She moved without waiting for my response, walked around to the side of the hill and started up, following a flagstone path that was now almost completely submerged in weeds. I followed.

When we got to the top of the hill, she moved over to the old well house and leaned against its side, facing the sun. Again I marveled at how completely hidden the house was, nothing but grass and soil evident beneath our feet, only the lip of a stone wall indicating the drop-off on the other side where the windows looked out on the pond. I walked to within a few feet of her and stood silently, arms folded, waiting. She seemed at ease, and for a while she just looked off at the sunrise and did not speak. When she finally broke the silence, she didn't bother to turn around.

"How many days have you been watching?"

"Quite a few."

She nodded. "This was going to be my last visit, you know. It will have to be. The house will have new owners soon. I can't very well come by then."

"If you know everything that's happened, why didn't you announce yourself, prove that you're still alive and keep the home? Why would you let it be sold?"

She didn't answer.

"Did you kill him?" I said.

Now she turned, wounded. "Of course I didn't kill him. Joshua? I loved him so much. So very dearly."

"Then what are you hiding from?"

She stepped away from the well house and dropped down to sit in the grass, cross-legged. It was tall grass, rising well above her waist, but she settled into it comfortably and pushed her sleeves up on her forearms. She was wearing dark jeans and a gray fleece jacket, and there were simple silver bracelets on both wrists. She had to be near fifty now, but she looked like a college student settling down outside of a dormitory. If she weighed more than a hundred and ten pounds I would've been stunned, and her skin was weathered but still smooth, every thin wrinkle looking as if it belonged and added something that you'd miss otherwise.

"Are you going to continue standing?" she said, looking up at me. "It makes me uncomfortable."

So I sat in the grass with her, felt the moisture of day-old rain leave the ground and soak through my jeans, and watched the sun rise behind her as she told me the story.

Alexandra's life was shaped very much by her father's, by the world of crime and violence that had surrounded her childhood. The money he'd left was something she'd viewed as an embarrassment at first and then decided to reinvest into the reentry program. Her vision for Whisper Ridge as a sort of work farm had not received the funding or support it needed. She decided to operate at a smaller level and use success to grow the operation in the future. It was at this point that she began to feel her husband's resistance.

"Joshua was not a direct man in times of conflict," she said. "He wouldn't come out and tell me flatly that he didn't want to open our home to this, but I knew it was the case, and I pushed ahead anyhow. I thought he believed in the ideals, and that time would take care of the rest. It was a selfish thing to do, maybe. I've wondered about that a lot, and I think that it probably was, but at the time I could not imagine . . . I'm sure you know I could not imagine what would come."

What came was an increasingly troubled marriage. Alexandra's version of events meshed well with John Dunbar's. She described Joshua as growing withdrawn and distrustful. Then Parker Harrison was hired, a move that exacerbated the problem at Whisper Ridge.

"My relationship with Parker was very close," she told me.

"I'd say that of all of them, of course, but not to the same level. Parker and I, we were similar spirits. I found his story truly tragic."

"I believe the family of his victim would agree," I said.

She stopped speaking and looked at me with a frown that was more sad than disapproving.

"To say one is not to dismiss the other," she said. "Can you understand that?"

"Can I hear the rest of the story?"

"As I said, my relationship with Parker was special. We were so close. I think that fueled the resentment that was already in Joshua."

"You say your relationship with Harrison was special. Was it also sexual?"

"No, no, no. Absolutely not. Although during the first six months Parker was with us, Joshua's personality changed. I now understand this was when he was in contact with the FBI and being pressured to inform on my brother, but I didn't back then."

"It wasn't the FBI," I said. "It was one retired agent with some bad ideas."

"Nevertheless, my husband was withdrawing, and I finally began to understand just how much damage had been done. Then we began to discuss who would replace Parker, and Joshua told me that he wanted to do the interviews and make the offer, which was something I'd always handled in the past. I was confused by that but agreed, because I was so happy to see his enthusiasm returning. Then he decided on Salvatore Bertoli, who was very far from the profile we'd agreed upon at the start."

"You didn't know Bertoli was associated with your brother?"

"No. Salvatore didn't know who I was, either, because my name was Cantrell, and my brother and I were not close. We saw each other, but only rarely, and we did not discuss his . . . associates. All of that is in the past, though. My brother's crimes. He served two years, and when he got out his life changed. He kept no ties. Many who would've posed the greatest problems to him were in prison themselves, and the others accepted his desire to step away. My brother has not been involved with a crime in fifteen years."

"There are police who would dispute that," I said. "I've met some of them."

Her arms unfolded and she leaned forward. "What proof did they show? What evidence? What did they tell you that was current, not historic?"

"Nothing," I said, and then, as the satisfaction crossed her face, "but some of those *historic* events included murder. There are people who feel those things are unresolved."

The satisfaction disappeared, and she dropped her eyes again. "I'm sure that's true. All I can tell you is that he's not been involved in anything criminal in years, that he's led a life that benefits others. He's a businessman now, a generous one. You should see the charities—"

"All due respect," I said, "I'm not here to evaluate your brother's tithing history. I'm glad you don't think he's killed anyone lately. I'd agree that's progress, but it's not what I'm interested in."

I expected that would get a rise, some defensiveness, but instead she just considered me calmly. It was a gaze that made me uncomfortable, as if I fit neatly into a mold she'd been studying her whole life and understood well. When she began to speak again it was without rancor, leaving the subject of her brother behind.

"I was losing trust in my husband and had none in Salvatore. I felt bad things coming into my home, and so I asked Parker to stay. I trusted him. That's the decision that put Joshua over the edge. I didn't see it at the time, of course, but apparently he'd had misgivings and was being bullied along by that FBI agent, Dunbar. When I said I wanted Parker to stay, though, it incensed him, and he decided to go ahead with it. The house became a very ugly place for a while, a distrustful, silent place."

"I've talked to Dunbar," I said, "and he said he conceived the whole thing because he is certain that Bertoli witnessed your brother killing a man named Johnny DiPietro."

"That's not true."

"According to your brother."

"No. According to Salvatore."

"What?"

"He told Parker," she said, "that he understood what Joshua was trying to do and that whoever had put him up to it was absolutely wrong, didn't understand who they should be after, but that it was someone who wouldn't hesitate to kill my husband."

"It seems logical that he'd say that."

"Perhaps, but Parker believed him, and Salvatore moved out."

"At which point Harrison reported all of this to you," I said. "I'm supposed to believe you never chose to confront your husband about it?"

"I did confront him," she said, "and we had a royal battle, a screaming raging fight, and it saved our marriage. It would have saved our marriage."

Her voice faded, tears rose in her eyes, and she dabbed them away gently without shame. She looked hauntingly beautiful in that moment.

"That night was when the silence broke," she said, "and everything that had been held secret was shared. He told me what he'd thought and what he'd done, and I told him how his silence had damaged us, and that night we made love like people *in* love for the first time in years—and we decided we were going to leave."

"For good?"

She shook her head. "No. For a few months, maybe a year. Joshua had been talking about it for a long time, urging for a trip overseas, and at the time I'd refused because I thought it would set us back in what we were doing here. That night, I agreed to it, because I thought that we had to get away to find a shared life again, so we could come back. Otherwise we were going to lose each other. Maybe we would have anyhow, but I like to think differently."

She stopped talking then, and her mouth became a hard line. For a moment I thought she was angry, but then I realized the tears were gaining on her again and she was determined not to be overrun.

"Joshua also thought we had to leave for safety. After what Parker told us, he thought we could be in danger."

"So you planned to leave," I said, "but you never made it. Your husband never made it, at least."

She nodded. "We made calls about arrangements for the house, for the mail, all those things you need to do before going abroad. The last time I saw him, I was heading out to talk to a travel agent and asked if he wanted to come, too. He said he had things to do around the house and I should go alone. I was gone for maybe three hours. When I came back here, I found my husband's body."

She was staring at the well house as if something were crawling out of it.

"He was outside. Just in front of the door. He'd been shot, and there was blood all over the stone, and when I saw his body I was sure that my brother had killed him."

"How did you know?"

"Dominic gave Joshua a present when we got married. It was a ring, this horrible ring with an enormous stone that surely cost a fortune but could not have been less like my husband. He was not a man who wore rings. My brother, at that time, was. He was loud and flashy and wore expensive jewelry and to him the gift meant something. Joshua hated it, though, and the only time he ever wore it was when my brother was around."

She folded her arms across her chest again, even though the wind wasn't blowing and the sun was warm on us through the bare trees, and said, "The ring was lying on his chest. Right there in the blood. It had been dropped in the blood and I understood what it meant. The ring had been a symbol to my brother, a welcome into our family, and Joshua had betrayed that welcome. So my brother killed him, and even as he lied to me about it, he left that ring as a message."

"He was murdered here," I said, "and his body was left at the door."

She nodded.

"Then could you explain how he ended up in the woods in Pennsylvania?"

She looked at me and then away, twisted her torso as if stretching her back, and spoke with her face turned from mine. "I took him there and I buried him."

"I'm glad you lied about that," I said. "Because it tells me how bad a liar you are, Alexandra, and that's going to help me believe the rest of what you've said."

She unfolded the stretch slowly, let her face come back around.

"Parker Harrison buried him," I said. "Now tell me why."

"To help me," she said. "To save me. He'd been gone that afternoon, and when he drove back in, with the truck all loaded up with mulch, he found me sitting there beside Joshua."

"Why didn't you call the police?"

"The police wouldn't bring him back, but they would ask me to stay here and face the investigation and the trial, to prosecute my brother, to deal with the media. All of that would happen if I stayed, and so much more. There were people like Parker, and like Nimir Farah and Mark Ruzity, and I knew the publicity would find them, and I thought that would be a terrible thing. I saw no good coming from it at all, and so much harm."

"What about justice for your husband?" I said. "That meant nothing?"

"Of course it did. My response was one of shock, I'll admit that. The idea of having to bear what would come . . . I decided I couldn't do it. That may seem like cowardice to you, and you may be right. I'll let you make that judgment."

"Mark Ruzity was seen with your brother after you disappeared, after Joshua was killed," I said. "And Parker Harrison called him. Why?"

"I asked Parker to pass along a message to my brother, to tell him that I was leaving, would never speak to him again, and that he should never look for me."

"What about Ruzity?"

She frowned. "Mark is such a good soul, but he struggles with his anger. He really does. He and Parker were close, and I told Parker that he could tell Mark only that I was leaving because of my brother's actions. I didn't trust his reaction to the details. Even so, I suspect Mark might have . . . given a more direct message to Dominic."

"I'm sorry?"

She looked up. "I suspect he threatened to kill him if he pursued me."

I thought of the chisel against my forehead, and then I thought of the photograph Dunbar had taken, the way Ruzity had clasped his hand around Sanabria's neck, pulled him close, and whispered in his ear. There weren't many people who would threaten to kill a mob boss, but Mark Ruzity seemed like he could be one of them easily enough.

"Harrison took the body," I said, "and you took off."

"Yes."

I shook my head, wondering now more than ever why he had decided to darken my door. He knew what had happened. What in the hell had he really wanted?

"Did he know where you went?" I asked. "Did you have any contact with him?"

"No."

So maybe he'd just wanted to find her. Maybe he'd been honest about that much.

"I had no contact with Parker," she said, "until this May. Until the day before Ken was murdered. That day, I called Parker to tell him not to trust you."

"What?"

"I told him that I was safe and well and that I knew he was looking for me but it would be dangerous for him to have any association with police and detectives. He'd buried my husband's body. It was easy to imagine he could be blamed. I said if anything happened, all he needed to do was ask me, and I'd come forward."

The day before Ken was murdered. That was the same day Harrison had told me to quit, but then he'd asked that final question, asked who Ken really was.

"Why didn't you explain Ken to him?" I said.

"Ken was the only person who knew how to find me, and had known for years. Couldn't the police have charged him with something for that? I wanted to keep him out of anything negative."

"Out of anything negative," I echoed. "He's dead. Your decision to leave your husband's murder unanswered is understandable, maybe even acceptable. This isn't."

"I agree."

"Yet you haven't contacted the police, haven't taken any action."

"I didn't know what action to take. I've been gone for twelve years. I have a new life, in a new place. I don't want to destroy that in the way my old life was destroyed."

"But you're the only person who knows anything."

"Here's all I know: that on the morning before he died Ken Merriman left me a message—"

"That's another lie. He didn't leave you a message, Alexandra. All the phone records were checked and rechecked."

"He didn't use his own phone, or mine. He understood my reluctance to give that out, and so years earlier he created an account with a phone message service, some anonymous thing, and he used pay phones and a calling card, just as I did. It was the only way we were in touch. Never in actual conversation, always through an exchange of messages. Now would you like to hear what he said that last day?"

"Yes."

"He said that he believed the two of you were getting close to the truth of my husband's murder, and that it had nothing to do with my brother, and more to do with a car."

Chapter Thirty-seven

"A *car*?" I stared at her, and I couldn't speak. A car. What car?

"You don't know what that means?" she said.

"No. I don't know, because he cut me out of it, went off alone on whatever theory he had and got himself killed."

"He cut you out of it because he was waiting for my permission to tell you the truth. To give full disclosure. He thought you could be trusted."

"Would you have given it to him?"

She was quiet for a while before saying, "I don't know. I suppose so. I've told you the truth now."

"Only because I found you." As I said it I realized Ken had told me *how* to find her. That constant insistence that she would return to the house if it were sold, that she'd have to see it one last time. *Let me tell you,* he'd said, the way he started so many sentences, *if she's alive, she'll come back for one more visit before the place is sold.*

"You told him you'd come back here," I said. "When you found out your in-laws were making a claim on the property, you told him you'd come back before it was sold."

"Yes."

He'd led me to her. Brought me here.

"He'd known for years," I said, "and kept the secret. Why?"

"All I told him was what I've told you, only with far less composure. It was my first trip back to the house, and I was already a wreck when he found me. Then that sense of being caught . . . he calmed me down, and he listened to me, and I told him the same story, only without some of the information I have now."

"You told him all of this and then asked him to just go on and pretend he had no idea where you were."

She nodded. "You disapprove, and I'm not surprised. Most people would share your opinion, I'm sure. Ken Merriman was not one of them. He understood when I told him that everything had been taken from me. There were two great loves in my life—my husband and my mission here. They were destroyed. Do you think the state would have continued to work with me? I'd gotten a man killed rather than rehabilitated. My work was destroyed, my husband dead, my brother responsible. I ran from it. I ran, okay? It was wrong, maybe, and weak, certainly, but it is what I did."

I didn't respond.

"I begged Ken Merriman to let me leave, and he did," she said. "He did."

This would have been after the newspaper articles and the public complaints of Joshua Cantrell's parents. After immense damage to Ken's reputation and to his career. He could have played the ultimate trump card by producing Alexandra, silenced every critic and bought himself some amount of fame. It was a hell of a story, a hell of a mystery, and he could have brought it to light. Instead he chose silence, went back to that career of infidelity cases and insurance work, of financial problems and low respect. I thought of the time he'd told me that his wife was right to leave him, what he'd said about making a decision that seemed absolutely right at the time, then seeing the way it affected your family and wondering if it was a selfish choice.

"Do you appreciate the losses he took for you?" I said. "What he gave up?"

"Of course I do. He damaged his own life to protect mine."

"It was the epitaph," I said. "That's what convinced him you'd come back?"

She nodded.

"Who did the carving?"

"Parker. At my request, and after I was gone. I wanted to leave some sense of a memorial, and I wanted the words to speak to my brother. I wanted him to know that *I* knew he'd killed my husband. Ken Merriman suspected something close, and he thought that if I viewed the house as a memorial, I might return to it. Probably around the last date, April twelfth. So he waited, and he watched. Every day for three weeks."

Three weeks. I wouldn't have lasted that long. I remembered now what Casey Hopper had told me when I called to ask him about Ken—*You know I was a sniper in Vietnam. So when I say somebody is patient . . .*

"You didn't come back on the twelfth?"

She shook her head. "I wanted to, but then I was afraid that might be expected. So I came later."

"He was still waiting."

"Yes. He said everyone told him how important this place was to me, how much hope and excitement I'd held for it, and between that and the epitaph he became convinced I'd come back."

"The house was almost new," I said, "and worth a fortune. You intended to just leave it empty forever?"

"There was nothing left for me here. There was no way I could continue to live here—but sell the house? I could never have done that. Never."

"It's gone now," I said. "I doubt you can reclaim it. It might be too late."

She nodded. "I won't try to stop it. Let them have their money. I owe them that much, surely."

"They did great damage to Ken's career."

"I know, and when he left a message telling me that you'd be inquiring about the house, I said I wanted to hire him to find out who you were working for. I was afraid it was them again, and that Parker would be at risk. I didn't imagine he was the client."

"When you found out, you asked Ken to hang around and keep an eye on things?"

"No. That was on his own. He'd evidently grown doubtful of my brother's guilt."

"You have no contact with your brother?"

"None. As I said, for so many years I believed he killed Joshua. Then Ken left that final message and said he thought I was wrong."

"And that the police needed to pay attention to a car," I said.

She nodded again.

"It needs to be finished," I said. "You have to realize that."

"Will the police be able to finish it?" she said. "After all this time?"

"I'll be able to," I said. "Hell, according to Ken, I already did. Now I just have to figure out *how* I did."

We stayed for another hour, sat there as the sun rose higher and our muscles stiffened, and she told me more of her story but nothing that compared to what I'd already heard. Eventually I asked her where she had been for the past twelve years. She gave more of an answer than I expected.

"I live in a small town not in this country but not so far away, either." She laughed. "How difficult of a riddle is that? Fine, so I live in a small Canadian town. I live under a different name, and I've worn a wig for so long that it feels like part of me. I make a modest living in modest ways and it's all that I need. In my new life, it's more than I need. I've never remarried, and I doubt that I ever will. I have friends whom I treasure, people who mean more to me than I can express, and none of them, not a soul, understands my past. I haven't lied to them, I've just asked for no questions, and they have respected that. Those closest to me have, at least."

I had so many questions myself, but it became clear that she had fewer answers, and after a time the conversation became stagnant and then disappeared altogether. I didn't want to let her go. I also knew we couldn't stay.

"I could hold you here," I said, "and call the police. There are many of them who would like to talk to you."

She didn't answer. Just held my eyes in silence.

"I'm not sure I want to do that," I said. "Maybe I will, soon, but not yet. I'm equally certain it would be a mistake to let you leave."

"Give me your phone number," she said. "I'll call you in a day. I promise I will do that. Whatever you want from me, I'll offer it."

"Including coming forward?"

Again, the silence.

"Ah," I said. "Whatever I want, except that."

"Maybe that. I'm not sure. I've been gone for many years, and I have a new life that would be sacrificed. Surely you know that's not a snap decision."

"No decision that takes twelve years to make is—but I'm not sure it's your decision to make, Alexandra."

We sat and looked at each other for a while, and then I got to my feet. My legs felt foreign. We'd been sitting for a long time.

"I can accept all of this as the truth, and a week from now realize it was a lie and feel a fool for believing you," I said.

"It isn't a lie."

"It may be," I said. "If it is, you can know this—I'll chase you. For as long as it takes me, and as far as it takes me, I'll chase you."

She stood as well, brushed off her jeans, and then stepped forward and offered her hand. I clasped it and held it and looked into her eyes as she said, "I'll say this one more time—it isn't a lie."

She walked away from me then, walked to that short ridge of stone that marked the rear wall of the house and looked down at the pond. She stood there with her hands in the pockets of her jeans and her shoulders hunched, looking down. I gave her a few minutes before I followed.

"I wish you could have seen it," she said when I was beside her.

"I can imagine what it looked like."

"No." She shook her head. "You can't. When Parker was tending the grounds, when everything was at its best, it was beyond what you can imagine. In the spring, when it was all in bloom . . . no, you can't imagine what that looked like."

She took her hands from her pockets and turned away. "It was everything I'd dreamed of. We could have done so much here. We could have done so much."

Chapter Thirty-eight

I walked up the drive with her, and neither of us spoke. When she reached her rental car, she turned and faced me.

"I'll call tomorrow," she said, "and we'll figure out how to move forward. You may not believe me, but it is the truth. If I don't call, keep your word. Start the chase."

"That might seem like a joke to you," I said, "but it is not to me. I don't care where you are, Alexandra, I'll find you eventually. Anyone can be found."

"Ken Merriman already taught me that." She took my hand again, squeezed it once, and then turned and opened the driver's door and climbed inside. I waited until she'd started the engine before I left and walked back up the road to my truck. I got inside, started it up, and drove to the highway. I stared at every vehicle that passed and thought, *He said all they needed to do was pay attention to a car.*

There was only one possibility coming to my mind, and Mike London had checked it out. The day Ken and I had lunch with him, he told us about a vehicle he'd seen near Bertoli's murder scene that had belonged to a chop shop affiliated with Dominic Sanabria. What had the owner's name been? Neloms. Darius Neloms. His alibi checked out solid, though, and the lead dried up. So what could Ken have possibly seen that Mike did not?

Unless it was a different car entirely. If that was the case, then I was as utterly clueless as I had been before talking to Alexandra.

I was halfway back to the city when my cell phone rang, and I saw the call was coming from the office. Joe.

"You're out there again, aren't you," he said when I answered, and then, before I could respond, "LP, you've got to let it go. You've got to stop."

"She came to the house this morning."

For a moment I didn't hear a thing.

"Tell me it is the truth," he said, "and that I don't need to begin searching for the proper institution for you."

I told him what had happened. By the time I was done, I was a mile from the office, and he hadn't spoken for a long time.

"I let her go," I said, "and I know you'll tell me what a terrible mistake that was, but I don't care. I'll find her again if I have to."

"If you believe what she told you, that's not the issue of the day," he said, and something inside me sagged with relief. He agreed with me. Alexandra was no longer the focus.

"I believe it," I said, "because I saw her lie today, and, Joseph, she is not good at it."

"And the car?" he said. "Do you have any idea what that means?"

"Maybe. If I'm wrong, then I've got nothing. We'll have to wait and see."

I hung up with him, and five minutes later I was behind my desk. I told Joe what I remembered from Mike London's investigation, then leaned back with my hands spread.

"That's the best I've got. Darius Neloms was an associate of Sanabria, but he was far from the inner circle. The guy painted stolen cars and sent them back out the door. It's not like he was Sanabria's right-hand man. Even if he was, Ken apparently was questioning whether Sanabria had anything to do with the murder."

"He said the car was important. So maybe he found out who else had access to it."

"Maybe. If it doesn't go back to that chop shop, though, then I have no idea what he was talking about. We talked to Mike the day before Ken was killed, so it would have been fresh in his mind, and if he was giving me credit for getting him to the solution, well, that's the only thing I got him to. Only London mentioned a car."

"Well," Joe said, "I'd say now's the time to call him."

So I called him. Put him on speaker while Joe sat with his chin resting on steepled fingertips and listened. I had not spoken to Mike London since Ken was killed. He'd called after he heard the news, more curious then distressed, and I had never called back.

I'd already decided I didn't want anyone but Joe to know that the new information had come from Alexandra, so I skirted that, told Mike only that Ken had evidently mentioned his belief that a car was the key to the case shortly before he was killed.

"The only car I ever heard mentioned," I said, "was the one you told us about. It belonged to a guy named Darius Neloms, right?"

"Right."

"Who had an alibi that was—"

"Airtight. Yes."

"There's no way you could have been wrong on that."

Silence. Then, "Brother, you want to check up on me, by all means go ahead. Hell, we probably still have the security tapes buried in some evidence locker. But I'm giving you my word that Darius Neloms was nowhere near Bertoli's death scene. A car belonging to him was. I did not find out who was driving the car. I tried, and I did not find out."

His voice was terse and biting, and Joe raised his eyebrows and gave me a little smile. I was stepping into dangerous turf now, with even a suggestion that Mike might have missed something.

"That's good enough for me," I said, trying to soothe, thinking that while I was still going to need to verify, there was no reason to call him out on it now. "I just don't know what the hell to do with this, Mike. If Ken was excited about a car, I think it had to be the one you told us about, but where that took him . . ."

"Like I told you back in the spring, Darius was connected to Sanabria."

"Evidently Ken wasn't sure the murder had anything to do with Sanabria."

"Then I quite simply don't know what to tell you, Lincoln."

I rubbed my forehead and squeezed my eyes shut, trying to think of the right question—hell, of *any* question. What could Ken have seen in that car that neither Mike nor I could?

"You traced the plate, and it ran back to Neloms directly," I said. "Right?"

"Right. Wait, no. It was registered to his shop, which doesn't really make a damn bit of difference. Ultimately still his vehicle. He claimed no idea of who could have driven it, said the keys were inside the shop and maybe somebody took them, then told us the car must have been stolen."

"But it had been returned."

"Uh-huh. I checked out every employee—most of whom were family or friends of his, cousins or nephews or whatever—and didn't get anything, but I don't think whoever was behind the wheel really had much to do with Neloms."

"You think they worked for Sananbria."

"Right. They had a history together."

All of this was recycled, the same damn conversation we'd had six months ago, and all of it pointed back to Sanabria, when Ken's final words pointed in another direction entirely.

"Look, Lincoln, I don't know what else to tell you . . ."

"It's fine, Mike. Don't worry about it. If I think of something else, I'll call."

I thanked him and hung up.

"Mike thinks one of Sanabria's guys drove the car," Joe said.

"Yeah."

We sat in silence and thought.

"This is going to sound crazy," I said, "but what if Bertoli drove himself there?"

He frowned. "His ghost got up off the pavement and drove

it back? The car was gone after he died, right? That's why Mike was looking at it as a suspect vehicle."

"Right," I said, "but he had to get there somehow, and whoever killed him would have known that. The guy had just gotten out of prison; it's unlikely he had his own car. So maybe he borrowed one from this Neloms guy. He drove that car to meet somebody, he got killed, and then someone else—maybe the guy who killed him, maybe not—drove the car back. Having the car gone from the scene is one less thing for the cops to look at, which is what they'd want, and they couldn't have known . . ."

My voice trailed off, and Joe said, "Keep going," but I didn't answer. The notion of Bertoli as the driver had tripped something in my brain, and I got up and went to the file cabinet and pulled out the sheaf of papers Ken had given me on the case. Copies of everything he'd had, or so he'd told me.

It took me a while, but I located the paperwork he'd brought into the office on the morning after our first encounter, the morning after my wild drunken dream about Parker Harrison watching me on the roof. Profiles of all the convicts who'd stayed at Whisper Ridge. I flipped through until I found Bertoli. Read the report once again, the details of his arrest for beating the truck stop manager and stealing his heroin. The police had arrested him within hours. Due to his car.

Chapter Thirty-nine

Bertoli used a stolen plate, but it was his own vehicle, an Impala with a custom paint job and chrome rims featuring cutouts in the shape of diamonds.

"Son of a bitch," I said, and then, without bothering to say a word to Joe's questioning glance, I pounded the redial button on the phone and got Mike London back on the line. He sounded weary when he realized it was me.

"One last question," I said. "The car you saw that night, it was an Olds Cutlass, not an Impala, right?"

"Right."

"You said it had custom features on it, though"

"Yeah, all that shit like in a rap video."

"This is a long shot, but do you remember the rims?"

"The *rims*?"

"Yeah."

"Well, they were spinners. You know, the kind that rotate when the engine's on?"

"Right. You remember whether there were diamond etchings in them? Cutouts in the shape of diamonds?"

Silence while he thought, then, "Yeah, maybe. Maybe there were. I'm not sure, but I think that sounds right."

"All right, Mike. Thanks. Thanks a lot."

I hung up with him again, and then I stood and brought the Bertoli report over to Joe's desk and dropped it down, waited while he read it.

"You're thinking that he got his car worked on down there?"

"Yes."

"Makes sense. Of course, we already know Sanabria's guys and Neloms had an association."

"Uh-huh, but read that arrest report again—who was in the vehicle with Bertoli the night he stole the heroin?"

"Unidentified juvenile."

"Right. Name redacted from Ken's report, because what Ken could access was public record, and the passenger was a minor. There's an original police report with that kid's name. I want it."

"I'll call."

Unlike me, he wouldn't use the speakerphone. I heard him say what he wanted and was sure he'd be told to wait for a call back. That's what it would have taken had I called—and if I didn't pick the right person to lean on for the favor, the wait might have extended into the next day. Instead, Joe was on hold for what seemed like all of thirty seconds. He murmured a soft thank-you into the phone, scribbled a name onto his notepad, and then hung up and held the pad a few inches from my face.

Alvin Neloms, black juvenile, sixteen years old.

"A son, probably," I said. "Darius has a son."

"Check on it."

I went back to my computer and ran a database search on Alvin Neloms and pulled up a family history. His father was listed as unknown. His mother had kept her own name, it seemed. According to the family chart the database offered, Darius Neloms was the boy's uncle, not his father. He was from East Cleveland, was now twenty-nine years old, and had been arrested just one time as an adult, for drug possession, charge dismissed. These were all things Ken could have found in a few minutes of research after he made the connection between the cars.

"You know anybody with East Cleveland PD?" I asked.

"Tony Mitchell did some task force stuff with them."

"Ask about this kid, would you? I want to know more before we talk to him."

"We're going to talk to him?"

"Bet your ass, Joseph. We're getting there. Getting *somewhere*."

So Joe got back on the phone and asked for Tony, and they exchanged cursory greetings while I waited impatiently.

"Use the damn speaker, Joe."

He ignored me, then told Tony he was calling to ask if the name Alvin Neloms meant anything to him. He listened for a while with no change of expression, then said, "Could you repeat that, please?" This time he finally hit the speakerphone button.

"I said Cash is the worst they've got," Tony said. "One of them, at least. And down there? When I say he's one of the worst, you know what I'm talking about."

"Cash?" Joe said.

"That's what he goes by, yeah. Comes from an old playground basketball nickname, everybody called him 'Cash Money' when he was a kid because he had a jump shot that just did not miss. In another neighborhood, another school, that kid plays college ball and goes to the league. No question. I've seen him play plenty. We had surveillance details on Cash for years, and even while waiting to bust his ass, I was impressed by his game. He played it like he loved it, you know? Then he'd go off and kill someone. It's sad, is what it is."

"What exactly is his story?" Joe said.

"Drugs and blood. He's top of the food chain out there now. Nobody moves a damn dime bag through East Cleveland that he doesn't know about."

"He's only been arrested one time? Charge dismissed?"

"The boy is *good*, got it? Runs a couple dozen gangbangers and pushers who take his falls for him and isn't a one of them says a word, because if they do, they just dug a grave that fits them nice and tight. Cash runs shit organized, runs it like the damn Mafia."

Joe cocked his head and looked at me. I didn't say anything, didn't respond.

"Unofficial body count credited to Cash Neloms?" Tony said. "Twenty. Maybe twenty-five."

My chest muscles suddenly felt cold and constricted.

"You ever heard of him actually having mob ties?" Joe said.

"Nope. It's all his show, Pritchard. His organization. And that shitty side of town drips with his blood."

"Supposing we wanted to talk to him—" Joe began.

"Talk to *Cash*? On what?"

"Cold case investigation. Twelve years old."

"Twelve years old? *Twelve?* Sweet mother, Pritchard, I'll tell you this one time and make it clear as I can—this ain't a man you *talk* to. Not a PI. I know you were police for a long time, but you're a civilian now, and that's a distinction that means something to Cash. Understand? You walk in that neighborhood asking questions about Cash Neloms, you better be wearing a damn vest and carrying with your finger on the trigger."

"I'm advised," Joe said. "Thanks, Tony."

He disconnected, blew out a breath, and said, "Where are we going, Lincoln? Where in the hell are we going?"

I didn't know. I stood in silence for a minute, trying to think, but there were too many pieces and too many ways they could fit, and I could not see the whole for the sum of its parts, couldn't even get close. Eventually I picked up the phone and held it in my hand, thinking of Quinn Graham. I didn't call, though. I hung up before the dial tone switched over to that rapid off-the-hook beep, and then I lifted the receiver again and called John Dunbar. I used the home number, and he answered.

"Hey," I said, "it's Lincoln Perry. You remember me?"

"You got something?" he said, and it was incredible how much anticipation was in his voice, how much hope.

"Yeah," I said, "I got a question. You have access to phone records from the Cantrell house in the last few months they were there?"

"I've got the actual records. I told you, I kept everything. There's nothing there. I've been over those—"

"Do me a favor," I said, "and go find them. Check and see

if there was a call to a guy named Alvin Neloms. Or maybe it was to an auto body shop on the east side. Look for either."

He set the phone down and disappeared. It was maybe five minutes before he came back, and his voice was lower.

"There were three calls to a place called Classic Auto Body, on Eddy Road."

"Were they all during Bertoli's stay?" I said. "The last weeks anyone was in that house?"

"Yes."

"Hang around, Dunbar," I said. "I'm headed your way."

I disconnected then and turned to look at Joe.

"The problem with this job," I said, "is that the guesswork always comes before the facts. I'm pretty sure that system put Ken in his grave."

Chapter Forty

I had to give John Dunbar credit—he didn't balk at the idea. In fact, what I saw in his face when I laid it out for him wasn't denial but shame. He actually seemed to wince when I showed him the police report that mentioned Bertoli's car at the time of his arrest and explained its similarities to a different car that had been near the death scene.

"I knew what kind of car he had," he said. "Of course I knew that, and I knew that's what got him arrested, but I didn't consider that it would have any importance beyond that. I didn't consider it."

He bit off that repeated line, angry, self-reproachful—*I didn't* consider *it*. Joe hadn't said much at all, but he looked at me when Dunbar said that, gave a small nod, showing that he thought it was legitimate.

"I knew it was Alvin Neloms who was in the car with Bertoli the night he was arrested," Dunbar said. "Of course I checked that out, of course I knew it, *of course* I did the same work you just did. Back then he was nothing more than a kid on the corner, someone who watched for police and maybe did a little muling. He was sixteen."

"He's not anymore," Joe said. "According to what we've been told, he's as close to a drug kingpin as the east side has. It's gang country out there; you do well to last six months. Neloms being around this many years later, that tells you something."

Dunbar's eyes flicked side to side but held distance, as if he were watching a film.

"DiPietro was providing some of the east side supply," he said, speaking slowly. "That was the point, see, that's when he and Sanabria had their first falling-out. Sanabria didn't trust drugs, and he certainly didn't trust blacks. His father was of that old school, racist, and I'm sure that stuck with Dominic. He did not want to be involved with the drug trade on the east side. We knew that, knew it from wiretaps and informants and a hell of a lot of work. We knew that Dominic was furious with DiPietro."

He paused and took a breath and then said, "Dominic killed DiPietro," but his voice had gone soft and he wouldn't take his eyes off the police report that detailed Bertoli's car.

As I watched his face, I felt tinged with sorrow. I was looking at an old cop who'd believed something very deeply and was now considering that it might have been wrong.

"You talked with a cop from East Cleveland," he said. "Someone who knows about Neloms."

"Yes," Joe said.

"Can you call him back?" Dunbar said. "Can you ask him a question?"

"What am I supposed to ask?"

"If he has any idea when Alvin made his move into the power structure. If he has any idea where the supply came from. A small fortune of drugs disappeared when DiPietro got whacked. They never turned up with the Italians again."

Joe took his cell phone out and called. He asked for Tony, waited for a few minutes, and then spoke again. He repeated Dunbar's questions, listened as Dunbar and I sat with our eyes on the floor, silent. At length, Joe thanked Tony and hung up. He put the phone back in his pocket and waited for a few seconds before speaking. He did not look at Dunbar when he did.

"The way Tony remembers it, Alvin was a lot like what you say, a corner kid, until he was in his late teens. Then he got his hands on some product. Nobody knew where, or how, but all of a sudden he had product, and then three major players were dropped in a drive-by over on St. Clair, and from that point on Alvin, while still a boy, was also the *man* in East Cleveland. This beginning when he was still in his teens. He was, Tony says, an ambitious young man."

I looked at Dunbar. "DiPietro controlled the drugs you were talking about, right? They were in his possession?"

"You know they were. I already told you that. We looked at every associate, looked at everyone who . . ." his voice faded, and then he said, "Alvin Neloms was a boy. A child."

"Tony also said Alvin and his uncle were tight," Joe said quietly. "Alvin's father is an unknown, disappeared when the mother got pregnant, and Darius looked after the family. Supported the family."

I nodded. "Supported them with a little help from the mob, is what Mike London thought. He said Darius was involved with stolen cars, changing their look and putting them back out on the street."

Dunbar shifted, smoothed his pants with his palms, swallowed as if it were a challenge.

"You never even considered the possibility, did you?" I said.

He looked up. "Neloms? Well, I had no idea—"

"Not Neloms. The possibility that it might have been anybody other than Sanabria, period."

"Of course I did."

"Really?"

His gaze focused again, went defiant. "Perry, that man would've killed anyone who collided with him. You don't understand that about him. I do. He had killed before, and I'd *had* him for it, okay? I told you that story."

"I know," I said. "I'm just wondering which murder you were really chasing him for. The new one you thought he'd committed, or the one he'd already beaten you on."

He held my eyes for a little while and then looked away and ran a hand over his mouth. His hands were dry and white and the blue veins stood out. They matched the strips of stark color under his eyes.

"So what we're thinking," Joe said, "is that Bertoli and Neloms were friends, probably from meeting at the uncle's shop. Neloms is along when Bertoli beats up the guy at the truck stop, but he doesn't go in, which means that as a kid he's somehow already got people doing the bleeding for him. It also means he was already looking for his own supply at that point, his own drug nest egg. He wanted to run the show, not stand on the corner for somebody else."

"The guy Bertoli beat up didn't have as much product as they thought," I said. "They overestimated his role. Bertoli got busted, but Neloms walked because he was a juvenile."

Joe nodded. "Right. After this, DiPietro is killed, a small fortune of drugs disappears, and suddenly a teenage kid became a deadly force. It was a power play, but one from a player nobody respected or even knew of at the time. This is the scenario?"

"That's the scenario," I said. "Ken Merriman got about ten percent of the way there. He got to the connection between the cars. I bet he didn't get farther than that, but he tried to. He tried to, and he died."

"What would he have done?" Joe said. "Once he connected the cars, what do you think he would have done?"

"Gone and asked about them," I answered, feeling a sick sadness. "He wasn't a street detective. He would have gone right down to that body shop and asked about the car, thinking that was the next step. He might have suspected Cash Neloms was involved by then, but I don't think he had a real sense of how dangerous the guy was. He would have gone down there to ask some questions, and he wouldn't have been very good at it. I saw him in action with interviews, and he was not very good at it."

"Suppose you're right on Bertoli," Dunbar said. "Suppose he was killed by Neloms. That doesn't mean Cantrell was, too. The styles of crime are entirely different. One was killed on scene and the body left without any concern; the other one was buried in another state. Those are two different killings, maybe by two different people."

On the surface he was right, but I understood what he didn't: how Joshua Cantrell's body had been transported, and why. The killings hadn't been different in style at all—both bodies were left where they'd fallen. Same style, same killer. Solve one and you've solved the other.

Thinking about that brought a realization to me. To whoever had killed Cantrell, the disappearance of his body must have seemed extraordinary. For twelve years, while the rest of the world wondered what had happened to him, one person wondered about the fate of his corpse. Wondered, no doubt, quite intensely.

"I want to talk to Darius," I said. "Not his nephew, not yet. Hit him with the only solid thing we have—that report on Bertoli's car—and see what he'll say."

Dunbar said, "I've got photographs."

"Pardon?"

"I've got photographs of Bertoli, and of his car. I've got photographs of damn near everybody's car, everybody that went near Sanabria."

"How soon can you come up with them?"

He stood up and went into the bedroom. From where I sat I could see through the doorway, and as I watched he opened a closet door. It was a small closet—every space in his house was small—and the clothes that hung in it were pushed far to the side to make room for a clear plastic organizer with drawers. It was the sort a lot of people had in their closets, usually for sweaters and old jeans, things they rarely used or for which they'd run out of shelf space. Dunbar's didn't hold any clothing, though, not a single piece of it. The thing was filled with manila folders, and I could see that each drawer was labeled with a date range.

He'd been retired for nearly fifteen years and had almost no closet space. I looked at that set of plastic drawers and I felt sad for him again.

It didn't take him long. First drawer he opened, first folder he removed. When he came back to the living room he had three photos in his hands; he passed one to Joe and two to me.

"These would have been taken just a few months before Bertoli was arrested, a little before DiPietro was killed. You can see the diamonds carved in the rims. They're tiny, but they're there."

Yes, they were. A half-dozen small diamonds. The car was an Impala, probably midseventies model, painted a metallic black. Bertoli wasn't visible in either of the photographs—the windows were up, and they almost matched the car's paint, clearly an illegal level of tint. Window tint like that pissed off street cops because you couldn't see what was happening in the interior as you approached. The entire car was basically a rolling request to be stopped and searched.

"This is perfect," I said. "Can we borrow these?"

Dunbar nodded, but his eyes seemed faraway again.

I stood up. "Thank you. For the pictures, and the insight."

"I've got some other things I'll go through," he said, not looking up. "I'll do some thinking. I'm not sure you're right . . . but I'll do some thinking."

Chapter Forty-one

Darius Neloms's shop, Classic Auto Body, was on Eddy Road, which was one of the few streets in the city that I would actively try to avoid while driving. It's an asphalt strip of neglect and anger, a place where as a rookie I'd been called to the scene of a fight and arrived to find a fourteen-year-old boy bleeding to death on the sidewalk from a knife wound to the neck. I'm not one of those PIs who loves to carry a gun, and I usually don't have one in my truck. Eddy Road, though, can make me regret that.

Today I had a gun, and I had Joe in the passenger seat, casting a dour eye over the neighborhood.

"It just gets worse, doesn't it?" he said. "I haven't been down here in a few years, but you can't pick up the paper without seeing something about this neighborhood. It just gets worse, poorer and bloodier."

"And more hopeless," I said, because that's how East Cleveland seemed to me, a legacy of poverty and crime and corruption drowning the people who tried to make a life there.

"Ah, shit, nothing's hopeless," Joe said. "Just ignored."

My mind wasn't on East Cleveland, though. I was thinking of Ken Merriman, of that spot in Mill Stream Run where his body had been dumped, and wondering whether he'd made a drive down Eddy Road on his last day alive. Joe had his face turned away from me, looking out at the neighborhood, and when I glanced at him I had a vision of the bullet holes that hid under his shirt, and then one of the steel security bar that rested across Amy's door.

"Hey," I said, and he turned back to me. "When we talk to Darius, I don't want to give him any names, all right?"

"You mean Cantrell and Bertoli?"

"No, I mean Pritchard and Perry."

He frowned.

"Like I said before, this is a scouting trip, okay? I want to ask the guy about Bertoli's car, drop Cantrell's name, see if we get any sort of response. Feel him out. Then I'll call Graham. It's still his case, you know."

His frown didn't fade. "What's that have to do with names?"

"Nothing."

"Then why—"

"Look, Graham got on my ass about this before, told me to stay out of his way. I don't want to deal with that again."

He looked at me for a long time, then nodded his head at the traffic light ahead.

"You've got a green."

It was closing in on six now, streetlights coming on, but Classic Auto Body was still open. It was an ugly, sprawling place of cinder block, with a stack of tires and a few stripped cars in the parking lot. From the outside it looked like a picture of poverty, but the garage doors were up and two gleaming cars were visible inside, one a new Cadillac and the other a pickup truck that had been painted gold and black and mounted on massive, oversized tires. Two young black men lounged on stools in the garage. A set of speakers stood behind them, playing rap music with a bass line I could feel in my chest.

"Hey," Joe said as we got out of the truck, his voice soft, and when I looked at him he nodded at the black-and-gold pickup truck inside. "Look at the wheels."

There were small diamonds cut out of the chrome rims.

One of the men inside the garage, a thin guy with darker skin and a shaved head, had moved his hand to rest beneath his oversized jacket when we drove in. Now that he saw us, he took it away and exchanged a look with his partner, who got to his feet and stepped over to a closed door. He opened it and said a few words, then shut it and came out to meet us. The guy with the jacket never moved.

"We closed," the one on his feet said, stopping at the edge of the garage. He wore a close-fitting, sleeveless white shirt, ridges of muscle clear beneath it. The music was even louder now, the sound of a ratcheting shotgun incorporated into the beat.

"Doesn't look that way," I said.

"Is, though."

"That's all right. Don't need any work done. Came to see Darius."

He reached up and scratched above his eyebrow, head tilted, studying me. "Darius a busy man."

"I'm sure of it. That's why we don't intend to keep him long. Got a picture to show him, a question to ask, then go on our way."

His eyes flicked over to Joe, whose look and demeanor said *cop* about as subtly as a billboard would.

"I'll give him the picture for you."

Joe shook his head. "We will. Thanks, though."

"Man, Darius ain't available."

"You work with him?"

"That's right."

"Then you know how to get in touch with him. Give the man a call."

While Joe talked, I found myself staring at the man on the stool, that hand resting near his waist. He wasn't looking back at me. He was looking at Joe.

"He ain't gonna answer," the guy in the sleeveless shirt said.

"How do you know that?"

"He busy."

"How about we call him just the same," Joe said.

"No," I said, and they both looked at me with surprise. I shook my head. "If he's not around, he's not around. We'll come back."

He nodded. "You do that, man."

"Thanks."

I turned and walked to the truck. I had the door open and was sitting behind the wheel before Joe even moved. He walked over slowly, got inside, and swung the door shut without a word. The guy from the stool got to his feet and came over to stand with the other man at the edge of the garage. They watched as I drove out of the lot.

"Maybe I misread the situation," Joe said after we were a few blocks away, "but I kind of assumed Darius was inside that office. You know, where the kid poked his head in before he came out to run us off."

"Could be."

"Uh-huh. You want to tell me what we're doing driving away, then?"

"I'm thinking we should pass this off to Graham," I said. "His case, his decisions to make. You saw those diamonds on the rims down here, that's enough, right? Between that and the phone calls, we've got enough. It's time to pass it to him now."

"That's a pretty different stance from the one you had this afternoon."

"Had a few hours to think about it."

"You've done some thinking," he said, "but it's not hours of it that are catching up with you now. It's months."

We didn't say much on the way back to the office. When we got there all he said was "Let me know if Alexandra calls" before he got into his own car and drove away.

I went home, too, called Amy and said I'd come over and I had some news, and then took a shower. Before I got into the water I stood at the sink and stared into the mirror for a long time, waiting for the man looking back to tell me what he wanted to do. What he needed to do. Then the steam spread across the glass and he was gone, no answers left behind.

I did not call Quinn Graham, as I had told Joe I would. I did not call anyone. That night I updated Amy, took her from my conversation with Alexandra Cantrell to my decision at the garage.

"You're really going to back off, pass it to Graham?" she said. "Then why were you there to begin with? Why spend two weeks watching for Alexandra?"

"Just to see if he was right. I had to know. That's all. Now I do."

"If who was right? Ken?"

I nodded.

"You said you were angry with him at first," she said. "Hurt and betrayed, because he lied to you."

"Sure. You think that's abnormal?"

"No. But you don't seem angry now."

"I understand why he did it now."

She nodded. "That makes it easier, doesn't it."

"Of course."

"You know you've been lying to me?"

"What?"

"For three days you've been lying to me. Said you'd given up on the surveillance, stopped going out there—and, unlike you with Ken, I don't understand why."

"I'm sorry," I said. "I didn't think of it as lying, even though it was. I just knew that you and Joe thought I should quit—"

"You told us you already had. Back in the summer, it was *you* who said you were done. Emphatically. Neither of us told you to give up your job, Lincoln, but you did, and then you went back to it in secret. Lying about it. I don't understand."

I didn't know how to make her understand. I couldn't explain to her that she was one of the reasons I'd had to quit, that Ken's murder had been one that hit too close to home. It could be her next time. Or Joe. My decision at the garage today had been made the moment the guy on the stool had reached under his jacket with his eyes on Joe. I understood some things in that moment, understood just how damn close we were to the one thing I could never allow to happen again. I would not bring those I loved into harm's way again. I couldn't.

So if I understood that, then why couldn't I stop altogether? Why had I ever gone back to that damned house in the woods with my camera and my binoculars?

I didn't have an answer for that one. It chilled me, but I

didn't. I'd ended up back out there, that was all. The absence of resolution, of truth, had tormented me for too many months. In the end, it won. I was weaker than I'd thought.

"Let me ask you one more thing, and this time, if you care about me at all, tell me the truth," Amy said. She was speaking very carefully, slowly, as if she needed me to feel the weight of the words. "If you don't tell me the truth, we're done, Lincoln. We will have to be done. Because I can't live with you otherwise."

"Ask the question," I said.

"Are you really going to pass this off to Graham, or are you telling one thing to me and Joe and planning another?"

I looked away.

She said, "Lincoln."

"I've got something left to do," I said. "That's the truth. It's something I'm going to do alone. Then I will give this to Graham and, yes, step away. I promise you, that is the truth. I've got one thing left to do."

"What is it?"

"I'm going to get Graham the tape he wanted me to get from Harrison, only this time I'll get it from the right source. I'm going to get him evidence, Amy, get him a case he can prosecute, a case that will end the right way. I don't want to pass this off to him until I know it's ready for that. I can't stand to let it fall apart the way it did with Dunbar and Mike London and Graham and everyone else. Do you understand that? I can't let it fall apart again."

She fell asleep around midnight. I sat beside her in the dark, looking at a pale shaft of light across the carpet that I liked to imagine was the moon but was really from a parking lot light pole. She had not pressed me for more details of what I had planned, and I hadn't offered them. It had been a quiet night. We didn't make love or even talk when we turned out the lights and got into bed, but she fell asleep with her hand wrapped tight around my arm.

After twenty minutes, when her breathing had slowed to the rhythm of true and deep sleep, I got to my feet and found my car keys. She was on her side, face turned into the pillow, and before I left I leaned down and kissed the back of her head, smelled her hair. Then I walked through the dark apartment and opened the door and stepped out into the night. There was no way I could fasten the steel security bar behind me. I regretted that.

I stopped at a convenience store on Rocky River and bought a large black coffee, then drove home, went upstairs, and found the wire I'd used in the early stages with Parker Harrison. I'd never taken it back to the office. We'd had no use for it anymore.

I tested it and then put it on, clipping the microphone lower, near the fourth button instead of the first, remembering the way Harrison had torn at my shirt, how completely exposed it had been then. Once the wire was in place, I got my gun case out of the closet and removed the stainless steel Beretta 9 mm. It had been a while since I'd handled that gun, but I had a shoulder holster for it, and I put that on now and slipped the Beretta inside. I put a jacket on over that, leaving it unzipped, and then I put the Glock into its holster, this one secured on my spine. The East Cleveland Ensemble.

With that preparation complete, I turned off the lights and left the apartment and went to the office. I fired up the computer and then took my PI license out of my wallet and went to the scanner, made a copy of the image and loaded it onto the computer, and made a few changes before printing out a copy. A little trimming work with scissors, a quick pass through the card laminator I'd purchased years ago for just this sort of thing, and then I was done. I tucked the new ID into my wallet in place of the old one, left the office, and drove back to Eddy Road.

Chapter Forty-two

One version of the neighborhood came to life at dawn, and another went to sleep. It hadn't been a quiet night of surveillance—I'd watched people stumble the sidewalks wrecked out of their minds, seen a fistfight flare and then vanish when a police cruiser drove by, heard the laughter and loud car stereos of those returning from a night at the clubs. That world slid away just before daylight, and then the traffic thickened and stores and businesses opened as the sun rose.

Classic Auto Body was quiet until almost nine, and then someone drove into the parking lot in a sleek black Cadillac CTS and pulled to a stop just outside of the office window, in an area not marked for parking. The driver's door opened and a large black man stepped out with keys in his hand. He unlocked the office door and disappeared inside.

I pushed the blackout curtain aside and climbed into the front seat of the truck and then got out and walked to the shop, tested the door and found it unlocked, and stepped inside.

I'd entered an empty office, but I could hear movement in the garage beyond, someone walking around snapping on light switches. A few seconds passed, and then the door from the garage opened and the Cadillac's driver stepped back into the office and saw me.

"You need help?" he said, not unfriendly, but not thrilled about seeing me there, either.

"Got a couple questions about a car you did."

"Yeah?" He walked around the desk and leaned on its edge, more intrigued now. "Like what you've seen out there, huh?"

"Oh, absolutely. Absolutely."

He was nodding along in agreement, confident in his work. "You got something classic you working on, or is it more of just getting it done up right, something newer but just don't have that *look*, that *style*?"

He appeared even bigger indoors than he had outside. Probably six-four and at least two hundred and sixty or seventy pounds, with a block of a head above a football lineman's shoulders. He looked about forty-five and had a pencil-line beard tracing his massive jaw. Wore baggy jeans and a black jacket open over a T-shirt. There was a chain of white gold or platinum with a glittering medallion in the shape of a diamond around his neck, hanging halfway down his chest.

"I've got some pictures of it," I said, pulling Dunbar's photographs out of my pocket. I nodded at his medallion before I handed them over. "That diamond there, any chance that's, like, your logo?"

"Yeah, man, like a signature, you know? Every artist puts one on their work." He was smiling at me now. "Keeps people from passing off their shit as mine, too. You got these kids, do something on their own, then they want people to think they spent the money, right? Want them to think they got the money *to* spend, so they say, oh, I took it down to Darius. But I got those diamonds I do by hand, man, and there ain't any of them going to try putting *those* on."

"Brand protection," I said. "Trademark."

"Yeah, exactly, a trademark." He put his hand out for the photographs. "What is it you've seen around? Which one of 'em caught your eye?"

I passed them over. "You probably won't remember this. Did it a long time ago."

He took the pictures and studied them one at a time. His face changed to a frown, but it wasn't suspicious, not yet. Just thoughtful.

"Man, you ain't kidding, this is a long time ago. I remember the car, though. This would've been ten years ago at least, got those old dubs on there."

"You did the work, though?"

"Oh, yeah. For sure. That's mine."

"You happen to remember the owner?"

His mouth twisted, and he hesitated, thinking, trying to remember. It took him a few seconds, but when he got it the frown came back, this time with a different quality, and when he spoke his voice wasn't as relaxed as it had been.

"It was an Italian kid, I think. Maybe not. I don't know."

He held the photograph out, and when I didn't take it immediately he gave it a shake to get my attention, as if he were in a hurry to get it out of his hand.

"I don't even know why that piece of shit grabbed your eye," he said.

"You don't like it?"

"You know, I did the work, that's all. People got their own ideas of what looks good, I try to listen. Now what kind of a ride you got? What are we talking about doing?"

"I'm afraid there's been some confusion," I said. "I'm not here to have a car worked on. I'm here about *this* car."

I lifted the photograph and gave it the same little shake he had, but he didn't look, just held my eyes. Now all the good humor was out of his face.

"You a cop?"

"Private."

"It's private whether you a cop?"

"No. I'm a private detective."

"Man, I don't got time for this. That car's so old, I don't remember nothing about it, don't know nothing about that Italian kid, all right?"

"That's fine, Darius. Maybe you could do me a favor, though?"

He waited, suspicious.

"Give your nephew a call, get him down here."

"My family got something to do with you? Man, go on and get out of here. I don't have time—"

"You got nothing to do with Alvin? With Cash, I mean?"

He was giving me flat eyes now, a response to police questioning that he'd spent some years perfecting.

"Maybe you could just give him a message," I said. "Write down my name, tell him that I was down here and that I'd like to speak with him if he gets a chance. That I'd appreciate it if he could give me a call."

"You want to talk to Cash, find him yourself."

"Darius . . ." I spread my hands. "You really want to make this a pain in the ass? All I'm asking is for you to give your nephew my name, tell him I was down here. You do that, and I'm gone."

He scowled and waved his hand at me, impatient. "All right, leave your damn name and get out."

"I'm fresh out of cards," I said. "So you'll have to write it down."

"Man, write it down yourself."

I ignored him, reached in my back pocket and withdrew my wallet, flicked it open to reveal the investigator's license I'd made, and passed it over. He glanced down at it, but it was a cursory look while he picked up a pad of paper and extended it to me.

"Write it here," he said.

I didn't answer, just kept holding the license in front of his face, and this time when his eyes went to it they lingered. He stared at it for several seconds. Too many to be comfortable. Enough to tell me what I needed to know.

"Like I said, you write it down yourself," he said finally, looking away from the license and back at me. His voice was much softer, his eyes much darker.

"Okay," I said, and I closed the wallet and put it back in my pocket and then wrote the name from the license in all capital letters across his pad—KEN MERRIMAN.

He watched me write it and didn't say a word when I dropped the pad on his desk.

"Are you sure," I said, "that you don't want to give your nephew a call right now?"

He looked up at me, and his jaw worked as he studied my eyes.

"It might be a good idea," I said. "Up to you, Darius, but it might be a good idea."

He didn't take his eyes off me as he withdrew his cell phone from the pocket of his oversized jeans.

"You wait," he said, and then he stepped out into the garage and closed the door behind him. I felt my breath go out of my lungs when the door closed, and I looked around the office and through the window out onto the street. Nobody in sight. I would be alone with them when Cash came, just as Ken had likely been. I was more prepared than he had been, though. I had my story ready, had the scenario I needed, and now it was just a matter of playing it through, getting the hell out of here, and handing Graham a case that was ready to close. Simple stuff. Simple. I reached inside my jacket and touched the Beretta once, a gentle tap, and then I dropped my hands back to my sides and waited.

Darius wasn't gone long. Two minutes at most. Then the door opened and he stepped through, face expressionless, eyes flat again.

"You in luck," he said. "Cash is in the area."

"Going to come by?"

He shook his head, and I saw he had his car keys in hand. "You are. I'm going to take you out to see him."

"No need for you to do that," I said.

"Man, I'm helpful like that."

"You want to leave, fine, but I'll wait for him here."

He shook his head again. "You want to see Cash, I take you."

"Maybe you don't understand," I said. "I'm going to wait for him here."

There was real anger showing in him for the first time now, the sort of look that probably didn't meet with opposition very often. He said, "He's not coming here, and you ain't going to stay on my property."

I dropped into one of the plastic chairs that lined the wall across from his desk, crossed one ankle over my knee.

"Try him again, Darius. I think you might be wrong. I think he might be willing to make the trip."

He hesitated. It wasn't me he was worried about, it was his nephew's response. Eventually he turned and went back into the garage, and this time it was almost ten minutes before he returned.

"All right," he said. "He's on his way."

"Terrific," I said.

"Sure is," Darius said. He crossed the office, reached for the blinds, and twisted the rod until they were closed again, and the street was gone and the office was dark. Then he went to the door and locked it and turned the sign to CLOSED.

"Sure is," he said again, and he went behind the desk and sat in his chair, opened a drawer, and withdrew a stainless steel Beretta that looked identical to the one I had under my jacket. He placed the gun on the desk without a word, not pointing at me but close to his hand.

Then we waited.

Chapter Forty-three

It was about twenty minutes before Cash arrived, and Darius and I did not speak during the wait. If you've ever wondered how long twenty minutes can feel, try spending them in total silence facing a man with a gun.

At some point while we waited, I realized that it was past nine but nobody else had arrived. Then I remembered the extra time that Darius had spent out in the garage before telling me his nephew was on his way. He hadn't turned the CLOSED sign over until after that. Made some extra calls, maybe, told his employees not to come in? I'd chosen to make my return trip out here in the morning for a reason, thinking the place would be more active, but that didn't seem to be the case. Of course, the only employees I'd seen here yesterday weren't exactly the type of guys whose presence would reassure me now. I wondered if much actual work went on down here these days, or if it had become a cover operation for Cash Neloms.

When a car finally pulled in, Darius got to his feet, taking the gun with him, and walked over to unlock the door. He stood beside it and waited, and after a moment the door opened and a slim, athletic-looking black guy stepped inside and shut the door behind him. He looked first at Darius and then turned to me.

"Morning," I said. "Thanks for making the trip."

He was the same height as Darius but about eighty pounds lighter, with a shaved head that glowed under the fluorescent lights in the office. The family resemblance was clear. Same skeptical, watchful eyes and hard-line mouth and strong shoulders. What surprised me most was how damn young he still looked. If I'd seen him on a college campus I wouldn't have even considered that he'd be anything but a student.

"D says you got a question for me?" he said. The words came slow, each one studied on before release.

"That's right." I went through the routine again, took the wallet out and opened it to my Ken Merriman ID and passed it over. With Darius, the idea had worked just as I'd hoped, maybe even better than I'd allowed myself to hope. I'd thought that questioning him and his nephew about Ken might not tell me what I wanted to know. They were used to questioning; they would know how to play the game by now. Pretending to be Ken, though, re-creating his visit as near as I could imagine it had taken place, seemed as if it might produce a different response, put a touch of déjà vu in the air that would be difficult for even veterans like the Neloms to ignore.

Darius had looked at the ID and been momentarily frozen. Cash had the advantage of being forewarned, though, and instead of looking at it he took the wallet right out of my hand, ignored the PI license entirely, and slipped two of my credit cards out. Read the name on them, then held one up for me.

"Looks like you a little confused. Got a couple names, huh?"

I didn't say anything. He waited for a long time, and then he slid the credit cards back into the wallet, closed it, and threw it at me. It hit me in the chest and dropped into my lap. I picked it up and put it back in my pocket, still silent.

Darius was standing by the door, the gun held down against his thigh. He was watching Cash more than me.

"So what you want, man?" Cash said.

I didn't answer.

"You going to speak?"

Again I was quiet. I sat in my chair and did not take my eyes from his, tried to ignore the desire to glance over at Darius and make sure that the gun was still down. I'd see him if he moved. I'd see him.

"Man, say whatever the fuck you got to say." Cash sounded agitated now.

I looked back with what I hoped was a steady, calm stare. He gave it almost a full minute before breaking the silence again.

"All right, then, get out. Come down here and waste my time, waste my uncle's time? Get the fuck out."

His voice was bridling with anger, muscles standing out in his neck. This was what I wanted. To see him frustrated. I wanted to drive him wild with silence. Have him unsteady by the time we got to the real talk.

"I'ma tell you *one* more time—" he began, but this time I spoke.

"I just have a few questions, Alvin."

"Don't call me that."

"My name's Ken Merriman," I said. "I'm a private investigator from Pennsylvania. I was hired by the parents of a man named Joshua Cantrell. He was murdered a few years ago. Twelve years ago, actually. Almost thirteen."

He looked away from me and at Darius, and it took everything I had to keep my hand still, to keep from reaching for the Beretta. Darius hadn't moved. His gun was still pointed down.

"Why you saying you somebody else?" Cash Neloms said. "Come down here and lie to us, you think that's wise? Think that's a good way to stay alive?"

"You're right. I was lying. I didn't come to ask questions. I came to give you some answers, if you wanted them."

"I don't even know who you are. You don't got no answers I need."

"I disagree."

Another look at Darius, and I knew now that this was how it would go. If Cash gave him the right look, that gun was coming up.

"I don't know what you been told, what you think," Cash Neloms said. "I'm *sure* I don't know what kind of fucking fool you are, coming down here, talking crazy shit like this, but, boy, go on and walk out. Right now."

"Don't you even want to know how Cantrell's body ended up in Pennsylvania?" I said.

That stopped him. His mouth closed and his eyes went hard and dull, and for a moment he seemed to have forgotten about Darius in the corner of the room. For a moment he seemed to have forgotten about everything but me.

"I thought you'd like to know that much," I said. "As far as Ken Merriman is concerned, well, I don't need to give you any answers to that one. You already know them. Same story with Salvatore Bertoli. Cantrell . . . I thought you might be curious about that one. Twelve years is a long time to wonder."

"I don't know . . ." It was supposed to be another denial, but he let it die, wiped a hand over his mouth and stared at me and tried to decide what to say. It took maybe ten seconds. "All right. I'm not saying I know what you talking about, but go on and tell it, if that's why you came down here. Go on and tell it."

"You know the name Dominic Sanabria?" I said.

"I might've heard it."

"Yeah, I thought so. He'd like you to do him a favor. Man like that can be a good person to do a favor for, you know?"

"I don't owe him any favors."

"No? He might argue that."

It was quiet again for a while.

"Well," he said, frustration showing again, "what is it, man? You got to say it."

"Dominic's sister has been gone for twelve years. Lot of people looked for her. Police, family, private detectives, reporters. By this time, it seems like if she had anything to say to anybody like that, she'd have said it. Don't you think?"

He didn't answer.

"I'll tell you what she told me," I said. "She has a new life now. Doesn't want to leave it. Doesn't want to come back here, to the questions and the attention."

"Why you telling me that?"

"The favor that Dominic would like you to do," I said, "is pretty simple. I'll put you in touch with her. Get you a meeting. You explain to her that Dominic had nothing to do with her husband's death. That's all."

I expected he might give me disbelief or confusion or anger—anything but acknowledgment—but instead of speaking, he just looked at me for a long time. When he broke that silence, it wasn't with an argument. It was a question, spoken soft and cold.

"Who are you?"

"You saw the name."

"Name don't mean shit to me."

"Here's all you need to know about me—I came here with an offer from Dominic. You've heard it. You going to take it?"

All I wanted now was out. The recorder was running, I had this whole conversation, and I could set up the meeting with Alexandra. There'd be plenty more than Alexandra there, more wires and more cops and a pair of handcuffs ready to fit around Cash Neloms's wrists. I was close now; I just needed to get it done and get the hell out. I just needed to make it through the door.

"Sure," Cash said after a pause. "I'll take it, man."

He was so casual when he said it, his face so utterly relaxed, that if I hadn't been reminding myself to be ready to move if he looked at Darius again I would've died immediately. As it was, I'd been ready for the look, and when he turned to Darius I was already rising, made it out of my chair before Darius lifted the gun.

I reached under my jacket for the Beretta, and I ran straight for Cash and the swinging door to the garage beyond. I was hoping to get behind him or at least close enough to him that Darius wouldn't fire, but that was a hopeless idea; it simply doesn't take that long to lift a gun and pull the trigger.

Darius fired before I cleared my gun, and the bullet hit me on the right side, hit me like the thrust of a metal stake that had been forged to a glowing red heat. The force of it knocked me forward, and his second shot missed high as I fell into Cash Neloms's legs.

I didn't hit him hard, or even intentionally—I was just

trying to make it to the door. My weight caught him around the knees, though, and while he didn't go to the floor he did fall backward into the wall, and for a brief moment we were entangled. He came off the wall with his hands reaching for my throat, and by leaning over me like that he blocked any chance of his uncle finishing me off with another shot. By then I had my gun out, and I twisted as his hands clawed at my neck. I saw nothing but the metal desk and Darius Neloms's feet and legs beneath it, but that gave me something to shoot at. I fired once, saw a spray of red burst out of the back of his calf and heard him scream, and then I shoved through Cash Neloms's legs and toward the swinging door that led to the garage. He slammed a punch into the back of my neck and tore at my hand as I went by, and the Beretta came loose and hit the floor. It spun away from me, back toward the desk, but I ignored it and kept scrambling forward. Then I was out of the office and onto the cold concrete floor of the garage. I kicked the swinging door backward as I went, heard it hit something, and then another shot was fired and I felt a second searing pain burn across my thigh.

It was dark in the garage, the doors down and the light off, and I rolled away and hit something that fell all around me, didn't realize until I touched one of them that I'd knocked over a stack of hubcaps. I pulled myself back with my hands, got my torso into an upright position, legs stretched out in front of me, and then I reached behind my back and removed the Glock from its holster. I was slow getting it out, but when Cash Neloms stepped through the door and into the garage, with a gun in his hand, he turned to the left first, reaching for the light switch, thinking that I was now unarmed.

I lifted the Glock and fired twice.

When he dropped, he went backward into the door and it swung open and his head and shoulders fell into the office, nothing of him left visible in the garage but his legs. They moved for a few seconds, heels scraping on the concrete, trying to get upright, and then they went still and it was quiet.

I sat in the pile of hubcaps with the Glock still pointed at the door and waited for Darius. It was hard to hold the gun up now, and the door seemed to be dancing in front of me, waving and undulating and blending with the shadows. I heard motion and fired again before realizing it had been the front door. Darius had just left the office and gone outside. He'd be coming around from a different direction, entering through a different door. I had no idea which way to look. It was his garage. He knew the layout and I did not and it was becoming hard to sit upright and hard to see.

The Glock dropped to my lap, not a mental decision but a physical one, my body giving out, and I twisted onto my side and reached into my pocket for my cell phone. It took two tries to get it out of my pocket. My fingers were slick with warm wet blood.

I got the phone out and open and then I dialed and spoke into it. I could not remember the address where I was, or even the road. All I could tell them was that I'd been shot and Darius was coming back for me. Several times, I said that I did not know what door he would use. That I would not be ready for him when he came.

The phone slid out of my fingers then and bounced off the concrete floor. I could not make myself reach for it even though it was close. There was blood in my mouth now and a terrible high hum in my ears and I could not reach for the phone or lift the gun.

I never heard the sirens.

Chapter Forty-four

The paramedics found the recorder and gave it to the police. When they listened to that and heard what Joe had to say, it wasn't hard to piece together what had happened. That was good, because I wasn't in any condition to talk.

By the time I got out of surgery, the first media report had leaked, and Alvin "Cash" Neloms was being identified as the alleged killer of Joshua Cantrell. Mike London and John Dunbar were called into the investigation. Quinn Graham drove in from Pennsylvania. The tape was solid, but there was no confession. They needed more. It was Graham who suggested they focus on Ken Merriman, the freshest case and the one that had the best potential for evidence. They found a variety of weapons while searching the properties affiliated with Cash and Darius Neloms, including a handgun and ammunition that were probable matches for Ken's shooting. They would later be proved conclusive matches.

All my concern over Darius Neloms and his unknown path of reentry into the garage turned out to be unnecessary—he'd tried to leave when he saw his nephew fall dead through the door into the office. Dragged his wounded leg along with him and went out and got into his Cadillac and drove away. About two minutes and ten blocks away, he passed out from pain and blood loss and drove up onto the sidewalk and into a telephone pole. They arrested him when he got out of surgery.

By the time the paramedics found me, I was unconscious and in shock. They didn't get me stabilized until I was at Metro-Health's trauma center, the same hospital that had saved Joe. In fact, I had the same surgeon, a Dr. Crandall, who was one of the specialists on gunshot wounds. My surgery was about six hours shorter than Joe's, though. Something he could hold over my head.

Oddly, the chest wound was the lesser of my troubles. Eight inches from being my end—*if it goes in on the left side in the same position, you're dead almost immediately*, Dr. Crandall told me—but the bullet took a ludicrously forgiving trajectory and passed through me, leaving behind a broken rib and some minor soft tissue damage. If it had gone in on the left side, it would have blown right through my heart.

The leg wound, which came when Darius fired at me as I fell through the door and into the garage, was much more serious. The bullet did some arterial damage, and the only reason I didn't bleed out before the EMTs arrived was that I was sitting upright and the wound was on the back of my leg, which offered some level of compression and slowed the bleeding. The crime scene photographs I saw later showed a spray of blood almost six feet from my body that had been released when I leaned onto my side to reach for my phone. If I hadn't rolled back over, pressing the wound against the concrete floor, I would've lost consciousness before I ever got a word out to the 911 operator.

Fall on your ass, save your life. It was a hell of thing to think about.

It turned out there was actually some talk of arresting me, too. I was a civilian, not a cop, and I'd taken a life. We tend to call that murder. The only thing that allowed me to avoid at least preliminary charges was the recording, which supported my story.

I was coherent enough to watch TV on the second day, when I stared through a fog of medication and saw an old booking photo of Cash Neloms fill the screen. He was dead, the anchor explained, but still the focus of several ongoing homicide investigations.

He was dead.

It was over, then. Wasn't it? I thought it was probably over.

No one heard from Alexandra Cantrell in the aftermath of the shootings.

They held me in the hospital for ten days. During that time I refused to see anyone except Amy, Joe, my sister, and the police. My sister, Jennifer, stayed for five days, the longest visit she'd had since she moved from South Bend to Seattle, and the first time she'd met Amy. The two of them seemed to get along well.

Gena came into town, too, and I was happy to hear that. I didn't find out she'd been there until the day she left—Joe told me he'd explained to her that I didn't want a large audience. That rule hadn't applied to her, but it was just like Joe to quietly respect it, no matter what. It was good to know she'd come when he needed her.

I spent a lot of those days asleep. The right kind of drugs will do that to you. I woke once and heard Amy crying in the chair by my bed, but something told me that I should not open my eyes, should not disrupt her. I listened to her cry, and after a while she stopped and reached out and put her hand on my arm, and then I fell asleep again.

Calls came in constantly, most of them from the media. A few other friends tried to call or stop by, and Amy told me that Parker Harrison had come by on three occasions and been turned away. He was holding a card each time, she said, but he would not leave it with the receptionists or with her.

An insider account of the shootings and the crimes that had led to them was released during my hospital stay. It included significant details but was largely unattributed, most of it laid at the feet of "an unnamed source close to the situation." Amy was the source. I'd told her that I wanted to get as much of the detail out as possible, and have it done as early as possible. I also didn't want to give any interviews. That wasn't the sort of balance that pleases the media, but she leaked the story to the right people, people she trusted, and they did the rest.

Darius Neloms was charged with attempted murder. We heard that his attorney would attempt a counterclaim alleging that I had fired first. Amy was worried about that. I told her we'd deal with it when it came. Then Darius and his attorney listened to the tape, and evidently found it more conclusive than they had hoped. By my fourth day in the hospital they were negotiating with prosecutors, suggesting that Darius could produce evidence proving his nephew was indeed the murderer of Cantrell, Bertoli, Ken Merriman, and others. Blood ties meant a great deal to Darius until he was in jail and his nephew was dead, it seemed.

According to Darius, Salvatore Bertoli had sought Cash out to warn him of Joshua Cantrell's attempts to get information about the murder of Johnny DiPietro. Bertoli still believed Cash Neloms to be a friend. In exchange for the warning, Cash killed him and then Cantrell. Housekeeping. His was a different world by the time Bertoli got out of prison; he had an empire to protect, and one did not rule an empire with a soft touch.

While all of this was the focus for me, the police and prosecutors were more interested in what Darius had to say about his nephew's associates. Cash was dead—his network was not. Mike London told me that he was hearing Darius might get a hell of a deal if he rolled on enough people.

I didn't know how to feel about that.

Joe was around often, but he wasn't himself. Anytime he spoke, it tended to be to make a joke, things like suggesting he and I be the stars of a TV commercial for MetroHealth's trauma unit. It was a forced sort of good humor, and while I knew he was worried about my condition, I also sensed something else in the quiet that filled in the spaces between jokes. He was angry.

It wasn't until the day before my release that he was in the hospital room alone with me. Always before Amy had been around, or my sister, or a cop or a nurse. That afternoon, though, Amy had left for a few hours, my sister was on a plane for Seattle, and the cops and nurses had other concerns. Joe sat in the chair under the window. We talked for a few minutes before he lost that false comedic air.

"This is how you like it, right?" He waved at the bed, at the monitors around me.

I smiled. "Sure. My bed at home doesn't have any of this stuff."

He wasn't smiling. "You're okay lying in that bed with me in the chair next to it. That's all right with you."

"What do you mean?"

"Exactly what I said—it's fine with you if you're in the bed and I'm on my feet. Just like you were okay going to see Alvin Neloms alone, nobody aware of what you were doing, because I wasn't there, Amy wasn't there, nobody you care about was there."

"What are you talking about, Joe?"

"You think that if there's nobody around you, then there's nothing for you to fear. If nobody gets hurt but you, then who cares, right? You can deal with that. You can't deal with the other."

"I have dealt with the other."

"Not too well," he said. "Not too well."

I twisted my head on the pillow, turned away from his gaze.

"You sent me home," he said, "and then went back over there alone. Why?"

I didn't answer.

"We could have talked to Darius," he said. "It's what we'd gone over there to do. Then you backed off, said it was a bad idea, that we should pass it to Graham. Told me that, went home and said the same thing to Amy, and then loaded your guns and went back alone, without a word to anyone. I'd like you to explain why you did that."

I reached up and rubbed between my eyes, sucked in a gasp of pain at the movement. It still caught me off guard. I'd spent six days lying here with nothing to think about but the damage the bullets had left behind, and still the pain caught me off guard.

"I guess you're not going to explain why you did it," Joe said. "So I'll go ahead and explain for you. You went down there alone because you're afraid for everybody around you, and not yourself. It's so much easier to isolate yourself, right? Nobody to worry about then. Well, there are a handful of people—poor misguided souls like Amy, like me—who would tell you that's a pretty damn selfish idea."

"You've got a hell of a bedside manner. Should have been a doctor, maybe a chaplain."

"I'm not worried about my bedside manner," he said. "You're fine. Took two bullets. I've taken two of them myself. So if you expect me to sit here and sponge off your forehead, forget it. You'll get better. You're getting better."

I turned back to him. "What do you want me to say, Joe? Apologize for not bringing you along to get shot again?"

"I don't want you to say anything. I want you to *understand* something."

"What's that?"

"What you're doing to yourself, LP."

"I don't know what that means."

"Let me ask you this. Why'd you decide to quit the job back in the summer?"

"I told you—I was tired."

"Tired of what?"

"Everything."

"No. You gave me the phrase, said it right to my face— collateral damage. Ken Merriman got killed, and it was too much. After what had happened to Amy, what had happened to me, it was too much. I understood that. Amy understood that. So we supported you, didn't question it, let you quit. I didn't think it was the right thing for you to do, but I—"

"*You* had already quit, Joe. Don't remember that?"

"I'm also sixty-two years old! I did thirty years as a cop; you did five. Don't see any differences there?"

Neither of us said anything for a few seconds. When he spoke again, his voice was softer.

"I didn't think it was the right thing, but I didn't argue because I don't know that there are many things more deeply wrong than one person telling another how to live. So I let you quit. Now, a few months later, you're in here because you *couldn't* quit."

"Should be a little easier to make it stick now."

Now it was his turn not to answer.

"You remember the way Dunbar looked when we went out there and showed him the Neloms connection?" I said. "You remember how he went into his bedroom and found his files, Joe? In his bedroom? A man who has been retired for years? He was obsessed. And wrong."

"And a different man than you."

"Yeah? I don't know about that. Don't know how different he is from you, either, if you hadn't forced yourself to disappear, forced yourself to quit this work. He's what waits at the end of the tunnel."

"Something you need to understand, Lincoln? There are a lot of tunnels, and you do your own digging."

Neither of us spoke after that. He stayed in the chair until a nurse came in and gave him an excuse to leave.

Chapter Forty-five

We didn't have another conversation like that. The next time I saw him, there were other people around and he was back to his forced cheerfulness. I'd never seen him so funny, in fact. He seemed like he should have his own late-night show.

I stayed at Amy's apartment after I was released. The stairs were easier to negotiate there, and her place was more open, had better daylight. That sort of thing matters to you when you spend most of the day sitting around.

I was coming back fast. That's what the doctors and the physical therapists told me. Coming back faster than I had any excuse to, in fact, largely because I'd been in outstanding shape at the time I'd taken the bullets. All those obsessive workouts were worth something, then. Good to know.

Amy and I talked about the shooting often, but always in a journalistic fashion—how strong the case against Darius was, what the potential legal ramifications for me might be, things like that. At first I wondered if she was keeping that sort of distance for my sake, and eventually I realized it was for hers. In the silence that grew after one of our conversations, I told her that I was sorry.

"You're sorry?" she said. "For what? Getting shot?"

"For putting you through all of this."

She gave a sad smile. "One of the last things you said to me, the night before you went over there, was that you had to do one last thing, and it had to be done alone."

"I remember."

"Look how well that turned out. In your head, I suppose you were protecting Joe. Probably me, too."

"Oh, no, Joe's shared his psychological insight with you."

"You think he's wrong?" she said. "You have the nerve to look me in the eye right now and tell me that Joe was wrong with what he told you in the hospital?"

I didn't speak.

"Exactly," she said. "You know that he's right—and you know that if a bullet went just a few inches in a different direction, I'd be alone right now, remembering that last night we were together. You think that would be a good memory for me? I couldn't stop thinking about it while you were in the hospital. I decided that it would have made a hell of a fitting epitaph for you. 'He had one last thing to do—alone.' Heaven knows it would be alone."

I didn't say anything.

"I don't think I can explain just how that memory resonated with me while you were in the hospital," she said. "How perfectly and tragically symbolic it seemed. If you had gotten killed out there, and you almost did, that moment would have stayed with me. You know why? Because it felt like you were telling me, '*I have this one last thing to do—alone—and then I can love you without walls.*'"

"Damn it, Amy, you know that I love you."

"I do, but I'm trying to tell you something that you need to understand—you can't protect everyone you love from harm. From the world. Trying to do that will break you, eventually. It will. And you know what? Something bad will still come for the people you love. You can't stop that, and it's not your job to try. It's your job to be there for us when it does."

It was quiet for a moment, and then she said, "Trust me, Lincoln, bad things will happen to the people you love. I'm staring at my boyfriend right now, and let me tell you, he's a pretty pathetic sight. Bullet wound, all bandaged up, can't even get off my couch under his own power."

"I can, too."

"Prove it," she said and walked to the bedroom.

* * *

On one of those long days while Amy was at work and I was sitting in her living room alone, I got out a legal pad and a pen, and I sat down to try writing a letter to Ken's daughter again. It came easier this time. I wrote five pages, five pages of apology and sympathy. Then I read through it and thought that it was all wrong, and I threw those away and started over. I left in a few paragraphs of the old stuff, but then I focused on the case. I told her as much as I could. I told her what sort of detective her father had been, how dedicated, how patient. How he had waited day after day to check out a hunch, and in the end the hunch had been right. I couldn't tell her more than that, but I could at least explain that much.

He was a good detective, I wrote, because he stayed at it. Because he craved the truth above all else, above even himself. Certainly above himself.

This time, I mailed the letter.

Late in the week after my release, Joe called to say that Parker Harrison was leaving daily messages at the office. I took down his number and called him back. He asked if he could see me in person, and I gave him the address, and he told me he'd be out in twenty minutes.

It took fifteen. I'd already made my way down to the door and was sitting on the bottom step waiting for him. The steps were difficult. My right leg still screamed if it took the bulk of my weight. I opened the door when he arrived, and I shook his hand, and we went back upstairs. It was slow going. He followed me and didn't say a word.

When we got up to the living room, I fell into my designated corner of the couch, and he sat on the chair across from me. He reached out and handed me an envelope.

"This first," he said. "I tried to bring it to you at the hospital."

I opened the envelope and found a handwritten letter inside. It was a woman's handwriting. Alexandra Cantrell. When I read it, I wanted to laugh. It reminded me so much of the letter I'd written to Ken's daughter—the tone, the words, even some entire phrases. There was a lot of gratitude there, awkwardly expressed. There was also, I discovered when I turned the page over, a phone number and a promise.

If you need or want me to speak to the police, to the media, to anyone, I will do it. This number will reach me, and all you have to do is make the call. I owe you more than I can express, and I feel deeper guilt and agony over the things that have happened to you than you are probably willing to believe. If there is something I can make right, then this is the number to use.

I finished the letter and then folded it again and slipped it back into the envelope. Parker Harrison was watching me.

"I know what she offered," he said, "and it was sincere. If you'd like her to come forward, she will. She wanted to at the start, but I talked her out of it. I told her to wait."

I nodded.

"Will you ask her to come forward?" he said.

"I don't really see the point. It wouldn't give anyone who matters anything new. It would take some things from Alexandra, though. She's already had a lot taken."

That seemed to please him. He looked at the floor for a moment and then leaned forward and said, "Lincoln, the things that happened—"

I held up my hand. "Stop, Harrison. I don't want or need apologies. You could explain some things to me, though."

"Of course."

"Why did you hire me to begin with? Were you worried about being connected to that corpse and wanted to find Alexandra in case you needed a witness?"

He smiled. "Do you know how many times you've asked me the same question? How many times you've asked why I came to you? I told you the truth the first day."

"Not all of it."

"No, not all of it. I apologize for that. My reasons, though . . . those were honest."

"Then why wait twelve years?"

"I'd thought about doing it earlier but always talked myself out of it. Then Joshua's body was found, and I thought it was time. I wanted to speak to her again."

"Ken tried to talk to you during his first investigation. He said you ducked him. Didn't you remember who he was, though?"

He shook his head. "That was twelve years earlier, Lincoln, and I never spoke to him, just ignored the calls and messages. His name meant nothing to me. Then Alexandra made contact, told me that the police were focused on me, and that you were working with them, and she thought I should probably stay away from you."

I recalled the day he'd fired me, how he'd gone straight to the phone when I left. It hadn't been Alexandra that he called.

"You talked to Dominic throughout this. Why?"

"When she left, Alexandra asked me to give him a message."

"To tell him that she wouldn't speak to him again, and he shouldn't look for her," I said. "Yes, that's what she told me. Why did Ruzity go to see him?"

"To threaten to kill him if he looked for her," he said. "I hope you understand that promise didn't come easily for Mark, or lightly. He loved Alexandra, though. The reason I didn't want you to visit him to begin with was that I knew it could go badly, for everyone. He's doing well, though. Ever since he left Alexandra, he has been doing well."

"Why'd you talk to Sanabria after you fired me?"

"To tell him that you'd been working for me but were not any longer, and if any harm came to you I'd hold him responsible."

He'd called, in other words, in an attempt to protect me.

"Quinn Graham said you two didn't have contact for years, but then you did again when the body was found."

He nodded. "I said that I wouldn't go to prison for him. That I'd talk to the police if they came to me, regardless of his sister's decision for silence. He told me then, as he had before, that he hadn't killed Joshua. I found myself, for the first time, starting to believe him. I needed to know the truth, and I needed to talk to Alexandra. So I came to you."

"Because you'd read about me in the papers."

"Because I thought you were the right person for the job,"

he said. "It's the same thing I told you at the start—it was about how you viewed the guilty. I thought you would be able to look past the things that others would not."

"I didn't, though."

He made a small shrug, as if it didn't matter, and I shook my head.

"No, Harrison. I don't think you understand how badly I failed to be what you hoped I would be. I distrusted you from the start. That never changed."

When I said that, he dropped his eyes and looked at his clasped hands and was quiet for a time.

"I've never asked anyone to forget what I did," he said. "I haven't tried to forget it, either. It demands to be remembered. I carry it with me. I deserve that."

"We all like the idea of rehabilitation," I said. "I just don't know how many of us actually believe in it."

That made him smile, for some reason. "It only takes a few, Lincoln. Alexandra was enough for me."

"Have you talked to her?"

"A few times. As I said, I talked her out of going to the police the day you were shot. I told her to wait."

"I'm glad," I said, and I meant that sincerely. I saw no gain from what would happen if she reappeared. Not for me, or anyone else. Let some mystery linger for the rest of the world. The world probably needed it.

"I have another question for you," I said.

"Yes?"

"What happened to Joshua's ring, the one Dominic left with the body?"

"It's at the bottom of Pymatuning Reservoir." He frowned. "You know, if Alexandra hadn't made the decision she made, her brother might have gone to prison. It was a good way to frame him. It might have worked."

"Yes. It might have."

There was a brief silence, and then he reached in his jacket and withdrew something wrapped in newspaper and passed it to me. It was heavy in my palm.

"What is this?"

"Mark Ruzity wanted you to know he could do other things with a chisel than what he showed you the first time. I think it's his version of a thank-you. Maybe even an apology."

I tore the paper loose and found a beautiful, small piece of granite. Across the front, carved in small but clear letters, it said, *Lincoln Perry, PI.*

"It's for your desk," Harrison said.

"Yeah."

When he got to his feet I started to do the same, but he waved me off.

"Don't make that trip down the stairs for me."

"The trip's good for me, Harrison. It's no fun, but I need it."

I followed him down the stairs, and when we reached the bottom I put out my hand and shook his.

"Thank you," he said. "For what it's worth, Lincoln . . . everything I hoped about you at the start, I still believe now."

He left then, and I turned and took a deep breath and started up the steps again. Back in the living room, I sat down and read the letter from Alexandra one more time, then picked up the nameplate Mark Ruzity had carved and held it in my hands.

Lincoln Perry, PI.

For my desk, Harrison had said. That's what Ruzity had in mind when he carved it, at least. I wondered, though, if it wasn't really the smallest headstone he'd ever done.

Chapter Forty-six

It was three more weeks before I went to see John Dunbar. By then I was moving better and had some of my weight back. I'd lost almost twenty pounds in the aftermath of the shooting, and it was depressing as hell to consider how weak I'd be when I could finally get back in the gym. I'd been at a strength peak before, and now I'd bottomed out. That's how it goes, though. That's always how it goes.

It was late November when I made the drive, and the lake was hard and cold and whipped into a fury by a strong front out of Canada. Winter on the way, and with it would go Joe. I hadn't been surprised when he told me he was planning on another departure in January, but I was surprised to hear it would be back to Florida, and not Idaho. It seemed Gena was stepping aside from her position and heading south to join him. I remembered what she'd told me about neither of them wanting to be selfish, and how the best thing might be to pick a place that was new to both of them. Florida would be that, and it was also the place where they'd found each other. Maybe they'd stay. Maybe he'd convince her to spend some of the year in Cleveland. It was too early to tell.

Sheffield Lake was quiet; not so many people interested in heading to the lake come November. When I got out of the car and walked to Dunbar's door, the wind was difficult to move through. It seemed to find the bullet wounds somehow, slip through them and carry the chill to the rest of my body.

Dunbar was home, and happy to see me. Ushered me in and took my coat and got me positioned in a chair by the fireplace. It was gas, not wood, but it threw some heat and made the tiny house seem like the perfect place to sit out a howling storm.

"You better let me get you some coffee," he said. "Maybe put in a touch of whiskey, too? Just a warmer. Today's a day for it, if ever there was one."

I said that sounded fine, and then he went out to the kitchen and fixed the coffee, and I sat and watched the storm. When he came back we drank the coffee together, and I listened while he talked about the case, offering updates and theories and connections I might not have heard.

Eventually he burned himself out and set his coffee aside and said, "Well, what brought you out here on a day like this? I'm sure it wasn't for my coffee."

"How sure are you that Alvin Neloms killed Joshua Cantrell?" I said.

He blinked. "Quite sure. How could I not be, at this point? I've heard your tape—he all but confessed. Then Darius provided the details. Why do you . . . I mean, you're sure of it, too. Right? You don't think something else?"

"If I had to guess," I said, "if I had to put every dime I have down on one bet, I'd say he did it, yeah."

"That's what I thought."

"I believe that because of what I saw. Because of how he reacted when I said Cantrell's name. Sometimes, though, I get things wrong. Sometimes I make an assumption based upon what I've seen, and it's wrong."

He was frowning at me, quiet.

"So here's what I have to ask you," I said. "Did you kill Joshua Cantrell, or did you just leave the ring?"

I waited a long time. He did not speak, did not move. Did not look away, either.

"Probably wouldn't have bothered me if I hadn't gotten shot," I said. "Or if it had bothered me, it would have slipped by easier. Since I did get shot, I've had a lot of time to sit around and think. I thought about the way Neloms had his uncle shoot me, the way he dumped Ken's body, the way he threw Bertoli off a roof. He was not a man who was interested in subtleties. He was interested in making people dead and moving on. Didn't care who got arrested for it, didn't care about framing people."

I leaned forward, feeling a tug in my chest but not the radiating pain that had once been there.

"Alexandra thought her brother killed him, or had him killed. She thought that because of the ring. It's why she left. While I can understand why she thought that, I can't imagine why in the hell Dominic would have left it. As a message? That would have served no purpose. She wasn't a mob rival, she was his sister, and she mattered dearly to him. If he had killed her husband, he wouldn't have left a calling card."

Dunbar's face was still impassive, but his eyes went to the wall above my head.

"It's possible that Joshua Cantrell told Bertoli about that ring," I said, "and that Bertoli told Neloms. Here's the thing, Dunbar: Even if Neloms were to think it wise to frame someone like Sanabria—and he wouldn't—and even if he did know about the ring, he wouldn't have known where to find it. Because Cantrell never wore the thing. I suppose Bertoli could have known, and could have told Neloms, but I don't think so."

It was quiet. Dunbar looked at me for a while, then away.

"Of course I didn't kill him," he said.

"That's your only denial?"

He nodded. "How do you know about the ring?"

"How, indeed."

He sat back in his chair, blew out a shaking breath.

"Tell me what you did," I said.

He turned his hands up. "You know what I did."

"I know you left the ring. I'd like more details."

"Joshua called me and told me that Bertoli was dead and he wanted out. Said they were leaving the country. I told him that he couldn't do that; he had to be a witness for the investigation of Bertoli's murder. He hung up on me. So I went to see him in person, and I found his body."

His mouth worked for a bit without any words coming out,

and then he said, "You can't know what I felt then. I can't explain that to you. I knew I was partially responsible, but I also knew who killed him."

"You *thought* you knew," I said. "You were wrong."

That made his jaw clench, but he nodded. "At the time I was *certain*, and I thought, no, I will not let this happen again. I will not let Dominic walk away from this, too."

"You knew where Cantrell kept the ring?"

"It was in a cabinet just inside the door. He kept it there in case Dominic made a surprise visit. So he could put it on at the last minute, you know? The ring was a big deal to Dominic."

He said "Dominic" the way most people say "poison."

"You had a key?"

"Door was unlocked. Open. His feet were still inside the house."

"So you went away, and waited for the discovery."

He nodded, and there was a tremor in his face, near his left eye. "Waited all night, and into the next day. Then I couldn't wait any more, and I went back. He was gone, and the stone was clean. I couldn't believe it. I thought I was losing my mind."

"You didn't call anyone," I said. "With the murder less than two days old, you did not call anyone."

"I had tampered with a homicide scene, and then I had left it."

"There was a murder to be solved. You were the only—"

"*I didn't think it would take twelve years!*" He shouted it at me, and now his hands were trembling, too.

I shook my head in disgust.

"I tried to help," he said. "Anybody would tell you that. I tried to guide things."

"Guide things right to Dominic Sanabria. Right to an innocent man."

"He is *not* an innocent man!"

"He was this time, Dunbar."

"If you had known what I knew—"

"I did," I said. "Me, and every other detective who's looked at it. We fell all over ourselves looking at Sanabria and Harrison and all the rest of them. Shit, there was no shortage of suspects. All of them had been guilty. None of them were this time. Nobody could ever get it, could ever see the forest because there were too many damn trees. Until Ken Merriman. He got it. Then he was murdered, and some of that's on your head, Dunbar."

"Everything you just said is true, but it wouldn't necessarily have changed because they had a corpse. They already had Bertoli's corpse. That didn't help."

"You're right," I said. "Why would another crime scene possibly have been a help? Why would Alexandra's testimony possibly have been a help? You know how long it took me to get to Neloms after I talked to her? One day. One *day*, you son of a bitch."

He said, "When you *talked* to her?"

"That's right, Dunbar. She's out there—and she's staying out there. You tell anybody that I've talked to her, and I'll happily distract them with the rest of this conversation."

"I won't tell anyone," he said. "I just can't believe . . . I never knew . . ."

"She ran away. Because of what *you* did, she ran away. It wasn't the murder. It was the ring and the message that it carried. Remove that, and you might have had an arrest within a week, might have had twelve fewer years of Alvin Neloms, might have had Ken Merriman alive."

My voice was rising now, and I wanted to hit him, but instead I reached out and ran my fingers over my shirt, near the scars.

"I hope it weighs on you," I said. "I hope that burden is terrible, Dunbar. It should be."

"You *hope* it is? You don't know?"

"I don't know much of anything," I said. "I just do a lot of hoping."

I got to my feet and went to the door, walked back out into the cold wind.

That night I took Joe and Amy out for dinner at Sokolowski's. I hadn't been there since that lunch with Ken at the end of the spring. It was edging toward winter now, and the view of the city's lights was hampered by rain-streaked windows. It was still beautiful, though. You just had to look harder.

I told them about my visit to John Dunbar. Joe's initial response was for a call to action—he wanted police, prosecutors, punishment.

"He's an old man now," I said. "A retired and highly regarded FBI agent. You think they'll ever actually let him get to a trial? For a charge of tampering with a crime scene, one that can no longer be proven?"

"It can be testified to."

"By Parker Harrison and Alexandra Cantrell. Those are the people who could testify to it. I ask you this—is it worth it?"

Joe didn't answer. Amy said, "No. I don't think that it is."

"Ken Merriman's daughter might disagree," Joe said. "As Lincoln pointed out, Neloms should have been arrested years before he had a chance to kill Ken."

"Should have been," I said. "Might not have been. Anyway, however corrupt Dunbar's actions, you can be sure he didn't want it to play out like it did. I've seen that man enough to know he won't be able to find peace with this, Joe. Alexandra and Parker Harrison have come closer, and they deserve it more. I suggest we leave them to that."

"What about you?" Joe said. "Have you found peace with it yet?"

"Sure."

He and Amy exchanged a look.

"You remember the conversation we had in the hospital," I said to Joe.

"Yes."

"You were right, of course. I was trying to make this case my life without letting it into my life. Maybe that doesn't make sense, but I don't know how else to phrase it."

"It makes sense," he said. "I've seen plenty of police do it."

"I have, too. They're the ones who eventually end up divorced and drinking and angry. You know that."

He nodded.

"So I see your point, is what I'm trying to say. Still, you

have to understand that I've had trouble dealing with what happened when some of these cases found their way into my home, Joe. Found their way to Amy, to you."

"He understands," Amy said. "As do I. Trust me, as do I."

"What are you leading up to?" Joe said. "Are you telling us you want to go back to PI work, or that you're ready to truly quit?"

"I'm telling you I don't have an answer yet. I need some time. There's a part of me that would like to move on. Maybe the largest part of me."

"What would the other part like?" Amy said.

"There are some people who have come to us because they really needed us. I'd like to think we've done some good in those situations."

"You *know* you have," she said.

"Hell," Joe said, "you don't have to look at it like such a crossroads, Lincoln, like it's a right turn or a left and you've got to make the decision now. Hang at the stop sign for a while. Keep it in idle. We still get calls for case work, you know that. Just because you take the calls doesn't mean you have to take the cases. You can listen, and then you can decide."

"That seems right," I said, and it did. For now, that sounded like enough.

I would answer the phone when it rang. I would listen.

Acknowledgments

This book and its predecessors wouldn't have existed without the faith, hard work, and keen eye of Peter Wolverton, who has been both an editor and a friend, and I'm deeply indebted. Thank you, Pete, and thanks to everyone else at St. Martin's, Minotaur Books, and Thomas Dunne—Andy Martin, Thomas Dunne, Matthew Shear, Katie Gilligan, Elizabeth Byrne, Hector DeJean, and all the rest.

Much gratitude is also due to:

David Hale Smith, agent extraordinaire.

George Lichman of the Rocky River Police Department, a friend and helpful resource.

Laura Lane not only offered a critical eye to the early pages but guided me to the genesis of the story several years ago. She had no idea of this, of course, but deserves credit nevertheless.

A pair of deeply valued early readers: Bob Hammel and Christine Caya.

Michael Connelly, for countless kindnesses.

Dennis Lehane, with a standard but important additional note of thanks to his Writers in Paradise conference at Eckerd College, www.writersinparadise.com.

Tom Bunger, who answered a lot of truly strange legal questions involving the missing, the dead, and their homes. If you're missing or dead and you have a home, I'd suggest you call Tom.

The many booksellers and friends who have been gracious hosts over the years, including but certainly not limited to Jim Haung, Robin and Jamie Agnew, Richard Katz, Jon and Ruth Jordan, Steve Stilwell, Barbara Peters, Otto Penzler, John and Toni Cross, Mike Bursaw, and so many others.

A motley band of assorted generous folks: Dr. J. D. Headdy, Ridley Pearson, George Pelecanos, Laura Lippman, Gena Asher, Lawrence Rose, Brad Petrigala, Tony Mitchell, George Juergens, Louise Thurtell, Robert Pepin, Roger Levesque, and my family.

Read on for a letter from Michael Koryta
in which he discusses the inspiration
behind the Lincoln Perry series and for the
first chapter of THE PROPHET, Michael
Koryta's nail-biting new thriller, available
in print and as an eBook from
Hodder & Stoughton.

Dear Reader,

Many thanks for joining Lincoln Perry in these pages, and I hope you enjoyed them. I am often asked questions about the origins of these stories, the differences between writing detective fiction and supernatural fiction, and, consistently: Why Cleveland?

In reverse order, then . . . My storytelling roots are found in Cleveland's west-side neighborhoods, on the sidewalks and alleys traversed by Lincoln and Joe in these books. My parents are from the city, and I spent a great deal of time there as a child, much of it walking the Clark-Fulton neighborhood with my father, who would tell me stories. They were true stories, or mostly true, as is the way with memories, and when I began to write fiction I turned to Cleveland. There's a great drama in Cleveland's story – once powerful, a manufacturing titan, home to more corporate headquarters than any city in the world . . . and, just a half-century later, one of the few cities in America with a declining population, wracked by poverty and crime, more famous for a polluted river that caught fire in 1969 than for its glorious history.

There was – and is – something decidedly noir about that backdrop. Broken dreams and faded glory, a city trying to redefine itself and recapture something that slipped away like a morning fog. The detective novelists I love – Chandler, Hammett, Connelly, Lehane – all capture that sense of a place working on a character, and I always found Cleveland in the heart of Lincoln's story.

The private detective novel was a natural form for me; I began working for a private detective as a 16-year-old student intern. It became a part-time job, and then a full-time job, until I eventually left it for writing. The detective novel was my first love. TONIGHT I SAID GOODBYE, the first in the series, was written when I was 20, published when I was 21. At that time I was a student at Indiana University, working 40 or more hours a week as a newspaper reporter, and moonlighting as a part-time private detective. Writing sessions fell between midnight and 3 a.m., and they never exhausted me; instead I felt recharged. The book was my battery, and I'll forever have fond memories of that one.

TONIGHT I SAID GOODBYE was born from the title line. I had that before anything else, and I knew that it would be the final diary entry of a young girl who had gone missing. I was haunted by the possibilities.

SORROW'S ANTHEM, which followed, is the most personal of the Lincoln books to me, because it connects back to my father's old neighborhood and all of those walks and shared memories. I wanted it to bridge eras and families and friendships. "True friends are precious, and lost friends are the kind of ghosts that never wander far away," says Lincoln, and in that was the seed of the story.

A WELCOME GRAVE is the product of a case I worked myself; a simple job tracking down missing heirs. But one man I traced reacted strangely, almost panicking, when I identified myself as a private investigator. His reaction planted in my mind that wonderful question that is a writer's best friend, the one that begins "What if . . ."

THE SILENT HOUR, the latest installment in the Lincoln Perry series, is my attempt to wrestle with the psychological dilemma of the detective, the notion that at some point the burden of the unsolved cases threatens to break him. "Every detective had his white whale," Lincoln thinks. "I wondered how many of them ever lifted their heads to see that the seas were teeming with white whales." I'd put Lincoln through an emotional gauntlet by this point in the series, and I wanted to show the weight of that. He's no superhero, is Lincoln. But he's trying. And in that way, he represents my own joy and struggle with writing. Like each case, each story has its challenges. You take them on and hope for the best.

Which brings us to the supernatural – why the shift? Why move from a private detective to a ghost story? In all honesty, that move never felt as significant to me as it did to others. They're all detective novels at their core – a protagonist is setting out to restore order by replacing uncertainty with certainty, lies with truth, chaos with control. As a writer, I think you've got to keep moving to produce anything worth reading. You have to find challenges, and adding layers of the supernatural provided that for me. The supernatural elements add a freedom to create rules of the universe, but with that freedom is a requirement to explain those rules, justify them, and sell them to the reader. That's the challenging part. There are moments in a supernatural story where I catch myself longing for the inherent logic of the detective novel. Then I shift back – as I recently have – to the world of the private detective and I find myself longing for the injection of cold fear that the uncanny provides. It's a fun back-and-forth for me, and I certainly hope it is for you as you turn the pages.

With gratitude,

Michael Koryta
January, 2012

Prologue

The town feels like home immediately, and he credits the leaves. It must be a pickup day. Plastic bags bursting with withered remains of life are stacked on the curbs, a few spilling over onto the sidewalks, flecks of crimson and copper that dot the white concrete like blood splatters on pale flesh. The air is that contrary blend: alive with a smell, but the smell is death.

Those who pass him have their heads down and shoulders hunched, turtles seeking their shells. He stands tall as he walks, embracing the cold wind, which is wonderfully unblocked by concrete walls, unmarred by razor wire fencing. He is grateful for that. There are other people in this town who have similar feelings, memories of days when one could not embrace the wind and longed to, no matter how bitter and chill. He knows some of them, and he knows that those very memories—realities—are in some cases exactly what chased them to this town, a chance to hide from the past.

At first glance, this town feels like a fine place for hiding from reality, too: impossibly quaint, with an actual town square and a brick courthouse. It could be the stage set from some Hollywood version of small-town middle America if not for all the empty buildings. Half the storefronts facing the courthouse have FOR RENT or FOR SALE signs in dusty windows. As he moves away from the square, walking north, toward the lake, stepping carefully around those swollen bags of leaves, he encounters vacant properties, once-tidy yards filled with brown weeds, vinyl siding begging for a hose and some bleach.

Hard times have come to Chambers, Ohio.

Five blocks farther north, the lake visible now, the smell of water pushed toward him by a steady wind, and he departs to follow the signs for the high school. Turns west, walks a few more blocks, and now he can see it. A two-story main structure with single-story wings sprawling in odd directions, indications that several additions have been made over the years.

Chambers High School, Home of the Cardinals.

A cardinal was the third creature he ever killed. Caught it beneath his grandmother's birdfeeder. He'd watched the cat's approach to this task and marveled. The cat didn't hide; it just waited with incredible, dazzling patience. There was no cover under the birdfeeder, nothing to shield a killer, and still the killer succeeded. As the cat approached, the birds would scatter. The cat was unbothered by that, content in his role and devoted to it, possessed of unusual clarity of purpose. The cat would simply settle down into the grass beside a dusting of fallen sunflower seeds and wait. And without fail, the birds would return. Even though they could see the cat, its lack of motion reassured them, convinced them that they were safe. The cat never reacted to those first birds. The cat would wait, and watch, and eventually they'd become so confident in their safety that one would come just near enough, and then there would be a blinding strike, and those around the victim would scatter.

Give them enough time, though? Then they would return. Always. Because the feeder was there, the feeder was home, and though they might be capable of remembering what had befallen one of their own in the same spot, they did not believe it could happen to them as well.

Unshakable confidence. Unshakable stupidity.

He is fascinated by the confident specimens of the help-less. He finds no fascination in the fearful.

The first bird took him longer than it took the cat, but not as long as he'd expected. The secret was in his stillness. The secret was in their stupidity. It took him only five days to get the cardinal. He killed the cat when that was done. There was nothing more to be learned from it.

He has patience for study, and hunger for it, in the way that only those truly devoted to a craft can ever possess. His craft is killing. His understanding of it is great, but he knows there will always be more to learn, and in that knowl-edge is his happiness. He has studied the behavior of killers, has spoken with them, has lived behind steel bars with them, and he has learned from them all.

Now, as the wind freshens and the smell of dead leaves fills air that is rapidly chilling with the promise of rain, he stares at the front of the high school long enough to observe the security guard in the parking lot, and then he walks down the block and turns the corner and the football field comes into view. Here the Cardinals make their claim to glory. It's a terrible name for sporting teams. Why not the Warriors or Titans or Tigers? How does one summon any level of confidence wearing the logo of a bird that can be killed by the squeeze of a child's palm?

There are half a dozen men sitting in the aluminum bleachers that border the field. He is not the only watcher today. They are undefeated, these Cardinals, they are the most intense pride of a town that once had many more reasons to be proud.

He slips in, leans beside the bleachers with hands in pockets, and waits for the coach to arrive. The coach, of course, is more than a coach. He has won 153 games for this school, this community. He has lost only twenty-two. On this field where his players are now stretching, limbering up against the wind and beneath the gray sky, he has a record of eighty-one wins against four losses. Just four home losses. He's more than a coach, he is a folk hero. A mythic figure. And not just because of the wins. Oh, no. Coach Kent Austin is about much more than football.

He proves it now, drawing silence as he walks across the field, still a young man and a fit one but always with the trace of a limp, the left knee refusing to match strides with the right, always yielding just a little more, a little too much. It only adds to the coach's compelling quality. Everyone else recognizes his wounds; the coach pretends not to.

It is not only the young players in uniform who fall silent as the coach makes his way across the field, it is the men in the stands, the watchers. There is a reverence about them now, because what happens on this field matters deeply to people who have not so much as walked across its surface. You take your pride where you can find it, and right now, this is where it can be found. Because hard times have come to Chambers. This much he understands well, reads it as a weather forecaster would read the dark clouds scudding in off Lake Erie. He is a forecaster in his own right.

A prophet of hard times.

The coach is far too focused to look up and see him, because the coach is at work, lost to the game that he insists does not matter, but of course it matters because it is all he really has, in the end. Empty games and empty faith. Hollow words and false promises. A child's preoccupations and distractions, carefully constructed walls to separate him from the reality of the world that owns him, that carries him in an open palm that could so swiftly turn into a closed fist. He needs to feel the first squeeze of that fist.

The prophet spent three years with a killer named Zane who murdered his wife and both of her parents with a ten-gauge shotgun. Quite a messy weapon, the ten-gauge.

Before he pulled the trigger, he gave all three of them the chance to renounce God. To say that Zane was their God. A promising idea, though poorly understood. Zane was not of proper depth for such a task, but he was to be admired for the effort nevertheless. The way Zane told it, two of the victims accepted him as their God and one did not. It made no difference in their fate, of course, but Zane was interested in their answers, and so was the prophet. At one time, he was even impressed. The idea of posing that question to someone facing the final seconds before entering eternity seemed powerful.

He no longer believes this, though. Consideration has shown him its weaknesses and ultimate insignificance. The question and its answer mean little. What matters, what Zane was unable to see—he was an impulsive man was Zane—is in the removing of the question from the mind entirely, and replacing it with certainty.

There is no God.

You walk alone in the darkness.

To prove this, to imprint it in the mind so deeply that no alternative can so much as flicker, is the goal. This is power, pure as it comes.

Bring him the hopeful and he will leave them hopeless. Bring him the strong and he will leave them broken. Bring him the full and he will leave them empty.

The prophet's goal is simple. When the final scream in the night comes, whoever issues it will be certain of one thing:

No one hears.

What he has been promised in Chambers, Ohio, is strength and resiliency. He has looked into a confident man's eyes and heard his assurance that there is no fear that will not bow to his faith.

The prophet of hard times, who has looked into many a confident gaze in his day, has his doubts about that.

I

Adam had his shirt lifted, studying the lead-colored bruise along his ribcage, when the girl opened the door. She turned her head in swift horror, as if she'd caught him crouched on his desk in the nude. He gave the bruise one more look, frowning, and then lowered his shirt.

"Want a lesson for the day?"

The girl, a brunette with very tan skin—too tan for this time of the year in this part of the world—turned back hesitantly and didn't speak.

"If you're going to tell a drunk man that it's time to go back to jail, you ought to see that the pool cue is out of his hand first," Adam told her.

She parted her lips, then closed them again.

"Not your concern," Adam said. "Sorry. Come on in."

She stepped forward and let the door swing shut. When the latch clicked, she glanced backward, as if worried about being trapped in here with him.

Husband is a good decade older than her, Adam thought. *He hasn't hit her, at least not yet or at least not recently, but he's the kind who might. The charges probably aren't domestic. Let's say, oh, drunk and disorderly. It won't be costly to get him out. Not in dollars, at least.*

He walked behind the desk, then extended a hand and said, "Adam Austin."

Another hesitation, and then she reached forward and

took his hand. Her eyes dropped to his knuckles, which were swollen and scabbed. When she removed her hand, he saw that she was wearing bright red nail polish with some sort of silver glitter worked into it.

"My name's April."

"All right." He dropped into the leather swivel chair behind the desk, trying not to wince at the pain in his side. "Somebody you care about in a little trouble, April?"

She tilted her head. "What?"

"I assume you're looking to post a bond."

She shook her head. "No. That's not it." She was holding a folder in her free hand, and now she lifted it and held it against her chest while she sat in one of the two chairs in front of the desk. It was a bright blue folder, plastic and shiny.

"No?" The sign said AA BAIL BONDS. People who came to see him came for a reason.

"Look, um, you're the detective, right?"

The detective. He did indeed hold a PI license. He did not recall ever being referred to as "the detective" before.

"I'm ... yeah. I do that kind of work."

He didn't think he was even listed in the phone book as a private investigator. He was just AA Bail Bonds, which covered both his initials and gave him pole position in the Yellow Pages as people with shaking hands turned pages seeking help.

The girl didn't say anything, but looked down at that shiny folder as if it held the secrets of her life. Adam, touching his left side gingerly with his fingertips, still trying to assess whether the ribs were bruised or cracked, said, "What exactly brought you here, April?"

"I'd heard ... I was given a referral."

"A referral," he echoed. "Can I ask the source?"

She pushed her hair back over her left ear and sat forward in the chair, meeting his eyes for the first time, as if she'd summoned some confidence. "My boyfriend. Your brother was his football coach. We heard from him that you were a detective."

Adam said, "My brother?" in an empty voice.

"Yes. Coach Austin."

"Kent," he said. "We're not on his squad, April. We can call him Kent."

She didn't seem to like that idea, but she nodded.

"My brother gave you a referral," he said, and found himself amused somehow, despite the aching ribs and bruised hand and the sandpaper eyelids that a full week of uneven hours and too much drinking provided. Until she walked in, he'd been two minutes from locking the office and going in pursuit of black coffee. The tallest cup and strongest blend they had. A savage headache had been building, and he needed something beyond Advil to take its knees out.

"That's right." She seemed unsatisfied with his response, as if she'd expected the mention of his brother would establish a personal connection. "I'm in school at Baldwin-Wallace College. A senior."

"Terrific," Adam said.

"It's a good school."

"I've always understood that to be true." He was trying to keep his attention on her, but right now all she represented was a delay between him and coffee. "What's in the folder?"

She looked down protectively, as if he'd violated the folder's privacy. "Some letters."

He waited. Could this take any longer? He was used to fighting his way through personal stories he didn't care to hear about, used to deflecting tales of woe, but he did not have the patience to tug one out just so he could *begin* deflecting it.

"What precisely do you need, April?"

"I'd like to get in touch with my father."

"You don't know him?" Adam said, thinking that this wasn't the sort of problem he could handle even if it interested him. How in the hell did you go about finding someone who'd abandoned his child decades ago? It wasn't like chasing down a guy who'd skipped out on bail, leaving behind a fresh trail of friends, relatives, and property.

"I've met him," she said. "But he was . . . well, by the time I was old enough to really get to know him, he was already in prison."

Adam understood now why she'd gone to the trouble of telling him that she was in a good school. She didn't want him to form his understanding of her from this one element, the knowledge that her father was in prison.

"I see. Well, we can figure out where he's doing his time easily enough."

"He's done. He's out."

Damn. That would slow things down.

"What I've got," the too-tan-for-October girl said, "is some letters. We started writing while he was still in prison. That was, actually, your brother's idea."

"No kidding," Adam said, doing his damnedest to hide his disgust. Just what this girl needed, a relationship with some asshole in a cell. But Kent, he'd have found that a fine plan. Adam's brother had gotten a lot of ink for his prison visits over the years. DRIVEN BY THE PAST, one headline had read. Adam found that a patently obvious observation. Everyone was driven by the past, all the time. Did Kent's past play a role in his prison visits? Of course. Did that shared past play a role in Adam's own prison visits? Better believe it. They were just different sorts of visits.

"Yes. And it was a *wonderful* idea. I mean, I learned to forgive him, you know? And then to understand that he wasn't this monster, that he was someone who made a mistake and—"

"He stopped writing when he got out?"

She stuttered to a stop. "No. Well, he did for a while. But it's an adjustment."

"It certainly is," Adam said, thinking *That's why most of them go right back.* She was so damn young. This was what college seniors looked like? Shit, he was getting old. These girls seemed to be moving backward, sliding away from him just as fast as he aged away from them, until their youth was an impossible thing to comprehend.

"Right," April said, pleased that he'd agreed. "So some time passed. Five months. It was frustrating, but then I got another letter, and he told me he'd gotten out and explained how difficult it was, and apologized."

Of course he did. Has he asked for money yet?

"So now he writes, but he hasn't given me his address. He said he's nervous about meeting me, and I understand that. I don't want to force things. But I'd at least like to be able to write back, you know? And I don't want him to be . . . *scared* of me."

Adam thought that maybe he didn't need coffee anymore. Maybe he needed a beer. It was four in the afternoon. That was close enough to happy hour to count, wasn't it?

"You might give him some time on that," he said. "You might—"

"I will give him time. But I can't give him anything more than that if I can't write back."

That's the point, honey. Give him nothing but time and distance.

"He explained where he was living," she said. "I feel like I should have been able to find it myself, honestly. I tried on the Internet, but I guess I don't know what I'm doing. Anyhow, I'd love it if you'd find the address. All I want to do is respond, right? To let him know that he doesn't need to be afraid of me. I'm not going to ask him to start being a *dad*."

Adam rubbed his eyes. "I'm more of a, uh, local-focused type. I don't do a lot of —"

"He's in town."

"Chambers?"

She nodded.

"He's from here?"

She seemed to consider this a difficult question. "We all are, originally. My family. I mean, everyone left, like me to go to college, and ..."

And your father to go to prison. Yes, everyone left.

She opened the folder and withdrew a photocopy of a letter.

"In this, he gives the name of his landlord. It should be easy to come up with a list, right? He's living in a rental house, and this is the name of the woman who owns it. It should be easy."

It *would* be easy. One stop at the auditor's office and he'd have every piece of property in this woman's name.

"Maybe you should let things take a natural course," he said.

Her eyes sparked. "I have plenty of people who actually know something about this situation who can give me *advice*. I'm asking you to give me an *address*."

It should have pissed him off, but instead it almost made him smile. He hadn't thought she had that in her, not after the way she'd crept so uneasily into his office, scared by the sound of the door shutting behind her. He wished she'd come in when Chelsea was working. Not that Chelsea had a gentle touch, but maybe that was why it would have been better. Someone needed to chase her out of here, and Adam wasn't doing a good job of that.

"Fair enough," he said. "May I see the letter?"

She passed it over. A typed letter, the message filling barely a quarter of the page.

Dear April,

I understand you're probably not very happy with me. It just takes some time to adjust, that's all. I don't want you to expect more of me than I can be. Right now I will just say that it feels good to be back home. And a little frightening. You might be surprised at that. But remember it has been a while since I was here. Since I was anywhere. It's great to be out, of course, just strange and new. I am living in a rental house with a roof that leaks and a furnace that stinks when it runs, but it still feels like a castle. Mrs. Ruzich—that's my landlord— keeps apologizing and saying she will fix those things and I tell her there is no rush, they don't bother me. I'm not lying about that.

It is my favorite season here. Autumn—so beautiful. Love the way those leaves smell, don't you? I hope you are doing good. I hope you aren't too upset about the way I've handled things. Take care of yourself.

Jason (Dad)

Adam read through it and handed it back to her. He didn't say what he wanted to—*Let it breathe, don't force contact because it will likely bring you nothing but pain*— because that argument had already been shot down with gusto. The landlord's name made it cake, anyhow. Ruzich? There wouldn't be many.

"I just want to write him a short note," April repeated. "Tell him that I'm wishing him well and that he doesn't need to be worried about my expectations."

Definitely beer, Adam thought. *Definitely skip the coffee and go right to beer.*

"Can you get me an address?" she asked.

"Probably. I bill for my time, nothing more, nothing less. The results of the situation aren't my responsibility. All I guarantee is my time."

She nodded, reached into her purse. "I'm prepared to pay two hundred dollars."

"Give me a hundred. I charge fifty an hour. If it takes me more than two hours, I'll let you know."

He charged one hundred an hour, but this would likely take him all of twenty minutes and it was good to seem generous.

"All right." She counted out five twenty-dollar bills and pushed them across the desk. "One other thing — you have a policy of being confidential, don't you? Like a lawyer?"

"I'm not a lawyer."

She looked dismayed.

"But I also am not a talker," Adam said. "My business is my own, and yours is your own. I won't talk about it unless a police officer walks in this door and tells me to."

"That won't happen."

She had no idea how often that *did* happen with Adam's clients.

"I just wanted to be sure... it's private, you know," she said. "It's a private thing."

"I'm not putting out any press releases."

"Right. But you won't even say anything to, um, to your brother? I mean, don't get me wrong, I really respect Coach Austin, but... it's private."

"Kent and I don't do a whole lot of talking," Adam said. "What I will do is find some potential addresses and pass them along to you. The rest is between you and your dad."

She nodded, grateful.

"How do I get in touch with you?" he said.

She gave him a cell phone number, which he wrote down on a legal pad. Beside it he wrote *April* and then looked up.

"Last name?"

She frowned, and he knew why she didn't want to give it. If she still carried her father's name, and he was betting that she did, then she was afraid Adam would look into what the man had done to land in prison.

"Harper," she said. "But remember, this is —"

"Private. Yes, Miss Harper. I understand that. I deal with it every day."

She thanked him, shook his hand. She smelled of cocoa, and he thought about that and her dark skin and figured she'd just left a tanning bed. October in northern Ohio. All the pretty girls were fighting the gathering cold and darkness. Trying to carry summer into the winter.

"I'll be in touch," he said, and he waited long enough to hear the engine of her car start in the parking lot before he locked the office and went to get his beer.

'A man in love with the woman who shot him. Who could possibly resist that story? Not me. Read on, and discover one of the **scariest** and most **touching** horror tales in years.'
James Patterson

THE RIDGE

A lighthouse in the middle of a desolate wood, hundreds of miles from the sea.

For many years it has been the source of amusement in Blue Ridge, Kentucky – until its eccentric builder is found dead.

Deputy Sheriff Kevin Kimble, a man already on the brink of a very dangerous relationship, is called to the odd beacon, which seems to contain disturbing proof that a long-held secret was somehow known to others.

Events soon convince Kimble that his secret is connected to the ridge, and that a terrifying evil might be on the other side of the divide between dark and light.

'The **excellent** Michael Koryta has established a formula of his own . . . one that mixes likeable protagonists with **imaginative** out-of-the-way settings and a dose of the supernatural.'
Daily Mail

'Michael Koryta is **a hot name** in the supernatural/crime crossover field . . . An enjoyable **blockbuster**.'
Financial Times

HODDER

In the best books, the ending often comes as a shock.
Not just because of that one last twist in the tale,
but because you have been so absorbed in their world,
that coming back to the harsh light of reality is a jolt.

If that describes you now, then perhaps you should track down
some new leads, and find new suspense in other worlds.

Join us at www.hodder.co.uk, or follow us on
Twitter @hodderbooks, and you can tap in to a
community of fellow thrill-seekers.

Whether you want to find out more about this book,
or a particular author, watch trailers and interviews, have
the chance to win early limited editions, or simply browse
our expert readers' selection of the very best books,
we think you'll find what you're looking for.

And if you don't, that's the place to tell us what's missing.

We love what we do, and we'd love you to be part of it.

www.hodder.co.uk

@hodderbooks

HodderBooks

HodderBooks